Praise for Leigh Greenwood

RWA Emma Merritt Service Award
RT Book Reviews Americana Historical Award

"Leigh Greenwood is one of the best."

—*RT Book Reviews*

"Leigh Greenwood continues to be a shining star of the genre!"

—*Literary Times*

"Greenwood's books are bo

"Leigh Greenwood remains
oned with in Americana romance."

—*Affaire de Coeur*

"Leigh Greenwood shows after all these years, he still knows how to write a breathtaking Western romance."

—*The Romance Reviews*

"If you haven't read Mr. Greenwood's books yet, you need to take a look."

—*Long and Short Reviews*

"Leigh Greenwood brings romance to an action-filled Western worthy of reading."

—*Fresh Fiction*

"I recommend any novel by Leigh Greenwood."

—*Night Owl Reviews*

Praise for Leigh Greenwood's Night Riders series

Heart of a Texan

"An emotional, fast-paced Western tale, full of realistic characters, authentic settings, nonstop action, back-stabbing villains, and rough justice."

—*RT Book Reviews*

"Another excellent Western romance to add to the ever-impressive list of novels penned by Leigh Greenwood."

—*The Romance Reviews*

"Strap yourself in for a wild ride with this cowboy and the stubborn love of his life."

—*Fresh Fiction*

"Rip-roaring, fast-paced high adventure...a delicious romance."

—*Historical Hilarity*

Texas Pride

"[An] entertaining high-stakes adventure."

—*Booklist*

"Another powerful, yet poignant saga in his Night Riders series...saddle up and read on!"

—*Fresh Fiction*

"A breathtaking Western romance."

—*The Romance Reviews*

"Greenwood is a word master."

—*Long and Short Reviews*

Texas Homecoming

"What more could we want? More cowboys!"

—*RT Book Reviews*

"Few authors provide a vivid, descriptive Americana romance filled with realistic angst-laden protagonists as this author can."

—*The Midwest Book Review*

"Greenwood's plot flows like paint across the canvas of a master. He reveals his characters with the skill of a diamond cutter, one facet at a time."

—*Rendezvous*

When Love Comes

"Complex and compelling. Full of cowboys and characters from the Old West, this book is like watching a John Wayne movie."

—*RT Book Reviews*

"Leigh Greenwood NEVER disappoints...always, always a guaranteed good read!"

—*Heartland Critiques*

To Love and To Cherish

LEIGH GREENWOOD

sourcebooks
casablanca

Copyright © 2014 by Leigh Greenwood
Cover and internal design © 2014 by Sourcebooks, Inc.
Cover art by Gregg Gulbronson

Sourcebooks and the colophon are registered trademarks of
Sourcebooks, Inc.

Published by Sourcebooks Casablanca, an imprint of Sourcebooks,
Inc.
P.O. Box 4410, Naperville, Illinois 60567-4410
(630) 961-3900
Fax: (630) 961-2168
www.sourcebooks.com

Printed and bound in Canada.
MBP 10 9 8 7 6 5 4 3 2 1

To Zachary Grayson Villela
Born January 18, 2014

One

LAURIE STARED NUMBLY AS HARD, DRY LUMPS OF DIRT fell into the open grave and struck the pine casket with hollow thuds. Her husband's death had been sudden and unexpected—a shock to the whole town. The doctor said his heart just gave out, most likely brought on by stress. To everyone else, Noah had seemed like a calm, quiet, sensible man who led a calm, quiet, sensible life married to a calm, quiet, sensible wife. Not even his brother knew that Noah lived on the edge of a precipice, petrified that any moment he would be catapulted into the abyss beyond.

Only Laurie knew that she was the abyss.

Laurie was surrounded by her parents, her cousins and brother-in-law, and by neighbors she had known all her life, but she had never felt more alone. The ice-cold wind blowing in from the desert failed to drive away the lead-hued clouds that hung low on the horizon. Not since the day she arrived had this land of pines and sagebrush felt so little like home, so much like an alien world into which she'd been pitched against her will.

On either side, her cousins Naomi and Sibyl gripped her hands tightly in theirs. Both knew Laurie had been forced to marry a man she didn't love, but neither knew how many times she'd prayed for his death. It had seemed the only means of escape from a life that was an impregnable prison despite the absence of walls. Guilt battled with relief. It was joined by fear of the future and a nearly mad need to escape the past. The conflict left Laurie weary, unsure of what to do, where to go, who to trust. For the first time since the day of her birth, her life was her own. The prospect thrilled and frightened her.

It had come too fast. She wasn't expecting it. Despite years of aimless daydreams about possible escape, she had no plan for what to do if it should happen, no goal beyond freedom from a marriage that was slowly smothering her. Even now, she found herself breathing deeply, drinking in the dry air in great gulps and feeling the bonds loosening and falling away. Her chest expanded as the air sank deeper into her lungs, sending oxygen to clear the mists from her brain, energy to the muscles that had dragged her body through each day with wearying effort.

Everything before her stood out in sharper detail, the colors more luminous, the textures more luxurious. She might as well have spent the four years of her marriage in hibernation. She had gone to sleep at seventeen and had awakened at twenty-one to find she didn't know who she was or who she wanted to become. Those years had left almost no trace—just a mist through which she'd wandered without a goal beyond escape.

"Noah would choose the coldest time of the year to die," Norman Spencer grumbled.

"I don't understand why he died at all," Laurie's father said for what had to be the twentieth time in the last two days.

"Doctor Kessling said his heart just gave out. It was most likely brought on by stress," Laurie told him. "I don't see why you can't accept that."

"But he was so young."

"Lots of people die young," Norman said, "but I never thought it would happen to Noah."

Norman believed he and his brother had been born of a superior race, one that was immune to the mental and physical shortcomings that prevented other people from achieving their same level of success.

"They can finish filling in the grave without us standing here freezing," Naomi Blaine said to her cousin. "Everything at Sibyl's house will be ready by now."

Laurie allowed Naomi to escort her from the cemetery despite Norman declaring that it was disrespectful for a wife to leave until the last bit of dirt had been piled on the grave. That didn't stop him from leaving, too. The wake was being held at his home. He wouldn't have considered allowing it to begin without his presence.

"I know you've been too grief-stricken to think about looking into the settlements Noah made in his will," Norman said to Laurie as he walked alongside her. "If you feel up to it, come by the bank in the morning and I'll go over everything with you."

"What's there to go over?" Naomi asked. "Laurie was Noah's wife, and they had no children."

"There is business to be discussed. I wouldn't expect you to understand."

Norman refused to believe a woman could do anything beyond keep house and take care of children.

"I'll be there." Laurie was eager to have the will read and Noah's estate settled. For the first time, she'd have money of her own and the freedom to decide what to do with the rest of her life. She was certain of only one thing—she would never marry again. Nothing could induce her to put herself under the control of any man.

The walk to Norman's house was short. Cactus Corner was a small place in the Verde River Valley that had been formed three years earlier when twelve families from Kentucky chose it as the site of their new town. In that short time, homes had been built, businesses had opened, and new families had come to settle either in town or in the valley. As her cousin's husband, Colby, said, the Arizona Territory was an empty place just waiting for people to fill it up. Noah had been excited about the arrival of new settlers. That meant more customers, more business, and more money. Laurie had been pleased because keeping Noah busy meant less time with him watching her like she was a small animal and he a hawk about to pounce.

She was relieved to arrive at Norman and Sibyl Spencer's house because Norman was forced to pay attention to his guests rather than her.

"How are you holding up?" Sibyl whispered as

soon as she could pull Laurie aside. "Are you sure you're up to meeting all these people?"

"I see them every day," Laurie said. "They didn't like Noah any more than I did. Why should it be hard to see them?"

Sibyl looked uncomfortable with Laurie's forthrightness. Naomi laughed, but that's what Laurie expected her to do. Naomi was married to a man who loved her deeply and believed there was nothing she couldn't do. Naomi had shocked many people when she'd insisted that they shouldn't start building houses just anywhere—they had to organize a real town with a street for business and areas for private homes.

Despite opposition from Norman, she took on the job of laying out the town and selling lots to the newcomers. Most men still had trouble getting used to talking to a woman about business, but Naomi's success had given Laurie hope that she might someday be equally independent. After four years of virtual imprisonment in a marriage that had been forced upon her, nothing but complete freedom would do.

Accepting condolences from people she'd known all her life and mouthing meaningless responses didn't take much thought, but Laurie was relieved when everyone had spoken to her and transferred their attention to the food and each other. Norman was presiding over the gathering, which allowed Sibyl and Naomi to stay at Laurie's side. No one would be surprised that Laurie's parents weren't standing with her. Her break with them was known to everyone. Laurie was only comfortable when she was with her two cousins, but there was little more that could be said today. So it was no surprise that, standing in silence with nothing more to do than watch people eat Norman's food, she was instantly aware of a stranger the moment he entered the house. He didn't look all that different on the outside, but she knew instantly he was unlike any man she'd ever seen before.

He was tall and so broad-shouldered he filled the doorway. He was handsome and eagle-eyed, with a presence so arresting that it penetrated even Norman's sense of superiority. But that wasn't what riveted Laurie's attention and caused her stomach to tighten. There was a sensuality about him that reached out to her from across the room. It couldn't have been any more powerful if he'd touched her. When his gaze found hers, she felt that he had.

"Who is that man?" she asked Sibyl.

It was Naomi who answered. "Don't you remember? His name is Jared Smith. He was with the traders we followed into Santa Fe after Colby left us. He bought a ranch about five miles up the river."

"I've never seen his wife in the store." Laurie had worked there every day of her marriage. Noah had said he didn't want to waste money hiring an extra clerk, but Laurie knew he required her to work alongside him because he was petrified she would run away if he let her out of his sight.

"He's not married. He just got out of the army. He worked at the fort."

"How do you know so much about him?"

"I met him when he was in town setting up an account at the bank. I tried to convince him to buy a lot in town, but he said he intended to live on his ranch."

"Norman hasn't said anything about him," Sibyl said, "so he can't be too prosperous. Norman can smell money faster than a coyote can smell a mouse."

Norman was tight-fisted when it came to money, but he'd been openhanded in providing loans to people to build homes and start businesses. His uncharacteristic generosity and the source of the money was still a topic of whispered conversations.

Laurie thought Jared Smith looked quite prosperous, but she was probably confusing financial prosperity with his physical prowess. The man was a testament to Mother Nature's ability to produce an exceptional being when she wanted. If he'd been a wild stallion, Laurie could visualize him sniffing the air and tossing his head in impatience, daring anyone to challenge his superiority. When he started toward Laurie, her whole body quivered.

The crowd that filled Norman's parlor seemed to make way for this man, enabling him to approach Laurie on a path as arrow-straight as his gaze. When he came to a stop before her, she felt dwarfed by his size as well as the energy that radiated from him.

"My condolences, ma'am," he said in a voice that was as deep as he was tall. "I didn't know your husband, but he must have been a fine man to have the whole community turn out for his wake."

How could a man who could make his presence be felt from across the room act so ordinary? She struggled to find words to respond, but none came.

"We're a small community," Naomi answered for her. "Many of us are related. We've known Noah all our lives."

"That makes the loss all the greater. As you know, I was in the army. I'm well acquainted with death. It's never easy no matter the time or the manner." He turned back to Laurie. "I'm a stranger to everyone here, so I won't stay."

Laurie found her tongue. "You won't find a better time to meet everyone outside of church."

Mr. Smith smiled, and Laurie felt a response awaken inside her that she'd thought long dead. "Some other time. I don't want to take time from your family and friends."

Sibyl tried to protest, saying everyone would be glad to meet him, but Laurie knew he wouldn't change his mind. He was a man who went his own way, chose his own goals, and required approval from no one. The odd thing was that she felt there was something familiar about him. That was ridiculous. Noah had done everything in his power to ensure that she never met a man, so she was certain she'd never seen him before today.

"Who is that man?"

Laurie turned to find Cassie approaching and smiled inwardly. If there was anyone who could sense the presence of a handsome man, it was Cassie Greene. The wonder was that Mr. Smith had left without being dazzled by the beautiful young widow.

"He's a rancher," Naomi told Cassie. "He's unmarried, so he's fair game."

Cassie laughed. "Maybe, but he's not for me. He couldn't see any woman in this room but Laurie."

Laurie didn't think she'd ever get used to Cassie's artlessness. There wasn't a mean or jealous bone in her body, but she didn't hesitate to put into words what another woman would hesitate to think.

"I'm sure that's only because he came to offer his condolences on Noah's death," Naomi said.

Cassie's look of wide-eyed innocence was as alarming as it was genuine. "I may have a prettier face, but Laurie has the kind of figure that keeps men awake at night."

Heat suffused Laurie's face. The person her figure kept awake had been Noah, but that hadn't benefited either of them.

"You've got to stop saying things like that," Naomi scolded Cassie.

"Why? It's true."

"I've told you a hundred times—"

"I know. *I've got to stop uttering every thought that comes into my head.* I wouldn't have said it to anyone but you." And anyone within hearing.

As a young girl, Laurie had been proud of her figure. She had confessed to her cousins that though she was careful to offer no encouragement, she enjoyed the looks the soldiers cast in her direction. Her husband hadn't liked anything about her body, had said it was so grossly out of shape that he couldn't bring himself to make love to her. He had complained that her breasts were so big they made her look top-heavy. He said her waist was so small in comparison to her hips that she looked deformed. He accused her of intentionally putting a swing into her step to attract the notice of any man who happened to walk by. She had become so paranoid she had done everything she could to disguise the shape of her body.

"I know this isn't a nice thing to say"—Cassie cast a defiant glance at Naomi—"but I'm glad there's another widow in town. I'm tired of being treated like a potential threat to every woman's marriage."

"We don't feel like that," Naomi assured her.

"You don't because Colby can't see any woman except you, but not every husband's gaze stays so close to home."

Laurie liked Cassie. The young woman's candidness was a breath of fresh air in her stale life, but she didn't intend to become a bosom friend. Once she had access to Noah's estate, she intended to change her life completely. The fact that she didn't know what those changes were going to be didn't matter. She might even go away. She'd never been allowed to go anywhere without her parents before her marriage, or her husband afterward.

It was hard to imagine doing anything on her own, but she was excited about the possibility and intimidated by it as well. The future was unknown, the possibilities limitless. She had never faced anything unknown or without limits. She didn't know if she could handle it. Maybe it would be better if she stayed in Cactus Corner and continued her life as it was. She would have her freedom. That's all she'd ever wanted.

"Some of the guests are getting ready to leave," Sibyl told her. "They'll want to say good-bye."

That seemed pointless since she'd see any number of them the moment she stepped outside, but she prepared to say all the proper things. After all, this was the last time she would have to do that. After she saw Norman tomorrow, she would be free. The thought buoyed her spirits so much that she had to caution herself to continue to appear grave. She wasn't going to pretend to be grief-stricken. Too many people knew about the condition of her marriage, but it wouldn't do to appear happy about Noah's death. Even those who knew the state of her marriage wouldn't accept that.

"I think everyone in town showed up," Norman announced when the last guest had left. "But that was to be expected considering the esteem in which everyone held Noah."

Norman found it impossible to believe anyone could think less of him and his brother than they did of themselves.

"Many said how much they appreciated the refreshments we provided," Norman said with pride.

Sibyl had been responsible for every aspect of the food's preparation and presentation, but Norman could never give his wife sole credit for anything. It was as though doing so would diminish his value.

"I have to get back to the bank. Noah would be the first to say I should never neglect business. Don't forget to come by tomorrow," he reminded Laurie. "We have a lot to talk about."

"I'd better go, too," Cassie said.

Laurie didn't see why turning over Noah's estate to her required more than a few sentences, but she was willing to let Norman talk as long as he wanted. Once she walked out of that bank, she would never have to listen to him again.

"Do you know how much money Noah left you?" Naomi asked.

"No, but Noah owned most of the store and part of the bank."

"At least you won't have to work in the bank like Cassie."

Norman didn't believe any woman was capable of understanding the simplest bank transaction, but he wasn't above using Cassie's looks to ensure every male within fifty miles used his bank.

"What will you do?" Sibyl asked.

"I don't know. I haven't had time to think about it."

"You don't have to decide right away," Naomi said. "I, on the other hand, have to get home right away. Colby is so crazy about that baby, he'll use any excuse to have him all to himself. That's why he's not here now. He said I could convey his sympathies better than he could. If I don't get home soon, I'm afraid my own son will forget who I am. If it weren't for Esther and Peter, I wouldn't get any attention at all."

Laurie tried not to be envious of Naomi's happiness, but Colby was the kind of husband every woman wanted and only one in a thousand found. She was glad that one had been Naomi.

"Are you sure you want to stay in that house by yourself tonight?" Sibyl asked. "You're welcome to stay here as long as you wish."

"I only stayed with you and Norman these last two nights because he insisted I was too upset to be left alone. He has no idea how long I've dreamed of being alone. Noah was cruel. I would never have done anything to hurt him, but I'm glad he's dead. Does that make me a bad person?" Her laugh sounded slightly hysterical even to her. "You don't have to say anything, but don't pretend you don't understand. Now before I say anything else, I'll leave. I have some shopping to do before I go home. I don't know if I can stay in that house without feeling Noah's presence in every room."

"What will you do if you can't?"

"Build another house. Or maybe I'll move to Tucson. Noah had plenty of money."

"You can't do that. Your family is here."

"Don't call my parents my *family*! If they'd loved me even a little, they'd never have forced me to marry Noah." Emotion choked off anything else she might have said. Before Noah's death, she hadn't spoken to either of her parents since her wedding day. She didn't know if that would change now. "For the last four years, I've died a little each day," she told Sibyl. "Now I actually feel alive, like I can take a deep breath, express an opinion, make a decision, do something as simple as get dressed without wondering if Noah will find some way to criticize me." She stopped and took a long, slow breath to calm herself. "Sorry, I didn't mean to say any of this. I'm more emotional than I thought. I should go."

"Are you calm enough to face other people?"

"I'm used to pretending. It's only with you and Naomi that I can let myself feel anything." She kissed her cousin's cheek. "Thanks for everything you've done, but I have to start getting used to living on my own."

She experienced a moment of uncertainty when she stepped outside. She'd never been on her own. Either her parents or Noah had made every decision for her. The prospect was a little frightening, but it was also exciting.

Her life was about to start.

ﾐﾍ

Jared told himself it was a waste of energy to lust after a woman he'd seen for barely more than a minute. It was downright uncivilized when that woman was a young widow who'd buried her husband only that afternoon. None of that stopped him from fantasizing about what it would be like to make love to her— something he'd been doing since he first saw her three years ago. When she left Santa Fe, he'd never expected to see her again.

He soon found himself very uncomfortable in the saddle, but even that didn't succeed in driving the pleasant fantasy from his thoughts. He had been a sensual person as far back as he could remember. He expected his surroundings to nourish his senses. That was especially true with women. No one could appreciate their shapes or their softness more than he. Considering that, it was out of character that he had chosen to settle in the Arizona Territory, a land noted for its harshness and its lack of women.

The land around him was a far cry from southern Texas, but he was a far cry from the young man who'd gone off to war seven years earlier. Fighting his fellow countrymen in Virginia and Indians in Texas had deprived him of most of his idealism. Now all he wanted was to find his two brothers. Six months spent in Santa Fe following up every possible lead had turned up nothing.

The family that had adopted him had returned to Texas in less than a year. The same could have happened to his brothers. Or they could have gone farther west. He had nothing to go on, but he couldn't rid himself of the conviction that he would find them west of Santa Fe. Consequently, he'd chosen to settle in the Arizona Territory. He had been able to buy a ranch that was already set up and running. At first, that had seemed like a good idea. Now he wasn't so sure.

Even though the land below the Mogollon Rim was covered in trees and riddled with creeks, it could be a dry, harsh land that wasn't hospitable to cattle. He had no intention of building a herd of the hardy Texas longhorns. They were lean and mean, fully capable of holding their own against most predators and surviving in harsh country, but he had set his heart on a herd of Herefords. They were equally hardy but carried more meat. He wanted a small herd that wouldn't overgraze the range but would still turn a profit. He had his land and he had his crew. What he didn't have was a herd of Herefords. He knew where to get them. He just had to find a way to pay for them.

He had to get a loan.

He didn't look forward to sitting down with that long-nosed banker. The man looked the type who would enjoy turning him down. He'd much rather think about the young widow, Laurie. She was the banker's sister-in-law, but she didn't seem to be anything like him. Scared. Subdued. Sad. Confused. Maybe all of those, but she definitely wasn't mourning her husband. He wondered why. He also wondered why she wore clothes that hung on her like moss on a tree.

He needed to stop thinking about Laurie Spencer,

though seeing her flanked by two equally handsome women was a hard picture to forget. He was a man used to feeding his carnal appetite on a regular basis. Coming to Arizona had changed that. Women were few and far between. They were either respectable women married to respectable men, or they were women of no reputation who followed the mining camps and whose time and bodies were for sale. He'd never had any problem satisfying himself with the latter, but Laurie Spencer had instilled in him a desire for a woman of a different type.

Specifically, Laurie Spencer.

Hell, if she was like the women back home, she'd wear mourning for a full year. He could dry up and blow away before then. As he expected from the first moment he saw her, he'd have to settle for someone less likely to start him thinking of marriage.

Laurie looked at herself the mirror. She'd been taught that vanity was a sin, but she was pleased with the way she looked. Well, more than pleased. She was delighted. The weather had made an abrupt change, enabling her to dispense with the coat she'd planned to wear. She wore a plain wool skirt that hugged her hips and cinched tightly at her waist. A simple cotton blouse covered her bosom without clouding its outline. Her only concession to the weather and modesty was a jacket that was fitted at the waist.

She didn't know if Noah had been right when he insisted that her body was an affront to female modesty and that she should do everything she could to disguise it, but she intended to find out. She tried on three hats before dispensing with all of them and pinning her hair atop her head. She liked the way it accented her neck. If she was going to be thought an immodest female, she wanted to provide plenty of ammunition.

She had no sooner placed her hand on the door-knob than she suffered a stab of doubt. What would Naomi or Sibyl say? What if Noah was right? Would any of the older women turn their backs on her?

Laurie's spine stiffened. She didn't care if no one liked the way she was dressed. They'd just have to get used to it. They didn't complain about Cassie anymore, and she did everything she could to make herself more attractive.

She opened the door and stepped out.

When Naomi and Colby had laid out the town, they'd insisted that only businesses should be on the main street. They reasoned that the noise and dust caused by steady traffic would make it an unsuitable location for private homes where quiet and cleanliness were important. Norman and Noah had built their homes on the western end of town because it had a higher elevation that allowed them to look down on the town from their upper windows. There were no buildings on the main street in front of their two houses because the brothers had wanted everyone to see that they owned the most imposing houses in Cactus Corner. Thus Laurie was forced to walk nearly the length of the town along the main street. She hadn't gone far before she got a partial answer to her question.

Two young men she didn't know were coming

toward her on their way out of town. They caught sight of her at the same time. The sight rattled them so thoroughly that they lost control of their horses and rode into each other. At first Laurie was afraid her appearance was so shockingly bad that the boys had been knocked senseless in horror. But Laurie hadn't forgotten everything about being young, pretty, and single. It was quickly apparent that the men liked what they saw. Laurie was certain she was a sinful woman, but the reaction delighted her. It was hard to hide her smile of satisfaction, but she hadn't the nerve to let them know she was aware of her effect on them. Noah was wrong about one thing—her appearance wasn't an affront to young men. With that bit of encouragement, Laurie held her head a little higher and walked with more confidence.

That confidence ebbed when Mae Oliver, her mother's second cousin, took one look at her, crossed the street, and marched straight up to her.

"Thank goodness you've stopped dressing like a nun. You must have gotten a good night's sleep. You look wonderful."

A tight knot of fear unraveled, and Laurie allowed herself to smile. "Are you sure? I'm not dressed too immodestly?"

"If I looked like you, I'd dress the same way. I used to wonder why you didn't, but then I realized that Noah didn't like it when other men looked at you."

Laurie felt vulnerable, like her veil of secrecy had been stripped away. Did everyone in town know of the hell she'd lived through? She wondered how many of her other *secrets* weren't secret.

"Don't look so shocked, dear. There's not a woman in Cactus Corner who hasn't offered a prayer of thanks she wasn't married to Noah. He was a fine man in many ways, but he was never the husband for a lively girl like you."

Laurie thought of several things to say, yet said none of them. There didn't seem to be a need.

"Now that you're free, you can look around for a nice man. With your looks and the money Noah left you, there ought to be a line at your door by the time you get home. I know I've embarrassed you, but there's no use pretending when the truth will serve a lot better. Now I have things to do, as I'm sure you do as well. I know you'll feel more comfortable confiding in Naomi or Sibyl, but if you ever need to talk to someone else, Elsa or I will be glad to give you what advice we can."

Laurie was relieved when Mae turned and crossed the street. Even though Mae and Elsa were her mother's cousins, Laurie didn't know what to say to Mae's kind offer. She couldn't imagine a situation that would have her going to either Mae or Elsa for advice. It took a few moments to recover her equilibrium, but she had regained her composure by the time she reached the bank.

Norman had insisted that his bank had to be the most impressive building in Cactus Corner. There was no need for a second floor, but he'd built one anyway. He said he found the idea of a false front insulting. How could his customers trust him if the front of his building wasn't honest? Inside, a bench-filled lobby was big enough to accommodate up to a dozen customers. The tellers' cages were made of dark mahogany and shone with a rich luster.

Cassie occupied the first cage. Ostensibly, her job was to direct each customer to the right person, but everybody knew Norman employed her to smile at the male customers, engage them in friendly conversation, and ensure that they would continue to do their business at his bank. Sibyl had told Laurie that Norman believed Cassie was worth every cent he paid her. Besides, providing a job for the young widow who had a small son to support made him look good in the eyes of the town.

"Are you here to see Norman?" Cassie asked when Laurie entered the bank.

"He told me to come by whenever I could."

"There's someone with him right now." There were no customers in the bank at the moment, but Cassie beckoned Laurie to come closer. "It's that man you spoke to at the wake yesterday."

"Which one? I spoke to a lot of men." She didn't really have to ask. Cassie could be referring to only one man.

"It's that Jared Smith," Cassie whispered. "I don't know what he wants, but I've heard him raise his voice a few times. I don't think he's going to be very happy when he comes out."

"Naomi said he's just arrived in the area. He's probably just talking about setting up his business with the bank. Naomi said he bought a ranch."

"I don't know about any of that, but I can tell when a man is angry."

Laurie didn't doubt that. Cassie had an

understanding of men that bordered on the supernatural. Fortunately, she was the most uncomplicated person Laurie knew. Cassie never said one thing and meant another, nor did she try to manipulate people. It was her open honesty that caused some people to avoid her.

A door in the back of the bank opened, and Laurie could hear Norman telling Mr. Smith that he was sorry that he couldn't help him, that maybe he ought to reconsider his plan.

"Would you accept my advice if I told you how to run your bank?"

"Of course not."

She could tell from the sound of Norman's voice that the mere suggestion was an affront to him.

"Then you can't expect me to accept your advice about how to run my ranch."

"When someone asks to use my money, he has to expect to listen to my advice."

The two men appeared around the far side of the clerks' cages. Mr. Smith was walking ahead with long, angry strides. Norman had to practically run to keep up. Mr. Smith turned around so unexpectedly that Norman nearly collided with him.

"Since you've made it clear I'm not going to be using your money, let me make it clear that I'm not going to be taking your advice."

"I hope this won't prevent you from using the bank for your business," Norman said.

"At the moment, I don't have any business. When I do, I'll think about it."

With that, he turned and strode from the bank

without appearing to notice either Cassie or Laurie. Norman looked after him in a kind of bemused surprise.

"I don't think I can smile brightly enough to bring him back to the bank," Cassie said.

"He'll have to come back," Norman said. "He can't find another bank without riding all the way to Jerome."

"Laurie is here to see you," Cassie informed him.

"You don't need to tell me. I can see her."

"She could have been here to withdraw money. She's got a lot of it now."

"I employ you to entertain the customers," Norman said, "not speculate on their business."

"I can come back if this isn't a good time." Laurie had hoped to prevent Norman from being sharp with Cassie, but the look he gave her made her wish she'd kept silent. His disapproval didn't need words to make itself known.

"Where did you get those clothes?" he demanded.

"At my own store. Where else could I have gotten them?"

"First, it's not *your* store. And just because an item is sold there doesn't mean you have to purchase it or wear it."

"I think she looks wonderful," Cassie said. "You could give her my job and you wouldn't have to pay me."

Laurie hoped some honest, upstanding man showed up soon to marry Cassie. She was too guileless for her own good.

"Your job would be unsuitable for my sister-in-law," Norman said.

Fortunately for everyone, a customer entered the bank. Norman beckoned Laurie to follow him and headed for his office.

Even more than his home, Norman's office reflected his opinion of himself. The room was furnished with heavy, dark furniture made of mahogany or covered in leather. Books he would never open lined the wall, and an oriental rug covered the space between his massive desk and the chair Laurie was to occupy. Sunshine flooding in a huge window lit the room.

"Mr. Smith seemed unusually upset when he left. I gather he didn't get what he wanted." Laurie didn't know why she'd said that. Mr. Smith's needs were none of her business. Besides, Norman never discussed business with women. There was no reason he would make an exception for Laurie. But he did.

"He wanted to borrow money to buy a herd of Hereford cattle. I told him longhorns would be better, but he insisted he wanted only Herefords." He glared at Laurie. "I can't understand why you would appear on the street dressed like that. Noah would never have allowed it."

Laurie had been ready to listen to Norman's criticism without comment, but that was too much. "Noah's no longer my husband, so what he would or wouldn't allow is beside the point."

She might as well have slapped Norman. He sat up in his chair and gaped at her with wide eyes. "As long as you bear the Spencer name, anything you do will reflect on the family's good name."

Laurie hadn't endured four years of marriage to

Noah to allow his brother to dictate her taste in clothes. "There's nothing amiss with any of the clothes I'm wearing. Just minutes ago Mae Oliver crossed the street to tell me how attractive she thought I looked."

"A widow shouldn't look attractive," Norman insisted. "You might as well announce that you'd welcome male attention."

"You can rest easy on that score. I will never marry again." She was pleased to see her answer had surprised Norman.

"Certainly you wouldn't marry again for several years. Noah deserves a suitable period of mourning, which your choice of attire fails to honor. You should wear only black for the next several months."

"We're not likely to agree on what's suitable for me to wear, but if it will make you feel any better, I'll be happy to consult Sibyl or Naomi when I go shopping again."

"I hope you don't intend to model your behavior on Naomi."

"I don't intend to model my behavior on anybody. I have enough intelligence to make my own decisions." She needed to get to the reading of the will. She was becoming so annoyed it was hard to keep it out of her voice or her expression. "Why don't you tell me what's in Noah's will? The sooner you hand over control of his estate to me, the sooner you can get back to work."

Norman assumed the pompous attitude that always made Laurie long to slap him. "It's not quite that simple."

"Why not? I'm his only heir."

"Noah left the house and its contents to you."

"I know that. What I need to know is how much money I have."

"You don't have any money. He left the rest of his estate to me to administer for your benefit."

For a moment, Laurie was afraid her heart would never beat again. She struggled to draw breath, but her body was paralyzed. She couldn't move or speak. She felt weak, so dizzy she was afraid she would faint. Norman's mouth opened. He must have been saying something, but it sounded like bees buzzing in her ears.

Then everything went blank.

Two

THE FIRST THING LAURIE WAS AWARE OF WAS A WET cloth on her forehead. She could make out the murmur of voices, but she couldn't understand what they were saying. She was lying down, but the bed was so hard she couldn't possibly sleep. Where was she? Noah would never have bought such a bed.

"She's coming around," she heard Cassie say to someone else in the room. "Watch what you say. If you make her faint again, there'll be hell to pay."

"I didn't *make* her faint. She did it on her own. And I won't have an employee of mine, especially a woman, using such language in my bank."

That was Norman's voice, but what was he doing here? And why did he think she was in his bank?

"Help me lift her into that chair. I'm not strong enough to do it alone."

"Why can't she remain where she is until she can lift herself?"

"Because it's not dignified for a lady, especially your sister-in-law, to be lying on the floor."

"She should have thought of that before she fainted."

"What did you say to her? It must have been awful."

"It certainly was not. I was merely discussing the provisions of my brother's will."

Laurie opened her eyes to see Cassie looking down at her, her beautiful young face a mask of concern.

"From her reaction, I'd guess he left everything to you."

"The contents of the will are no concern of yours."

"I expect everybody in town will know before nightfall." Cassie helped Laurie sit up. "How are you feeling?"

"A little dizzy. What happened? Why am I on the floor?"

"Mr. Spencer said something to make you faint."

"I did no such thing," Norman protested.

"Help me up. I can't stay sitting on the floor."

Norman tried to help her up, but he was so tentative he was more of a hindrance. Once in the chair, Laurie smoothed her hair and straightened her skirt. "Thank you, Cassie. I'd have been in a sad way without your help. Now Norman has to tell me why I fainted."

"Are you sure you're strong enough?"

"Yes." What choice did she have?

"I think you ought to see the doctor when you leave. A healthy young woman like you ought not to faint."

"I'll be all right. I'm sure it was the stress of Noah's death and the funeral."

"If you faint again, I'm calling the doctor myself."

After the door closed behind Cassie, Laurie turned to Norman. Her strength was returning. Along with it came seething anger. "Now I remember. Why would Noah leave everything to you? Did you force him to do it?"

Norman was incensed. "I have never forced my brother to do anything. It is a perfectly ordinary thing to do. No woman is capable of handling an estate on her own."

"I've worked in the store, so I know how it's run. I don't see any reason why I can't have my money."

"You *do* have your money. It's just that I've been left to manage it for you."

"How do you intend to *manage* it?"

"As I said, he left you the house and its contents."

"Can I sell it?"

"No. Why would you want to?"

"Then I don't have a house any more than I have any money." Noah was controlling her from the grave.

"You have a house and you have money. I'll make you a suitable allowance each month."

"How much?"

"I'll decide that once I've had a chance to go over Noah's household accounts."

"I can tell you how much I need."

Norman took on the appearance of a prune. "Noah's will directed *me* to make all decisions about your money."

"I would like a hundred dollars immediately. I need to buy new clothes and some new furnishings for the house." She might as well have told Norman she wanted to throw everything in her house into the street. He puffed up like a hot pastry.

"What's wrong with the house?"

"Nothing. I just want to replace some furnishings I don't care for."

"Noah chose everything in that house."

"That's why I want to buy some new ones. He chose them, not me."

"Do you intend to purchase more clothes like the ones you have on?"

"There's nothing wrong with my clothes. I already said I'd talk to Naomi or Sibyl before I buy anything more."

"I believe it would be better if I went along to approve your purchases."

"You don't trust my cousins? Not even your own wife?"

"There are a lot of single men who come through our town. They are not the kind of men who are likely to think well of a woman dressed as you are."

Laurie didn't need Norman to say anything further for her to know he intended to use her money to control her as tightly as her husband had done. She had been given freedom just long enough to taste it before it was snatched away. She had to do something to keep this from happening, but she didn't know what it would be. In the meantime, she was so angry she'd say something to make the situation worse if she didn't leave. "How much money will you give me? I will need to buy food."

He reached inside a drawer in his desk and withdrew a handful of silver coins. "Here's twenty dollars. Since you will have your own money, you won't need to buy anything from the store on credit."

He really did intend to supervise everything she

bought. She accepted the coins with a shaking hand. She put them inside her purse and rose. "I'll let you know when I need more money."

"We haven't discussed—"

"I don't see any need to discuss anything further when you've made it clear you plan to make my decisions for me. Should I let you know when I'm close to starvation, or can I expect twenty dollars next week?"

"I don't think you need that much money a week just for food."

If she stayed any longer, she'd throw something at him. "I'm surprised you didn't decide to keep the money and send me what food you think I need."

She left his office while he was speaking, but she didn't need to hear what he was saying to know she'd exchanged one prison for another. She couldn't be sure this one wouldn't be worse. At this moment, she was sure of only one thing—she didn't know what she would do or how she would do it, but she would *not* live one day longer than necessary under Norman's thumb. On her way out, she walked by Cassie with no more than a curt good-bye, but courtesy would have to wait. Right now she needed to get as far away from Norman and his bank as she could.

She looked about, but there was really no place to go. If anyone saw her wandering about the countryside, they'd be sure she was distraught over Noah's death and refuse to leave her alone until they'd peppered her with enough questions to satisfy themselves she wasn't going to hurt herself. If they only knew! Nothing could hurt her more than the marriage she'd endured. She would go home. She needed to think.

Laurie didn't know how long she'd sat staring into space before she heard a knock at the door, and Naomi let herself in.

"Cassie said Norman said something to cause you to faint this morning. Are you all right? I thought you went to talk about the will."

It took Laurie only a few minutes to explain the situation. It wouldn't have taken as long if Naomi hadn't interrupted so many times to express her indignation and anger.

"How can Norman do that?"

"Norman didn't. Noah did, and I'm certain it can't be changed."

"I'll talk to—" She stopped.

Laurie knew Naomi had started to say she would talk to Vernon Edwards. He was a lawyer, but he was also Norman's father-in-law. They could expect no help there. In all probability, he'd written the will for Noah.

"There has to be something you can do," Naomi insisted. "If nothing else, we can try to bring enough pressure on Norman to embarrass him."

"It won't do any good. Norman will claim he was only doing what Noah wanted, which we all know is the truth. You can't go against a dying man's wishes."

"A *dead* man, and what he wishes is cruel. You have a lot of people on your side. We'll figure out something."

But Laurie didn't need *everybody* else to figure out something. She wanted to do it herself. She'd been given her life back. She didn't plan to let it slip out of her control again.

"What would you like to do?" Naomi asked. "Run the store?"

That's what Laurie had assumed she wanted to do, but as soon as the words were out of Naomi's mouth, she knew she wanted nothing to do with that store. It was as much part of Noah's prison as the house she would be forced to live in. "As far as I'm concerned, my father can take it over."

"Do you think Norman will let him? Everybody knows your father is a lousy businessman. We also know he forced you to marry Noah so Noah wouldn't kick him out."

Could her humiliation be more complete? "I don't care what happens to the store. If Norman had any sense, he'd turn it over to Mae Oliver and Elsa Drummond. Nobody knows more about what everybody in this town likes, and their husbands would help them. If they put Ted Drummond behind the counter, every woman within a hundred miles would come in just to look at him."

Naomi laughed. "If he and Cassie got married, their children would be so beautiful they'd blind you."

Laurie grinned, but only briefly.

"If you could do anything you wanted, what would you really like to do?" Naomi asked again.

"I'd like to own a ranch." The answer surprised even Laurie. She didn't know anything about running a ranch. Why would she want to own one?

"Are you sure you don't mean a farm?"

"If you mean like people had in Kentucky, no." She was sure it was a ranch.

"You don't have any money, and I know Norman would never give you money to invest in a ranch. Besides, the only rancher I know is Jared Smith, and he may not be here much longer. I heard Norman turned down his request for a loan to buy Herefords."

An idea struck Laurie that was beautiful in its simplicity. She had a lot of money no one knew she had. It was a guilty secret, but she'd kept it against the day when she had no choice but to use it. That day had come. She would lend Jared Smith the money he needed, and she would become his partner.

❦

"Where are you going to find the money?" Jared's nephew, Steve, asked. "If you don't have it when the Herefords get here, the owner is just going to keep going."

"I know that," Jared said. "I was sure that snotty-nosed banker would be happy to lend me the money, but somebody's convinced him the only cows that will survive in the Arizona Territory are longhorns."

"I think you ought to give up on Herefords and keep the longhorns we have. We don't know how those fancy cows will do out here."

Out here had a lot in common with where he'd grown up in Texas. It was hot, dry, and it would take thirty-five acres to support a single cow, but he had the advantage of a ready market in the troops at Fort Verde. He had seen his first Herefords in Virginia during the war. Their traits of economy in feeding, natural aptitude to grow and gain weight from grass, rustling ability, hardiness, early maturity, and prolificacy were exactly what he needed if his ranch was to be a success. But Herefords were scarce. It was pure luck that a man was crazy enough to attempt to trail a herd through Arizona to California. If he didn't buy this herd, he might never get the chance again.

"They'll do just fine."

"Are you sure he will sell to you?"

"No, but it's a long way to California. Money in hand is better than money he can only imagine. If I can offer him an acceptable price, I believe he'll sell me the herd." But that was the problem. He was certain the man would only sell the *whole* herd. What would be the point of selling part of a herd if he still had to make the dangerous journey with those left unsold, especially when he'd get twice as much for them if he could make it to California?

Jared had known leaving the army to invest in a ranch was a gamble. He had grown up in Texas and knew all about longhorns, but the previous owner had made only a small profit with only longhorns. Jared knew he needed good stock he could make still better through selective breeding.

"We don't have the money, so you might as well stop thinking about it," Steve told him. "Now we've got work to do. You coming?"

"I have some things I need to do in the office. I'll join you after lunch."

Steve made a rude sound. "If you can consider anything Odell cooks food. I don't know how you can eat it."

"It's better than what I ate during the war."

"I didn't fight in the war, so I'm not used to eating stuff that would cause dogs to turn up their noses."

"If you can find a better cook, I'll hire him. Until

then, you'll have to eat what Odell cooks or cook it yourself."

"Then I would starve. I know why you came to Arizona, but I don't see why we have to stay here now that you haven't found any trace of your brothers. It's worse than Texas."

Steve's departure left Jared with too many questions and too few answers. If he couldn't buy the kind of cows he wanted, could he afford to continue to ranch? Was it fair to keep Steve in a place he disliked and a thousand miles away from his mother's family? Maybe most important of all, was he wasting time in his search for his brothers? Why was he so determined to find two men he could barely remember and who might not remember him or want to be found?

His adopted parents had told him Logan had been four and Kevin one when their birth parents died. That was twenty-nine years ago. More than enough time to have built a life that had nothing to do with him, that probably had no place for him in it. What did he *really* expect to do if he found them? They would be strangers. Beyond birth parents he barely remembered, he would have no more in common with them than a man he met on the street.

Yet he couldn't stop looking. His adoptive parents had been loving and kind, but he'd always felt incomplete, like a part of him had been lost when his parents died and their boys had been adopted by three different families. Maybe he just wanted to know his brothers were alive. At thirty-two, he'd already lost two sets of parents, a brother, and a sister-in-law. All he had left of his family was Steve. Maybe he was reaching out because if something happened to Steve, he would be alone. There was no single reason. It was simply something he had to do.

But right now he had a desk covered in work that needed to be tackled.

Jared didn't know when he became aware of the sound of a buggy approaching the house. That in itself was unusual. The trails through the valley were so rough that many could only be navigated on horseback. That meant the buggy must have come from Cactus Corner. That name immediately conjured up an image of the young widow, Laurie Spencer. He'd tried without success to put her out of his mind. He'd had two dreams that were so real he'd come awake in a state of arousal that was as uncomfortable as it was impossible to gratify.

It was foolish to taunt himself with thoughts of her. He had nothing to offer such a woman. She was related to half the people in Cactus Corner and was a wealthy and beautiful widow. He wouldn't be surprised if she left Arizona altogether. Endowed with looks and money, she would be a success just about anywhere. He should put her out of his mind. He needed to finish this last letter so he would be ready to greet his visitor. He was the only one in the house.

When he stepped out on the porch, he was convinced the sun had to be in his eyes or that he was seeing who he wanted to see. But it took only a minute before he realized he wasn't mistaken. Laurie Spencer *was* driving the buggy that even now was slowing down as it approached his house. His mind went blank. What could she possibly want with him, and why was it so important that she would have driven all the way from town by herself?

Rousing himself from his stupor, he hurried down the steps. When the buggy came to a halt, he tethered the horse to the hitching post and moved to help Laurie alight.

"Welcome to Green River Ranch." He held out his hand to help her down. "You shouldn't have come alone. There's still danger from Indians."

"I didn't want company. I have business to conduct with you alone."

Jared couldn't imagine what business she could have with him, but he'd have listened to the most outrageous proposal just to sit and look at her. It was pathetic, it wasn't good for him physically or emotionally, but nothing could have caused him to tell her to get back in the buggy and go home.

"I'm surprised. You know nothing about me."

"My cousin, Naomi Blaine, spoke well of you. I trust her judgment."

"You'd better come inside and get warm."

A weak winter sun struggled to shed some warmth, but a harsh wind swallowed it. Laurie was wrapped up head to toe in a heavy driving coat. She had wound a thick woolen scarf around her neck, but her hat and veil provided little protection. She had to be chilled to the bone.

"Thank you. It was a chilly drive."

He didn't know if she was just being polite, or if she really didn't mind the cold. After growing up in south Texas, he had suffered during the winters he spent in Virginia. He hoped he'd never see snow again.

He felt self-conscious about the state of his house as they went inside. The army had taught him to be neat and organized, but two men lived here who didn't have the time or interest in furnishing their home attractively or in keeping it clean.

"I apologize for inviting you into my office, but it's the only room with a fire."

"You don't have to apologize. You had no way of knowing I would be coming."

Nor any idea why she had. "Can I offer you some coffee? There's still some in the pot on the stove."

"No, thank you, but I would appreciate some water."

What did you put water in when you served it to a lady? All he had was an assortment of coffee cups, tin and earthenware. He returned, embarrassed to present her with a cup and saucer. "Sorry, but we don't have any glasses."

She smiled and his knees nearly gave out under him. "I don't mind. After what we endured on the trip to Santa Fe, I'll never quibble about what I drink from as long as it's clean."

He couldn't be absolutely sure the cup was clean, but he thought it best not to mention that.

She took a long drink before setting her cup down. "Thank you. That's just what I needed. I still haven't gotten used to the weather being so dry."

"You're from Kentucky, aren't you?" That's what one of the people in her train had told him.

"Nearly everyone in Cactus Corner is from the same village, Spencer's Clearing. It was all we could do to keep Norman from naming our new town Spencer's Corner."

He could believe that. "He's your brother-in-law?"

"He *was* my husband's brother."

He wondered why she'd chosen such an odd way to answer his question. "Your husband must have been well thought of. It looked like everyone in town turned out for his funeral."

"As I said, nearly all of us came from the same place. We've known each other for years. It would have been odd not to attend the funeral."

Again, she'd avoided answering his question.

"Do you mind if I take off my coat? I'm getting rather warm."

"Not at all. I should have asked you if you wanted me to take it when you came in."

"I was still cold then."

She stood and shrugged out of her coat before he could offer to help her. Next she removed her hat and veil. "Your office is very cozy."

The potbellied stove didn't qualify as *cozy* in his mind, but maybe she was talking about the warmth and its small size. "I don't spend a lot of time here, so I don't need much space."

"What's it like being a rancher?"

Normally he wouldn't have had any trouble answering that question, but normally he was not in the room with a beautiful woman whose lush body caused his brain to turn to mush. Not even her relatively modest clothes could hide the generous curves that belonged to a woman at least a decade older. It was her face that said she was young, probably no more than early twenties. Yet there was something about her eyes that said all her years hadn't been happy ones. But how could he concentrate on her eyes when her mouth was so wide and her lips so full and red? It was enough to cause a man to do something stupid.

"I suppose being a rancher is a lot like other jobs," he said, trying to concentrate on her question and not her body. "I get to spend a lot of time outdoors on a horse, but I still have to pay bills."

"You don't make it sound very exciting."

"It's not, but I grew up on a ranch in Texas. Cows aren't much fun."

"Would you rather do something else?"

Why all the questions? It was like she was questioning him to see if he passed some sort of basic requirements before she decided whether to discuss her business. Still, what kind of business could this young widow have that could concern him? He had no connection with her late husband's mercantile or her brother-in-law's bank.

"I've spent seven years in the army, four fighting a war in Virginia, and three fighting the Comanche in Texas. Fighting and ranching are all I know. Of the two, I much prefer ranching."

"How much land do you have?"

"That's difficult to say. I can't *buy* enough land to ranch, but I can use all I can claim and control."

"How much is that?"

"Twenty thousand acres. Thirty if I need it."

She seemed surprised. "Isn't that a lot?"

"Not when it takes thirty-five acres to support one cow."

She paused only briefly before replying, "Then

your twenty thousand acres could only support something over five hundred and fifty cows. Is that a lot?"

She might not know much about ranching, but she was certainly good with math to be able to figure that out in her head so quickly. "It's not a lot by Texas standards, but Texans have longhorns. I'm hoping to buy Herefords."

"Why?"

"Because they gain weight quickly on grass, are hardy, mature early, and reproduce quickly. They carry more weight and the meat is a better quality than a longhorn. For the same investment of time and resources, I can get twice the profit."

"Do you have any of these cows? What do they look like?"

"They're red with white faces, but I don't have any yet."

"How do you plan to get them?"

"A man will be passing through Arizona in a few weeks with a herd he's taking to California. I've heard tell he now realizes it was a foolish thing to do, but he's come too far to turn around and go back. If I can buy his whole herd, I believe he'll sell it rather than attempt to make the rest of the journey and risk losing more of his cows."

"How many cows does he have?"

"He started out with five hundred. I expect he has fewer than four hundred left. He got hit by Indians and stampedes, wolves got a few, and some just died."

"How much will they cost?"

"If he makes it to California, they'll go for more

than thirty dollars a head. He'll sell them to me for twenty, but I'm hoping to get him down to fifteen."

After another quick calculation, she said, "At twenty dollars, it would cost you eight thousand dollars to buy four hundred."

"That's why I'm hoping to get him down to fifteen a head."

"That's only six thousand dollars, but you don't have that much money, do you?"

Jared was finding it difficult to concentrate. Being so close he could reach out and touch her was driving him nuts. It had been years since he'd been with a desirable woman, but no woman he'd ever been with or seen could compare to Laurie Spencer. Arizona weather was much harder on women than Texas, yet her cheeks were soft and pink, her skin as creamy and rich as a magnolia blossom. The skin around her eyes might reveal hardship and unhappiness, but the eyes themselves were large orbs of pure white and the most vivid blue he'd ever seen. She faced him with a wide-open gaze that invited confidence yet demanded distance.

He forced his thoughts back to her question. "No, I don't have all the money I need. I had hoped your brother-in-law would give me a loan for the rest, but he won't."

"I would prefer that you not refer to Norman Spencer as my brother-in-law. That connection ended with my husband's death."

"Anything you wish." He imagined Norman Spencer could be a difficult person to have in the family. "Why have you come to see me? Why are you asking these questions? We can't possibly have any business to conduct."

She paused and lowered her gaze to her lap before raising it again. "I would like to invest in your ranch. I've asked these questions because I need to know whether my money would be invested wisely."

"Why haven't you asked your brother-in…Norman Spencer to advise you? He would know a lot more about potential investments than I do."

"Norman doesn't know I'm here, and he knows nothing of what I intend to do. If he did, he'd do everything in his power to stop me. Part of our agreement, if we are able to reach one, will be that you can never tell anyone the details of our arrangement."

That made Jared uneasy. "You're going to have to explain that. What you've told me makes me reluctant to enter into any arrangement with you."

Laurie twisted her hands in her lap and looked resigned. "I was hoping you wouldn't require an explanation, but it's only fair that you receive one. I have some money of my own. Norman doesn't know about it, and you're not to tell him where you got it. Except for my house, my husband left his entire estate in his brother's control to manage for my benefit. He will use that to force me to do what he wishes. I refuse to be under Norman's thumb. If I don't invest my money with you, I'll look elsewhere."

Jared had never seen a woman look more determined. If Laurie hadn't been so controlled, he wouldn't have been surprised if she'd shouted the words at him. "Any business deal between us would be private. No one would have a right to know the details."

She relaxed visibly and took another drink of water. "How much money do you need? I'm not a rich woman."

"You've already done the calculations. I will probably need eight thousand. I have five."

When she smiled, he knew that she had at least three thousand.

"I can provide the difference and a little more. When will you need it?"

After her businesslike approach, he hadn't expected her to jump to the end so quickly. "Don't you want to talk about a contract, know what you can expect in return?"

"Certainly I will require a contract. I shall go over it most thoroughly. I merely asked because I wanted to know when you expect the herd to arrive."

"It's still in New Mexico. I won't need the money until it reaches Arizona. Will it be in gold or bills?"

"It'll be in bills." Her laugh was unexpected. "You couldn't hide that much gold from Norman. He could smell it." She sobered quickly. "Norman has been exceedingly generous in providing loans to everyone in our town, but my husband was quite different with me. Norman will be the same."

"Do you know anything about ranching?"

"No."

"How do you know I won't try to cheat you?"

"You are an honorable man."

"You can't know that."

"I know you've been staring at me in a manner that indicates you have some very improper thoughts in your head. Yet you've done your best to make sure it doesn't show."

Jared was disgusted that he'd been so transparent, but he was impressed Laurie was so forthright. "You're a very attractive woman. No, you're a beautiful and voluptuous woman. Surely you're so used to men staring at you that you no longer take offense."

It appeared that he'd upended her calm. She blushed in a shy manner that made him fear he could fall head over heels in love in a single moment. She wasn't nearly as worldly as she tried to pretend if a mild compliment could cause her to blush so brilliantly.

"I have two cousins who are more attractive than I am. We've known the same people all our lives. I'm related to half of them. No one thinks of any one of us as beautiful, and certainly not voluptuous." She regained enough composure to laugh. "They don't hesitate to remind us of the years when we were straggly and boney with uneven teeth and unsightly bumps." She leaned a little toward him. "I appreciate your compliment, but you mustn't say anything like that again."

"If I agreed to do that, I won't be talking very much. How about the men who work for me? Are they equally forbidden to express their admiration for your beauty?"

"I'm sure they're all gentlemen. Otherwise, you would not have hired them."

"I don't know what kind of men you've been around, but they must have been like your banker— bloodless and full of conceit. I have a fifteen-year-old nephew. If you think you can muzzle him, you're welcome to try. I've never succeeded. My men are as hot-blooded as any men who've gone a long time without enjoying the company of a beautiful woman. They're likely to stare and be unable to speak without stuttering, but they're gentlemen." Laurie looked uncomfortable, but if she wanted to go into a partnership with him, she had to know the kind of reception she could expect. Dumbfounded amazement would just be the beginning.

"I'm sure you exaggerate," Laurie said self-consciously. "Now we ought to talk about the terms of the contract."

"Naturally, the terms of the contract won't come into play until I have the money, but they can be straightforward. Depending on how much of the purchase cost you provide, you will own that percentage of the herd."

"Do you mean I will own so many animals and you will own the rest?"

"No. We will each own the same percentage of each cow. When we sell one, we both make a profit. When one dies, we both lose."

"When would you plan to sell?"

"That's hard to say. I would like to build the herd, select the best bulls, and sell the rest. I would do the same with the cows."

"So you don't anticipate a major sale for up to a year?"

"Not of Herefords, though I'll be gradually selling off the longhorns. Is that a problem?"

"No. Since we're going to be partners, I want to know your plans for the future of the ranch."

"You didn't say anything about being a partner, only investing in my herd."

"I said I wanted to invest in your *ranch*. That encompasses more than the cows. It includes the house, the land, even the equipment."

This little lady didn't know what she was asking. No man took a woman as a partner, not even a silent one. "I can't do that."

"Why not?"

"It would require more money."

"And if I have the money?"

"Do you?"

"I won't know until you tell me how much the ranch is worth."

He tossed out a figure he was certain she couldn't meet. "But it won't make any difference if you have the money. I don't want a partner."

"Why?"

"Do I need a reason?"

"A reasonable man would have one, and I believe you're more than reasonable."

Jared had always considered himself a rational man, so it came as a shock to realize he *didn't* have a reason for not accepting a woman as a business partner. He'd never known it to happen and had unconsciously assumed it wouldn't work. But what would a partnership with Laurie entail? Nothing but an infusion of money. She wouldn't live at the ranch, she wouldn't ride with them, and she wouldn't know enough about ranching to make the business decisions. Since she was obviously gifted in math, she would probably want to see the books to make sure she was getting her fair share of the profits, but that would be the extent of her involvement. Partnership with her would be the perfect solution.

"I'm ashamed to say I don't have a reason beyond never having seen it happen before."

"Then if you will give me a *realistic* figure for the cost of a full partnership, we can discuss terms."

Jared was so curious he had to ask. "Where did you get your grasp of business? The women I've known haven't been interested in anything beyond babies and what to cook for supper."

"My father owned the mercantile with my husband. I've heard the two of them and Norman discuss business at the supper table for years. Since I was *only a woman* who couldn't understand anything they said well enough to repeat it later, they talked about everything."

Jared's father had done much the same. "Okay, here's what I paid for the ranch." The figure was so low she raised her eyebrows in surprise. "It covers only the land, the house, and the other buildings. The range is free to anyone who can hold it."

Her enthusiasm disappeared. "I can't meet that figure and pay for my share of the herd."

He was relieved. He much preferred that her involvement be limited to the herd. "That's okay with me. I only wanted enough money to buy the stock."

"It's not okay with me. If I can't be a full partner, I won't be a partner at all."

Jared could see his dream was about to crumble if he didn't do something quickly. "Why is being a full partner so important to you? You said you know nothing about ranching."

At first, Laurie seemed reluctant to answer. Was his question too personal? Was she hiding more secrets she didn't wish to share? Whatever the reasons for her reluctance, she appeared to set them aside. She spoke with a directness that left no room for doubt or insecurity.

"I've been ignored my whole life for the simple fact that I'm a woman. It was assumed I had no intelligence and wouldn't have wished for any. I was told what to do and was expected to be grateful for it. *That will not happen again.*"

Jared couldn't believe such a beautiful woman had been treated so badly. He'd have willingly turned himself into a slave to be able to make love to a woman like Laurie. Noah Spencer must have been a complete and utter fool.

"A limited agreement wouldn't mean that you were ignored. You would have access to the books so you would know the exact amount of all costs and profits. You would be welcome to come inspect them at any time."

She was unmoved. "I can't accept that. I would feel like an outsider asking permission to see what was my own. I wouldn't know what was happening with my investment. This is all the money I have. If I lose it, I'll be a prisoner for the rest of my life." Her agitation was growing. She spoke as though to herself, "I was so sure this was the answer."

"It can be. It's a safe investment. Herefords are nearly as indestructible as longhorns, which is why I was surprised Mr. Spencer turned down my request for a loan."

"If I didn't know it was impossible, I'd believe Norman knew I was going to approach you and turned you down just so I could fail and remain under his control."

That didn't make any sense to him, but he could see Laurie was upset. He could also see that the money he needed was about to disappear. "You'd be welcome to come out to the ranch at any time. If you'd prefer, I could go into town once a week to tell you what we're doing. If you had any questions, you could come see for yourself. Or you could ask someone you trust to come in your stead."

"You don't understand. *I* want to do this. I don't want to be told by you or anyone else." She started to rise.

"Don't go." He had to do something to make her stay, something to keep her from withholding her money. If he changed his mind and said she could have a full partnership for the same money, she wouldn't trust him. She'd probably believe he would treat her like her husband had. He had to find some way for her to believe that she was paying for her share of the partnership. Only one solution came to mind.

"You can have a full partnership if you'll cook and clean for us."

Three

Jared knew immediately he'd said the wrong thing. "Our cook is so bad we can hardly eat anything he fixes. My nephew was complaining about him just before you came." He had to try harder, because she wasn't looking any happier. "The army taught me to be neat and organized, but I don't have the time to keep the house clean. I tried to arrange for one of the wives from Fort Verde to help, but no one would do it."

"And you think I would?"

How did he say he wasn't suggesting anything improper without putting it into words? "As a full partner, it would be in your best interest to make sure your investment was being properly managed and your workers well cared for."

Her smile was cynical. "Very cleverly stated, but what you're proposing is to turn me into a drudge."

"Do you cook for yourself, clean your own house?"

"Of course I do, but I don't live I-don't-know-how-many miles from town without a woman or relative around. My reputation would be ruined. I'm surprised you didn't know that's why no army wife would take your job."

He did, but he'd hoped the hardships of living in the West would knock some sense into the outdated social customs of the East. They'd managed it in Texas. Why not Arizona?

Laurie got to her feet. "Thank you for talking to me and answering my questions so frankly. I regret we couldn't reach an agreement."

"Are you sure?"

"Absolutely. I hope you find some way to purchase your Herefords. They sound like the best stock for this range."

Jared wanted to keep arguing, but he could tell Laurie had made up her mind. It was still possible he might come up with a solution, but it wouldn't be today. Yet he was encouraged by the fact that she'd offered the money and was unhappy that it hadn't worked out as she'd hoped. She wanted the partnership. He just had to find a way to make it acceptable to her.

On the other hand, maybe it was best things hadn't worked out. He would have done his best to control his urges, but being around Laurie for hours at a time would have put a severe strain on him. Even now he could practically feel her full breasts in his hands, imagine how it would be to kiss that lush mouth, to sink into her body with—

He had to stop before he embarrassed himself in front of her, which would guarantee that she'd never set foot on the ranch again.

"I'm sorry we couldn't reach an agreement, but I'll

try to think of a way we can work together. I hope you will, too."

"My terms won't change."

Her brother-in-law ought to give her a job in the bank. She was a tough negotiator.

He followed her out and helped her into her buggy. As he watched her drive away, he owned he'd do whatever was necessary to make this partnership a reality. Laurie Spencer was simmering with untapped passion. She'd been kept under such tight restraint she probably didn't realize it herself. He needed her money to stock his ranch, but she needed him to bring her back to life.

Still, he wasn't going to give his ranch away. It was all he and Steve owned in the world. If she wanted a partnership, she would have to pay for it one way or the other.

❧

Laurie had suffered many disappointments in life, some of tragic proportions, so she wasn't prepared to find herself so frustrated that her proposed partnership with Jared Smith hadn't worked out. She couldn't think of any other way she could invest her money, certainly not one where she could keep the origin of the money secret. And she needed to do that, she thought, as she remembered how she had gotten the money.

Everything had been in chaos the night Naomi shot the man who'd killed their grandfather. On one hand, the men were trying to sort out what happened and figure out how to keep the army from punishing them for killing one of their soldiers. On the other hand, they were trying to keep the women and children from knowing what had taken place. Everyone was focused on Naomi and the two dead men, which left Laurie and Sibyl to clean up as best they could.

When Dr. Kessling was cleaning up the blood, he threw the soldier's saddlebags at Laurie and told her to see if he had stolen anything from Grandpa Brown. She knew more about the house than the doctor did. She found several items the soldier had stolen, but there was a packet of bills at the bottom she knew didn't belong to her grandfather. The men were too busy worrying about the bodies to be interested in the contents of the saddlebags, so she kept the money for herself.

Not until she overheard Noah and Norman talking about bags of money found in their and Sibyl's father's houses did she realize the money had been part of a Union Army payroll. Had anyone from the army found the money there, the men would have been arrested and possibly shot. Too afraid to think of using it yet unable to turn it in, Laurie had hidden the money in the bottom of one of her trunks. She'd kept it hidden for five years. Only Noah's death had made it possible for her to use it. But the question was how?

A partnership with Jared Smith was the only practical plan she had. He was a stranger who wouldn't think it unusual that a wealthy widow had access to so much money. Anyone who knew Noah would demand to know where she got it. If Norman found out, he would be certain she'd stolen it from her husband and insist that she give it to him. She was so nettled she flicked the whip over her horse's head. She regretted it immediately. The road was so full of rocks and holes that the extra speed threatened to shake the buggy to pieces. She slowed the horse to a trot.

Being allowed to learn to drive had been one of the few concessions to independence Noah had allowed.

She couldn't help but draw comparisons between Noah and Jared, even though there was no common ground on which they could be judged. The two men were nearly opposites in every respect.

Noah had disliked her physical appearance and had forced her to try to disguise it. However, it had been immediately apparent that Jared Smith had not only liked her appearance, but had been strongly aroused by it. After four years of being told her appearance was an affront to Noah's mother's memory, Jared's reaction was a great relief. She hadn't chosen her body. It had been chosen for her. There was nothing she could do about it. Noah had made her feel even worse by saying her body gave her the appearance of a woman who would encourage men to harbor unsuitable thoughts. She'd spent years trying to disguise the outlines of her figure and avoiding places where she would be noticed by strangers.

She reluctantly admitted that she enjoyed knowing Jared appreciated her looks, but it was a little unsettling to know carnal thoughts sprang so readily to his mind. Even more disturbing, his interest in her had given rise to a few such thoughts in her mind. She'd never thought she was the lustful creature Noah had accused her of being. Nature had designed men and women to be attracted to each other. How else could the race be perpetuated? She would never yield to it, but it couldn't be *wrong* to feel such an attraction to a man like Jared. Naomi had told her that's how she felt about Colby. It had shocked Laurie at the time, but now she understood.

She wondered what it would feel like to have such strong arms around her. Noah had said a lady should preserve decorum at all times. Apparently that forbade all touching. Once, she'd felt so desperate she'd asked Noah to touch her. His response made her feel like a tramp. After that, she never asked again.

She approached a shallow crossing of the Verde River. Its waters were the lifeblood of the valley it meandered through on its way to the Salt River. Along its banks, oaks, willows, and cottonwoods commingled with a smattering of black walnut and box elder. A hundred feet downstream, a mule deer drank from the crystal clear water. Upstream, a heron stood like a statue waiting for an unwary fish to wander within its reach.

Laurie's horse plunged into the shallow water without hesitation. Despite a cold wind that chilled her cheeks, the desert sun's rays burned their way into the fabric of her navy coat, making her feel too warm. Or was it the result of thinking too much about Jared Smith?

Her horse climbed up the far bank, splashing water onto the parched soil. Despite the sun's warmth and the river's shallow depth, streams flowing from the Mogollon Rim kept the water cool even in summer. The youngsters loved swimming in it.

She wondered if Jared ever swam in the river. The image that created in her mind was so vivid and unnerving she decided she wouldn't think about him anymore—and then proceeded to do it anyway. She found him very attractive. Any woman would. He had a way of looking at her that made her feel he couldn't see anyone else. It was evident he liked what he saw. While that made her slightly uneasy, it also excited her.

After years of being fearful of being thought attractive, it gave her a heady feeling to have a handsome man look at her with lust in his eyes. It was even more intoxicating because she could sense a connection between them. He was a big, powerful man, thoroughly masculine, but there was a sensuality about him that was so palpable it was practically visible, so strong that leaving his house was like being released from bondage. If she were alone with him for any length of time, she wouldn't be able to vouch for her behavior.

That's why she couldn't accept his offer to cook and clean in exchange for a full partnership in his ranch.

Now she didn't know what to do with the money. She could use it in small amounts to take the edge off Norman's parsimony, but that wouldn't give her the complete independence she wanted. If she moved to Tucson or Phoenix and was very careful with her money, she had enough to survive for years, but she didn't want to leave her family and friends. She could look for a job, but that wasn't easy for a woman. She needed to find a new investment, but it would have to be with a stranger to keep from having to explain where she'd gotten the money. There were no other strangers in the valley she felt she could trust, no one she *wanted* to trust.

She had to be careful not to let physical attraction get in the way of pragmatic thinking. This was her future. She wouldn't get a second chance. She had plenty of time to look for another investment. Living under Norman's thumb wouldn't be pleasant, but it wouldn't be forever.

∾

Laurie stared at the paper in her hands, unable to believe what she was seeing. It was a list of typical menus for one week and the cost of each meal.

"I used that to determine your food allowance," Norman was saying.

Her allowance! He made it sound like she was a child. "There are things on this list I don't eat, and it makes no allowance for guests."

"I figure you'll eat with others as often as they eat with you."

"You can't determine the cost of a meal merely from the price of the meat and vegetables on the plate. There's butter, oil, flour, seasonings, dozens of other things that go into the preparation of a meal. And that doesn't include soap for cleaning up."

"I'll talk with Sibyl to see what extra costs she thinks are necessary."

"Why not talk to *me*! No one knows better what it will cost to feed me."

"Noah's will made it quite clear that he wanted me to make these decisions for you. I can't go against his wishes. Even if I wished to do so—and I do not—I'm legally bound to follow his instructions."

"I don't believe *making all decisions for my welfare*

extends to deciding how much salt I need, or whether I should eat chicken rather than goose."

"That's what I interpret it to mean."

She didn't believe that. She was certain he couldn't resist the chance to have her completely in his power. He'd tried to do that with his own wife and had failed. Now he was trying to feed his ego by doing it to Laurie. "What if the prices go up?"

"Bring me any bills in question, and I'll see about making adjustments."

Laurie could see herself keeping every bill and adding up pennies to prove a point Norman was as likely as not to ignore. "What about the rest of my expenses?"

"Noah left meticulous records of what it cost to run his house. Since there's only one of you rather than two, I've cut that figure by half."

Laurie ground her teeth. If Norman had paid any attention to those *meticulous records,* he wouldn't have had to make up those ridiculous menus. "The house doesn't care if there are two or twenty people living there. It takes the same amount to keep it furnished, clean, and heated, and repairs made."

"Bring me any pertinent bills, and I'll look at them."

That was probably all he would do. "What about the rest of my allowance?"

"The only other major item is your clothing allowance."

He looked with disapproval at what she was wearing. She'd dressed more conservatively than she had the day she came to see him about the will, but she was never going back to the tent-like dresses Noah had insisted she wear.

"I'm certain Noah would find your present outfit too revealing."

"This dress is no more revealing than the ones Sibyl or every other woman in this town wears."

"We're not talking about other women. Noah had very definite ideas about what he thought was suitable for his wife, and it's up to me to follow those."

"I'm not Noah's wife any longer. I'm his widow."

"That doesn't change anything."

"It changes *everything*."

"As long as it's Noah's money that supports you, I believe we have to follow his wishes as closely as if he were alive. According to his accounts, he provided you with a generous amount for clothing. Do you really need that much?"

Noah had spent more than necessary on her clothes because he was never satisfied with what he could find in made-up dresses. When a seamstress came to Cactus Corner three months before his death, Noah had immediately engaged her to make clothes for Laurie. He'd been enraged when the woman refused to make the kind of dresses he required. She said if women saw Laurie parading around town in a dress that fit no better than a sack, she wouldn't have a single customer.

"If I'm going to wear the black or gray dresses you insist I wear for the next six months, I need extra money. I don't own any suitable dresses." The only positive side of Noah's taste in clothes was that he hated to see her in black. He said with her blond hair and pale complexion, the color made her look like she was ill.

"I'm a very busy man, but I think I can manage to find the time to help you choose your dresses."

Laurie looked at Norman like he'd lost his mind. "I'm not letting you decide what I can and cannot wear."

"Noah did. He would expect me to do the same. He certainly wouldn't approve of that dress as a model for mourning wear. I have half an hour this afternoon between two and two-thirty. I've instructed Amber to have a selection of dresses for us to view."

That was too much for Laurie. Something inside her exploded, making it impossible to remain in Norman's office a moment longer. Without a word, she snatched up her hat, surged to her feet, and stalked from the room with all the dignity she could muster.

"Come back. We're not finished. You can't walk out…"

She didn't need to hear another word to know Norman was going to be *more* controlling than Noah. A sense of desperation seized her. She felt crushed, suffocated, hemmed in with nowhere to turn and no one to help her. Everyone in town could agree that Norman was being unfair, could insist he was perverting Noah's will to feed his own need for control, but no one had the power to change Norman's mind. She was a rich woman, but she would be treated like a beggarly dependent. She wouldn't be allowed to choose her own clothes, probably not her food, either. She might as well be living in Norman's house for all the control she would have over her own home. She couldn't live that way.

The moment she appeared in the lobby, Cassie took one look at her and rose from her chair.

"You look too upset to be alone."

"I'm all right. I just want to go home."

"I'll go with you, but you ought to have someone stay with you until you feel better."

"I'll never feel better." Laurie moaned. "I wish I were dead."

Cassie grabbed her coat and caught up with Laurie just before she reached the door to the street. "That would be a great waste. You'll make the right man a wonderful wife."

"I don't want anything to do with men. I especially don't want to be a wife."

Laurie knew she needed to get herself under control before she left the bank, or she would attract unwanted attention. But rather than rein in her emotions, she itched to tear up that wicked will and tell Norman he was a slimy toad. It would have given her great satisfaction to scatter papers and pull down books he'd never read, anything to destroy the obsessive orderliness of his office, but that wouldn't have changed anything. She had to think, and she had to calm down before she could do that.

"You don't have to accompany me home," she said to Cassie as they headed down the boardwalk. "I don't want you to lose your job."

"Norman won't fire me. He likes money more than he dislikes having a woman work for him. Besides, Frank Oliver made giving me a job part of the memorial to Toby. Frank lost a son in that Indian attack, but I lost a husband and father-in-law."

It was a shame the Indians didn't get Norman instead. Everybody had liked Toby, but they were all grateful to Norman for the loans to build their homes and start their businesses. Laurie didn't understand how he could be so generous to everyone else and so miserly to her. It wasn't his money. If he got his way, she wouldn't be allowed to spend even a quarter of her income. What was he planning to do with the rest?

"Why don't you ask Sibyl to stay with you a while?" Cassie asked when they reached Laurie's house.

"I'd rather Naomi. I don't want my anger with Norman to spill over onto Sibyl. She suffers enough having to live with him."

"Beats me why you two let your fathers force you to marry men you couldn't stand."

Cassie was nothing if not forthright. "Now that you mention it, it beats me, too. But what's done can't be undone. Now if you don't mind, see if you can find Naomi."

But that wasn't necessary. Laurie barely had time to remove her coat and move into the parlor before Naomi was at the door.

"Sibyl said you came out of the bank looking like you were going to be sick. What's wrong?"

"Norman is what's wrong," Cassie informed her. "What did you expect? Now that you're here, I'm going back to work. I might even give Norman a piece of my mind."

"Tell me what happened," Naomi said as soon as Cassie had gone.

Naomi let Laurie talk without interruption, which was a great help. By the time she'd finished, she'd talked out her rage and was in a better frame of mind to think rationally.

"You know what I think of Norman," Naomi said, "but I never thought he could be that cruel."

"He insists he's following the spirit of Noah's will, and I think he probably is."

"That's still no excuse. What are you going to do?"

"I don't know, but I won't allow him to ruin the rest of my life."

"You could always get married. Then Norman would have to hand over your money to you or your husband."

"Who do you suggest I marry? As far as I know, Jared Smith is the only eligible man this side of Fort Verde. I hope you aren't going to suggest I marry a soldier."

"I'm not suggesting you marry anyone in particular. I just meant that marriage would free you from Norman's control."

"Getting married would be no more than transferring control from one man to another. I want to be free to make my own decisions about what I eat and what I wear. I wouldn't be surprised if Norman expects to approve of my undergarments."

That caused both women to laugh, which made Laurie feel better.

"Why would you mention Jared Smith?" Naomi asked. "I thought you didn't remember him until you met him at the wake."

"He's not an easy man to forget." Naomi didn't need to know about Laurie's visit to his ranch. "You don't have to be young and single to think he's attractive."

Naomi's gaze intensified. "Are you interested in him?"

"Just because I think he's attractive doesn't mean I'm interested in him. I don't even know him."

"I remember you said you wanted a ranch, and he's a rancher."

"Just because I want a ranch doesn't mean I want a rancher to go with it."

"You don't know anything about running a ranch."

"You learned how to lay out a town and sell lots. Cassie learned to work in the bank, and Amber could manage the store if my father would give her the chance. Why couldn't I learn to run a ranch?"

"Cassie's job is to attract men, which she can do just by waking up each day. Amber knows what people want because she's known them all her life. You've never been on your own, you don't ride, and you don't know the first thing about cows. I didn't know anything about laying out a town, but I had Colby to help me. Who would you have?"

Jared. The name came unbidden.

"I have to do something. It's not just the money. I can't live the rest of my life under Norman's thumb. I'm not sure I can last the next month."

"I'll try to think of something. Maybe Colby will have some ideas."

Laurie shrugged. "All he can think about when he gets back from one of his trips is you and the children."

Naomi grinned like a lovesick schoolgirl. "I suspect he's going to have another baby to think about before long."

Laurie was excited for her cousin despite being envious of her happiness. "Does he know?"

"I didn't begin to suspect until after he left on this trip."

Naomi had three children and a husband she adored. Sibyl wasn't in love with Norman, but she had a precious daughter everyone in town was determined to spoil. What did Laurie have? A house that didn't feel like it was hers, and a dead husband who had managed to find a way to ruin her life from the grave. No matter what she had to do, she wasn't going to let that happen.

∽

"There's a woman driving up to the house," Steve announced when he came into the kitchen. "A damned good-looking one, too. What does she want coming here?"

Jared nearly stumbled over his own feet getting to the front door. He got it open in time to see Laurie Spencer drive into the ranch yard. He scrambled down the steps to tie her horse to the hitching post and help her down from the buggy.

"I didn't expect to see you back."

"I didn't expect to be back, but I am. Can we go inside?"

He was so shocked he hadn't realized he was standing staring at her. "Of course. Would you like some coffee?" he asked once she was settled in the parlor.

"Please. It's rather cool out today."

"There's some on the stove. I'll be right back."

Steve was standing in the hall, his jaw dropped so low it practically touched his chest.

"Keep your eyes in your head and your mouth closed," Jared told Steve. "She's not some trollop to be ogled by a horny boy."

"You were doing some ogling yourself," Steve shot back. "The way you stumbled getting to the door, I'd think you hadn't been walking more than a week."

"We don't get many female guests, especially not ones like her."

"We *never* had one like her," Steve declared. "There ain't a female at the fort who can touch her. Who is she? What's she doing here?"

Jared searched for a coffee cup that wasn't chipped or cracked. "Her name is Laurie Spencer."

"Is her husband that sidewinder who wouldn't give you a loan?"

"That's her brother-in-law. Her husband has just died, and she's looking to invest some money. I'm hoping she'll invest it in our ranch."

"What does a woman like that want with a cow ranch?"

"I don't know, but I intend to make it sound like the most wonderful place in the Territory. Now I'm going to take her this coffee before it gets cold. You keep out of sight."

"If she's thinking about investing in the ranch, I should meet her. This is my ranch, too."

Jared had to agree with Steve, but he would have preferred to introduce the boy later. He didn't know why Laurie had changed her mind, but she didn't look happy about it. It might not take much to cause her to change it again.

"Give me fifteen minutes. If she agrees to give us the money, I'll introduce you. If not, there's no point in you meeting her."

"Can't I just sit and listen? I've never been this close to a woman who looks that good."

"She's already nervous about coming here. Having you stare at her like you'd never seen a woman before would scare her away for sure."

"I *haven't* seen one like her."

"Neither have I, but we can't act like it. Now I've got to go. I promise I'll introduce you no matter what she decides."

Laurie was sitting rigid as a hitching post when Jared returned. "I brought sugar," Jared told her. "The cream is fresh from the cow this morning."

"Thank you."

Laurie didn't look at him or speak while she fixed her coffee and took the first sips. Jared decided to wait for her to speak first, but the suspense was terrible. Was it really possible he would be seeing her in his house every day of the week? She would have to stay here. Surely she wouldn't consider driving back and forth each day. Where would he put her? There wasn't enough room in the house to give her any real privacy.

Laurie finally looked up at him and broke her silence. "I'm sure you're wondering why I've come back. You need to know I didn't want to, that I consider this a last resort."

He didn't like knowing she was so unhappy, but he couldn't be sorry that something had forced her to return. "Why did you come back?"

"My husband left control of his estate in the hands of his brother. Norman is determined to impose conditions I find intolerable."

"More unbearable than cooking and cleaning for us?"

"I never said cooking and cleaning for you would

be unbearable. I said it was certain to cause a lot of talk and speculation, neither of which would do my reputation any good. Members of my family are bound to oppose it as well."

"But you've changed your mind?"

"If we can come to a mutual agreement."

Jared thought he'd probably agree to anything, no matter how foolish. He shouldn't allow this woman to affect him so powerfully, but he couldn't help it. "I've already told you what I want. Now it's your turn."

"I'll give the house a thorough cleaning once a week."

Laurie didn't look like she'd ever had to do more than dust a table or wash a plate. How was she going to manage the heavy work she was taking on?

"I will also prepare two meals a day, six days a week. I won't be here on Sunday."

"That's more than fair."

"In exchange, I want a full partnership in the ranch. I want to know what you're doing and why. I want to know about any significant financial transactions and have a hand in making the decisions."

That was more than Jared was ready to give up, but he expected she'd lose interest after one or two discussions. "I'm afraid you're under the mistaken impression that I'm the sole owner of this ranch. My nephew and I own it together. He should be part of this decision."

The apprehensive look she shot him told him he should have told her about Steve sooner, but he wasn't able to think clearly when he was with her.

"He's young," Jared said as he got to his feet,

"but you can depend on him to honor your request for privacy."

As he expected, Steve was hovering just outside. He was through the door before Jared could invite him in. Once inside, however, Steve couldn't do anything but stare.

"Mrs. Spencer, this is my nephew, Steven Smith. Steve, this is Mrs. Laurie Spencer. She's going to buy a full partnership in our ranch. As part of the bargain, she'll cook and clean for us."

Steve attempted to speak. His lips moved, but no sound came out.

"Steve is nervous around strangers," Jared said. "We grew up in Texas, in a small town where we knew everybody."

"I did the same," Laurie said to Steve, "but I find I like meeting new people."

"I like meeting you," Steve managed to say in a reverential voice. "I like it a lot."

Laurie blushed. "I'm sure you would like meeting some of the young people in Cactus Corner. Maybe you can come with your uncle the next time he comes to town."

"He's not my real uncle," Steve said. "He was adopted."

Jared ruffled Steve's hair. "Adopted or not, I've been your uncle your whole life."

Steve ducked away from Jared but didn't take his eyes off Laurie.

"Do you work with the cows?" Laurie asked.

"I have to with Jared being locked away in the office all the time."

"I'll be cooking breakfast and supper," Laurie told him.

"She'll be cleaning and washing, too," Jared added. "From now on you'll have to keep your room neat."

"You can have my room, ma'am," Steve offered. "I've been aiming to move into the bunkhouse."

"I won't need anyone's room," Laurie said. "I'll go back to town each night."

"You can't do that."

Four

LAURIE REACTED AS THOUGH HE'D MADE AN IMPROPER suggestion. "Under no circumstances will I stay here. I'm surprised such a possibility would even occur to you."

Jared hadn't meant for his objection to sound like an order. He certainly didn't mean to suggest anything improper. "Despite the presence of soldiers at the fort, it's not safe for a woman to travel alone at night. You'll have to set out in the dark to get here in time to get breakfast on the table before we head out to work."

"Then I shall prepare the midday meal instead."

"We don't usually eat then. Most of the time we're on the range, and it's a waste of time to ride back just to eat."

"Then I will limit myself to supper."

"But breakfast is the best meal of the day," Steve protested. "But not when Odell fixes it."

"Can't you eat breakfast later?"

"No."

Laurie thought for a moment. "Suppose I do the washing?"

"I do that," Steve told her. "I had to learn when Mama got sick."

"Do you have a suggestion?" she asked Jared.

"I know!" Steve danced with excitement. "I can go home with you. That way you won't have to drive here by yourself."

"But you would have to get up in the middle of the night to get to my house each morning," Laurie pointed out.

"I meant I would *stay* at your house," Steve explained. "That way you'd have somebody with you both ways, and Jared wouldn't have to worry."

An objection was on Jared's lips, but he swallowed it. He didn't know if Laurie would agree, but there was too much at stake for him to raise any objection that didn't have to do with her safety. Laurie didn't appear to find the idea appealing, but she seemed to be considering it.

"Can't nobody object to somebody as young as me staying in your house," Steve eagerly buttressed his solution. "It'd be like having your own nephew. I could do stuff like chop wood and haul the heavy stuff."

The longer Laurie remained silent, the more the tension in the room grew.

"A nice lady like you shouldn't be alone in a house." Steve watched Laurie intently. "You never know what might happen."

"Cactus Corner is a small town. I have neighbors close by."

"They won't do you any good if you're in no position to call them, will they?"

Laurie turned to Steve. "Why are you so willing to stay at my house? You'll have a long ride twice a day."

Jared thought the boy was going to melt under Laurie's gaze, but he managed to keep his wits about him.

"You're the only chance Jared has to get his Herefords and for me to get some food that's fit to eat. Every bit of money we have is sunk into this ranch. It's got to be successful, or we're liable to be asking you for a job."

That was not the way Jared would have put the argument, but Laurie hadn't rejected it outright. He could almost hear the arguments going through her mind. Did she want to make such a long drive twice a day? Would she be comfortable with a boy she didn't know sleeping in her home? Was investing in his ranch worth this much trouble? What would family and friends say about her decision?

What would he do if she changed her mind? The ranch wouldn't be profitable if he couldn't change over to Herefords. Limited land meant a limited herd. It would take four hundred longhorns to produce as much meat as two hundred Herefords, and the Herefords would require only half the grass.

But he needed to do more than just make a profit. Steve wasn't cut out to be a rancher. He should go to school back East before deciding what to do with his life. He had to have Laurie's money. Steve's future depended on it. Jared wanted a bigger house in preparation for the day he would marry the girl of his dreams—a shy, upright girl of unimpeachable morals, a girl different from the kind of woman his adopted mother turned out to be. But Laurie was so beautiful he couldn't even picture another woman.

Laurie's voice cut through his abstraction. "I'll do it."

A smile split Steve's face, and he shouted, "Yippee!"

Jared had been so deep in thought it took a moment for Laurie's words to register. "Are you sure?"

Having made up her mind, Laurie favored him with a smile so glorious he was in danger of losing his ability to think. "I've said for many years that our community needed more new people, particularly people who weren't related to us."

"We're not moving to town, are we?" Steve asked.

"I'm not, but it looks like you are."

"I'll just be sleeping there, not moving there, right?"

Steve wasn't the secure, self-confident boy he pretended to be. The humiliation caused by his grandmother's behavior had scarred him as deeply as it had Jared. Jared had insisted Steve join him in Arizona to get him away from the taunting and scorn from people who should have tried to help him.

"There's no reason you can't get to know people while you're there," Jared told Steve. "You can help Mrs. Spencer with her shopping and running errands."

Steve wasn't so overcome by Laurie's beauty that he was ready to be part of what he would call *female doings*. Much to Jared's surprise, Laurie caught that immediately.

"I don't think there'll be much need for shopping or errands. I'll be eating here, and I don't need new clothes to clean and wash. I expect it'll be time to go to bed when we get home, so you probably won't have to chop wood, either."

Steve looked relieved. "I don't mind chopping wood, ma'am. You can't go to sleep in a cold house."

"We'll see." Laurie turned to Jared. "When do you want me to start?"

Steve didn't wait for Jared to answer. "Tomorrow."

Jared laughed. "We ought to give Mrs. Spencer a few days to make any arrangements she might need before starting. After all, she'll be here virtually all the time."

"I won't need more than a day or two," Laurie said. "Since we're going to be partners, I would like you to call me Laurie."

"How about I call you Miss Laurie?" Steve asked. "My mother would haunt me if I was to call a lady by her first name."

"Miss Laurie will be fine. I'd hate to be the cause of a haunting. I'm told it's bad for sleeping."

Jared was relieved to discover Laurie had a sense of humor. He knew undertaking this partnership was a big step for her, but if she could laugh, it would be easier on all of them. Well, maybe not for him. The attraction had been strong from the beginning, but now that he knew he would be seeing her each day, it had leapt to the front of his mind. He had to remember this was a business arrangement. If she even guessed at some of the thoughts in his head, she'd back out.

"I promise you'll have the money when you need it," Laurie said, "but Norman can't know anything about it. No one can."

"I'll write down the terms of our agreement so we'll have a firm contract," Jared told Laurie. "Do you want to show it to a lawyer?"

"No. The only lawyer in Cactus Corner is Norman's father-in-law. I don't want him to know anything about it. There are other people I trust."

"When do you want to go to the bank to transfer the money?"

She looked uncomfortable. "The money isn't in Norman's bank, but it's somewhere safe. I'll give it to you when it's time to buy the Herefords."

Now it was his turn to be uneasy. He had no reason to believe she had lied about the money, but he wouldn't feel entirely comfortable until it was deposited in his account. This whole situation was a little too cloak-and-dagger for his peace of mind.

"While I write up our agreement, you and Steve can talk about traveling back and forth."

There wasn't a lot to put in the agreement and it wasn't complicated, but Jared had difficulty keeping his mind on what he was doing. Knowing Laurie was in the next room, knowing that she would be in the next or the same room for the foreseeable future, played havoc with his concentration. He had to start over twice before he completed a copy without a mistake. He was almost as bad as Steve, and he didn't have youth or inexperience as an excuse.

He was a very sensual man and had been with more than his share of women over the years, but none had affected him as Laurie had. She was like a physical force pulling him toward her. He knew she was aware of this. He just didn't know how she felt about it. He would have to be careful. Until he got the money in his hands, she could back out of the deal and there was nothing he could do about it.

When Jared reentered the parlor, Steve was asking if he could handle the reins. "I wouldn't feel right being driven by a lady."

"As long as you don't turn me into a ditch, we can share the driving. I'm not fond of horses, but I like to handle the reins myself."

"Do you have your own horse?"

"Yes, but he's kept at the livery stable. They harness him and bring the buggy to the house."

"I can do that for you," Steve said. "No use wasting money."

"You'll have plenty of time to work out such details." Jared handed the agreement to Laurie. "See if that's satisfactory. You don't have to decide now. You can bring it with any changes you want when you come to work."

Laurie read quickly. "It looks fine just as it is, but I'll keep it a little longer in case I think of something else." She rose. "I should be going. I won't fix breakfast on my first day. I'll need time to settle in first."

"That's up to you," Jared said. "If you need more time before you start, let me know. By rights, you don't need to start until you give me the money." He had struggled with himself over whether to say that, but honesty won out over lust.

"I thought about that, but a full-time housekeeper wouldn't cost you nearly as much as my share of the ranch is worth. I'll start in two days."

He tried not to show his relief, but Steve wasn't so circumspect.

"Hot damn!" he exclaimed. "Now I won't have to starve."

Laurie laughed softly, and Jared thought his insides would melt.

"You haven't sampled my cooking yet," she told Steve.

"Anybody as beautiful as you has to be a great cook."

It delighted Jared to see Laurie blush at things he felt but wouldn't dare say.

"We'll see. Now I'd better be getting home. I have a lot to do in two days."

Jared didn't know what that might be, but he hoped nothing would cause her to change her mind. He wasn't sure he could stand the disappointment.

⁂

"You did what?" Sibyl exclaimed.

Naomi was in complete agreement with her cousin. "You can't possibly do anything that crazy. You have to sit down immediately and write him saying you've changed your mind."

"I haven't changed my mind, and I'm not going to," Laurie insisted. "I thought about this a long time."

"You couldn't have," Sibyl said. "Noah's only been dead two weeks."

"I thought about this long before Noah died. Not this exactly, but doing something to escape his control."

"But you have escaped his control," Naomi reminded her.

"Norman is even worse. I told you what he said."

"He'll change his mind after a while," Sibyl said. "You know it's all about power. Once he feels you'll do what he wants, he'll forget you and start thinking about something else."

"I don't want him to think I'll do what he wants,"

Laurie protested. "All my life I've done what some-body else wanted—first my parents and then Noah. I'm not going to add Norman to the list, and I want everybody to know it."

"There must be some other way," Naomi said.

"I'm not going to work in the mercantile. I refuse to work with my father."

"You could work in the millinery shop with Mae Oliver or in the bakery with Polly Drummond."

"I don't like to sew, and I don't bake better than any other woman in town."

"If you insist on working, there must be something you'd like to do."

"Nothing that would get me a partnership." She bit her tongue. She hadn't meant to say that. Neither Sibyl nor Naomi knew about the money.

Both cousins pinned her down with their gazes. "What partnership?" Sibyl asked.

"Jared is going to give me a partnership in the ranch for working for him."

"When did working as a housekeeper start being worth a partnership?"

"When I made deal with Jared that said it would," Laurie answered back. "I knew you wouldn't like it, but I'm telling you because I want you to know. I'm going to need your support once everybody in town hears about it."

"But I'll agree with them," Naomi said.

"Me, too," Sibyl added. "How could we not?"

"Because I'm your cousin," Laurie replied. "Because I've been miserably unhappy for years. Because I want to be in control of my life. Because I want to have something of my own that Norman doesn't give me just because he's gotten tired of torturing me and is looking for another victim."

"You can't be getting much of a partnership just for cooking and cleaning," Naomi said.

"It doesn't have to be that much," Laurie said, "as long as it's something Norman can't control."

"I'm sure if you talk to Mae—"

"I don't want to talk to Mae or anybody else in Cactus Corner. I'm tired of being surrounded by people who think they know more about what's best for me than I do. I even considered moving to Tucson."

"That's out of the question," Naomi declared, "but I'd like that better than your being at Jared Smith's ranch all day. You can imagine what people are going to think."

"Yes, and I'll think less of them for it. I've done nothing in my whole life to warrant such suspicions."

"It's human nature," Sibyl said. "You're a beautiful woman, and Jared Smith is a mature, virile man. Two such people shouldn't be alone all day."

"We won't be alone. He has a fifteen-year-old nephew who'll stay with me so he can drive me back and forth."

"That's something else I don't like. Do you think it's safe?" Naomi asked.

"He's fifteen. He's only a boy."

"A boy who's only a few years away from being a man," Sibyl pointed out.

"He's still a boy. The only other solution was to have me move out to the ranch."

Laurie was glad she said that. Her cousins were so

horrified over that possibility that they objected less to Steve staying in her house. She was tired of trying to convince her cousins to approve of something she knew they never would. She knew they were worried about her, but she didn't intend to let that hold her back. The moment she put her signature on that agreement, a great weight had been lifted from her. She no longer had to worry that someone would find the money and force her to tell where she got it. She didn't have to worry what Norman did or didn't do. She would finally have something of her own that neither Norman nor her father could take from her. There would be purpose in her days, new people in her life, new things to learn.

She would finally feel like a person instead of a possession.

"You're determined to do this, aren't you?" Naomi asked.

"Yes."

"And nothing we say is going to change your mind?" Sibyl asked.

"Nothing."

The two cousins looked at each other and sighed. "I don't know that I can defend you," Naomi said, "but I'll try."

"I can't in good conscience," Sibyl said, "but I know what it's like to live under Norman's thumb. If you can do this without a scandal, I'll stand by you. You still have to face your parents and Norman," she warned.

"I know, but I want to hold off until I've worked a few days so I can show them there's nothing they have to worry about. So you can't tell anybody yet."

"I won't lie to Colby," Naomi said.

"Then it's good he's away on a trip. Besides, I know he'd support me."

"Not until he'd been out to that ranch and met every man who works there."

"I hope he will," Laurie said. "His assurances would do more to convince people than anything I can say."

"Nothing is going to make people understand why you're doing this or how it should earn you a partnership in that ranch, no matter how small it is."

"Then I guess they'll just not understand."

Laurie's arguments hadn't swayed her cousins, but she could count on their support. It would be more difficult to explain the partnership. She couldn't tell anybody about the money. It had been a long time, but if the army found out, they might arrest her. And if they arrested her, they'd have to arrest Norman, her father, and probably several other men. And what about Naomi killing that soldier? Once they found out about the stolen payroll, no one would believe she'd done it in self-defense.

"I'm coming over here after your first day of work," Naomi informed her, "and I expect to hear every detail of what happened."

"I'll be here, too," Sibyl said.

"How will you get away from Norman?"

"You let me worry about that."

Laurie had always been jealous that Norman gave Sibyl more freedom than Noah had given her. "Okay. Just promise you won't tell anyone until I'm ready."

"As long as I think you're safe," was as far as Naomi would go.

That was all Laurie needed. Now she just had to make sure everything worked out the way she planned.

~⁂~

This was the third time Laurie had driven up to Jared's ranch, but today was different. On one hand, she was doing something that would draw the disapproval of everyone she knew. On the other, she was taking the first step toward establishing her independence. Yet it was more than that. She was going to be in a close relationship with a man she found attractive, and who found her attractive. She didn't intend for it to stray beyond professional boundaries, but just having the freedom to form such an association was a heady experience. For the first time in four years, she felt like a beautiful woman.

By everyone's standards except Norman's, she was not dressed provocatively. At the moment she was covered from head to toe in a thick coat to protect her from the cold, and a grossly unattractive hat to keep her head warm and her hair on top of her head. Underneath she wore a simple gray skirt and a wool blouse with long sleeves and a high collar. It might be warm in the kitchen, but she expected the rest of the house to be cold.

She wasn't surprised when Jared came out to meet her. She'd expected to see Steve, too, but Jared was alone. He looked at the box in the boot of the buggy.

"What have you got there?"

"Things to clean with, some seasoning for cooking, and few things for the kitchen."

"We should have everything you need."

He held out his hand to help her down from the buggy. She'd been aware of his strength before, but today she was aware of more than strength. A kind of nervous excitement traveled through his hand into hers, instantly communicating with the rest of her body. The shock caused her to stumble. Jared caught her.

"Are you all right?"

Of course she wasn't. She was practically in the embrace of a man she barely knew. "I guess I'm stiff from the cold. It's a long ride."

"Are you okay now? Let's get you inside."

"You can release me. There's nothing wrong. I just stumbled."

Jared practically jumped back from her. "I'll carry the box."

Laurie hoped this awkward beginning wasn't a harbinger of the rest of the day. She followed Jared into the house. He put the box down inside the door.

"Where you do want to begin?" He looked as uncomfortable as she felt.

"Why don't you show me the house?" They stood in a wide hallway that ran from the front to the back of the house.

"There's not much to see. It's a small place. You've seen the parlor. We rarely have visitors, so I use it as my office. Across the hall is the kitchen. I'll save that for last. The two bedrooms are in the back." He opened the door to a large and neat room. "This is my room. Steve's is across the hall."

Seeing Jared's bedroom had a strange effect on her. The room was plainly furnished with a large wardrobe, a chest of drawers, a chair, and a table with a shaving stand.

"That bed was left by the previous owner. I'd never have hauled anything that size from Texas."

A huge bed covered by a handmade quilt dominated the room. The thought of Jared asleep in the bed—did he wear long underwear or did he sleep naked?—caused her stomach to clench. Appalled at the direction of her thoughts, she turned her attention to the windows. "You need curtains and some pictures on the wall."

"I'm never in this room except to sleep. You really don't have to clean it. I can take care of it myself."

"I said I'd clean the house, and that's what I'll do. Your job is to make sure the Herefords prove to be a good investment."

He smiled. "I can see you're going to be a demanding business partner. I'm going to sell off the longhorns while I build the Hereford herd. There won't be much profit right away, but we won't starve."

"What will I live on?"

"You're a full partner. You'll get a share of everything I sell starting today."

"But I haven't given you the money."

"Because I don't need it yet. The partnership started the minute you signed the contract. Of course, either of us can back out until I get the money and buy the Herefords."

That's how it worked in the mercantile, but she hadn't known if ranches were the same.

"Steve's room is a mess. I'll have him straighten it up for you."

"I'll do that. I never had any brothers or sisters. It'll give me a chance to see what I missed."

Jared opened the door to a room that was smaller than Jared's bedroom and as disorderly as his was organized. "Is this something you regret missing?"

Laurie laughed. "It's not so terrible. It's not like there's a half a dozen of him."

Jared shivered. "I love my nephew, but I cringe at the thought of even one more like him."

"Don't you hope to marry and have children?" The question was ordinary enough, but under the circumstances it felt too personal. Fortunately Jared didn't appear to mind.

"I've been in the army for the last seven years so I haven't had a chance to do anything about it, but I do hope to have a family. However, I will not spoil my children as badly as Steve's mother spoiled him. He was an only child."

Laurie had washed, folded, and put away Noah's clothes, but doing that didn't have the same impact as the thought of handling the clothes of a teenage boy who was as sexually vibrant as Noah had been quiescent. "Maybe you could ask him to pick up his clothes."

"I have. You see the results."

She supposed she'd have to get used to it. There were bound to be times when she would have to handle Jared's clothes, too. She hadn't expected this response. She hoped it wasn't going to be a problem.

"I can't tell you much about the kitchen," Jared said as they left Steve's room and headed back up the hall. "Odell does all the cooking. We eat in there as well."

He opened the door to a room that was the same size

as the parlor. A stove stood against the far wall, but most of the room was occupied by a large table furnished with benches. A counter with cabinets beneath ran alongside the wall that separated the kitchen from Steve's bedroom. A single window opened onto the front porch.

Jared pointed to a door at the end of the counter. "That door leads to a storage room. All I know about it is that's where Odell keeps the coffee grinder."

"According to my cousin's husband, coffee is more necessary to western men than food."

"I like my food, but coffee is essential to get the day started."

"My husband drank tea. His mother hated coffee, but I'm partial to it myself."

"Good. I'm not sure the boys would trust your cooking if they thought you didn't like coffee."

"How many men work for you?"

"Four, counting Odell. They're all ex-soldiers, so they're used to taking care of themselves."

"Where do they stay?"

"In the bunkhouse, but they got used to tents in the army. They sleep out except when it's cold."

"So I have to cook enough for six men."

"And one woman," Jared reminded her.

"I haven't forgotten. Do you know if Odell has anything planned for supper?"

"Fix anything you find in the larder. We eat mostly ham and beef, chicken if we can keep the coyotes from getting them first, and fish if Steve can catch any. There's canned and dried fruits and vegetables. Odell made a hill for the potatoes, but I'm told it rarely gets cold enough to freeze, so they might be in the pantry."

"Where do you keep milk, butter, and eggs?"

"Right now it's cold enough to keep everything in the pantry. I don't know what he does when it gets hot. What else do you need to know?"

"I think that's enough for now. You can go back to whatever you were doing before I arrived and leave me to get acquainted with everything."

"I have to ride out in about an hour. We're getting a shipment of longhorns ready to take to the fort."

"I'll be okay. I'm used to being in a house by myself." Not that she'd ever been alone very often. Noah had been so jealous, he'd forced her to work in the mercantile so he could keep an eye on her. She'd had to go to the store with him in the morning and stay there until he left in the evening.

"If you do need anything, ring the gong. Someone is bound to hear it."

"What time do you expect supper?"

"How about six? We like to get to bed early so we can make an early start."

"I'll expect all of you then."

Jared lingered, like there was something he wanted to say.

"Did you forget something?"

"I just wanted to say we're glad to have you here. I mean for more than the money. It'll be nice to have a woman's touch to the place."

"I didn't come here to change anything."

"We could use a little change. We get in a rut when it's all men."

"Well, I won't change anything for a while yet... except the food so Steve won't starve."

They both laughed, but neither sounded quite natural.

"I'll leave so you can settle in. Where do you want your box?"

"Bring it in here."

Jared was back in moments with the box, which he placed on the end of the counter. "If you find you need anything we don't have, make a list. In a few days we can go into town and pick up everything."

He stood there for a long moment, as though he was waiting for her to say something. When she didn't, he nodded and left the room.

Laurie let out a big breath and felt her whole body relax. Her first day as Noah's wife had been more stressful, but at least she had known him all her life. She just disliked him. She was certain she would like Jared and Steve, but she knew nothing about them or the four men that worked for them. They might be uncomfortable or resent having a woman in the house.

She was uncomfortable. She had only agreed because she doubted she'd ever have a better chance to establish her independence. She'd certainly never have a better chance to use the money without anyone demanding to know where it came from. She *had* to make this work.

But something else unsettled her. Jared was attracted to her, and *she was attracted to him*.

Her father had been afraid the soldiers attracted by her charms would lead her to do something that would ruin her. That's the reason he gave for forcing her to marry Noah at seventeen. She had been prepared to be a dutiful wife, but it was clear on

their first night together that Noah was repulsed by
her body's opulence rather than attracted by it. He'd
never come to her as a husband. He'd been certain
her opulence was proof she harbored a carnal appetite
that he said was disgusting in a lady. As a consequence,
she'd spent years attempting to expunge any trace of
physical desire.

Now her release from that purgatory was followed
almost immediately by a physical attraction so strong
it scared her. If it was wicked for a wife to long for
and enjoy the embraces of her husband, how much
more wicked would it be for her to lust after a man
who was a virtual stranger? She hoped he would leave
after breakfast and not return until supper. If they were
never alone, she would be safe.

Laurie had steeled herself for the men's return, but
hearing them ride into the ranch yard caused her
stomach to clench. She wasn't worried about the food.
She was a good cook. Noah had demanded it. It was
simply that she would be meeting four men she'd
never seen. They would be judging her, her cooking,
her reasons for being there. Men were such creatures
of habit; they were nearly always resistant to change
in their routine.

Steve was the first through the door. "What's for
supper? It smells good."

"Ham. Have you washed up?" The question was
merely polite. From the looks of him, he hadn't been
near water since morning.

"I don't need to wash to eat."

"You need to wash if you expect to eat at my table."

It was clear a battle was going on inside Steve. Did he allow his admiration for her to cause him to yield and wash, or should he stand up for his male prerogatives? If he chose the latter, would the wonderful smell of food vanish as suddenly as it had appeared? Being fifteen, his schoolboy crush and the demands of his stomach carried the day.

"I'll tell everybody. They come in here smelling worse than their horses."

Laurie questioned whether she'd done the right thing, but she couldn't endure sitting down to supper surrounded by the smell of horses mingled with human sweat. She had found little to like about Noah, but he had insisted on cleanliness.

She waited the five to ten minutes she thought were enough to wash up and maybe change a shirt. When no one had entered the kitchen, she started to get nervous. She walked to the window, but it looked out over the front of the house and she saw nothing but the road that led to town. She opened the side door, but that part of the yard was empty. She heard no sounds. She might as well have been the only person at the ranch. That had been a comfort earlier. Now it meant something was wrong.

The wait stretched so long she worried that the food would be cold and dry before they sat down to the table. What could be keeping them? They weren't getting ready for a formal dinner or a party. This was just supper after a long day's work. She had become so tense that the opening of the door between the kitchen and the hallway caused her to jump. She spun around to see Jared standing in the doorway, the look on his face one degree short of murderous.

"We've cleaned up. May we come in?"

Five

"OF COURSE. YOU DON'T HAVE TO ASK TO ENTER YOUR own kitchen."

"Steve said that *you said* now there was a lady around the house, we had to act like gentlemen."

"All I said was he needed to wash up before he sat down to the table."

"You didn't say we needed a bath and to change our clothes?"

"Of course not. Why would I want you to take so long that the biscuits have gone cold and the ham dry? I expect the coffee is strong enough to walk out of here by itself."

Jared's expression forecast a stormy session ahead for Steve. He called behind him, "Come in, fellas, before the food gets any colder."

Steve nearly bounded through the door, but the four men who followed marched in as solemnly as if they were going to their own execution. All six men were dressed like they were ready to go to church or attend a wedding. She was certain Jared and two others had taken the time to shave. Her hopes for a good beginning evaporated. No meal, regardless of how delicious, could make up for the humiliation she'd put them through. Jared must be desperate for her money to have agreed to it. She'd have to find a way to make up for it, but nothing could help her right now. She indicated the table that was covered with empty plates and bowls of food. "Sit down and serve yourselves. I'll pour the coffee."

Except for Steve, you would have thought they were being served their last meal. They moved to the table only to take up a position in front of a plate.

"Sit down."

"We can't," Steve announced. "You aren't seated."

Laurie started to protest that it wasn't necessary, but she could tell from Jared's expression that it was. She quickly took her seat. The men sat, but when the severity of their expressions remained unchanged, she sighed and accepted defeat. "Please serve yourselves."

"We have to wait for you," Steve announced.

That was too much. "No, you don't. I have to be up and down serving coffee and refilling bowls. Serve yourself from the bowl in front of you, then pass it to your left."

Steve wasn't ready to give up. "Mama said a gentleman never served himself before a lady."

"I'm not the lady of the house. I'm here because fixing supper is my job. If one of the soldier's wives had fixed supper, would you wait for her to sit down and serve herself?"

Steve was backed into a corner. When he didn't answer, Jared answered for him.

"No, he wouldn't. Nor would he make up a list of

demands and pretend they'd come from you. In the future, it would be better if you communicated your requirements to me." His gaze was frosty enough to freeze boiling coffee.

Could this first meal be going any worse? "My only *wish* at the moment is that you will enjoy your supper. The coffee is on the stove. I would serve it, but I need to be excused for a moment."

She left the room with as much of an appearance of calm as she could manage, but she nearly burst into tears the moment the door closed behind her. She looked for somewhere to hide, but she didn't want to go into the parlor because it was too closely associated with Jared. She escaped to the front porch and moved to the end farthest away from the kitchen. She couldn't understand why she was so upset. She'd endured years of disapproval from Noah. She should be immune to it by now. Why was tonight so different? She barely knew Jared and Steve. She knew nothing about the other men. She might as well have been cooking for strangers. The opinion of people she didn't know had never bothered her before. Why should it matter now?

Steve had substituted his own requirements and attributed them to her. Now that she had explained everything to Jared, it would be all right. But what was *all right*? And why was it so important? Was it because she found Jared attractive? If so, what was she hoping would come of that attraction?

Nothing. Thanks to that hateful will, she hadn't fully escaped from Noah. She certainly wasn't looking to get involved with another man.

The front door opened, and Jared came out onto the porch. When he saw her, he came toward her. "Are you all right?" His expression showed concern.

"Do you care? I cooked your supper. That's all you want from me." That was unfair, but she was feeling aggrieved.

"Steve admitted he made up what he said *you said* about taking a bath and dressing up. The boys would like to thank you for supper. It's very good."

"It would have been much better thirty minutes ago." There was no need for her to say that now. "I'll be careful what I say around Steve. He probably thought that's what I wanted."

"He's at a very impressionable age, and he didn't want to leave Texas. He wants everything to be like it was before he lost his parents. In his mind he knows nothing can be like it was before the war, but he's still struggling emotionally."

Knowing that made her feel small and self-centered.

"The men understand you're still trying to adjust to the loss of your husband."

She wasn't going to allow herself to use that as an excuse. "I can't expect you or your men to take my personal life as an excuse for not doing my job. You wouldn't accept that from a man, so I don't want you to accept it from me. Ours is a business relationship. I have entered into an agreement, and I intend to uphold my part."

Jared's expression softened still more. "Coming in as you have must be difficult. It will take a while for you to become used to us, and for us to become used to you. I promise the men will like you as soon as they know they don't have to take a bath and shave before they eat."

Laurie's sense of being wronged disappeared. "Why did you believe Steve? Surely no one does that."

"His mother did. She came from a wealthy family that lost everything in the war. When her husband was killed, she gave up and died."

Noah had dressed for supper and taken a bath each night, but she didn't expect that of anyone else. Heating Noah's bathwater each night and washing his back had been a burden. Even now she could visualize his pasty white, baby-soft skin with its smattering of black hairs. She'd be glad when she could forget it.

"I don't expect exaggerated manners, but I don't want the men coming to the table smelling so strong they overpower the aromas of the food. Smell is part of the enjoyment of eating."

"Everything smells wonderful. Now, before the men eat it all up, we need to get back. I'm hungry, and I expect you are, too."

She hadn't been, but she could feel her appetite returning. It had been a long day, and she'd worked hard.

"The men are anxious for me to introduce them to you. They're going to be a little stiff around you for a while, but don't let that bother you. They'll all ex-soldiers and haven't seen much of women for the last seven years. At least not good women."

She didn't need to have that explained.

The men were busy eating when they returned. They looked up, unsure of what to do. When one stood, the others started to get to their feet.

"Don't get up," Laurie said. "If you get up every

time I do, you'll never finish your meal. Does anybody need more coffee?"

"The pot's empty," one man said.

"I have another pot. It'll be ready in ten minutes." She took a pot from the counter and set it on the stove. "There are more biscuits keeping warm in the oven."

That caused an instant thawing in the atmosphere. A tentative smile appeared. "Odell never made extra biscuits," one man said.

"'Cause you wouldn't eat them," the man she took to be Odell responded.

"That's because they were inedible."

"Let me introduce you to this cantankerous crew," Jared said. "The man with the thin, sour face is Odell Staples. He was our cook, but he prefers to ride horses. He comes from Texas. He says he went into the army so his neighbors wouldn't shoot him. The one next to him is Nick Benaras. He says he's from Europe somewhere, but I think he was born under a cactus. He's always complaining about the food, but he can't boil water without burning it.

"Clay Charpiot is from Louisiana. He's one of those Cajuns you hear about. He's still trying to adjust to not living in a swamp. That hang-faced old dog on the end is Loomis Drucker. He hails from the Shenandoah Valley in Virginia. He says he didn't want to go home to a burned-out farm, so he came out West where everything is burned by the sun."

Odell did look a little sour, but Laurie thought the other three men were nice-looking.

"I hope you mean to stay a long time," Nick said.

"This is first decent food I've had since I had my feet under my Ma's table."

"I wish you were back at your Ma's table," Odell grumbled.

"Can't. The Yankees burned it. Besides, I never liked farming."

Laurie took her place at the table. The men were quick to pass everything. Once they started eating, the conversation became general with the men discussing their work and taking jabs at each other. It didn't take long for her to realize the men were good friends who had a solid respect for each other. Jared was the owner and their boss, but that didn't prevent them from sending a few barbs his way. Steve spent so much time staring at Laurie she worried he wouldn't eat enough.

The men went through the second pot of coffee, all the biscuits, and the peach cobbler she'd prepared for dessert.

With the meal over, Nick sighed and leaned back. "Before you arrived, ma'am, I was thinking Arizona was as close to hell as I could get without actually going there."

"You're going there all right," Odell assured him. "Then you'll know how wrong you were."

Nick ignored Odell. "Now I'm sure it's a little slice of heaven."

Loomis spoke up. "If you're going to believe anything that lying coyote says, you're not as smart as I take you for."

"I don't know. I think I could grow to like being thought of as an angel."

The men laughed, but Steve sat up straight, his expression changed from bemused to serious. "You're so beautiful you should be an angel."

"You should read your bible, boy," Loomis said. "All those angels were men."

"There must have been some girl angels," Steve insisted.

Laurie decided it was time to end this conversation. "I'm sure you're right, but I have to put the food away and wash the dishes before I can go home. I don't think there were any angels who had to do that."

"I can help," Steve offered.

"We can all help," Jared said. "It's the least we can do in exchange for such a delicious supper."

Laurie tried to object, but Jared stopped her.

"You have to come here in the dark. You shouldn't have to go home in the dark, too."

"Are you going to fix breakfast, too?" Nick asked.

"I've agreed to fix breakfast and supper six days a week."

"Hot damn!" Nick exclaimed. "I'll wash the dishes myself as long as you do the cooking. Hell, I washed them during the war, and what we had to eat wasn't fit for hogs."

"We've all done mess duty, so washing a few dishes won't upset anybody," Loomis said. "You go on home."

Laurie turned to Jared.

"I agree with Loomis. Is there anything you need done for tomorrow?"

"I may bring a few more things from home, but I think I have everything I need."

"You shouldn't have to use your own supplies or

equipment. Make a list of what you need. We'll go into town in a few days."

"I'm a partner, not a hired housekeeper," Laurie reminded him. "You shouldn't be expected to provide everything."

Laurie noticed a sudden stillness in the other men. Apparently Jared hadn't told them about the partnership, and she didn't intend to do it for him. "Are you ready, Steve?"

The boy jumped to his feet. "I'll have the buggy ready in a jiffy." He dashed out the door without a backward glance.

"You'd better remind him to get a coat," Laurie said to Jared. "He'll be shivering long before we reach town."

By the time she'd finished directing the men where to store the little food that hadn't been eaten, Steve had the buggy at the door.

"Don't let him drive too fast," Jared warned Laurie.

"We're going to share the driving." Being allowed to drive a buggy was the one freedom she'd wrung from Noah. She didn't intend to give it up entirely for a mere stripling. It was too bad if Steve would be disappointed, but he'd get over it.

"Are you sure you won't have any trouble driving here in the morning? It'll still be dark."

"I know the road. Today was my third trip out here."

"Still, I'll worry about you."

She hadn't expected that. "Don't. Steve and I will be fine."

She had the stupid feeling she ought to be kissing

him good-bye, like she was leaving her husband rather than a partner. She didn't know where that feeling came from, but she had no intention of kissing Jared for any reason. That was asking for trouble. She might need to sit close to the fire to keep warm, but there was no need to stick her hand into the flames.

She let Jared help her into the buggy. "Hand me the reins," she said to Steve.

He started to protest, but Jared stopped him. "From the moment you leave here until you return, you're to do everything she asks without any objection."

Steve sulked, but didn't say anything.

As Laurie drove out of the yard, she decided that the first day had gone remarkably well. Once she gave the house a thorough cleaning, it wouldn't be difficult to keep it clean. It was more important that she fix meals the men could enjoy, but if tonight was any indication, that wasn't going to be a problem. There were only two things that worried her. One was dealing with the reaction people would have to her working at the ranch and having Steve sleep in her house each night. She could just imagine how Norman was going to react. The second was keeping her attraction to Jared from growing any stronger. That just might prove to be the more difficult of the two.

❧

The men were waiting for Jared when he returned to the kitchen. They didn't waste time getting right to the point.

"What did she mean when she said she was a partner?" Loomis asked.

"You know the banker turned me down for the loan I needed to buy the Herefords."

"Yeah, but what has that got to do with her being a partner?"

"She's going to give us the money to buy the whole herd."

"Where'd she get that much money?" Clay asked.

"Why does that mean she had to be a partner?" Nick wanted to know.

Odell asked, "How's that going to affect us?"

Jared knew he should have discussed this with the boys ahead of time, but as much as he liked them, they couldn't agree on anything without long and often strident debate. He had been afraid they would scare Laurie off or take so long she'd decide to invest her money elsewhere.

"Maybe you'd better put on another pot of coffee," he said to Odell. "This is liable to be a long evening."

"It doesn't have to be," Loomis said. "I'm glad you found the money."

"So am I," Clay added. "Do you have it already?"

Clay always thought of money first and anything else later. "She'll give me the money when it's time to buy the herd. She's the widow of a very wealthy man, so there's no problem about where she'll get it."

"If she's that rich, what's she doing cooking for us?" Nick asked.

"She refused to invest any money at all unless she got a full partnership," Jared explained. "She didn't have enough money for that, so she agreed to cook and clean until she could make up the difference."

"How is that going to affect our shares?" Clay asked.

Jared was reluctant to answer that question, but his men deserved the truth. If they decided to take their money and leave, he couldn't blame them. "It will cut into everybody's share. I know I promised you more, but this is the only way I can get the money to buy the herd."

They sat in an uncomfortable silence as the news sank in. He hoped he could take their silence to mean acceptance.

Odell spoke first. "I don't think it's right for a woman to own half your ranch. Why wouldn't she agree to go partners on the herd? That's what we did."

"I can't tell you that. I just know that those were her conditions."

"I can't blame you for what you did, but why didn't you tell us about it?" Loomis asked.

"She turned down my first offer so there was nothing to tell. When she came back, I was afraid if I didn't agree at once she'd go away and not come back. I don't mind giving up part of my share. If we can get that Hereford herd, our profits will more than make up the difference."

The discussion didn't end there. They covered the issues of being left out of the bargaining, their discomfort with a woman owning half of the ranch, and not wanting to see Jared and Steve lose part of their ownership.

"The whole setup was your idea," Loomis said. "You decided which ranch to buy, made the purchase, and got us all out here. All we did was give you a little money."

"I wouldn't have had the courage to do any of that

if I hadn't known I'd been working with men I could trust with my life," Jared said. "Your presence is even more valuable than your money."

"That's not saying much in my case," Odell said.

"Me, neither," Nick added. "I'd have wasted it drinking and whoring."

"I don't like her driving at night," Loomis said.

"Neither do I," Jared told him, "but she flatly refused to stay here. She offered to fix lunch and supper, but I told her breakfast was our most important meal. The only way she could do that was to get here early. I wouldn't let her drive in the dark alone, so Steve offered to stay at her house."

"What good is that kid?" Loomis asked.

"He'd not as irresponsible as he appears," Jared said. "And he knows how to use a gun."

"I don't think he ought to be staying at her house," Loomis said. "What are people going to think?"

"I doubt they'll think anything at all. He's still a boy."

"I don't like it, either," Clay said.

"If it makes you feel any better, I don't like it. So if you can come up with a better plan, I'll be glad to hear it. Now that the kitchen's cleaned up and the coffeepot is empty, I say we go to bed. We've got to start clearing the range of longhorn bulls. I'm not going to spend fifteen dollars a head for Herefords to have them dropping longhorn calves."

"Is fifteen a head enough?" Clay asked.

"Probably not, but I'm hoping he'll be so desperate to get rid of the whole herd that he'll drop the price some."

"What if he won't?"

"Then I guess we'll have to pay more per head."

"Where will you get the money?"

"I don't know."

"What will you do if she works here all that time and we don't get the herd?"

"I'll cross that bridge when I come to it. Now unless you've got something that needs to be discussed tonight, I'm going to bed."

The men grumbled, but they headed out, leaving Jared alone. It felt odd not to have Steve in the house, but the biggest difference was Laurie. All she'd done was fix supper and do a little cleaning, but already her presence seemed to have penetrated every corner. It was the smell of peach cobbler in the kitchen, the well-ordered neatness of the parlor, and the lack of dust in his bedroom. Even the smell was different. It must have been from the cleaning solution. Or was it from her perfume? He laughed at what a woman would think of a man who could confuse her perfume with her cleaning solution. It didn't say much for his knowledge of women.

He left the kitchen and went to his desk in the parlor.

Laurie wasn't like the women he was accustomed to. It wasn't just that she was a lady, or that she had money of her own. Though she was nervous about it, she was determined to establish her independence, and she wasn't afraid to run counter to some rules to do it. She had enough backbone to drive a hard bargain, but she wasn't afraid to roll up her sleeves and get to work.

He wondered why she had bothered. She apparently had so much money she didn't need to work to support herself. And if she did need to work, she could have found other jobs that wouldn't have gone against people's ideas of what was suitable for a young widow. He had no problem with Steve sleeping at Laurie's house, but he was certain there were many who would consider any male above the age of twelve a danger to a woman's honor. They ought to be glad *someone* was looking out for her. No woman as young and attractive as Laurie should be alone. If he were her father, he'd be tempted to build a fence around her. A woman like that could cause a man to do crazy things.

Could cause crazy thoughts to chase each other through his head until he felt dizzy…and desperate. It was a good thing Steve was the one staying with Laurie. Jared was sure he couldn't survive a single night.

Naomi was on Laurie's doorstep before she could open the front door. "Peter, why don't you and Esther show that young man where to put the horse and buggy?"

The six-year-old boy and his twin sister ran up to Steve, both chattering at once.

"I can't believe they're the same children who came here after their mother died," Laurie said to Naomi. "Colby must be very proud of them."

"Colby is so proud of them he's silly sometimes, but you're not going to get me off track. I want to know every detail of your day at Jared's ranch."

"It's not very interesting, but you'd better come inside and get little Jonathan out of the cold. You've got to be tired of holding him." The baby was a year old, but he was big enough to be twice that.

"He's like Colby. Nothing seems to bother him. Now stop stalling and tell me what happened."

"Come into the kitchen. I need to make some coffee to warm up." Laurie kept her coat and hat on while she set about grinding the coffee beans and putting water on to boil. "There's not much to tell. Jared showed me around when I arrived, then left to join the others. I did a little cleaning, but mostly went over the house to see what needed to be done. I spent the rest of the time fixing supper. After supper was over, the men volunteered to clean up because Jared didn't want me driving home in the dark." She poured the boiling water into a pot containing the coffee grounds. "I told you it was nothing exciting. Would you like some coffee?"

Naomi set Jonathan on the floor. "You're not going to get away with as scrawny a tale as that. How did Jared treat you? What were the other men like? Did they like supper? Can you trust that man who came with you?"

"His name is Steve. He's only a boy, but I can trust him."

"He's got to be fifteen or sixteen. That's a man out here."

"He may do a man's work, but he's still a boy." She laughed. "He said I was so beautiful I had to be an angel. Would any man say anything so silly?"

"Hundreds would if they were talking about you. When are you going to believe you're a beautiful and desirable woman?"

"When I can forget years of being told my body was an affront to decent women." She handed Naomi her coffee and picked up Jonathan. "What do you feed this child? He weighs as much as a calf."

"If you ate as much as he does, you'd weigh as much as a cow. Stop stalling and talk."

Laurie sighed and put the baby back down. He hadn't learned to walk yet, but he scooted across the floor on his hands and knees. "Jared was kind and thoughtful enough to leave so I wouldn't be uncomfortable poking my nose in their lives. The men are all ex-soldiers. They were a little rough on each other, but they were very polite to me and said the food was wonderful. They were even concerned about me having to travel so far each day."

"I'm glad to hear that. Maybe one of them will escort you instead of that boy."

"He would have to stay here so he could drive back with me in the morning. Jared couldn't afford to put them up in a hotel even if we had one."

Naomi was frustrated. "Obviously that wouldn't work. Jonathan, stay out of that cabinet. You don't have to do this. I can talk to Norman, get him to change his mind."

"Norman's not going to change his mind, and I won't have anyone begging him to for my sake. I intend to get everything that belongs to me one way or the other. In the meantime, I'm going to prove to him that I don't need his approval or Noah's money."

"How will you live?"

"I have a little bit of money."

"How? You told me Noah accounted for every penny."

"Norman gave me twenty dollars."

"That's not enough."

Laurie grinned. "Noah kept extra cash in his desk. That's one thing he didn't put in his will. Besides, I'll eat my meals at the ranch. Steve has promised to cut enough wood to heat the house. That ought to give me enough time to figure out what to do about Norman."

"You forgot to include what Jared's paying you."

That was easy, since he wasn't paying her anything. "Yeah, that, too."

Jonathan pulled himself up on one of the chairs.

"I didn't know he was walking," Laurie exclaimed in surprise.

"He's not. His legs aren't strong enough yet, but he will be soon. I'll either have to tether him to a post, or get Peter and Esther to watch him. Peter's impatient with him, but Esther thinks she's his mother." Naomi stood. "It's time to put the children to bed, but I'll be back tomorrow and every day after that until I'm satisfied you're safe."

"The most dangerous thing I ever did was marry Noah, and I survived that."

"You know what I mean."

Laurie gave her cousin a kiss on the cheek. "It's sweet of you to worry about me, but I'll be fine. It's just a job. I go to the ranch, do my work, and come home. What could be dangerous about that?"

Naomi returned her kiss. "A lot, but I'm relieved to see you looking more energetic and less haunted. Maybe this will be good for you."

"It will be. Now go find your children and send Steve inside. I want a fire."

Laurie tried to calm her nerves, but the closer they came to Cactus Corner, the more tense she became. She and Jared were coming to town to buy supplies. When she'd handed him her list of what was needed, she'd said he didn't need her and could go alone, but Jared had insisted she come with him. He'd said he wasn't used to shopping for a household and would make so many mistakes it would probably require a second trip to correct them.

Despite the first days of spring being nearly a week away, the weather had taken one of its abrupt turns. The sun shone from a cloudless sky with such brilliance Laurie had left her coat at the ranch. She felt so warm she wanted to undo the top button of her blouse that buttoned under her chin, but she didn't dare. The blouse fit her body with unaccustomed snugness. She hoped the high collar and long sleeves would prevent her from appearing immodest, but the look Jared had given her when she arrived at the ranch that morning caused her to doubt it.

Still, she wouldn't have changed her blouse if she'd had the chance. After years of Noah telling her she was unappealing, she needed to feel desirable, to feel that men looked on her with approval.

"It's hard to realize Cactus Corner is less than three years old," Jared said as they approached the outskirts of town. "They've done a remarkable job in a short time."

That first summer they spent in Arizona had been one of unrelenting hard work for everyone. Colby and Naomi had organized the layout and building of the town, and Norman had paid for it. Many people still disliked him, but everyone admitted their success wouldn't have been possible without his help.

"I'm glad to see the buildings have been painted a variety of colors. A town of weathered buildings is a dreary sight."

Colby had insisted on that, too. He'd said a desert landscape needed color.

"Where is the mercantile?"

Noah had refused to pay for a sign. He'd said everyone already knew where the building was.

"It's the large, red building." Even though Noah hadn't wanted a sign, he'd wanted the store to stand out from all the other buildings.

Jared chuckled. "You can't miss it. You'd have to go in out of curiosity if nothing else. I should have been shopping here instead of Fort Verde."

The moment they entered the main street, Laurie felt as if the eyes of the whole town were on her. Few people had seen her during the last week because she'd been at the ranch all day each day. Now she was reappearing with Jared. Since no one other than Naomi and Sibyl knew she was working for Jared, her sudden appearance in the company of a handsome man would start the gossip mill running at high speed. As much as she hated knowing everything she did would be whispered about and misinterpreted, people would learn the truth sooner or later.

"After we finish at the mercantile, I have business at the bank and the lawyer's office," Jared told Laurie. "Why don't you use that time to catch up with your friends?"

Naomi had been as good as her word and had been at the house every evening. Sibyl had been with her two of those times. There was no one else Laurie wanted to talk to. "I think I'll catch up on my housework. By the time I get home at night, I'm too tired to do much more than crawl into bed."

"Traveling back and forth each day is too much."

She didn't let him continue. "There's no other solution, so there's no point in talking about it. You can stop in front of the store, but if you've got a lot of business to do, it'll be easier to collect everything and load the wagon from the back."

"I keep forgetting you used to work here."

She hadn't forgotten it, but she was trying. Even in the store, Noah's judgmental gaze had never left her.

Jared helped her down from the wagon. She stepped up on the boardwalk only to be confronted by Mae Oliver. Mae looked Laurie up and down before favoring Jared with an equally thorough inspection.

"I haven't seen you all week," she said to Laurie. "Have you been sick?"

There wasn't any help for it. It was time everybody knew, and Mae would make sure they did. "I've been working for Mr. Smith at his ranch. I haven't been here much."

"What kind of work? All you've ever done is work in the store."

"I cook and clean. I've done that, too."

"I don't think we've met," Jared said to Mae. "I'm Jared Smith. I own the Green River Ranch."

"Everybody knows who *you* are. I'm Mae Oliver. I'm Laurie's mother's second cousin."

"How would everybody know me?" Jared asked. "I just bought the ranch a few weeks ago."

"Several people in town do business with Fort Verde. They know your ranch provides beef for the fort. They also know Norman wouldn't give you the money to buy Herefords. Nobody can figure out why. I think it would have been a good idea."

Jared didn't look pleased that his business appeared to be widely known, but he forced himself to smile. "You wouldn't happen to have a few thousand dollars you could lend, would you?"

Mae laughed. It was hard to remain unbending with Jared when he made up his mind to be friendly. "Not even a few hundred. Now I'm sure you have more important business than gossiping with an old woman, so I'll let you get on with it."

"You're not old, and we're just getting to know each other."

Mae turned to Laurie. "You'd better watch this man. I don't think he can be trusted."

Thinking of her father and late husband, Laurie said, "What man can?"

"Ladies, ladies," Jared said in mock horror, "don't judge me before you get to know me."

Mae simpered—actually *simpered*—before saying, "I'm not sure that would be safe. I'd better get along before my husband begins to wonder if I've been kidnapped."

"With a woman like you, that must be a constant worry," Jared said.

Mae tried unsuccessfully to hide a pleased smiled. "Now I know you can't be trusted. Beware of him, Laurie. Drop in when you're done. We need to catch up."

Laurie nodded without promising anything and Mae went on her way. "Let's go inside before we get waylaid again. Everybody in this town wants to know everything about everybody else."

Laurie started toward the store, then turned when she realized Jared wasn't following her.

"Who is that man?" he asked.

"What man?"

"The man driving that wagon?"

"He's Colby Blaine. Why?"

"I was too young to remember my father all that well, but Colby looks exactly like I remember him."

Six

AFTER SPENDING NEARLY SIX MONTHS IN SANTA FE without finding a single clue as to the whereabouts of his siblings, Jared had almost given up on finding his family, so it was a shock to see a man he was certain was one of his lost brothers. "What does he do?"

"He is a trader who transports goods and brings timber for building. If you want anything moved from one place to another, Colby will do it for you."

"Do you think he looks like me?" He was annoyed when Laurie didn't appear to see the resemblance at once.

"I'd never thought about it."

"Well, think about it now."

Laurie gazed at Colby. "Maybe I can see a slight resemblance. Why is that important?"

"I think he might be my brother. We were adopted by different families when my parents were killed on the Santa Fe Trail."

Laurie's attention intensified. "Colby was adopted after *his* parents were killed on the Santa Fe Trail."

"There couldn't have been that many couples killed

on the trail who had boys who needed to be adopted. What was the year?"

"I don't know. I'm not sure I ever knew."

"I've got to know."

"Why don't you ask him?"

"I will." Jared knew there was no way he could prove that Colby looked like his father. Some would even doubt that a three-year-old child could remember anyone except possibly his mother, but Jared had carried that picture of his father in his memory his whole life. He did remember, and that memory was so vivid he couldn't ignore it. Combined with the fact that Colby had also been orphaned on the Santa Fe Trail, well, the similarities seemed too much of a coincidence. "Will you introduce me?"

"Sure. You need to meet Colby anyway. If this town could be said to have a mayor, it would be Colby. If you want to know how to do anything except farm or run a bank, Colby is the man to see. He even chose the location for the town and laid out the streets."

Laurie waved to Colby. He pulled the wagon to the side of the road and stopped. "Are you doing okay? Do you need me to do anything?"

"I'm fine. It just takes a little while to adjust. I want you to meet Jared Smith. He recently bought a ranch between here and Fort Verde."

"So you're the man who bought the Green River Ranch." Colby leaned over and extended his hand. "Glad to meet you. If you need anything hauled out to your place, let me know. I not only give the best deal, I'm the only deal."

Colby shook hands, showing no indication that Jared was any different from any other man he'd met.

"Laurie tells me you lost your parents on the Santa Fe Trail some years ago. Do you mind telling me what year that was?"

"It was '39. Why do you want to know?"

"I also lost my parents on the Santa Fe Trail in '39. I had two brothers, one older and one younger, who were adopted by other families. I think you're one of them. Do you mind telling me how old you are?"

"I'm thirty, but I can't be your brother. We don't look a thing alike."

"I think we do. Do you know your real name?"

"Colby Blaine."

"Are you sure it's not Kevin Holstock?"

"Positive. Look, I'm sorry you couldn't find your brothers, but it wouldn't do any good if we were related. I don't know anything about you, and you don't know anything about me. We're absolute strangers. We don't even resemble each other."

"I think we do."

"What do you think?" Colby asked Laurie.

Laurie looked uncomfortable being put on the spot. "Your mouths and chins might be similar, but everything else is different."

"Okay, we might have similar mouths and chins, but the same could be said for dozens of men. Look, I hope you find your brothers, but I'm sure I'm not one of them. Now I'd better make this delivery, or my customers will start looking for someone else to do their hauling."

"You said you were the only one."

"And I don't want to give anybody a reason to want that to change that. Good to see you, Laurie." He winked and grinned broadly. "I always knew there was something worth looking at under those tents Noah made you wear."

Jared was so tied up with his disappointment he almost missed Laurie's blush. "Why are you blushing? What did he mean? Why would your husband want you to wear a tent?"

Laurie didn't meet his gaze. "My husband disliked my body and preferred that I conceal my shape as much as possible."

"Was he crazy?" Shock and disbelief were written large on Jared's face. "Most men would do anything to be married to a woman who looked like you. Hell, I'd sell half my ranch." Laurie blushed so vividly he was sorry he'd spoken so freely. "I didn't mean to embarrass you. It's just that I can't imagine how any man could find you unattractive."

"We'd better do our shopping. If I blush like this again, people are going to think you're making very improper suggestions."

Jared chuckled. "Do men in Cactus Corner often make improper suggestions in the middle of the street? I think I'd like to get to know this town a lot better."

Laurie relaxed enough to laugh. "You know they don't. Now stop wasting time. If we don't get our shopping done, we won't get back to the ranch in time for me to fix supper."

Jared looked to where Colby's wagon was turning the corner onto a side street. "I'm certain that man is my younger brother. It's too much of a coincidence that we both lost parents the same way in the same year. The odds against that happening to two men who're unrelated are phenomenal. I need to know more about him."

"I can talk to his wife—she's my cousin—but he's told you just about everything anybody knows."

"There must be something else."

"Not that I ever heard. Now are we going to shop or stand in the middle of the boardwalk so everybody can gawk at us?"

"We're going to shop until we have every item on your list, but I'm not going to stop trying to find out more about Colby Blaine. I know he's one of my brothers." Just as he turned to go into the mercantile, a young woman who was so blond her hair looked almost white came out. She smiled and greeted Laurie.

"Good morning, Mrs. Spencer. I hope you haven't been sick. I haven't seen you in at least a week."

"I have a new job. I'm working as housekeeper for Mr. Smith." She indicated Jared. "He bought the Green River Ranch."

The information appeared to catch the young woman by surprise, but she recovered quickly and turned to Jared. "How do you do? My name is Martha Simpson. My father is the preacher and newspaper editor."

Jared grasped the hand she extended. It was as slim as her boyish figure. "Pleased to meet you. My name is Jared Smith."

"Pleased to make your acquaintance." She turned back to Laurie, her perfect brow creased with concern. "I didn't know you had taken a job. Is anything wrong?"

"Nothing at all. I just wanted to be independent,

and the best way seemed to be to have a job. I've been keeping house most of my life, so that seemed the most logical thing to do."

Martha paused as though she wanted to say more. Instead, she smiled and turned to Jared. "You must be very kind to Mrs. Spencer. She's one of my favorite people."

"I certainly will. She's already become one of mine."

"I'd better be going. Will I see you in church Sunday?" she asked Laurie.

"Yes, and I'll be bringing a young man with me."

"How exciting." She turned to Jared again. "My father will be delighted to see you in church." She blushed. "So will all the women."

Laurie laughed. "I don't mean Jared. It's his nephew, Steve. He's very nice, but he's only fifteen."

Martha's mouth twisted in a wry smile. "Don't tell Mother what I said. She thinks I'm too forward."

"I'm sure you're a perfect lady," Jared said.

Another wry smile. "Regrettably so. Now I really must be going. Glad to have met you."

Jared's gaze followed her as she walked away. "I gather she's single and regrets the scarcity of men," Jared said to Laurie.

"Every single woman laments over the shortage of men to choose from. Being a preacher's daughter just makes it more difficult."

"Maybe for her. Any unmarried man would be proud to have her for his wife." Odd that he didn't feel that way. She was certainly pretty enough. Nice, too, it seemed, but she didn't spark his interest the way Laurie could just by being in the next room.

❧

"Colby told me Jared thinks they're brothers," Naomi told Laurie, "but he says that's impossible."

Laurie had talked to Naomi as she'd promised Jared, but got the answer she expected. "I wish it were true. Jared said he spent six months in Santa Fe trying to find any trace of his family. He heard that one family went farther west, but nobody remembered the name or knew anything about them. He was told a man whose wife was back East somewhere took the older boy. They expect that's where he still is."

"Then it couldn't have been Colby. His family went south to Albuquerque."

"Do you see any resemblance between Jared and Colby?"

"Maybe a little. What about you? You've seen Jared more closely than I have."

"Not much, but the coincidence of the date when they both lost their parents is enough to make it worth considering."

Naomi shook her head. "It's not enough for Colby. He said hundreds of people died each year from Indian attacks. He'd love to find his brothers, but it would be cruel to raise his hopes without solid proof."

"What kind of proof would that be?"

"I don't know. Colby's parents wanted him to forget he was adopted. If there was anything that would have provided a connection with his family, they would probably have destroyed it."

Laurie sighed. "Jared will be disappointed. He lost his adopted family, and his nephew lost both his parents. Each is all the other has."

"I'm sorry, but I hope he doesn't bring up being a brother to Colby again. It won't do any good and will just upset him."

"I'll tell him, but he's convinced Colby is his brother."

"Then he'd better have some more to go on than a feeling that Colby looks like a man nobody around here has ever seen and that everyone probably doubts a three-year-old boy could remember." Naomi changed subjects. "Do you really like working for him?"

"I like working for *all* of them," Laurie assured her. "They appreciate everything I do. After years of being told how far I came from measuring up to Noah's mother, that's a really nice change. I know this makes me sound vain, but I enjoy being looked at with pleasure. No one has done anything improper," she hastened to add, "but it's nice to have a man look at me with approval."

"I could kill Noah all over again for the things he did to you," Naomi said angrily.

Laurie laughed. "And I'd help you, but that's all over now, and it'll never happen again. Now I'd better go. Jared should be finished with his business by now. We have to get to the ranch in time for me to fix supper."

"Are you sure you want to do this?"

"You ask me that every day, and my answer is always the same."

"I know, but I don't understand it. It's a long ride two times a day. I'm not entirely comfortable having that young man staying in your house."

"He's a boy."

"He's practically a man, and he looks at you with stars in his eyes."

Laurie's laughter was as bright as the smile in her eyes. "No, he doesn't."

"Yes, he does. He's got a crush on you. Can't you tell?"

"If he does, he'll get over it as soon as he meets Amber or Garnet Sumner."

"They're pretty, but you're gorgeous. Besides, they're girls and you're a woman."

"All the more reason it can't be anything serious. Don't worry. Everything's fine."

⁓

Jared threw his pencil down with a grunt of disgust. He'd been trying for the last hour to concentrate on his work, but he couldn't take his mind off Laurie. He knew every part of the house she'd been in during the morning and how long she had stayed in each room. From the sounds he heard, he could even make a good guess as to what she'd been doing. He didn't care about dusted furniture, made beds, or swept floors. He didn't care whether the windows had curtains, though he *did* want them to be plain rather than a floral design. He wasn't thinking about his house at all.

He was thinking of Laurie.

He'd always been a man who enjoyed women. He'd managed to survive the deprivation of his years as a soldier without undue stress, but he'd never had a beautiful, desirable woman within twenty feet for hours every day. He could hear her, see her, smell her, and it was driving him crazy.

There was nothing immodest about her dress, but it would have been impossible for anything but a tent to disguise the glories of her body. Most men he knew said they judged a woman primarily by her face. Jared wasn't one to underestimate the value of a beautiful face, but women were more than just a face to him. He loved their hair, eyes, skin, and lips. Just visualizing the nape of Laurie's neck caused his body to harden. He could imagine kissing it, caressing it, inhaling her scent.

But it was her body that kept him awake at night. If she had chosen to stay at the ranch rather than drive back to town each night, he probably wouldn't have gotten any sleep at all.

He should have stayed out on the range with the men, but he couldn't leave all of his work for the hours after Laurie had gone home. Besides, he had to study. Ranching in Arizona wasn't the same as in Texas, even though both were dry and hot. The previous owner of the ranch had failed because he hadn't appreciated the peculiarities of Arizona's climate and had overestimated the productivity of longhorns.

Jared didn't intend to make the same mistakes. He was studying the man's records to see what he could learn. He'd talked to the soldiers at the fort to learn how they managed to find forage for their horses season after season. He was learning which grasses were most nutritious. He had to be sure how many acres were needed to support one cow. He needed to know when it rained, when it didn't, and which canyons could provide forage until the rains came again. Most important of all, he had to make certain he didn't overgraze any of his range. In these desert-like conditions, it might never recover.

He couldn't do any of that very well when he couldn't think of anything but Laurie. He wasn't getting anything done here, so he might as well see if she needed any help with supper. Who was he fooling? Despite his years in the army, he knew next to nothing about cooking. He just wanted to be near her.

There was nothing so terrible about that as long as he didn't let his lust—he hated to admit it, but he couldn't call it anything else—become obvious. That was one way to send her scuttling back to Cactus Corner to stay.

He found her in the kitchen peeling potatoes. They'd bought a sack full. She looked up when he entered the kitchen. She greeted him with a smile that nearly ruined all his good intentions.

"Supper won't be ready for an hour yet."

"I know. I got tired of studying records of failure. I could help you with that. I'm a terrible cook, but I can peel a potato."

"You didn't hire me so you could peel potatoes."

"I didn't *hire* you. You're a partner, remember? That means we have equal responsibilities."

"That may be, but since I'm a woman, we don't have the same work. You ride horses and chase cows—or whatever it is you do—and I cook the meals."

She was as beautiful and feminine as any woman could be, but Jared had the feeling Laurie was no mere woman. It had taken a lot of courage to propose the partnership. It had taken even more to agree to cook and clean for six men on a ranch five miles from town.

Her family couldn't have been happy about it, yet she hadn't missed a single day or been late. Steve sang her praises, but the boy was suffering from an advanced case of puppy love.

A better indication of her character was the respect with which the other men treated her. Nick's teasing was a poor foil for his infatuation, while Loomis would have thrown down his cape for her to walk on if he'd had one. Clay dredged up all the gentlemanly behavior of his Cajun background. Even Odell had gotten over his pique at being replaced. Jared was afraid to put his feelings into words. As long as they remained unacknowledged, maybe he could keep them under control.

"Peeling potatoes isn't cooking. How about letting me help?"

"Why do you want to help? Men don't do that. My father wouldn't even bring in water from the well."

"All of us learned to do new things during the war. Some cooked, and some took care of the wounded. We found it didn't hurt us."

"Maybe Colby *is* your brother. He's the only man in Cactus Corner who doesn't feel out of place in a kitchen." Laurie stood. "The potatoes are all yours, but don't be surprised if the men think there's a funny taste to them."

"As long as they can look at you, they could be eating sawdust and they wouldn't know the difference. If they did, they wouldn't care."

Laurie looked uneasy. "You shouldn't be saying things like that."

"Why not? It's the truth." Jared seated himself and

picked up the knife and a potato. "My father always told me the truth never hurt."

"I'm not sure I agree with him, but I know it can make people uncomfortable."

He fixed his gaze on her. "Do I make you uncomfortable?"

"Only when you talk like that."

"I thought women liked to be told they were attractive."

"I expect most women do, but I was taught that being too attractive could lead to trouble."

Jared couldn't help but smile. "There's no such thing as too attractive when it comes to women. There's not a single man alive who would complain if every woman looked like you."

Laurie turned her attention to a pot on the stove. "Then we'd all be equally plain."

A long spiral of potato peel dropped into the bucket between Jared's feet. "Equally beautiful. But if it bothers you so much, I won't say anything about it again."

"I would prefer that. How would you feel if women went around saying how handsome you were?"

"I'd love it. Do you think I'm handsome?"

Laurie's interest in the pot became more intense. "You don't need me to tell you that you're a very attractive man. I'm sure plenty of women are eager to do that."

Jared laughed. "Not as many as I would like. Do you think I'm handsome?"

Laurie turned to face him. "Yes. Now stop trying to embarrass me and peel those potatoes. The men won't be happy if supper's late."

Jared reached for another potato. "How many do you need?"

"Half a dozen. All of you eat like you have hollow legs."

"They didn't eat half as much when Odell was cooking. Of course, he's not half as pretty as you."

"Are you saying looking at a woman makes men hungry?"

"Yeah, and not just for food."

She turned back to the stove. "Maybe I should eat by myself."

"Definitely not. You've improved the quality of our language and our pleasure in eating. Haven't you noticed that the men like to sit over their coffee talking about nothing in particular and everything in general? It has improved our relationships. The five of us lost nearly everything we had in that war. Having you here has given us something else to think about."

"I'm not sure—"

"You're a lovely woman, a very desirable woman, but you have nothing to fear from any one of us."

"I know. I just feel uncomfortable when you talk about my…desirability."

"Why?"

Laurie turned toward him, the look on her face one of pain as well as anger. "My father married me off at seventeen because he said he was afraid my body would get me in trouble. My husband forced me to wear oversized clothes because he said my body was an affront to good women. He said I had a pretty face but my body disgusted him."

Without warning, Laurie burst into tears and hurried from the room.

Jared couldn't follow immediately because he had to wash the potato starch from his hands. When he found her, she was in the parlor staring out the window, her arms wrapped around herself, crying softly. He didn't know what to do so he relied on instinct. He walked up behind her and turned her around until she faced him.

"Your father was cruel not to see your strength of character, but I can't imagine what was wrong with your husband. He must have been a very disturbed and unhappy man not to be able to see that you're beautiful in face, body, mind, spirit—in every way a woman can be beautiful. You should be loved—you *will* be loved—so completely that you'll never again doubt your worth."

Her gaze seemed fixed on a button on his shirt. "Thank you."

"You don't have to thank me. You don't even have to believe me. All you have to do is look in a mirror. Even better, watch the reaction of men when they see you."

"I've been told that what they're seeing is the evil in me."

"My God, woman, who would say anything as cruel and stupid as that?"

She looked up. "My husband."

Jared had never met Noah Spencer, had heard very little about him, but he couldn't imagine why a man would say that about his wife, especially when it was manifestly untrue.

"He said he was sorry my father had talked him into marrying me."

It was fortunate the man had fathered no children. They didn't need any more insane people in this world. "I'd have wanted to marry you so quickly the engagement wouldn't have lasted any longer than it took to find a preacher. I'd have been unable to keep my eyes off you by day and my hands off you by night. I'd have been so proud of you I'd have made sure you were dressed so beautifully every time you went out that men would be filled with jealousy that you belonged to me and not them. I would trust you implicitly, but I wouldn't want to be separated from you for even a minute."

Laurie gave a watery chuckle. "Not even Colby acts like that toward Naomi, and he adores her."

"Then he can't be my brother. Of course, she can't hold a candle to you even if she is your cousin. You're the most beautiful woman in Cactus Corner."

Apparently he'd insulted her family, for Laurie was quick to come to Naomi's defense. "She most certainly can. She's beautiful and talented. And so is Sibyl, so you can't go around saying I'm the most beautiful woman in Cactus Corner."

"You are to me."

Laurie was embarrassed. "You shouldn't say that."

"Why? It's true."

"You shouldn't feel that way about a business partner."

"You're a woman, and I'm a man. That trumps any business arrangement."

Laurie looked unable to believe him.

"I don't know how you can believe anything that's so clearly untrue, but I haven't had anyone drumming into my head how unattractive I was. I find you incredibly attractive. I've wanted to do this since the moment I set eyes on you."

Then he kissed her.

Seven

SHOCK HELD LAURIE IMMOBILE. SHE WAS TWENTY-ONE years old and had never been kissed by a man. She didn't know how she was supposed to feel, didn't know how she was supposed to react. She felt on fire and as cold as ice. About to explode or shrivel up and die. She couldn't decide whether she wanted to run away or to throw her arms around Jared and hold on to him forever. It didn't matter. She couldn't move. She was paralyzed, barely able to breathe. She wanted to embrace Jared's vision of herself, but she couldn't block out Noah's venom-laden strictures. Hope collided with fear.

It all came to an end when Jared broke the kiss.

He jumped back with a look of shock and horror. "I shouldn't have done that. I'm sorry."

She was terrified. Maybe Noah was right. "You didn't like it?" She shouldn't have asked that question, but she felt like her life hung in the balance.

Jared looked at her like she'd lost her mind. "Are you crazy? Of course I liked it. I meant it when I said I've wanted to kiss you for days. You're the most beautiful woman I've ever met. I've dreamed about holding you in my arms, kissing you, making love to you. What man wouldn't?"

That was more than Laurie was ready to absorb. It frightened her but excited her as well. Noah *wasn't* right. A handsome man, strong and independent, thought she was beautiful and wanted to make love to her. "Is a kiss that important?" She was still too confused to know what to say.

"How can you ask that?" He seemed genuinely shocked.

"Nobody has ever kissed me. Not like that. I didn't know how I was supposed to feel."

She didn't know whether Jared thought she was trying to fool him or was simply lying. "Once I started to grow"—she couldn't think of a suitable word for what she wanted to say—"my father never let me go anywhere alone. My husband didn't even kiss me on our wedding day." She wasn't trying to sound pathetic. She just wanted him to understand.

"You have no idea what a kiss should be like, what it can mean?" Jared asked.

She shook her head. She wanted him to show her, but she didn't have the courage to ask. He must have sensed her reluctance because he didn't wait for her.

"Then it's time you learned."

Jared put his arms around her and drew her close. Lowering his head, he kissed her. Laurie was disappointed because he barely brushed her lips with his, using so little pressure she wasn't sure their lips had actually met. When he used the tip of his tongue to trace her lips, she realized he was beginning slowly.

He kissed the side of her mouth and teased her by kissing the end of her nose, but he was going too slowly. She wanted to feel the impact of their kiss like a physical force. Instinctively, she leaned in to him.

The response was immediate. His arms tightened around her, drawing her hard against his chest. His lips abandoned all attempts at subtlety and captured her mouth with the impact of a lasso pulling a full-grown bull to its heels. She was sure her lips would be bruised, that her body would be broken from the force of his embrace, but she didn't care. For the first time in her life, she felt alive. Her body no longer felt dead. A wellspring of desire washed through her with the force of a springtime flood. Hot and flushed, weakness caused her legs to threaten to go out from under her, but she fought it off. Nothing was going to make her forego the wonderful pleasure of being held in a man's arms and kissed as though he thought she was the most desirable woman in the world.

The sound of his men riding into the ranch yard caused Jared to break the kiss, release her, and step back. He looked as though he didn't quite know what to say. Was it embarrassment? Regret?

"I'd like nothing better than to keep kissing you until you believed you were the most beautiful woman in the world, but it wouldn't do for the men to see me doing that." He laughed without amusement. "They might think badly of you, and I couldn't endure that."

Laurie was so beset by opposing emotions that she hardly knew what to say. "I'd better get back to the kitchen, or supper will be late."

"And I'd better finish the potatoes."

"I'll do that. You'll need to talk with the men about what they've been doing all day." He had to leave. If he stayed in the kitchen, she'd never calm down enough to know what she was doing. Even now she was bombarded by so many emotions she felt dizzy.

"I promised six peeled potatoes, and that's what you'll get. Do you feel ready to go back to work?"

"This has been a shock, but I'll calm down sooner if I get back to work. I'll have plenty of time to think about it later."

"If you want to learn more about kisses, I'll be happy to help."

Considering the way he was looking at her, he probably had something more in mind than a kiss. Thinking about it caused her to go warm all over.

"If you don't stop saying things like that, I'll be so flustered the men will think something improper has been going on."

"They might think it of me, but not of you."

Maybe, but she didn't mean to take the risk. She gave herself a mental shake and pulled herself together. "Okay. Finish the potatoes, but after that you have to leave the kitchen. I'll never get supper on the table if you don't."

❧

The sun had disappeared over the horizon and a sharp wind had sprung up, but Laurie didn't feel it. Nor did she see the lengthening shadows cast by the cottonwoods that lined the bank of the Verde River. The sound of the horse's shod hooves on the rocky ground was muted and seemed far away. Her mind was too filled with the feel of Jared's kiss and his arms around her to have room for anything else.

She had barely had enough thoughts to spare to finish fixing supper without burning anything. She'd listened to the chatter of the men as though she was a disembodied presence. She had no idea if her responses made any sense. She was halfway home before she was aware they'd left the ranch.

She'd told herself over and over that Noah had lied to her, but she'd never been able to shake the fear that he was right. Surely Jared wouldn't have kissed her twice if he hadn't found her attractive. He had no reason to lie about his reasons. If he'd just wanted to comfort her, he could have done so without kissing her. All he had to do was ignore her until she pulled herself together.

But he had kissed her a second time and said he'd have liked to keep doing it. Surely he wouldn't have said that if he didn't mean it.

She couldn't yet embrace this new image of herself with complete confidence, but she desperately wanted to. It would change her whole outlook on life. For the first time in years, she could be happy about herself, could look forward to each day with eager anticipation rather than in fear. When she got back to town, she was going to withdraw all the money Norman had deposited in her account and spend every penny on new clothes. She was going to be proud of the way she looked, and she wanted everyone to know it. Norman would be furious, but she could count on Naomi and Sibyl to support her.

"I might as well have been talking to my horse for all the answering you've done," Steve complained. "Are you mad at me?"

Laurie turned to look at the young man and saw in his face worry and maybe a little fear. "Of course not. What could you have done to make me angry?"

"Nothing, I hope, but you haven't done more than nod your head or mumble agreement since we left the ranch."

"I've got a lot on my mind."

"Is it about the Herefords?"

"No. I'm going to let Jared worry about them."

"It can't be about your cooking. Everybody would starve if you left."

She was almost able to envy Steve. He couldn't think of anything more serious to worry about than cows or his stomach. He probably didn't know what mental anguish was. Yet as soon as that thought crossed her mind, she knew she was being shortsighted and unfair. He'd lost his parents and his grandparents, and had been forced to leave his home. He probably knew more about true anguish than she did.

She put her arm around Steve's shoulder and gave him a hug. "No one could ever be upset or angry with a sweet boy like you. I've just been thinking about some things that have troubled me."

"Just tell me who it is. If I can't get rid of them, Jared will."

If only things could be that simple. "It's not any-body. I'm just trying to forget some ugly things that were said about me."

"Who could say anything ugly about you? You're

beautiful. You're perfect. Tell me who said that. Jared will make him wish he was dead."

"He is dead."

"Oh." Steve thought a moment. "Was it your husband?"

"Yes."

"Then he deserves to be dead."

Laurie gave him another hug. "If you weren't so young, I'd marry you. You'd always make me feel beautiful."

She immediately wished she hadn't said either of those things. She didn't want to put any foolish ideas in his head, and she didn't want him to think all she was concerned about was feeling beautiful. It's just that not feeling ugly was such a relief it was hard to think of anything else.

"Forget what I just said. It makes me sound like a silly and vain woman."

"I'm not that young." He sounded like his feelings were hurt.

"Maybe not, but I'm that old. And I'm a widow to boot."

"Jared doesn't care that you're a widow, and I don't, either."

"I'm glad. Now tell me what you're going to do on Sunday. You'll have a whole day without any work to do."

"You mean I don't have to cut wood?"

"I forgot that. I meant work on the ranch. Do you want to go to church?"

"Do I have to?"

"No, but you might meet some very pretty young girls."

"None of them will be as beautiful as you."

It was quite possible she'd underestimated the strength of Steve's crush on her. She was certain it would burn itself out before long, but she had to be careful to do nothing to encourage it. Even if he hadn't been so young, she would have had absolutely no romantic interest in him. She couldn't say the same for his uncle.

◆

Laurie had barely had time to get a pot of coffee on after coming home from church when she heard a ferocious knocking on the front door. She opened it to find Norman standing on her porch looking more infuriated than she'd ever seen him. He must have heard she was working at Jared's ranch. She hadn't told him because she hadn't wanted to endure a tirade, but she had known it was coming.

"Come in, Norman, before you explode and make a terrible mess on my front porch."

"I'm in no mood for levity."

"I can see that, but you don't look like you're in the mood for rational conversation, either. Sit down. Would you like some coffee?"

"I would if you have some."

"I just put on a fresh pot. It won't take a minute." She resisted the temptation to take longer than necessary. The sooner she got this conversation over with, the sooner Norman would leave her house. She handed a cup of coffee to Norman and took her seat. "I hope you've come to tell me you're increasing the money I have each month." She knew he wasn't, but she wanted to remind him at every opportunity that he was keeping money that wasn't his.

Without giving his coffee time to cool, Norman took a big swallow and got burned. He shook his head, made a face, and rested his cup in his lap. She resisted the temptation to smile.

"I'm not here about your money because I see no reason to increase it. I am here because I overheard Mae Oliver and Elsa Drummond saying you'd helped Jared Smith buy supplies when he came into town yesterday. I told them they were mistaken. You would have no reason to help him or know what he needed."

This was the perfect opportunity to get it all out at once. "I did more than help him choose his supplies. I made out the list."

"That's ridiculous. You couldn't—"

"I knew what to put on the list because I'm cooking and cleaning for him."

Norman started so badly he spilled his coffee. He managed to control his trembling hands long enough to set his cup down before his anger exploded. His color rose to an alarming shade of red. His hands shook so badly he had trouble wiping up the coffee with the cloth Laurie handed him. Once he regained his seat, he tried to speak, but he sputtered. The words finally shot from him like a small explosion. "Are you insane? Do you know what people will say when they find out?"

"They'll probably say you're so stingy with *my* money that I had to take a job so I could have food to eat and keep a roof over my head."

If possible, Norman turned even redder. "I made a

very careful study of your needs. You have more than enough money to support yourself, but that's not what I meant. You're out there with men you don't know and no woman to preserve your reputation."

Laurie sat bolt upright in her chair and directed an indignant look at Norman. "Are you implying that I would do anything dishonorable?"

"Of course not," he snapped, "but a woman is not always in control of herself. Surrounded by so many men, and far away from those who have her best interests at heart, she might be persuaded to do something she would never have done otherwise."

"And just what would that be?" Laurie was too accustomed to Norman to spend time being truly angry with him. It would be a complete waste of energy.

"Men are prone to flatter single women, especially attractive women who have money."

"I am single, though being a widow qualifies that somewhat. I never knew you thought I was attractive—your brother didn't—and you know better than anyone I don't have any money. You have it all."

Norman's complexion assumed an alarming shade of purple. "I don't have your money, and I'll thank you not to go around saying that I do."

"I'll say what I please. I don't have to depend on you any longer."

"I'll reduce your allowance."

"Cut it off altogether. It won't make any difference to me."

"I'll take your house."

"I've read Noah's will so I know you can't do that, but it wouldn't matter if you did. I'd just move out to the ranch and become Jared's full-time housekeeper. He would like that."

For a moment Norman didn't know what to say. He was so used to controlling people with money that he didn't know what to do when that failed. The longer he went without speaking, the closer his color returned to normal. "I'm not going to reduce your allowance or force you out of your house." He didn't look like he'd accepted defeat but was instead trying a different tack. "I was just trying to show you how imperative it is that you give up this job. No woman is safe when she's surrounded by men. None of them are married. Who's there to protect your reputation?"

"I don't need anyone to protect my reputation. I go to the ranch, do my work, and come home. The men work away from the house all day. When they come in to eat, they're very respectful."

"Men have needs that women don't, that they have difficulty controlling."

"Are you implying that one of those men might rape me?"

The word shocked Norman. "No, just that a man's nature might cause him to do something improper."

They were interrupted by the front door opening. Steve came directly into the parlor, his mouth open to say something, when he saw Norman. "Who's that man?"

"He's Norman Spencer, owner of the bank and my former brother-in-law. Norman, this is Steve Smith, Jared's nephew."

Norman was immediately suspicious. "What is he doing here?"

Steve took a protective stance. He moved between Laurie and Norman. "I'm staying here. What are *you* doing here?"

Norman ignored his question. "What does he mean *he's staying here*?" he asked Laurie.

"Ranchers eat two meals a day, breakfast and supper. Preparing those two meals means I have to leave before dawn each morning and return home shortly before dusk. Jared wasn't willing to let me do that by myself, so we decided Steve should drive back with me after supper, sleep here, and drive back with me in the morning."

"You must be insane!" Norman exclaimed.

"Nobody calls Miss Laurie insane," Steve said. "Take it back."

"You let him call you Laurie? What else do you let him do?"

"Stand up!" Steve shouted.

"I'm not talking to you, boy."

"I'm talking to you, old man. Stand up before I punch you in the face right where you sit."

Norman looked so shocked that a boy would challenge him that Laurie nearly burst out laughing. "Ignore him, Steve. Norman doesn't mean what he's saying."

"It sounds like it to me." He turned to Norman. "I won't allow anybody to insult Miss Laurie. Now take it back."

"Take back what?"

"What you said."

"I didn't say anything."

"For Pete's sake, Norman, tell him you didn't mean it when you said I must be insane."

"Maybe not insane," Norman equivocated, "but you've lost all sense of what is proper for a woman in your position."

"My position is that of a woman with more expenses than income. I consider my actions quite sensible."

"Miss Laurie is very smart," Steve said. "Jared said she's the cleverest woman he's ever met."

"I have no regard for your uncle's opinion," Norman stated. "Or yours. Laurie is a member of my family. I expect her to act like it."

"Loomis says Miss Laurie's a perfect lady," Steve declared. "He comes from Virginia so he ought to know."

"We know what a lady is in Kentucky."

"Loomis told me Kentucky used to be part of Virginia. He says Virginia got rid of it a hundred years ago because you were nothing but a bunch of backwoods yokels who were so ignorant you thought it was okay to eat a coon."

Laurie didn't know whether to laugh at Norman being rendered speechless by a teenager or to be amazed at Steve's willingness to face down anyone he thought was threatening her. It was a novel situation, one she wouldn't have minded enjoying a little longer, but she wanted to end this confrontation.

"I need some wood for the kitchen if you want any supper," she said to Steve. "I'd appreciate it if you'd bring it in now."

"Is he going to stay here?" he asked, indicating Norman.

"He's said what he came to say so he'll be going home soon."

Norman glared at the boy, but Steve glared right

back at him. "I haven't said all I was going to say. If you really think it's necessary, I'll increase your allowance."

"I don't want you to increase my *allowance*," Laurie told him. "I want everything turned over to my control."

"That's impossible. The terms of Noah's will won't allow me to do that."

Laurie stood. "Then we have nothing more to say to each other. I'm sure you don't want to be late for your midday meal. Sibyl is an excellent cook."

"So you won't give up this job?"

"You give me no choice."

"Your reputation is in danger."

"Not from anybody at the ranch," Steve said.

The boy was a regular knight in shining armor. "I'd rather have a lost reputation than starvation. Now you'd better go. I have to prepare something to eat for Steve and me."

"I'll send Sibyl to talk to you."

"I'm always happy to see my cousin, but nothing she can say will change my mind as long as you insist on keeping my money."

"I'm not keeping your money!" Norman shouted. "I'm doing what Noah wanted."

"Which is to keep my money. Go home, Norman. I don't want to talk to you any more than you want to talk to me."

Norman took a final swallow of coffee and stood. "I will be back. You must not be allowed to do this."

Laurie wanted to tell him that never again was any man going to *not allow* her to do anything, but it would be a waste of breath. Norman would only believe that when he couldn't believe anything else.

"Do your parents know what you're doing? They wouldn't wish it."

"My parents weren't interested in my wishes when they forced me to marry your brother. I have no interest in theirs now."

"You're upsetting Miss Laurie," Steve said. "It's time for you to leave."

Norman looked down his nose at Steve. "I am about to leave, but certainly not at your behest."

"I don't know what a 'behest' is," Steve said. "I don't think I have one, but I can see that you leave."

Laurie spoke up when Norman looked as though he was about to take issue with Steve. "Leave before you cause any more trouble."

"I'm not *causing* trouble. I'm trying to prevent it. If Jared is as ignorant as his nephew—"

"Neither Jared nor his nephew are ignorant. Now go."

Norman's expression turned mean-spirited. "I don't know why Noah married you."

"Neither do I. He certainly didn't like me."

"You were never like this with him."

"I should have been."

"I'll talk with your father before I decide what to do about this."

Laurie didn't reply. It would only cause Norman to stay longer.

"I hate that man," Steve said when the door closed behind Norman. "I was mad at him for refusing to give Jared the money to buy his Herefords, but I hate him for what he said about you."

Laurie returned to the parlor, picked up the empty cups, and headed to the kitchen. "Don't pay attention to anything Norman says. He tries to control everybody and gets angry when they won't do what he wants."

"I'm not going to let him control you."

Poor Steve. He had no idea the kind of power Norman wielded over the people of Cactus Corner. Laurie was thankful she had the means to escape it. Well, most of it.

"Thank you. Now, what would you like to eat? You must be starving."

෨෨

Jared knew he had been making excuses to stay at the ranch during the day while the rest of the men were away, but he had kept doing it. It wasn't that there wasn't plenty of work that needed to be done. It was just that he would have come up with reasons to stay if there hadn't been any work at all. Today it had been working on the windows so they would keep out the cold air. Winter had returned and there was a threat of snow. Snow wasn't any more likely than it had been in southern Texas. But when it did snow there, it was so light it melted within a few hours. Today, however, was cold and windy, much colder than he'd thought possible in the Arizona Territory. If it snowed, it would stick.

Laurie opened the door to Steve's old bedroom and stuck her head in. "I hope you're done with that window. I can feel the wind all the way to the kitchen."

"You're a Kentucky girl. A little cold shouldn't bother you."

"I didn't like the cold when I was in Kentucky, and I don't like it here."

"I'm almost done. Some hot coffee would be nice."

Laurie smiled and his heart pounded against his rib cage. If she didn't stop that, he was going to drop dead from heart failure. He'd been without female companionship for extended lengths of time before, but he'd never had temptation in front of him every day. It was affecting him worse than Steve.

"I've kept a pot going all day. It was the only way I could stay warm."

He'd smelled it, but hadn't gone near the kitchen. After the kisses they'd shared just a day ago, he wasn't sure he could control himself. All he could think about was kissing her again. It was barely past noon. He didn't know how he was going to get through the rest of the day until the men returned.

He turned his attention back to the window. He'd tightened the strips that held the windows in place as snugly as he could without making it impossible to open them. Cold air would still get in, but not as much. That normally wasn't a problem, but there were no fireplaces in the bedrooms. If it fell below freezing tonight, they'd be bitterly cold. Not that it mattered. No one would be using this bedroom because Steve had no intention of ever moving back from the bunkhouse. The men would be warmer than Jared because they had a potbellied stove they'd keep going all night.

He gathered up his tools and carried them to the shed. The previous owner had spent a lot of money to make sure the ranch was well-equipped. Maybe that's why he hadn't been able to make a go of it. Jared was determined he wouldn't make the same mistake. His problem was that he'd had to spend so much of his and Steve's money to buy the ranch that he didn't have enough left to buy the kind of cattle he wanted. Laurie's money was going to make that possible.

Yet his feelings toward her were far from gratitude. Not that he didn't feel grateful. It was just that other feelings were more powerful. So powerful he thought it would be a good idea to stay outside a little longer and let them subside. That wasn't likely to happen unless he was forced to think about something else, so he decided to check on the horses.

He had a couple of good mares he'd bred when he was in Santa Fe. Both had gotten in foal, so he kept them in a large corral that had a shed to keep them out of the worst weather. That's where he found them, their heads under the shed with their rear ends facing the weather.

"What's wrong, Gracie?" he asked a long-legged sorrel who didn't turn her head to greet him. "You think it's going to snow?"

In answer to his question, a flake floated down from the leaded sky and settled on the thick hair of Gracie's winter coat. It was quickly joined by another. And another.

"Looks like you're right." He turned to the other mare, a short-coupled, muscular bay with the typical Morgan clean-cut head and arched neck. "What about you, Mandy? Are you afraid of snow?" Gracie was from Texas mustang stock, but he'd bought Mandy from a Union soldier after the war. Mandy turned her head, her huge brown eyes focusing on him.

"You take care of that foal you're carrying," he told

her. "I'm counting on it being a colt good enough to use as a stallion. The army will pay well for mounts with Morgan blood."

Unimpressed by her pedigree or Jared's wishes, Mandy turned away from him.

Jared looked out at the snow that was coming down so hard it threatened to obscure the ranch house. "Looks like you were right about the weather. I expect the boys will be in shortly."

By the time he reached the house, the snow was coming down heavily. He scraped his boots on the steps and stamped them on the porch to shake off the snow. Laurie had swept the hall just that morning. She wouldn't thank him for tracking in mud. When he entered the kitchen, he was enveloped by the heat and welcomed by the smell of freshly brewed coffee.

"You'd better think about heading home," he said to Laurie. "It's snowing quite a bit."

"It won't last long," she said. "Colby says it never does out here."

Jared looked out the window at what was rapidly being transformed into a white landscape. "It doesn't show any sign of slowing down."

"I've been here three winters, and this is the first time I've seen enough snow to cover the ground." She looked out the window. "Every time I complain about the warm winters or months with no rain, Colby reminds me that we're living in a desert."

Jared was used to the mild winters and a long, dry season from his years growing up in south Texas, but he wasn't used to such an abrupt change in the weather. When he'd gotten up just seven hours earlier, it had been sunny and warm. He went to the stove and poured himself a cup of coffee. It was strong and hot, just the way he liked it. "It used to snow like this in the Shenandoah Valley. Sometimes it would get three feet deep. The drifts were even deeper."

Laurie didn't look up from what she was stirring in a big pot. "We had lots of snow in Kentucky. I hated it."

The smell from the big pot was so enticing Jared had to know what was in it. When he looked in, all he could see was a thick, brown soupy mixture with lumps. "What is that? It smells delicious, but it looks like mud."

Laurie chuckled. "It's beans and beef with tomatoes, garlic, and other seasoning. Colby taught me how to make it. He said he practically lived on it when he was on the trail during the winter."

Jared inhaled deeply. "Can I taste it?"

"It's not done yet. The flavors need time to mingle."

He inhaled again, but this time he was so close he caught Laurie's scent. All thoughts of beans and beef went out of his mind. If he didn't move, he was going to touch her. He forced himself to back away and take a seat at the table. It would be impossible to touch her from there. It would also hide the effect she had on him.

"I had been planning to make this when it turned cold."

"Looks like you chose the perfect day."

A sudden gust of wind sent a cascade of snowflakes crashing against the windowpanes. Warmth from the kitchen melted the flakes, and drops of water raced down each pane. If it kept snowing, there'd be icicles hanging from the roof. The water in the troughs would freeze overnight, and they'd have to heat drinking water for the horses. Even though the river was shallow, he doubted it would freeze. The longhorns would have no trouble finding water. All they had to do was find a way to keep warm.

"I could tell by mid-morning it was going to be cold, but I didn't think it was going to snow."

Jared sipped his coffee and worried about her getting home. He wasn't anxious about her safety. He would make the drive with her. It was the cold that troubled him. It was a long way to town, and the wind was winding up to a good blow. It was crazy to consider an hour-long trip with snow blowing in her face and the cold knifing through her coat. The only alternative was—

The kitchen door burst open, and Loomis entered in a cloud of snow.

"It's a gol-darned blizzard out there," he said.

Eight

LAURIE DIDN'T TURN AROUND. SHE KEPT STIRRING, trying to calm the storm inside her. She couldn't spend the night here! It would give rise to exactly the kind of gossip Norman had predicted. She couldn't give him the satisfaction of being right.

"Did you hear me, ma'am?" Loomis asked. "The snow's coming down so hard you can't see more than ten or twenty yards."

"I did hear you, Loomis." She kept stirring. "I know it looks bad now, but it never snows long here. I wouldn't be surprised if it clears up in less than an hour."

It didn't. Two hours later, it was still snowing. Odell and Steve returned from bringing in a load of wood.

Steve's eyes glowed with excitement. "If this keeps up, there's going to be a foot of snow on the ground." He turned to Laurie. "You'll have to stay the night here. You'll never get home through that. I wouldn't be surprised if the river freezes."

"It's never done that," Laurie said.

"According to the soldiers at the fort, it's never

snowed like this," Jared said. "This is one of those freak storms that doesn't follow any rules. I can't let you go out in that storm."

The men had been gathered around the table for the last two hours, eating, talking, smoking, and drinking coffee. The awareness that she couldn't venture out into the storm had been circulating in the room for hours, but Steve putting it into words gave it a weight it hadn't had until now. Everyone stopped and turned to look at her.

"You can sleep in my old room," Steve offered.

"I can't," Laurie protested. "I don't have anything to sleep in." Why had she said that? She couldn't spend the night here. She should have asked how they were going to get her home if it didn't stop. She should have left earlier. The men could have handled supper by themselves. All they had to do was keep the pot simmering until it was time to eat. Instead she'd stayed, certain the snow would stop like it always had. Now she was stuck.

She hadn't brought anything from her house because she'd never intended to stay here past suppertime. The last three winters had been mild with no more than a smattering of snow. How could she have anticipated a blizzard?

"We can find you something to wear," Jared assured her.

"What?" Steve asked.

"I don't know yet," Jared said, "but we should be able to think of something."

Odell stood. "I'm heading to the bunkhouse before the snow gets any deeper. I expect we'll be in the saddle early tomorrow. Texas longhorns don't know what to do with this much snow."

"Jared's Herefords would," Steve said. "That's why he wants them."

"I want them because they carry fifty pounds more meat per animal," Jared said. "Being able to rustle about in the snow is an added advantage."

During supper the men had argued the virtues of one breed over another, but the moment Laurie washed the last dish, they stood and headed out of the house. She was left with Jared.

"We should have been prepared for something like this," he said.

"I wouldn't have agreed to come out here if I hadn't been certain I could go home every evening." She dried her hands and hung the towel up to dry. There was nothing else to require her attention. She turned to face Jared, her heart pounding against her rib cage. "Are you sure I can't get back to town?"

"If this were an emergency, I'd bundle you up in enough blankets to survive a snowstorm three times this bad, and the six of us would try to get you home. But it's not an emergency, and I don't want to endanger my men and horses. Not to mention endangering you."

Laurie had known what the answer must be. She supposed she'd asked to convince herself. At least she could tell Naomi and Sibyl she hadn't had a choice. "Do you want some more coffee?" she asked Jared.

"No. I'd better get to bed. Odell is right about the longhorns. They're used to heat and drought, not cold and snow. You don't have to go to bed yet."

She didn't want to think of going to bed. The idea of sleeping across the hall from Jared filled her with alarm. She was sure he'd be a perfect gentleman, but she wouldn't get a wink of sleep thinking about him less than a dozen steps away. She'd had trouble concentrating all day. Even when both of them were busy in different places, she could almost feel his presence. She would never be able to forget his kisses. They had awakened her body as well as her soul. Now just looking at him would cause her temperature to rise. She'd been able to console herself with the assurance that she could go home and get herself under control before she had to face him again. Now she wouldn't have that chance to calm down, to force herself to think of something else. He'd be close by with no one between them.

"There's no point in staying up," she told him. "Keeping the kitchen warm will just waste wood. Besides, you'll need a hot breakfast before you ride out tomorrow." It took an act of willpower to force herself to face leaving the safety of the kitchen. She picked up the single kerosene lamp that had dispelled the gloom in the kitchen from the center of the table. "You really don't have to find something for me to wear. I can sleep in my undergarments."

Jared held the door for her to precede him into the hallway. "I know enough about women's undergarments to know they won't keep you warm."

She would have guessed that, but she wished he hadn't told her. Now she couldn't stop thinking of how he'd obtained that knowledge. She paused in the hall long enough for Jared to fetch and light a lamp that had been sitting on his desk in the parlor. The extra light penetrated the dark corners and lifted her spirits. They stopped outside the door to Steve's room. She'd cleaned the room and changed the sheets earlier in the week in case Steve wanted to return to his bed. She'd never imagined that she'd be using it.

"If you don't have enough quilts, there are more in the wardrobe. I'll be in as soon as I find something for you to wear."

She wanted to tell him that was unnecessary, but she was afraid he'd explain why her clothing—she was sure he could name each item and describe it in detail—wasn't sufficient to keep her warm. Unable to think of anything to say, she went into the room and closed the door behind her.

There was nothing about the room to indicate that a young boy had lived there. She guessed the furnishings had belonged to Steve's parents' bedroom. The bed was a four-poster covered with a bedspread of tufted cotton and lace trim. A patchwork quilt lay across the end of the bed. She took a second one from the bottom of the wardrobe. The curtains at the window were floral.

Several quaint sayings such as "God Bless Our Home" had been stitched into bleached cloth, framed, and hung on the walls. A table more suitable for the parlor than a bedroom held several small pictures of people she assumed were Steve's parents and grandparents. A round table with a pitcher and basin profusely decorated with pink and blue flowers stood on the other side of a bed. Laurie wasn't surprised that Steve preferred the bunkhouse to such a room. She was spreading the quilts on the bed when Jared knocked on the door.

"Come in."

Jared was holding two garments. "This is a pair of long johns," he said, holding up clothes large enough for two of her. "And this is a nightshirt." It looked far too big as well, but it didn't need to fit her the same way the long johns did. "I never thought to keep any of Steve's mother's clothes."

She was certain both pieces of clothes belonged to Jared. Just the thought of encasing her body in clothes that had covered Jared's body caused her breath to snag. How was she supposed to sleep?

"You don't have to decide now," Jared said when she didn't speak. "You can try both and decide which one you want."

Laurie jogged her brain to make it work. "I'll take the nightshirt." She hoped her voice didn't sound as unsteady as she felt.

"Are you sure it will be warm enough?"

"I have two quilts on the bed."

"It's awfully cold."

"I'm from Kentucky. I don't like the cold, but I'm used to it."

The nightshirt was made of coarse homespun. It ought to be more than enough to keep her warm. "This is all I need."

"If you want something else, don't hesitate to call. I'm right across the hall."

He didn't have to remind her. That's precisely what she was trying to forget. He seemed reluctant to leave the room, like he was waiting for her to say something, but her brain was frozen. The only thoughts in her head were ones she didn't dare give voice to. After another moment, Jared nodded and withdrew.

Once the door closed, Laurie took a deep breath and tried to calm her nerves. She was safe. Nothing would happen if she didn't want it to happen. But that was the problem.

She wanted something to happen.

She could try to deny it, but that wouldn't do any good. All she could think about was Jared kissing her again, the feel on his hands on her body, the heat that washed over her like a wave, draining her of energy. Noah had rarely touched her. When he had, it had made her feel cold inside. Jared's touch had been so different it wasn't like the same thing. Was that the way a man's touch was supposed to feel to a woman who found him attractive?

There was no use torturing herself with these questions or memories. Besides, it was too cold. She ought to undress quickly and get to bed and go to sleep as soon as possible. Morning would come soon enough, bringing her face to face with half a dozen hungry men who would spend the day in the snow and the cold looking after their cows. It had been the same in Kentucky. The stock came first. Everything else came after that.

She removed her shoes and stockings. The floor was so cold she could hardly stand still long enough to undress. She threw her clothes on a chair upholstered in floral print, pulled the nightshirt over her head, and jumped in the bed. That wasn't any better. The sheets were icy cold and the quilts weighed her down.

She curled up in a ball and tucked the covers tightly under her quivering chin. Her whole body shook, but gradually the sheets warmed and she slowly uncurled until she was stretched out. The one advantage was that for a few minutes, thoughts of Jared hadn't been foremost in her mind.

But once she was comfortably warm, they came flooding back. She drifted off to sleep dreaming of being wrapped in his arms.

⤳

Jared tossed in the bed until the sheets were knotted around his feet. Completely frustrated with himself, he threw the covers off and unwound the sheets. He welcomed the bite of freezing cold on his overheated skin. He hoped it would help get his mind off Laurie, but it didn't. It just made him wonder if she was warm enough. Blizzard-driven wind howled around the corners of the house, forcing its way in at every crack between boards and around windows. The snow had continued to fall until everything was covered in a thick mantle of white.

He worried about his cows. They weren't used to snow. If he hadn't been in Virginia during the war, he would never have seen enough snow to cover the ground. Would Laurie be trapped here one day or for longer? Would she be so upset she'd never come back once she reached her home? Was she sleeping well? Was she worried about her house? Her reputation?

Probably all of those. What could he do to help her? Nothing if he stayed in bed. The thought of going to check on her sent his blood pressure soaring.

He had tried to control his desire for her, but two kisses had made that beyond possible. He could hardly think about anything but her.

What did she think of him? He felt fairly sure she liked him. She said she thought he was attractive, but that didn't mean she wanted him to be anything more than a business partner. Still, he couldn't get rid of the feeling that she would welcome a closer relationship. Despite her description of the relationship between her and her husband, Jared was certain Laurie's quiet and almost meek appearance hid a passionate and physical soul. It wasn't in her words or her behavior. It was in her eyes, banked heat waiting there to be released. Maybe she didn't know it, but she had a warm nature. The men had taken to her immediately, and it wasn't only because she was beautiful. She had a friendly, open personality that accepted everyone as they were without a trace of reserve. You felt she truly liked you and wanted you to like her.

His feelings for her were much more than *like*.

Unable to remain still, he sat up. The cold was so biting he was about to slide back under the covers when he thought he heard a sound. His breath stilled as he listened intently, waited for it to come again, but the wind shrieked so loudly he couldn't have heard her if she'd cried out. Unable to go back to sleep without knowing she was safe, he got out of bed, walked to his door, and opened it quietly. He listened again for that sound he was positive he'd heard, but the wind continued to howl around the house like a pack of hungry wolves. He had no option but to go to her room.

The hall floor was so cold he might as well have been walking across ice. The glass knob on her door felt just as icy to his touch. He turned the knob, opened the door slowly, and peered into the room.

❧

Laurie sensed Jared was outside before he opened the door. She hadn't heard anything. She just knew. Had she been expecting him, or had she wanted him to be there? Now that he was here, what was she going to do? She sat up in the bed but didn't speak. He looked like a ghost, his white long johns barely visible in the near pitch-dark of her room. When he moved toward her, he seemed to float. She should have lighted the lamp, but she couldn't move.

"I came to see if you were all right. Are you cold?" His voice sounded disembodied, lacking the substance visibility lent to it.

"A little." Shivering made her voice sound breathless, lacking any substance at all.

He moved closer. "There's another quilt in the wardrobe."

"It's already on the bed."

"I could bring you one of mine."

"Then you'd be cold." She was sure he was freezing, standing there next to her bed, his feet bare and nothing on his head. Were his long johns warm enough?

"I could stay here until you got warm."

She shivered, felt colder than ever. Was he suggesting they share the bed? That was impossible, but she couldn't interpret what he said any other way. Words jammed in her throat. Part of her wanted to tell him to leave, that he shouldn't be in her bedroom in the middle of the night, but the words wouldn't come out. Another part of her, one she hadn't had to face until now, wanted to invite him to warm her bed with his presence. That part of her didn't pretend that what it wanted wasn't scandalous. It just didn't care.

"I won't stay all night."

He shouldn't stay even one minute, but she couldn't say that. The thought of him *warming her bed* had deprived her of the power of speech. The blood was pounding in her ears so rapidly it drowned out the howling wind. She could only look at him, waiting for him to make a decision. She felt like a silly, spineless girl, and she hated it, but the conflict inside her was paralyzing. Everything she'd been taught she ought to do and feel stood in direct opposition to what her body and soul longed for. Regardless of her decision, she would lose something valuable.

Jared made the decision for her. "This house wasn't built for weather like this." He approached the bed. "I think the bed is strong enough to support the two of us."

Having spent the last four years sleeping with a husband she didn't want to touch her, Laurie had taken the left half of the bed out of habit. Jared crawled into the right side.

For several minutes, they lay there, neither speaking nor moving. Laurie couldn't tell whether she was hot or cold. Both temperatures raced through her, one after the other.

"We need to be closer to share warmth."

She knew that, but she was powerless to move. How had she become such a nonentity? She had opinions. She had desires. She could think. She could speak, though apparently not right now.

Jared moved closer until their shoulders touched. "Did you have blizzards this bad in Kentucky?"

She nodded her head, even though she knew he couldn't see in the dark.

"We never did in Texas, but the winters in Virginia were worse than this. We sometimes slept back to back to share body heat. Do you think we ought to do that now?"

Her head nodded without consulting her or her heart, which was beating so rapidly it felt like it might burst from her chest.

Without waiting for her answer, Jared turned over and backed up to her. She might as well have backed up to a hot stove. The places where his body touched hers felt like they'd been set afire. Yet cold shivers caused her to tremble. She was petrified with cold fear and aflame with a churning hunger.

"You're still cold."

How could she explain that she was too hot and too cold at the same time? It didn't make sense even to her.

"I'll turn over so you can back up to me."

The bed quivered under the weight of his body as he turned over and moved closer to her. When she felt his hand on her shoulder, she reacted awkwardly.

"I'm not going to hurt you. I just want you to back up against me. It's probably the only way to keep warm when it's this cold."

She didn't know whether she moved—she didn't think she did—or whether Jared moved closer, but their bodies touched, and his heat suffused her entire being in a great wave that drove every vestige of cold from her. Jared had put his arm on her shoulder. She was in his virtual embrace. She lay perfectly still, afraid to breathe, afraid of what might happen if she did.

But was she *really* afraid? Would she have allowed Jared in her bed if she were? Those were daunting questions because they called into question her basic nature. Was she the kind of woman who would allow a man who wasn't her husband to make love to her?

Maybe not, but she wanted Jared to make love to her. It didn't matter that she wasn't married to him. Did he want to make love to her? Why would he be here if he didn't? It wasn't that cold.

The movement was only slight, but even through the heavy homespun she was instantly aware when his fingers began to move against her. His touch was so slight it felt more like a feather, but it was as clear to her as if it had been an angry grasp. She lay still, wondering what he would do next. Noah had never touched her like this, had never made love to her. She didn't know what men wanted. Should she continue to lie still—or did he expect her to do the same to him? Naomi could have told her, but Laurie had never dared ask for fear she wouldn't have been able to endure another day with Noah.

Jared's feathery touch moved down her arm to her elbow, then up to her shoulder. Shivers ran through her, but they had nothing to do with the cold that filled the room. When his hand opened and lay upon her shoulder, her stomach turned over. The tips of his fingers pressed against her, then relaxed, pressed again, and relaxed. The effect was soothing, calming. Her breathing came a little easier, but her heart raced faster than a cow pony chasing a runaway steer. Should she lie still and pretend she wasn't aware of what he was doing? Should she say something? If so, what? Should she turn over and face him?

"Do you want me to stop?"

Jared's whispered question shattered the paralysis that gripped her. She could no longer remain silent, pinned down by questions she was afraid to answer. Jared had made it easy for her. All she had to do was say yes.

She moved her lips, but the word—she couldn't be sure what it was—was inaudible.

"I don't want to stop," Jared whispered. "I've wanted to do this since the moment I met you. You're the most beautiful woman I've ever seen. Your husband must have been the most envied man in Cactus Corner."

To be thought beautiful by a handsome man, to be desired by him, filled Laurie's heart to overflowing. A feeling of gratefulness, so great it kept her speechless, caused tears to come to her eyes. She brushed them away, afraid if Jared knew, he'd think she was unhappy. She hardly knew what she felt, but she was positive it had nothing to do with unhappiness.

The feel of his lips on the back of her neck was such a shock she started violently; his kisses sent shivers racing through her body like a thousand shooting stars. She knew he would not stop now. It was only the beginning.

"I didn't mean to hurt you. I won't do that again."

Fear that he would be a man of his word unlocked her lips. "It didn't hurt. It's just that no one has every kissed me there before."

"I find that hard to believe. Your neck and shoulders would do justice to a goddess."

Laurie didn't know anything about goddesses—they sounded like something pagan to her—but she hoped they were beautiful. She very much needed to feel beautiful.

"My mother says a woman should never expose her neck and shoulders."

"Not unless she wants to drive men insane."

"I wouldn't want to do that." She paused. "Does it drive you insane?"

"Very nearly."

She was certain it was wrong to be pleased, but she was starved for the kind of appreciation he was giving her. Nor could she deny that she wanted more.

"How? Why?" She hardly knew what she was asking.

"It's how any man would feel when he beholds extraordinary beauty that he can't have. It's like a starving man being forbidden to approach a table laden with his favorite foods."

Laurie wasn't sure she liked being compared to food, favorites or otherwise, but she liked the sentiment behind it.

"Men are faced with things they can't have all the time."

"That just makes them want them all the more. It's like forbidden fruit."

Back to food again! What did he think she was, a

ripe peach or a plump melon? Much more of this, and she would turn over—to tell him to go back to his own bed.

His laugh was a soft rumble. "I'm sorry. I thought I was good at talking to a woman, but I'm making you sound like something to be served on a platter. Believe me, I'm more likely to think of you as someone to set on a pedestal. You're perfect."

Laurie knew she wasn't perfect—Naomi was smarter and Sibyl was more elegant—but she liked that he thought so. Jared was kissing her neck and shoulders again. She wanted him to kiss her lips, but she knew that turning to face him implied acceptance of what he was doing, of what she was certain he wanted to do. She wanted it, too. Otherwise, why would she have allowed him in her bed? But she was afraid.

Why?

She wasn't afraid of what people would say. Once they found out she'd spent the night at the ranch, they'd probably think it anyway. It certainly wasn't out of loyalty to Noah or deference to Norman. No, she was anxious because she was fearful she wouldn't live to up Jared's expectations. He was probably so experienced he would be appalled at her naivety. He wasn't going to stop unless she asked him.

And she wasn't going to ask him.

"Your neck and shoulders are beautiful, but I'd much rather kiss your lips. I haven't stopped thinking about that since this morning, and I'd very much like to do it again."

There it was. She must either stop now or go forward to the end.

Hoping she wasn't about to make the second biggest mistake of her life, she turned over.

Jared smiled and gave her a quick kiss. "You're so beautiful I sometimes find it hard to believe you're real."

"I don't know why. I'm here. Besides, I'm not that beautiful."

"You are to me."

"I've never driven anybody insane." Well, maybe Noah, but not for the same reason.

Rather than try to persuade her she was wrong, Jared kissed her. Laurie decided that was a more convincing argument. Certainly one she enjoyed more, enough so that she kissed him back. His reaction wasn't what she expected. He drew her into his arms and kissed her so hard she was sure he'd bruised her lips. She didn't care. From that moment, it was impossible for him to do anything wrong.

Jared could kiss her all night and it wouldn't make up for the barren years of her marriage. She was ready to do just that, but it quickly became apparent Jared wasn't. His embrace had brought them into full body contact, making it impossible to ignore his erection that pressed against her thigh. Jared didn't give her time to worry about its size or the heat it ignited in her own body.

He covered her with kisses. No part of her face, neck, shoulders, or arms was neglected. It was as though he was afraid he would leave some part of her unkissed. Laurie put her hands on either side of his face and pulled him up until she could look into his eyes. "I want to kiss you, too."

"That's the easiest wish I've ever been asked to grant."

Without removing her hands, Laurie drew Jared to her and kissed *him*. It was the first time she'd ever kissed any man other than her father. It was just as wonderful as she'd hoped it would be. His cheeks were covered with stubble, and his abundant hair looked to be at war with itself, but his lips were warm and firm. She couldn't get enough of him. It was the most wonderful feeling she'd ever experienced. She wanted to cover his face with kisses, but he stunned her by thrusting his tongue between her parted teeth. When shock caused her jaw to slacken, his invasion was complete.

Now she knew she was dreadfully unprepared to make love to this man, but she wasn't going to admit it and give up. If he could do this, so could she. When she attempted to invade his mouth, his tongue parried her attempt. They jousted, first attacking, then retreating, then attacking again. While their tongues were locked in battle, their bodies struggled to find unison. They pressed against each other. The more desperate the battle of their tongues, the harder they pressed against each other. Finally, Laurie fell back exhausted by the intensity of their kisses.

Rather than being exhausted, Jared was energized. He covered her face, neck, shoulders, and arms with more kisses. It was as though he couldn't get enough of her to satisfy him. More demanded still more until she thought he would consume her. She wanted to do the same to him, but she was unable to summon the energy—or the desire—to combat him. She knew there was more, and she knew that Jared would share it with her.

She was shocked when he unbuttoned her night-shirt and covered her breasts with his hands. But her body wasn't shocked. It, rather than she, wrapped her arms around him like she never wanted to let go. It, rather than she, pressed hard against him, causing him to push back until their flesh felt like it had merged. His hands cupped her breasts while his lips covered them with kisses. When he took her nipple into his mouth and sucked gently, a moan escaped her. She'd never believed such feelings were possible, but they had to be because they were happening to her. When he took her nipple between his teeth and nipped it, her moan became a shout that sounded equally of pain and exquisite pleasure.

Jared drew back abruptly. "Did I hurt you?"

It was difficult to collect her thoughts enough to answer. The words wouldn't come out, so she shook her head.

"Do you want me to stop?"

"No." The thought of him stopping was more frightening than anything else. "It's good," she managed to say. "I just didn't know what to expect."

"Didn't your husband kiss your breasts?"

This was no time for the truth. "Not like that."

"Then he was a fool." Jared kissed each breast and suckled each nipple. "They're magnificent. *You're* magnificent."

There was no need to answer, for Jared had turned his attention to her abdomen, scattering kisses down one side of her body and up the other. Laurie squirmed with pleasure. She was amazed that her whole body seemed to be capable of giving her this unforeseen pleasure. How could Noah not have known? Why had he denied her such pleasure?

That thought vanished almost before it was complete, for Jared had placed his hands under her buttocks and pressed her firmly against his arousal. The groan that tore from him seemed to come from the depths of his soul. In a series of quick movements, he removed her nightshirt and she lay naked before him.

She didn't know what to do. She'd imagined being in this position, but it had never happened.

"You don't have to be afraid. I won't hurt you."

She hadn't realized her body was rigid. She attempted to relax, but between the cold and apprehensiveness, it was a nearly impossible task. Her mind's eye followed Jared's hand as it moved down and along her thigh, over and between, until it paused.

"Open for me."

First she had to relax. Her body was as rigid as stone. She told herself there was nothing to fear. While Sibyl never spoke of what passed between her and Norman, Naomi made no secret that she enjoyed making love with Colby. Laurie was sure it would be as good for her with Jared, but she had to relax and let it happen.

She closed her eyes and tried to concentrate on how wonderful it was to have a man love her body, to find it beautiful, to want to make love to her. She had wanted this for years, had been afraid it wouldn't happen. Now it was, and she would know what Naomi said was one of the most wonderful experiences of her life.

Gradually her body relaxed enough to allow Jared's fingers to enter her. Anxiety and discomfort caused her to tense and utter a tiny gasp, but Jared didn't pull back this time. Instead his finger moved deeper inside her and began to caress her with gentle, unhurried strokes. Gradually all feeling of discomfort left, taking with it any anxiety and giving way to wonder and expectation.

A kernel of heat started to grow and expand until it spread to her entire body. Rather than feel cold, her body seemed to radiate heat. Wave after wave swept over her, each hotter than the one before. A second finger penetrated her. Maybe a third—she didn't know—but it didn't matter. She was on fire and no longer able to remain motionless or silent. Her body moved from side to side as a series of increasingly loud moans escaped her. She hadn't expected this mixture of pleasure and discomfort. It was almost as though pain had become pleasure. Then Jared did something, *touched* something, that nearly lifted her off the bed.

She cried out, then reached down and gripped his shoulders so fiercely he grunted.

Before she had time to recover, he moved up and entered her.

A second later he pulled back with a startled oath.

Nine

LAURIE'S EUPHORIA VANISHED LIKE VAPOR INTO THE air, and fear returned like a suffocating blanket. He felt the same way Noah did! He found her body offensive. She should have known not to believe everything he said.

"You're a virgin!"

"What?" She knew what it meant, but she didn't know how he knew.

"You never slept with your husband. Why?"

All hope that the last four years could be erased from her mind disappeared. There was no point in lying or telling half stories. "My husband never made love to me. He said it was because he found my body offensive. He said I was unfeminine and insisted I wear clothes that would disguise my body as much as possible."

There was a moment of dead silence during which the last of Laurie's hopes died.

"Was the man insane? You're not only beautiful, you're the most feminine woman I've ever met. My God, there must have been something wrong with him. What did your parents say?"

"I never told them."

Moving back to her side, Jared rolled up on his elbow and looked down at her. "Why not?"

"My father forced me to marry Noah because he was convinced I would get into trouble if I stayed single any longer."

"And your mother allowed that?"

"She agreed."

Jared took her in his arms, pulled her to him. "If I ever meet your father, I'll be tempted to knock him down. I have no doubt your looks caused many a man to think things he wouldn't put into words, but your character is too pure to be swayed." He kissed her gently. "You're crying. Why?"

"When you pulled away, I was sure you felt like Noah."

"There's not a man alive who could see you like Noah did. And I'm going to do everything in my power to prove that to you."

It took a while to reach the previous emotional plane a second time, but now that Laurie was certain Jared truly believed she was beautiful, she was an eager and enthusiastic partner. It wasn't long before she was panting for breath.

"It may hurt a bit when I enter you, but it will be over quickly, never to happen again. Do you trust me?"

"I will always trust you."

He rose above her and positioned himself at her entrance. He kissed her at the same moment he entered her. The pain was sharp but brief. He continued to kiss her as he moved within her. In moments she was caught up by the fire that was driving him.

Rather than lie still, she rose to meet him, fell away, and rose again. She'd found what it was like to be with a man, and it was wonderful. Never again would she believe she was ugly. Never again would she cringe before a man's gaze. Jared thought she was beautiful. He desired her.

Finally sure of herself, she abandoned herself to the ecstasy that enveloped her.

❧

Laurie couldn't sleep. She wasn't sure she'd be able to sleep ever again. So many conflicting thoughts clamored for attention. How could she justify having slept with a man who wasn't her husband? That was exactly what her father said he feared when he forced her to marry Noah. She didn't even have the excuse that they were in love. She didn't care what her father would think, but she did care what Naomi and Sibyl would think. They were more than cousins. They were her only real friends.

Despite what some might say, she was not a fallen woman. She was an adult, a woman free to make her own decisions. She'd accepted the attentions of a man she found attractive, a man who found her attractive. She didn't owe allegiance to anyone but herself. Moreover, she was willing to accept the consequences of her actions. So far the consequences had been far more wonderful than she could have imagined.

Maybe it was of vain of her to be so concerned about her looks, but Noah had made her feel so ugly it had been difficult for her to leave the house in those horrible dresses. The pitying looks of her cousins and the other women had made it worse. They insisted that she wasn't ugly, but the fact that most men did avoid looking at her gave undeniable credence to Noah's allegations.

She didn't have to believe that any longer. Jared found her so attractive he couldn't resist making love to her.

Her body still hummed with the aftermath of his attentions. He'd gone back to his bedroom a short while ago, but they'd made love again before he left. She hadn't thought anything could be so marvelous, so transforming as the night spent in Jared's arms.

She looked out the window. Although the lower portion of each pane was covered by snow, she could tell the ground was completely covered. But soon the sun would come out, and the snow would start to melt. Even if it was winter, this was a desert.

She would have to get up in a few minutes to start breakfast. She didn't know how she was going to face Jared, or how he would feel about facing her. She wasn't ashamed of what she'd done, but it could be awkward. Outside of finding her beautiful and wanting to make love to her, how did he feel about her? What were her feelings for him?

Other than feeling strongly attracted to him, she wasn't sure. She'd spent so many years trying not to feel anything, ignoring feelings she couldn't crush, it was hard to feel anything but fear and inadequacy. She liked Jared. He'd accepted her as a partner and had been kind to her. He showed concern for her safety as well as her reputation. He appreciated everything she did for him and the men. He'd come to her room tonight because he was worried she wasn't warm enough. She smiled to herself. She was certainly warm now. The glow she felt might never wear off.

The gray light of dawn filtered in at the window. The men would be up taking care of the horses and other livestock in preparation for a rough day in the saddle. They would need a big breakfast and plenty of hot coffee to fill their canteens. She threw back the covers and left the bed. The floor was so cold it was like stepping on ice. She hurried to put on her clothes. She wouldn't be warm until she got the fire going in the kitchen.

❧

Laurie had been a virgin.

The phrase kept drumming in Jared's head. He'd never deflowered a woman. Not even his first partner had been a virgin. Despite anything he said to himself, a feeling of guilt rode him hard. He hadn't forced Laurie. She'd been a willing and enthusiastic partner. She hadn't asked him to go back to his own bed. She'd been content to snuggle in his embrace. So why did he feel so guilty?

Did he feel he was supposed to protect her, that because she was his partner and was working in his home, he should have protected her from men like himself? It hadn't been her choice to spend the night at the ranch. Had he taken advantage of the snowstorm to do what he'd been dreaming of doing since the first time she came to his ranch? Could any man have resisted making love to such a beautiful and desirable woman once he knew she was willing? Had he done anything to make it difficult for her to send him away?

He might find the answers soon, but he wouldn't

find them now. He could make better use of his time by getting this load of firewood to the kitchen.

He'd risen before dawn and dressed in a room lit by a single candle. Snow had drifted up to three feet against the door that led from the kitchen to the bunkhouse. It was nearly a foot deep in the wind-swept area in between. He was glad the woodshed was against the side of the house. Even at that, he'd had to shovel through a deep snowdrift before he could get to the wood. Loaded with all he could carry, he headed for the kitchen. He intended to get the stove going before Laurie got up. He had dumped his armload into the wood box and was knocking the snow from his boots when Laurie entered the kitchen.

For a moment they froze, each staring at the other. Laurie was the first to speak.

"Thanks for bringing the extra wood. That will give it time to dry before I need to use it." She picked up the ash bucket and began to remove the ashes from the stove.

"I can do that," Jared volunteered.

Laurie didn't look up from her work. "It'll be enough if you empty the bucket for me."

"You'll need more wood."

"No need to get it now."

"All of us will be in the saddle most of the day. I don't want you to run out before we get back."

"The sun will come out and warm things up. It never stays cold here, even in the winter."

"I don't know what usually happens, but that sky looks like the bottom of a lead pan, and the snow is so powdery it blows around like sawdust."

Laurie finished emptying the ashes and handed him the bucket. "It has to melt. I have to go home tonight."

"I'll check the trails when we're out today, but it looks too deep."

"I *have* to go back to town."

Jared was about to go back outside, but he turned back to Laurie. "Are you afraid to stay here?"

She didn't answer.

"I mean after last night. Are you afraid of me?" There, he'd said it. Now neither of them could avoid talking about it.

Laurie turned from where she'd been opening a drawer to get the matches. "I've never been afraid of you, not even after last night. I have to go home because everyone will be worried about me. I know Norman will think the worst, but so will some of the others."

"So it's just your reputation? You would feel comfortable staying here if it weren't for that?"

Laurie's gaze met his and held. "I'm not ashamed of anything I've done, but I don't want to make staying here a habit. It wouldn't be good for me, and it wouldn't be good for the men. It would cause needless speculation."

What she said made sense, but it irritated Jared. Didn't she think he could control himself? She was a beautiful, desirable woman, but that didn't mean he couldn't stay away from her. Then again, maybe she was right. After last night, it would be even more difficult to corral his need for her. "I'll check the trails, but right now it looks pretty bad."

The kitchen door opened, and Steve dashed in and slammed it behind him. "It's colder than hell out there."

"Hell's supposed to be hot," Jared said.

"Whatever. Hurry up with that fire," Steve said to Laurie. He was more interested in getting warm than arguing over a theoretical point.

"Didn't you have a fire in the bunkhouse?" Jared asked.

"Of course we do, but every water trough is frozen solid. The boys have to melt snow so they can water the horses."

"The fire's going," Laurie said, "but it'll take a while before the water's hot enough for coffee."

"Have you finished with the livestock?" Jared asked Steve.

"No."

"Then why aren't you helping them?"

"Clay sent me in to ask when breakfast would be ready. He said his Cajun blood was about to freeze in his veins. He wants enough pepper in his eggs to cause steam to come out of his ears."

"He better hope the eggs haven't frozen," Laurie said. "Or the water and the rest of the food in the larder. Otherwise, he won't get anything but coffee until tonight."

Steve panicked. "Don't make me go back out there and tell them that. Odell is as bad as Clay."

Laurie went into the pantry. Jared could hear her rustling around inside.

"What's she doing?" Steve asked.

"We'll find out when she comes out," Jared told him.

Laurie emerged with a basket of eggs. "The water froze." She turned to Jared. "I'll set the bucket on the stove. The ice will soon melt, but first see if you can chip out enough ice to start a pot of coffee. I wrapped the eggs up last night before I went to bed. Let's hope that was enough to keep them from freezing."

Steve watched eagerly as Laurie cracked an egg. It was so thick Laurie had to scrape it out of the shell with a spoon, but it wasn't frozen. Jared was more interested in the coffee. He took a hammer and pick and attacked the ice. It was slow going, but by the time he managed to chip out enough to melt for coffee, the stove was hot. He put the bucket on the back of the stove so the rest of the ice would melt. Some of the food in the larder had frozen and some was shot through with ice crystals, but Laurie had scraped out and thawed out enough for a decent breakfast by the time the men had finished their chores and entered the kitchen.

Clay cast an accusing glance at Jared. "You told me it never snowed in Arizona. I wouldn't have come if I'd known I was going to freeze to death in my own bed."

"I didn't tell you it *never* snowed," Jared said to Clay. "The colonel trying to recruit troops for the fort said nobody had heard of it snowing here."

"It hasn't snowed like this since I've been here," Laurie told him.

Clay backed up to the stove, shivering and rubbing his hands together even though he was bundled up in a fur-lined hat and sheepskin coat. "If I don't show up at supper, it'll be because my frozen carcass is somewhere out there being chewed on by wolves."

Nick and Loomis made fun of him, but Odell and Steve sidled up to the stove as well.

"If you don't leave room for Laurie to cook, you won't get any breakfast," Jared said. "Sit down at the table and wait."

He was in a bad mood, and he couldn't explain why. He ought to be relieved Laurie wasn't upset over last night. He ought to be thrilled to have found such a beautiful woman who liked him well enough to sleep with him, maybe enough to do it again. The men liked her. She worked hard and was an excellent cook. In addition, she'd provided the money to buy the Herefords he needed to make the ranch successful. He'd even found a man he was certain was one of his lost brothers. Everything was looking up for him. Why was he so irritable?

"Coffee's ready," Laurie announced.

Five cups were immediately thrust in her direction. Laurie gave the men a saucy smile. "I've got to serve the boss first. Don't want to lose my job."

"No man in his right mind would fire you," Loomis said.

"Not if he'd tasted your cooking," Steve added.

Jared accepted his coffee and watched irritably as Laurie poured coffee for the other men. He wanted to punch Loomis. The man treated Laurie like a porcelain doll, not like a real flesh-and-blood woman. Couldn't he tell she had enough life in her for a dozen women? She wasn't the kind of woman to be put on a shelf and admired. She had a lust for life that should cause any red-blooded male long to take her to bed and stay there until he was too exhausted to get up.

Watching his nephew stare at Laurie with his tongue hanging out amused and exasperated Jared. He could remember his own first crush, but it was on a girl his own age, not a woman who'd been married and widowed. What did Steve think was going to happen?

Jared told himself to stop acting like a fool. Steve wasn't an idiot. He knew nothing would ever come of his crush on Laurie. Being infatuated with an older woman was the sort of thing young boys did. She was safe. He could admire her, dream about her, and lust after her without worrying anything would be required of him. He wasn't like Jared.

"Breakfast is ready," Laurie informed everyone.

There was a clattering of feet as the men settled onto the benches on either side of the table. Loomis carried two bowls to the table for Laurie, then waited until she was seated before taking his own seat. Jared could tell Laurie really liked that. The smile she gave Loomis could have melted a twenty-foot snowdrift, and that *really* irritated Jared. He should have been the one to carry the bowls to the table and wait for her to be seated. Only he hadn't thought of it because none of the men he'd been around growing up had treated their wives like that. If they were all like his own mother, he wasn't surprised.

"I hope you got more of this coffee, ma'am," Nick said. "I've already finished my cup."

"Get it yourself," Jared barked. "The pot's on the stove."

Nick stood up. "I was planning to. I just wanted an excuse for Laurie to look my way and smile the way she smiled at Loomis."

Laurie turned to Nick and favored him with a smile that made Jared's temperature shoot up at least ten degrees. "I don't need an excuse to smile at a charming young man like you," Laurie told him. She swung her gaze to encompass the whole room. "Or any one of you."

"Don't waste your time on Odell," Nick advised. "He's still angry that he has to work like the rest of us rather than stay here cooking things we can neither recognize nor take a chance on eating."

"I don't like it when it's cold," Odell said, "but I like her cooking better than mine."

"We all do," Loomis said.

"Stop trying to embarrass me." Laurie got up and went to the stove. "The ice in the bucket has melted. I'll make enough coffee to fill your canteens."

Fortunately for Jared's rising temper, the men concentrated on eating while Laurie boiled water for more coffee.

"What do we have to do today?" Nick asked Jared.

"You can tell the man knows nothing about cows," Loomis said. "Where in Europe did you say you were born?"

"Sicily," Nick answered. "We had lots of cows but no snow."

"We have to check on as much of the herd as we can," Jared told him. "Longhorns are pretty self-sufficient, but they can be buried in drifts or bunched in a canyon to get out of the wind. We'll have to break ice so they can find water. Be on the lookout for wolves and cougars. Right now the snow slows them down more than the cows. If it crusts over hard enough for them to walk on it without breaking through, the herd will be at their mercy."

"I'll need more than one canteen of coffee," Nick told Laurie.

"I'll keep a pot going all day."

"Don't let me see you showing up here every hour," Jared snapped.

"You aren't riding with us?" Loomis asked.

"Of course I am. Those are my cows."

"Mine, too," Steve reminded him.

Jared ignored Steve. "Why did you think I wouldn't be riding with you?"

"From what you said to Nick, it sounded like you planned to be here all day."

"Well, I don't. Now all of you eat up and get in the saddle. Those cows have had all night to get themselves caught in a drift. And don't forget to take your axes with you."

"Supper will be early tonight," Laurie said. "I expect most of the snow will melt today, but I want to start for home well before dark. The trail is bound to be messy."

"I'm not sure the snow is going to melt," Jared said. "We'll have to wait and see."

Laurie stilled, then looked directly at him. "I *have* to go back. Under no circumstances can I spend a second night here."

Her statement was so unequivocal, her look so determined, that the men turned toward Jared with questioning looks. Could they be thinking he'd made some unwelcome advance? Did Laurie's resolve to return to town regardless of the weather mean she was afraid he'd demand a repeat of last night?

"I'm related to half the people in Cactus Corner,"

Laurie explained, "but that won't stop them from speculating on the reasons why I would stay here rather than return home. None of you has to live in Cactus Corner. I do, and I don't want everyone gossiping behind my back."

"We'll make sure you get back even if it takes all of us," Loomis assured her.

Jared made a mental note to break Loomis's neck as soon as he got the opportunity. "We don't have to make any decisions now, but we do have to get into the saddle. I want as many of the cows as you can find headed toward the river. The snow is likely to melt there first so they will be able to find something to eat. I doubt the river will freeze so they'll have water without us having to climb through canyons to find pools covered with ice." He stood. "We ride out as soon as you fill your canteens."

All six men hurried to finish their breakfasts. As soon as they saddled their horses, they were back to fill their canteens. By the time the last man came back for coffee, the kitchen floor had been tracked with snow.

"Don't worry about it," Laurie told Jared. "It'll dry."

"I'm not worried about the floor. I'm worried about you. Don't bother with the rest of the house. Stay in the kitchen where it's warm."

"I'll be fine," Laurie assured him. "I lived through snowstorms like this every winter in Kentucky.

"Well, you're not in Kentucky, and there's nobody here to look after you."

"I'm your partner, not your wife," Laurie reminded him. "You don't have to *look after me*."

"I still feel responsible."

"Don't. Tell the men I'll have supper ready by four o'clock. That ought to give me plenty of time to get home before dark."

"You don't have to leave. I'll stay in the bunkhouse if it will make you feel better."

"I really can't stay, but if I did, I wouldn't force you to sleep in the bunkhouse. You didn't make me do anything I didn't want to do. Now you'd better get going, or the men will accuse you of using your position as boss to stay close to the fire."

If she only knew. The fire wasn't half as tempting as she was.

❧

Laurie stirred the beef stew to keep it from sticking. The men had been in and out all day to spend a few minutes getting warm and to refill their canteens with hot coffee. Jared had been in only once. He said the herd was in good shape, but it was going to take more than a single day to get them out of the canyons, down off the rim, and into the valley next to the river. He also said the snow wasn't melting. It hadn't been above twenty degrees all day. The sun had stubbornly remained behind a thick cover of clouds. How was she going to get home?

She wasn't afraid of Jared. Just the opposite. She was so strongly attracted to him that she was certain she would let him make love to her again. But she needed time to think, and she couldn't do that while she was in his house. Certainly not when he was sleeping across the hall. She wasn't sure what she had to decide, but she knew there was something she had to straighten out in her mind before she could decide what to do next.

She didn't want to get married again. Four years with Noah had been more than enough for a lifetime. When he died, she'd expected to have enough money to be independent, but Noah's will had destroyed that chance. In a way, this partnership with Jared was even better. If the ranch was successful, she would have more money than ever and she would be out of Norman's control. Maybe she would have enough money to move to Preston or Tucson. She would hate to leave her cousins behind, but then she would be truly free. The prospect was exciting, but she couldn't get ahead of herself.

She wanted to know what kind of income the ranch could generate. She would never spend more than she had because that would give someone else control over her. Her father had sold her, her husband had humiliated her, and Norman wanted to manage her. She would never let that happen again.

The door burst open, and Steve entered on a wave of icy air. He slammed the door behind him and went straight to warm himself by the stove. "I don't know why Jared insisted we leave Texas. We never had to put up with anything like this."

"I thought he came west to find his brothers."

"He did, but he could have hired a Pinkerton. Then I wouldn't be dragging cows out of snowdrifts above my head."

"Where is everybody else?"

"They're coming. They told me I could quit first because I was the youngest, but I know they're just as cold. I wouldn't be surprised if Clay heads back to Louisiana as soon as the snow melts."

"Did it melt any today?"

Jared entered in time to hear her question. "Not a single flake as far as I can tell." He walked to the stove, rubbing his hands together to get them warm. "You're still snowed in."

Laurie was dismayed but not surprised. She'd gone outside several times to collect snow to melt for coffee. All the coming and going had trampled the snow between the house and the bunkhouse, but the drifts against the house hadn't diminished. The snow hadn't begun to fall from the limbs of the cottonwood trees. The weight of it bent juniper limbs nearly to the ground.

"I'm glad it didn't melt," Steve said. "I like having you here."

"I like being here, but that isn't the issue."

"What is?"

"She's already told you," Jared told his nephew.

"I don't know why you care what anybody says," Steve said to Laurie. "Everybody knows you're perfect."

Laurie wondered if she'd ever been so innocent. She'd known her parents weren't perfect long before she reached her fifteenth birthday. "I feel better sleeping in my own bed each night." Which wasn't quite true because that bed reminded her of the hundreds of nights she'd spent next to Noah.

"We can bring your bed here."

Jared laughed. "That would cause enough gossip to reach Tucson."

"Maybe not Tucson," Laurie said, "but certainly

Prescott." Only she didn't care about either of those cities. Just Cactus Corner.

"Well, nobody had better say anything bad about you to me," Steve declared.

"Or me," Jared added.

Laurie didn't know how to respond to such declarations, so she was relieved when the other men entered the kitchen. They headed straight for the warmth of the stove, leaving a trail of snow across the floor. She didn't say anything. It would melt, soak into the wood, and tomorrow you'd never know the floor had been wet.

Nick forced his way into the circle around the stove between Clay and Loomis. "I've been up to the rim and down to the river, and nothing's melting."

"We've dragged cows out of drifts up to their horns," Clay said. "I didn't know there was this much snow in the whole world. It was never like this in Louisiana."

"It's so cold, every water hole we opened will freeze over tonight," Odell added. "You'll be stuck here for the better part of a week."

"If Miss Laurie wants to go home," Loomis said, "I'll see she gets home."

"It would take hours," Steve said.

"Then they'll be hours I spend in her company. I can't think of a better use for them."

Laurie knew she ought to say she wouldn't let any of them take the time to escort her home after being in the saddle all day, but she really wanted to go home. Her gaze cut to Jared. She was surprised to find him glaring angrily at Loomis.

"If Laurie needs anyone to help her get home, I'll be the one to do it."

"It ought to be me," Steve objected. "I always do it. Besides, you can't stay in her house."

"I can stay in a hotel."

"There's no hotel in Cactus Corner."

Jared turned to Laurie. "There must be someplace for people to stay."

"They've got some rooms above the saloon."

"Then I'll stay there."

"You don't have to go," Steve told his uncle.

"I should go," Loomis said. "Steve is too young, and Jared needs to be here because it's his ranch."

"I'm not too young," Steve insisted.

"This is my ranch so Laurie's safety is my responsibility," Jared said. "I'll see she gets home safely."

"It's my ranch, too," Steve said.

Laurie was flattered that everyone was so concerned about her safety, but she didn't want this to degenerate into an argument. As important as it was to get home, she'd stay here before she caused trouble for Jared. A loud knock caused everyone to turn toward the door.

"Who could that be?" Steve asked.

"Open the door and see," Jared told him.

Nobody was more shocked than Laurie when Colby stepped into the kitchen.

"I'm here to take Laurie home," he announced.

Ten

COLBY WASN'T FAZED BY THE CONFUSED AND
unfriendly response that met his announcement.
"My wife is Laurie's cousin," he explained. "She and
just about every woman in Cactus Corner—half of
them related to Laurie—spent most of the night at
my house worrying about her. The only reason they
aren't here themselves is that I promised to bring her
home tonight."

"By the time we realized the snow wasn't going to
stop, it was too late," Jared said.

"You can't be any more concerned for her safety
than we are," Loomis added.

"That's why I ride with her every morning and
night," Steve said.

"It's as much a question of my sanity as your
safety," Colby said to Laurie. "Do you know what it's
like having a houseful of women imagining such horrible things happening to you that I was nearly ready
to come after you when it was so dark I couldn't see a
dozen feet in front of me?"

"It's my fault," Laurie said. "I was so sure the snow

would stop and melt before nightfall that I stayed until it was too late to try to go home."

"It's no one's fault," Colby said, "but Laurie has to go home tonight. In case you're wondering, everyone is concerned about her safety rather than her reputation."

Jared was surprised at the anger he felt. Being married to Laurie's cousin meant Colby would automatically be concerned about Laurie's safety, as would other members of her family. Since there was nothing in Colby's demeanor to indicate he thought anything improper had occurred, Jared had no reason to be upset. But he was. Was it because he thought Laurie was his responsibility and resented Colby's intrusion?

"How did you get here?" Laurie asked Colby. "Jared said the snow hasn't started to melt."

"I had a load to take to the fort. There's nothing like eight oxen and a wagon to break a trail through the deepest snow."

"Did you drive your wagon up to the house?" Jared asked.

"He sure did." Steve had rushed to the window. "Can I drive them on the way to town?"

"When they're headed home, those oxen don't need anybody to drive them. They know the way." Colby turned to Laurie. "You'd better bundle up as much as you can. It's bitter cold out there."

"I can't leave until the men have had their supper."

"We can serve ourselves, ma'am," Loomis said. "You get on home."

"I'm going with her," Steve announced.

"Me, too," Jared said.

"You don't have to do that," Laurie said, "not with Colby making sure I'm safe."

"Someone has to drive your buggy," Steve reminded her.

"I'm responsible for your safety from the moment you leave your house until you return." Jared knew there was no real need for him to accompany Laurie to town, but staying here felt like he was shirking his responsibility, like he wasn't properly concerned about her safety. He'd been the one to insist that she had to work at the ranch to earn a full partnership, so he had to make sure nothing happened to her.

"You can't go without eating your supper," Laurie said. "You've both been in the saddle all day."

"You need to eat, too," Jared said. "It's a long, cold ride."

Laurie hesitated.

"Colby should eat with us as well," Jared said.

"Naomi will have supper for me when I get home."

"You look like a man who could eat two suppers."

Colby grinned. "It's been known to happen."

"Grab a plate and help yourself. If I know Laurie, she's made enough for a crew twice this size."

Once Colby accepted the invitation to sit down and eat with them, Jared started to relax. He couldn't understand why he resented Colby's concern for Laurie, but there was no use denying that he did. Maybe he believed the secrecy of their business arrangement gave him a right not shared by anyone else. Maybe he felt everyone from Cactus Corner shared responsibility for Laurie's unfortunate marriage. Or maybe he was just jealous of any man who showed attention to Laurie. That would explain his reaction to Loomis and Nick. In all likelihood, he was overestimating the importance of their shared intimacy. Laurie wasn't acting like anything had changed.

And that irritated him because, for him, everything *had* changed.

"What possessed you to buy a cattle ranch in the Arizona Territory," Colby asked Jared, "especially when this particular ranch had already failed? Naomi tells me you gave up a successful army career."

"I came out here looking for my brothers," Jared said. "I'd finally gotten tired of the army, but I didn't want to go back East. I figured Arizona wasn't all that different from south Texas. I already knew about running cows in near desert conditions, so I decided to stay. Anyway, I'm going to buy Herefords. They're much better for beef than longhorns."

That led to a discussion of range conditions versus cattle needs that involved everyone at the table. Jared was surprised at how much Colby knew about ranching.

"Why didn't you go into ranching yourself?" he asked Colby. "You know enough."

"Never liked messing with cows or staying in one place."

"You're staying in one place now."

"I've got four very good reasons to change my mind." He turned to Laurie and favored her with a broad grin. "I suspect Laurie knows I have a fifth one on the way." He laughed at her embarrassment. "The husband is always the last to know."

"Naomi didn't want to say anything until she

was sure," Laurie told him. "She knew how excited you'd be."

"My wife and her cousins believe I'm so desperate for family I'd do something reckless if this was a false alarm. Even without my birth family, I've got more than any man could hope for. And don't start in about us being brothers," Colby said to Jared. "That used to be all I could think about, but not anymore."

Laurie had told Jared what Naomi said about Colby having given up trying to find his brothers, so Jared called back the words he'd almost spoken. Colby was in no mood to listen to anything Jared said, and this wasn't the time to try to change Colby's mind. Jared wasn't going anywhere and neither was Colby. Something would happen, some opportunity would arrive, for him to get Colby to reconsider. Jared could wait. He was certain he'd found one brother. That was enough for now.

Colby finished his supper and stood. "It's time to get going. With no sun, it'll be dark early."

Laurie was bundled up and ready long before Steve could have a horse harnessed to the buggy and Jared could saddle a fresh horse, so Colby told Jared he would start and they could catch up. In light of how slowly oxen moved, it was a sensible thing to do, but it only served to make Jared angry all over again. He was going to have to learn to control his feelings about Laurie.

He'd only known her for a few days, and while they'd slept together, it had only happened once and she didn't seem anxious to have it happen again. Nor did she stop giving the other men as much attention as she gave Jared. He'd never reacted like this with any of the other women he'd been involved with, so why should it happen with Laurie? It wasn't like he was looking for a wife. Yet he must be looking for something to become this upset. What was it?

❧

"Of course I don't mind you staying with us," Naomi said to Jared. "We have two bedrooms that aren't being used." She cast a coy glance at Colby. "At least not yet."

"I appreciate your hospitality, but I can stay at the saloon. Colby says they have rooms upstairs."

"It's time we got a decent hotel," Naomi said, "but until we do, you can stay here whenever you're in town. Are you hungry? I don't think Colby's supper has burned up yet."

Colby shared a conspiratorial grin. "I'm starved."

"I'd like some coffee if you have it," Jared said.

"Come into the kitchen. You can keep Colby company while he eats."

"Where are the children?" Colby asked.

"They went to bed early. Peter and Esther had never seen snow," she told Jared. "They wore themselves out playing in it. Morley Sumner made snow cream for everybody. They can't wait for it to snow again."

Jared smiled and tried to pretend that he wasn't thoroughly out of temper. The trip into town had been miserable and, in his mind, completely unnecessary. Laurie would have needed twice as much clothing to have stayed warm. Steve was exhausted after a day in the saddle, and Jared was feeling worn out himself. It had been impossible to talk during the trip. With the wagon squeaking, harnesses jangling, and twenty sets of hooves crunching through the snow, they didn't need the wind to drown out conversation. But it had been windy, and Colby was the only one to arrive in town not looking like an icicle. Laurie had dashed into her house without giving Jared a chance to say more than a hurried good night.

"Now that we've caught each other up on the day's events," Naomi said to Jared, "we can stop boring you. Don't pretend you're not bored and tired. You can go to bed now if you like."

"I'll go soon, but I'd like to talk to your husband for a bit."

Colby's expression wasn't encouraging. "Not about us being brothers, I hope."

"Why are you so against considering the possibility? You said yourself that it was all you could think of for years."

"I ran away from the couple that adopted me, and I had no friends or relatives. I had nothing to think about but the family I'd lost. All that changed when I fell in love with Naomi and the twins came to live with us. Now this whole town is like my family."

"But they're not your *real* family, not your blood kin."

Colby swallowed the last of his coffee, and Naomi refilled his cup. "First of all, you have no proof that we're brothers. Even you admit it was a feeling, a hunch. Even if you're certain I look like your father—which I doubt. How could a three-year-old remember what anyone looked like?—that wouldn't be proof."

"There's got to be proof. All we have to do is find

it. It can't be coincidence that both of us lost our parents along the Santa Fe Trail in the same year."

"Hundreds of people die on that trail every year."

"But how many couples with three small boys who were adopted by three separate families?"

"Why are you so anxious to find your brothers? It's not like you don't have family."

"Ever since I can remember, I've known I had two brothers. I've always felt like a part of me was missing. The need to find them grew stronger after my father and both of Steve's parents died."

"I used to feel that way, too, but not anymore."

"So you're not going to help me?"

"How can I help you?"

"You must have something from before our parents died. A toy, a blanket, something that I might remember."

"Didn't you hear me say I ran away? My father beat me, and my mother tortured my mind. There wasn't anything, but if there had been, I wouldn't have kept it. I didn't want anything to remind me of them. If there had been anything, they'd have destroyed it. They didn't want me to be reminded of my family."

Jared was trying to come up with a counterargument when Colby spoke again.

"What difference would it make if we were brothers? For the last twenty-nine years we've lived totally different and separate lives. We're strangers who know nothing about each other. I'll be happy to be your friend, but it would be better for both of us if you stopped trying to make us brothers. We'll never have proof. Without it, it will just lead to a lot of frustration."

"I understand what you're saying, but I can't give up. All I ask is that you keep an open mind."

"I'll do that if you won't mention it again until you have that proof."

Jared wasn't sure he could do that. "I'll try. Now I'd better get to bed."

"Not so fast," Naomi said. "I've got a few questions of my own."

"The man's tired," Colby said to his wife. "Let him go to bed."

"This won't take long. I just want to know what he did to make Laurie work for him when she knows everybody is against it."

Jared had expected to face some questions, but he hadn't expected anyone to be so direct. What could he say to convince Naomi without revealing Laurie's secret?

"I didn't do anything to convince her. Actually, she came to me. The part about traveling back and forth was the only problem, but we worked it out."

"Laurie says she wants to be independent, but I know there's more to it."

"You would have a better idea of that than I would. All I know is Laurie had a horrible marriage. Because of that, she refuses to let Norman control her the way her husband did. I don't know why somebody in this community wasn't able to do something about Noah and isn't able to do anything about Norman."

"Those are good questions for which I don't have answers," Naomi said. "I tried to help Laurie—Sibyl, too—but she wouldn't let me. I mean to do something about Norman. I haven't decided what yet, but I'm working on it."

"You haven't said anything to me about that," Colby said.

"Because I don't know what I want to do. Now I think we ought to let Jared go to bed. He has to get up early in the morning."

"Not before light," Colby said. "I can't stop Laurie from working at your ranch, but I won't have her traveling in the dark."

"At least that's one thing we agree on. Now if you will show me my room, I think I would like to go to bed."

Jared was jealous of Colby's house. It was bigger and better built. Cold didn't seep in around windows and blow through cracks. The furnishings were sparse, but what they had was of good quality. It was the kind of house he wanted when he finally had enough money to get married.

"There's nothing in here but a bed and a chair," Naomi said when she showed Jared to his room, "but there are enough quilts to keep you warm." She laughed. "They haven't been out of the trunk since we left Kentucky. I was beginning to think I'd never have to use them."

"Laurie said Kentucky winters could be bad."

"We got snow like this all the time. If you need anything, let me know. I'll wake you. The children never sleep late. They'd miss seeing Colby if they did."

"Are they that crazy about him?"

"No worse than he is about them. If they didn't wake up, he'd wake them."

"When did Colby stop wanting to find his brothers?"

"When he got a family of his own."

"I understand how important that must be to him, but wouldn't he still like to find the rest of his family?"

"I'm sure he would, but there's no way to prove the relationship. Rather than go through more years of pain and disappointment, he wants to concentrate on what he has."

"I understand, but I can't give up looking."

"Then you'd better look somewhere else. If you upset my husband, you'll have to answer to me, and you won't like that."

When Jared didn't respond, Naomi left the room.

Jared didn't immediately get ready for bed. He was certain Colby was his younger brother. He was equally certain there was some way to prove it if he could only find it. Much to his surprise, he had no idea what he would do if he did find the proof. Twenty-nine years had passed, and Colby had been a baby when their parents died. They had no memory of each other. There was nothing to connect them beyond the knowledge that they had had the same parents. They had no shared experiences. They didn't even know anything about each other. How would knowing they were brothers change anything?

Jared didn't know. He was just certain it would.

❧

Laurie knew she shouldn't be spending so much time with Jared in his study, but she'd finished her work and enjoyed his company. She wasn't especially interested in the war—it had come too close and brought too many unpleasant consequences—but she enjoyed hearing about other people and other parts of the country. Despite traveling more than a thousand miles, she felt she'd never been anywhere and didn't know much of anything.

"I thought about moving to Tucson when Noah died," she told him. "I might have if Norman hadn't withheld my money. In any case, I might not because I would hate to leave my family and friends. I don't know anyone else."

"You'd make friends wherever you went," Jared said, "but I'm glad you didn't. I would never have gotten my Herefords."

"Is that all you think about, cows?" She had meant it as a joke, but she realized immediately that she'd strayed into dangerous territory. Fortunately, Jared noticed a horseman riding toward the house.

"I wonder who that can be? It's not one of the men, and it's not Colby."

It took only one look for Laurie to know. "It's Norman," she said with disgust.

"What's he doing coming all the way out here? Do you think he changed his mind about lending me the money?"

Laurie was certain he had an entirely different purpose. "He's come to spy on me. He thinks me working for you is disrespectful of Noah's memory and prejudicial to the way he sees himself."

"How's that?"

"Norman is certain he's the most important person in Cactus Corner. As his brother's widow, anything I do reflects on him. Working for you is just about the worst thing I could have chosen to do."

"Do you want me to tell him to leave?"

"No. He'll only corner me when I'm at home. Don't get upset by anything he says. Nobody listens to Norman unless it's about money."

"I'm not going to let him abuse you."

"Neither will I. I can tell him to leave. It's a lot harder at home."

By this time, Norman had reached the house and dismounted.

"That's a beautiful horse," Jared said to Laurie. "Where did he buy it?"

"Somewhere in Kentucky."

"Do you think he'd let me use it as a stud?"

"You'll have to ask him."

When Jared opened the front door, Norman's sour expression made it clear this wasn't a social visit. "What brings you out this far?"

Norman stalked into the house without a greeting. "I came to see exactly what my sister-in-law is up to."

"I'm no longer your sister-in-law," Laurie told him from her position in the center of the hall, "and I'm not up to anything. And if I were, it wouldn't be any of your concern."

Norman didn't bother to answer her. Instead he peered into the study before crossing the hall to open the kitchen door. "I stable my horse in a barn that's better than this," he said to Jared. "How can you expect a decent woman to work here?"

"I don't live here, Norman. I just work here."

"It's a disgrace. You don't need to work."

"Have you changed you mind about the provisions of the will?"

"Of course not."

"Then I need to work. Say what you have to say, then go. I have a supper to fix before I go home."

"Then why weren't you in the kitchen?"

"How do you know I wasn't?"

"I could see you through that window," he said pointing to the parlor window overlooking the porch. "You can't cook in there."

"My job is to cook and clean. However, I wasn't doing either. I finished cleaning early, and Jared and I were talking. He was telling me about some of the places he's been and some of the things he's done."

"A woman shouldn't be interested in things like that. Her entire focus should be on her home and family."

"Since I have neither, I can't be accused of neglecting either."

"Where did you sleep the night it snowed?"

"That's none of your business." Jared looked angry enough to throw Norman through the door.

"I'll tell him," Laurie said. "If I don't, he'll just make something up."

Norman was incensed. "I'm a banker. We do not *make things up*."

"Well, see that you don't start." Laurie led him to Steve's bedroom and opened the door. "This is Steve's old room. He moved to the bunkhouse."

Norman sniffed in disdain. "It's hardly bigger than a closet. Where did *he* sleep?"

"I slept here." Jared opened the door to his room. "A slightly larger closet, but adequate for my needs."

"That's too close," Norman said.

"The house has only four rooms. There was no other choice."

"Don't say I should have gone home," Laurie warned. "Even Colby agreed it would have been dangerous. I'm surprised you're here. It's a long ride."

"Now that the sun is out and it has turned warm, the snow is melting rapidly."

"Which is why you needn't have bothered. Steve and I will be back before dark tonight."

"I don't like you being alone with that boy. There's no telling what ideas he might get in his head."

"He's only fifteen, but I expect you know very well what ideas get into his head. However, he's smart enough to keep them there."

"Steve adores Laurie," Jared said. "He wouldn't let anyone hurt her."

"Norman knows how protective Steve can be." Laurie smiled at the memory. "Now that you've seen where I work, you can go back to your bank."

Norman didn't move—he even appeared to be at a loss for what to say next. He looked around as through reassessing something. Finally, he turned to Jared. "I'd like to see your ranch."

"Why?"

"I might change my mind about giving you that loan."

"Why would you do that?" Laurie asked.

"I haven't said I would. I said I might."

"Do you think that'll make me stop working here?"

Norman's attitude turned superior. "This is a financial matter. It has nothing to do with you."

"I think it does," Jared said

"I don't see why it should." Laurie glanced meaningfully at Jared. "I only work here."

Jared returned her look. "With more money, I can build a bigger house, hire more men. My need for a cook and housekeeper would be even greater."

"Don't start making plans yet," Norman cautioned. "I haven't decided to give you the money. I've got to see your operation first."

"That means you'll be in the saddle most of the day," Jared told him.

"My horse is a Morgan. He's easy to ride."

"I want to talk to you about breeding him to a couple of mares."

"There'll be time enough for that later. Right now I want to see your ranch."

Laurie watched Jared and Norman leave the house with a deep sense of misgiving. Norman never did anything without a reason, and that reason was nearly always to his advantage. She didn't understand why he should have changed his mind or what he hoped to gain by it.

She was more worried about what Jared would do if Norman lent him the money. Would he decline her offer to be his partner? Jared had never said he wanted a partner for the ranch. It would decrease his control as well as his share of the income. Regardless of how much he liked her cooking and having a clean house, control of the ranch was more important.

No man she'd ever known accepted a woman on an equal basis unless forced. Having been forced into it, Jared would probably like to get out of the situation at the first opportunity. She could no more imagine Noah having giving her control of the mercantile than she could Norman letting Sibyl run the bank. Why should Jared be any different? Even Colby was more comfortable now that Naomi was spending most of her time at home with the children.

What would she do if Jared said he no longer needed, or wanted, her money?

She wandered into the study and sank down in the chair next to Jared's desk. There was a lot more at stake than just a safe investment for her money. This was her first chance for real independence. If she failed, she might not find another opportunity that suited her so well. She couldn't just sit at home and spend money without people asking where she got it, any more than she could invest in a business in Cactus Corner. She would have to leave, go as far away as Santa Fe or Albuquerque. Preston was too close. Tucson probably was, too.

Yet she didn't want to leave her family to live among total strangers. She longed for independence, but not the kind that distanced her from everyone she knew and loved. She wanted to watch Sibyl's daughter and Naomi's three children grow up. She enjoyed being *Aunt Laurie*. She wanted to feel free to make her own decisions, but she needed the support, the love and companionship of friends and family. She wasn't a rebel, nor did she suffer from wanderlust.

Then there was Jared. Not that she felt she had any claim on him. She was certain everyone she knew would say she'd made a terrible mistake by sleeping with him, but she was grateful it had happened. He'd restored a part of her that Noah had nearly destroyed. For the first time in many years, she felt like a whole person.

She got up and headed to the kitchen. Worrying wouldn't achieve anything. Besides, she was certain Norman had an ulterior motive, one so shameful it might cause Jared to refuse the loan if it was offered. She would wait to see what Norman decided.

∽

Jared had already known Norman Spencer was a man whose acquaintance he didn't want to pursue. After spending the better part of a day in the banker's company, Jared was certain he didn't want to know him at all. He gave Norman credit for being a shrewd businessman, but the man was a lousy human being. He was so cocooned by his own sense of superiority that he had no idea how offensive he could be. None of the hands had ridden with them for long. Steve took one look and rode off in the opposite direction.

"You seem to have a good operation here," Norman said as they headed back toward the ranch house. "Why do you want to buy Herefords when everybody else is running longhorns?"

"Grass here is limited. Herefords carry more and better-quality meat than longhorns, and they can do it on the same amount of graze. You come from Kentucky. Surely you're familiar with several superior breeds."

"That was in Kentucky, not in the desert."

It hadn't looked like a desert today. The abrupt change in the weather overnight had caused the snow to melt with such rapidity that only patches remained where drifts had been the deepest. Water poured off the rim above in cascading ribbons that glistened in the sun. Dry washes ran fetlock deep in water. Creeks overflowed. Pools had become lakes.

"Eastern breeds of cows need a lot of water," Norman said, "and you won't see this much water again in ten years."

"I'm planning on a small, select herd that won't cause overgrazing," Jared told him. "I learned the importance of that in Texas."

"I don't have much opinion of Texas," Norman declared. "My uncle died in the war down there."

Jared decided there was little point in defending Texas to a man whose opinions were as inflexible as they were arbitrary. He was relieved to be reaching the house. He felt compelled to invite Norman to stay for supper—he hoped he would refuse—but then he would be rid of the man. All he wanted now was to know if Norman was going to lend him the money to buy the herd.

Would he take it? If he did, what would he do about Laurie and her investment in the ranch?

If he borrowed the money, he would have to pay interest, but he wouldn't lose half his ranch. That had been a difficult decision that he'd made because he had no other choice. He had given away half of all that he and Steve had managed to salvage from their ranch in Texas as well as everything he'd saved from his years in the army. He'd be eager for the opportunity to get it back.

Borrowing from Norman would mean he could give the men bigger shares. That would be important when they left and got married. He'd never expected that they would stay with him forever. The ranch was to be their means of reestablishing themselves in the world. Giving Laurie half of the ranch would make that more difficult, if not impossible.

But what about Laurie?

She had taken a risk in offering him all her money. If they failed, she would end up with nothing and be forced to depend on Norman's barely discernible mercy. She'd taken a further risk when she agreed to work at the ranch. No matter how long people had known her, there was bound to be speculation about the temptations facing a woman who spent her day in the company of single men without a female companion. Norman had practically accused her of immorality just for sleeping in the bedroom across the hall.

There was no question that Jared and the men would want her to stay, no matter what the situation. It was more than her cooking. It was more than having an attractive woman to look at. They liked her, and she enjoyed being with them. Mealtimes had turned into the time of the day everyone looked forward to most eagerly. The men cleaned up without anything being said. They were polite, treating her more like a guest than a cook. In turn, she was fascinated by their lives.

She said it was because she'd never been anywhere, but Jared thought it was because she was truly interested in each of them. She remembered their stories as well as the names of family members and lost sweethearts. She didn't ask so much what they did but how they felt about it. Her caring had invested their evenings with the kind of thoughtfulness that had been missing. Sharing the pain of horrific events and terrible losses lightened the burdens all of them carried. Losing her would be a painful loss.

And what about him? How would he feel about losing her?

That was hard to say because he hadn't thought about it. He was certainly attracted to her and could still feel her in his arms as if he were back in that memorable night. She was a beautiful, desirable woman, and any man would do whatever he could to keep her. But he wasn't in love with her any more than she was in love with him. Their situation was merely one of a man and woman finding each other attractive and desirable.

He hardly knew her, and she knew even less about him. He didn't want to get married just yet, and he doubted she was considering it after suffering through a difficult marriage. She was here only because she needed a way to establish her independence. There was some mystery about the source of her money, but surely she could trust Colby enough to let him help her find another investment. Jared would feel guilty about backing out on her. If he did, he'd pay her for the work she'd done.

But he'd miss her far more than he would miss the food. She was brave and strong and resourceful, but she was also frightened and insecure. Despite a large number of relatives, she was alone in ways he never had been. At times he thought he understood her better than anyone else. Maybe because he hadn't known her all her life—just the last few weeks. She was neither the young girl they'd known growing up nor the woman who'd married Noah Spencer. Jared doubted she knew who she was. She needed time to grow, to learn who she was and what she wanted, but she needed to feel safe before she could do that. The security of their partnership was something she needed, something apparently only he could give her. Could he turn his back on all of that?

Norman's penetrating voice jerked him back to the present.

"I don't know why you want to be a rancher," Norman said. "Spending the day on horseback is a miserable way to earn a living."

They were wading through a dry wash below the corrals that was running a foot deep in water.

"And I would hate being stuck inside all day. I don't even mind the heat as long as I can breathe the pure air from atop the rim. We had nothing like it in Texas."

Norman rode up to the front of the house and dismounted. Jared resigned himself to inviting the man to supper, but he figured it was a small price to pay if Norman would give him the loan. "Why don't we go inside and talk business?"

"I'm not ready for that," Norman said. "I want to see more of this operation before I make up my mind. And I'm not sure you're smart to be sinking so much money into Herefords when you already have a herd."

"I think I can convince you that Herefords are worth the money. We can go to my office. I've got some information there—"

"Not now. I want to have supper with you so I can get to know more about the men who work for you. Knowing the quality of the help is just as important as knowing the boss."

Jared hoped Norman wasn't stupid enough to call his men *the help*. He had explained that the men were all partners in a limited way, but apparently Norman didn't remember that or didn't care. Laurie was alone in the kitchen.

"Did you find out what you needed to know?" she asked Norman.

"Not yet." Norman seated himself at the table. "I'd like some coffee."

"It's not ready."

"Why not?"

"I don't put it on to boil until I see the men ride in. By the time they clean up and come up to the house, the coffee's ready."

"I want some now."

Laurie faced him squarely. "You'll get your coffee when the men get theirs. After they've worked hard all day, I wouldn't think of serving them cold coffee." She turned her back on him. "Considering the way you've treated me, I'm surprised you have the nerve to ask me for anything."

Norman's shock amused Jared.

"I'm only following—"

Laurie began to ladle hot stew into a large serving bowl. "You're using Noah's will as an excuse to punish me, though I have no idea why."

"I'm not—"

"I don't have time to listen to you tell me the same lies again."

Norman reacted as though he'd been poked with a cattle prod. *"I don't lie!"*

Laurie spun to face him. "You've been lying for years.

You got away with it because nobody had the courage to call you on it. Well, I'm doing it now. You're a liar, Norman Spencer, and you always have been."

Jared doubted this exchange would help him get his loan, but he was enjoying it too much to interfere. Before it could escalate, Steve came running into the kitchen. He turned to Norman.

"You can't go back to Cactus Corner tonight. The river's flooded."

Eleven

JARED DECIDED SOMEONE OUGHT TO SHOOT NORMAN and put the rest of the world out of its misery. The way he talked, you'd think someone had arranged for the river to flood just to keep him from his own bed. Jared had seen people who acted like they were the center of the universe, but never one who actually believed it.

Never one to believe what he had not verified with his own eyes, Norman had mounted his horse and ridden off to check the river for himself. He must have searched for a crossing for some distance in each direction because by the time he returned, the men had finished their supper. The moment he entered the kitchen, they left. Except for Steve, who had apparently appointed himself Laurie's protector. He let Norman rant and rave without saying a word, but the moment he tried to vent his temper on Laurie, Steve was on him like a terrier on a rat.

"If you hadn't been so ill-advised as to take a job out here, I wouldn't be in this predicament," Norman said to Laurie.

"It's not Miss Laurie's fault," Steve fired back. "Nobody asked you to come out here. Nobody *wanted* you here. I already told you we were taking care of Miss Laurie just fine."

"I'm not in the habit of taking counsel from boys your age."

"Maybe you should. At least people don't want to hide or get sick to their stomach when they see me coming."

Before Norman could fire off a response, Jared sent Steve to the bunkhouse. Laurie chose that moment to get ready for bed, which left Jared alone with Norman. Jared spent the better part of an hour explaining why buying Herefords was a good business decision, but he doubted Norman paid attention to half of what he said. Nor did he give any indication of what he'd decided to do about the loan.

"I'll take your bed."

Norman's announcement was as unexpected as it was abrupt.

"We have extra beds in the bunkhouse," Jared told him.

Norman looked as though he couldn't believe his ears. "You can't expect me to sleep in a bunkhouse."

"It's the only free bed I can offer."

"Your bed would be free if *you* slept in the bunkhouse."

Jared was willing to do a lot to coax Norman into giving him the loan, but leaving him free to continue his battle of emotional and financial warfare against Laurie wasn't one of them. "This is my home. I don't see why I should be expected to give up my bed."

"Not even to the man with the power to give—or withhold—your loan?"

Jared swallowed hard but answered, "No."

Anger twisted Norman's features. "You can't think I'm going to leave Laurie alone in the house with you. There's no telling what you might do to her."

Jared decided not to utter the words he wanted to say. "Laurie has already survived one night here. I'm sure she can survive one more."

"Nobody can verify that."

"Laurie can."

"If anything had happened, she'd be too ashamed to admit it."

To hell with the loan. A man could only put up with so much. He had a choice: He could knock Norman down and throw him out of the house, or he could offer him a place to sleep and hope he didn't have reason to kill him before morning. As much as he hated it, Jared said, "I have a very large bed. You can share it, you can sleep in a chair in the study, or you can choose the floor. The decision is yours."

Norman was outraged. "I can't sleep in the same bed as you."

"I'm not happy about it, either, but I refuse to leave you alone to keep on bullying Laurie. Now I'm going to bed. I have a nightshirt you can use. If you choose the chair or the floor, I have extra quilts."

With that, Jared turned and left the study. He picked up a lamp from a table in the hall but didn't light it until he reached his room. He sank down on the bed and tried to calm himself. He had been tempted to think Laurie had exaggerated about

Norman. Now he realized he didn't know the half of it. He was furious at Norman for holding his feet to the fire about this loan, but he was certain Norman was using the promise of a loan to manipulate Laurie. Since Norman didn't know about her money, how did he plan to do that?

Jared decided it was a waste of time trying to plumb the depths of Norman's twisted mind. Instead he should get to bed and be rested for tomorrow. With or without the loan, they would have a full day's work repairing damage done by the flood. He'd just finished changing into his nightshirt when Norman entered the room.

"I would appreciate the use of a nightshirt." His voice was icily formal. He looked like he'd rather sleep with his horse.

Jared handed Norman a nightshirt. "I'll leave you to get dressed while I lock up."

He didn't need to lock up, but he did need to give Norman some privacy. He knocked softly on Laurie's door.

"Who is it?" Laurie whispered.

"Jared," he whispered in return.

She opened the door a crack. "Where's Norman going to sleep?"

"He's going to share the bed with me."

Laurie giggled.

"He wouldn't leave me alone in the house with you, and I wouldn't leave *him* alone with you. I don't think much of my chances of getting that loan."

Laurie sobered. "Are you upset?"

"I'm not happy about it."

"Why? I told you I'd give you the money."

"We don't have time to discuss it here. I just wanted to make sure you were all right and let you know where Norman was sleeping." He paused. "I'm not sure I'll get any sleep, and it's not because of Norman."

"Don't even think about it. I wouldn't be surprised if Norman can read minds. His brother could certainly read mine."

"You're not serious."

"We don't have time to discuss it. Good night, and thanks for putting up with Norman."

It was unnecessary to tell her he'd done it as much for his benefit as hers.

Jared checked both doors even though he knew they were locked. He looked out the window at the sky filled with stars and a nearly full moon. Then he went to his study to make sure he hadn't left anything out he didn't want Norman to see before he left in the morning. When Jared couldn't find anything else to delay him, he returned to his bedroom. Norman was already in bed. It didn't surprise Jared that the man had taken up more than half of the bed.

"I couldn't find anywhere to hang my clothes," Norman complained. "They'll be wrinkled tomorrow. I never wear the same clothes two days in a row."

Jared could think of no useful reply, so he didn't attempt to make one.

"This house should be torn down as soon as you can afford to replace it. But if I give you a loan, you aren't to spend a penny doing it. I'll put that in the contract."

After spending the four years of the war living in a tent or bivouacking on the open battlefield, any house was a luxury. Tearing this one down would be a senseless waste of money Jared could use to buy quality stock.

"You ought to keep your longhorns in case the Herefords can't survive here."

"They will," Jared replied.

"I hope you don't snore."

Jared hoped he did.

"Don't move around. I'm a restless sleeper. I'm going to sleep now."

Jared hoped so. He didn't know if Noah had been anything like his brother, but if he had been, Laurie must have nerves of steel. He turned on his side away from Norman and hugged the edge of the bed. He hoped he'd be able to sleep. But between thinking of Laurie just across the hall and Norman on the other side of the bed, it wasn't likely.

❧

"I told you it wouldn't do any good," Laurie said to Naomi as they walked back to her house. "He won't change his mind."

"He can't be allowed to treat you like this," Colby said. "We'll find some way to force him to give you your money."

"I hope you aren't doing this so I'll quit working for Jared."

"I was hoping you would," Naomi said, "but we're really doing it because it's the right thing to do."

Laurie hadn't made any firm plans for her Sunday afternoon, but she hadn't wanted to spend it talking about Norman. She still shuddered when she thought about the time the flooded river had forced him to spend the night at the ranch. Jared's cowhands told him they hoped he wouldn't get the loan. If Norman started coming out to the ranch on a regular basis—something he might do with a loan that large—they'd have to quit.

"Why don't you come home with us?" Naomi asked. "The children haven't seen you for weeks except in church. Esther asks about you all the time."

"Naomi's father and brothers are there now," Colby added for an extra inducement. "They'd like to see you, too."

Laurie was happy to accept the invitation. Working for Jared had effectively cut her off from the community. Catching up on Sunday wasn't enough.

The house was full of activity when they arrived. Peter was trying to convince Ethan he was old enough to work with him and Colby, Dr. Kessling was helping Jonathan learn to walk, and Esther was practicing her wiles on Ben. The moment Laurie entered the room, Esther let out a squeal, abandoned Ben without a backward look, and threw herself at Laurie.

"Aunt Laurie! Aunt Laurie!"

"Don't knock her down," Colby cautioned. "She's an old lady."

"She's not old," Esther said. "She's beautiful. I want to be like her when I grow up."

"I told you she missed you," Naomi said. "I'm just the woman who makes her behave."

"I love you, too, Mama, but I see you all the time."

"Make a note of that," Naomi teased Laurie. "If

you leave your children six days out of seven, they'll appreciate you more."

Laurie spent the next half hour listening to what the children had done during the week and answering questions about the ranch. But children could only be interested in adult activity for a limited period of time, and when Steve showed up, Peter and Esther went off with him and Naomi's younger brother, Ben, in hopes of finding more excitement. After Jonathan was put down for his afternoon nap, the adults were left to entertain themselves. Inevitably the subject of Laurie working at the ranch and Norman's denying her the use of her inheritance came up.

"There's no use talking about it," Laurie said. "I don't like the long ride to and from the ranch, but I like working there."

"You're not thinking of moving there, are you?" Naomi looked aghast at the prospect.

"Of course not," Laurie responded. "Not that I wouldn't be just as safe there as I am here. I like coming back to my house. I know it's an illusion, but it makes me feel independent."

"It wouldn't be an illusion if Norman would give you access to your own money."

"There's no use talking about it. He won't budge, and he's got the will to back him up."

"There ought to be some way to force him to loosen the purse strings."

"The only way anyone is going to force Norman to do anything he doesn't want to do," Laurie declared, "is to start a new bank."

After a moment of shocked silence, Naomi declared, "Why didn't one of us think of that?"

"We did," Colby told her, "but nobody has the money."

"And nobody wants to go up against Norman," Dr. Kessling added.

"I didn't mean that seriously," Laurie protested. "I just meant—"

"I know what you meant, but you're exactly right," Naomi's brother Ethan said. "Money is the only hold Norman has ever had over us. Once we break that, he'll have to treat us like equals."

"You can stop dreaming about that," Dr. Kessling said. "He holds loans on everybody in town."

"Not us," Colby said. "We paid him off with the money Elizabeth left for the children."

"I don't owe him any money," Ethan said.

"Neither do I," Laurie said, "but what does that gain us?"

"Stop teasing yourselves with all these questions," Dr. Kessling advised. "Nearly everyone in town would have to transfer their accounts to the new bank to have any effect. That can't be done because no one has enough money to start a new bank."

"You don't have to have a lot of money," Colby said. "All you need is sufficient deposits to grant enough loans to cover your costs of operation. The deposits for the Fort Verde payroll alone would be enough for that."

"Where are you going to find anyone with the time to solicit everyone in the valley, the guts to face down Norman, and the standing to convince people to trust him?"

Every gaze in the room focused on Dr. Kessling.

"Don't look at me. I have no desire to tackle Norman."

"You're the only one who can," Ethan urged his father. "Everyone in town loves and trusts you."

"They trust me as a doctor. Not a banker. I don't know about the love."

"You know everybody loves you," Laurie told the doctor, "but don't let anyone talk you into doing this for me. I'll be fine."

"It's not about you being *fine*," Naomi said. "It's about Norman doing what's right."

"You're not the only one he bullies," Colby said.

Laurie turned to Dr. Kessling. "I'll help you any way I can, but don't do this on my account. I'm going to be fine."

"I don't call being forced to work cooking and cleaning house fine," the doctor said. "Jared can't be paying you much. Certainly not as much as you should be getting from Norman."

"How much is he paying you?" Naomi asked.

"You can't ask her that," Colby said.

"I just did."

"Well, you can't expect her to answer."

"I don't care about the money. I'm worried about her because she's my cousin."

Laurie had known this was going to come up sooner or later. Since she couldn't tell the truth, she would give them a story that was as close to the truth as possible. "Between what I'm paid and what Norman gives me, I have enough money. I eat my meals at the ranch, and someone invites me to eat with them nearly every Sunday. I have very few expenses."

"It's still not right," Naomi insisted.

"I agree, but now can we talk of something else? Have you told Colby your news?"

∽

"What's wrong?"

Laurie had been so distracted she hadn't been aware that Jared had returned. She struggled to hide her tears, but it was too late.

"Nothing. I was just feeling sorry for myself."

Jared tossed his hat and gloves aside. He sat down next to her at the table and took her hands in his. "I'd believe that if Nick hadn't told me he saw Norman riding back to town. He's been here, hasn't he?"

There wasn't much use denying it. "He left about half an hour ago."

"What did he say to cause you to cry? I swear I'll knock the man down if he comes here again and upsets you."

"It's not that. I was so angry I told him I hoped his bank would fail. I was crying because he can't take his anger out on me, so I know he's going to make life miserable for Sibyl and her daughter."

"What's this about his bank failing?"

Laurie shook her head. "It's not going to fail. This whole mess is just a misunderstanding. It's my fault."

"What misunderstanding? How is it your fault?"

Laurie withdrew her hands long enough to dry her eyes. "Naomi and her family were trying to think of ways to force Norman to give me my money. I told them the only way was to start a new bank. I didn't mean for anyone to take it seriously."

"I think that's a great idea. What happened?"

"They decided Dr. Kessling was the only one everyone loved and trusted enough to consider going against Norman. He's the only doctor this side of the fort. I was sure he'd be too busy to talk people into giving him their money, much less actually running a bank."

"What did he do?"

"He went straight to Norman and told him people were urging him to start a new bank because of the way Norman had treated everyone. Norman decided I was the one who'd put Dr. Kessling up to it. He threatened not to give me any money at all until I quit working for you."

"Can he do that?"

"I told him I'd take him to court, but his father-in-law is the justice of the peace." Laurie tried to hold back the tears—she wasn't even sure why she was crying—but to no avail. Tears streamed down her face. When Jared pulled her to her feet and took her in his arms, she folded herself into his embrace. "I just feel so helpless," she told him. "I know that sounds foolish when I have so many relatives in Cactus Corner, but Noah was so jealous he practically cut me off from everyone. I was afraid to do or say anything he didn't like because it just made living with him worse. Now Norman's determination to control me has practically made me leave town."

"You have lots of friends here. Steve would

attack Norman with his bare hands if he hurt you. I think Loomis or Nick would resort to a more effective method."

"What would you do?" Was that fair to ask? She didn't know, but she had to ask it anyway.

"Whatever is necessary. You're very important to me, too."

Impulse caused Laurie to stand on her tiptoes and give Jared a kiss of thankfulness for his support. What she unleashed was quite different. Jared's arms tightened around her with a suddenness that left her dazed, but it was his kisses that left her breathless. She hadn't forgotten the night she spent in his arms. The night Norman stayed at the ranch, she had lain awake for hours imagining what might have happened if Norman hadn't been there. It had left her tired and fretful the next day.

"I've been thinking about holding you in my arms, kissing you, making love to you every minute since the night it snowed," Jared whispered. "I even imagined following you home and making love to you all night long."

"I thought of the same thing," Laurie confessed. "Does that make me an awful woman?"

"No more than it makes me an awful man," Jared assured her.

Despite Jared's assurances, it wasn't easy to forget all the things Noah had said about her. She held Jared more tightly, hoping that his nearness and acceptance would drive out all memory of Noah's words. It was so much easier when his arms were around her, when she felt safely sheltered in his embrace. His kisses made her feel desirable.

She didn't object when he lifted her off the ground and carried her to Steve's old bedroom.

She had expected he would want to make love to her immediately. Instead, he lay down beside her, put his arms around her, and started kissing her once more.

"I could stay here all afternoon," Jared said.

She wished they could, too, but it wasn't possible. "I don't need all afternoon. A kiss and your arms around me can make me forget just about anything."

"Even Norman?" Jared asked.

"Especially Norman."

They both laughed.

Jared nuzzled her neck. "Do you really like me kissing and holding you?"

She tried to sit up, but he wouldn't let her. "If I didn't, I'd have slapped your face and demanded that you find Steve so he could take me home at once."

"I would stop if you asked."

"I don't want you to stop. I thought that was clear."

"I just wanted to be sure."

"I've never felt as alive or been as happy as when I've been in your arms. It's the only time everything seems right with me. The rest of the time, something is always out of alignment."

"You're too beautiful to feel like that."

"Beauty has nothing to do with it, and I wish you'd stop saying that all the time. It makes me wonder if you can see anything but my face or my body."

"There's a great deal more to you than that, and every one of us here at the ranch is aware of it. I can't tell you what a difference you've made since you've been here."

"I'm glad. I like the men."

"They like you." He kissed her. "More than I would like. One of these days I may have to have a talk with Loomis."

"Don't you dare. He's a sweet man."

"Am I a sweet man?"

"That's not a word I'd use to describe you."

"What words would you use?"

"I'll have to think about that. A kiss might inspire me to think faster."

The longer Jared's kiss lasted, the less Laurie wanted to think about anything but kissing him back. After being afraid of a man's touch, it was hard to believe she couldn't get enough. It was like there was a deep hole inside her that needed filling.

"Have you thought of the words yet?"

"I don't want to think. I just want you to kiss me until I can't think at all."

Jared took her at her word. By the time he came up for breath, she wasn't sure she could breathe. It wasn't just that his lips touched hers or that his warmth flooded her body. It felt like he had staked a claim to her, that he wanted her to know she belonged to him. It wasn't that he would hold her by force. She would belong to him because she didn't want to be anywhere else.

A thrill raced through her when his hands covered her breasts. His heat penetrated her clothing as though it wasn't there. She trembled all over when his kisses traveled across her jaw and down the side of her neck. She couldn't wait for him to undo the buttons down the front of her dress, so she undid them herself. A quick tug at the tie holding her shift closed exposed her breasts to his hungry gaze. His hot hands on her heated flesh ratcheted up the tension until she felt ready to snap.

"I love your breasts," he murmured. "They're perfect."

He covered one breast with kisses before moving to the other. Laurie was unable to lie still. Her body writhed in an orgy of deliciously sensual sensations. She pressed herself against Jared, loving his strength, his heat, his need for her. It was all so new, yet it felt so right. How could Noah have thought anything about this was indecent? It was the most wonderful experience of her life, a revelation of what the relationship between a man and a woman should be. Noah had let his prejudices deny him the chance to discover a part of himself that should have been as natural as breathing. For the first time, she could find it in her heart to feel sorry for him.

Or she would have if she'd had the ability to give him more than a passing thought. Jared's attentions to her breasts had become more assertive. Unwilling to confine his attention to kisses, he had begun to lave her nipples with his tongue. She wanted to tear his clothes from his body, to cover it with her hands and her kisses, to wrap herself around him and never let go. There were needs she couldn't gratify, feelings she didn't understand, wants that remained tantalizingly beyond the edge of conscious thought. Yet despite the confusion and lack of answers, she'd never felt more alive, more eager to discover what life had so far withheld from her.

With Jared, all of that seemed possible.

"I thought I knew what making love to a woman was all about," Jared whispered, "but I didn't understand anything at all until I met you. I was just going through the motions, waiting for someone to make me understand what they meant."

"I've been locked away somewhere, unable to move forward or backward, unable even to breathe, waiting for you to come along and tear open the prison door. I feel liberated. You've given me my life back. I'll be eternally grateful for that."

Jared paused. "You make me sound better than I am."

"Not to me."

The kisses they shared were sweeter than ever, more tender than before. Need was still there, but so was compassion, a sharing of what they had come to mean to each other. Laurie wished she could remain right where she was forever. No more doubt or the need for constant proof of her value as a person in her own right. She didn't have to be someone's wife or daughter. Jared had helped her feel she finally was a whole person.

Laurie flinched when Jared took her nipple into his mouth. It was a strange sensation, one that was slightly uncomfortable as well as very sensual—a feeling that made her want more and less at the same time. A wave of desire swept over her only to crash and evaporate at an unwelcome sound.

"Miss Laurie, where are you?"

Twelve

JARED FROZE. WHAT WAS STEVE DOING HOME SO early? Pulling away from Laurie, he scrambled to his feet and straightened his clothes. "Stay here," he whispered to her. "I'll think of some reason why you had to lie down."

She looked horror-stricken. He could choke Steve for making Laurie feel this way.

"You're…" She gestured to his crotch.

It was obvious he was highly stimulated, but shock would take care of that in seconds. "Stay here as long as you need."

"What are you going to tell him? He's bound to see you come out of this bedroom."

"I'll think of something."

Hoping he now looked presentable, Jared left the bedroom barely in time to keep Steve from going in.

"What were you doing in there?" Steve asked. "Where is Miss Laurie?"

Jared closed the door before Steve could look inside. "Let's go to the kitchen."

"Why?"

"Laurie isn't feeling well so I told her to lie down."

"Is she sick? I can go for the doctor."

"There's no need for that. I think it's her time of the month."

"Her what?"

"You know. It has to do with women being able to have babies."

"Oh. I see."

Jared wasn't sure he did. That part of Steve's education might have gotten overlooked in the upheavals of the past few years. "I was just checking on her. She says she's feeling better and will be up before long."

"I don't think she ought to get up," Steve said. "I think she ought to stay here until she gets well."

"Let's hope she feels better soon, or we'll have Norman out here to make sure nothing happens to her."

"I'd rather have Colby."

"So would I. What brought you back to the house so early?"

"Odell wanted me to tell you he saw some puma tracks. He thinks we ought to set up a night camp to see if we can catch it."

"Did he find any kills?"

"One."

"Cougars come back to their kills, so we'll set up a camp somewhere we can watch for it. Otherwise we'd probably never see it again."

"Can I stay out with Odell?"

"I think Nick had better do it. He's used to hunting in the Louisiana swamps at night. I think he can see in the dark."

Cheated of his chance for adventure, Steve's

attention turned back to Laurie. "Are you sure she's all right? Maybe you'd better check on her."

"I was in there just a few minutes ago."

"She could have gotten worse."

"She said she was better, and that she'd be up soon to start supper."

"I think we ought to cook and take her supper to her."

Jared laughed and felt more relaxed. "I doubt she could eat anything we fixed. If she tried, it would probably make her feel worse."

"Don't we have some leftovers?"

Laurie entered the kitchen in time to hear Steve's question. "We have plenty of leftovers, but not enough to feed this crew."

Steve rushed over to Laurie. "Are you sure you should be up?" He moved closer until they were nose to nose. "You look a little pale."

"I told him it was your time, you know."

Fortunately Laurie was able to guess what he meant. Then she did go pale, but Jared was sure it was from embarrassment.

"I knew it," Steve declared. "You're about to faint."

Laurie pushed him away. "I'm not about to faint, but if you don't give me room to breathe, I might."

Steve jumped back. Jared felt guilty for putting the boy through this. It was his fault. If he had kept his lust under control, Steve wouldn't be worried and Laurie wouldn't be embarrassed. He decided right then that he was going to control himself. What would have happened if Steve had come looking for them without calling out first? He didn't even want to think about it.

Steve looked confused about what to do next, but that changed quickly. "Odell found puma tracks. I wanted to stay out to see if it turned up tonight, but Jared said Nick ought to stay on account of him hunting in swamps at night."

"I can imagine few things worse than hunting in swamps, day or night, or waiting around for a cougar to decide whether it wanted to eat me or a cow with very long horns and sharp hooves. Since I don't have either, it would probably choose me."

Steve laughed so hard both Laurie and Jared smiled. With that, the tension melted away.

But Jared's desire remained unsatisfied.

Later, Jared tossed his pen aside with a curse and pushed back from his desk. He didn't like what he saw, but the figures didn't lie. If Laurie got half the income of the ranch, it would leave too little for the rest of them to divide. He wouldn't have enough to ultimately buy out her half, the men wouldn't have enough to go out on their own, and Steve would end up with less than he had before they left Texas. If Jared could avoid the mistakes the previous owner had made, would he be better off sticking with longhorns? Even if he didn't make much money, all the income would be theirs. But would that income be more than he'd make with Laurie owning half the ranch? That was a question he couldn't answer.

The better solution would be for Norman to give him the loan. With the full income from the ranch,

Jared could pay off the loan and have more left for himself, Steve, and the men. He hated to think of letting Laurie down, but the future of six men was at stake. He couldn't let sentiment, or lust, cloud his judgment. Besides, it wasn't like he was taking anything from Laurie. She would still have her money to invest in a different way. There was no other solution. He had to go to Cactus Corner and see if he could talk Norman into granting the loan.

Jared had argued with himself the whole way into town, but he kept coming up with the same unsatisfactory answer. His thoughts were derailed when he reached the main street and saw Martha Simpson struggling to hold on to her hat in the wind without dropping her packages. Amused, he quickly dismounted and tied his horse to the rail.

"Let me help you."

Martha Simpson's smile was dazzling. "Thank you so much. I was hoping some gentleman would come along and offer to help. I would pick the time when everyone is having lunch to do my shopping."

Jared took both packages. "That's a pretty hat. It would be a shame to lose it."

Martha readjusted her hat and tied it securely under her chin. "Especially since I just bought it. My father said it was far too expensive, that it was a sign of vanity." She sighed. "I fear I must plead guilty. But a girl needs to look her best if she wants to attract the attention of the right man, doesn't she?"

Maybe others did, but Laurie didn't need fancy hats or dazzling smiles to start his heart racing. "Yes, I agree."

Her hat securely on her head, Martha retrieved her packages. "I'd better hurry home. I'm sure at least half a dozen people are watching us this very minute. To see an unmarried young woman blushing as she walks with a man—especially one who has just offered to carry her packages—will start half the town gossiping. By suppertime everyone will believe we're walking out. By breakfast tomorrow we'll be engaged."

Jared was surprised she appeared so ill at ease with that eventuality. "I'm sure you wouldn't make such an important decision that quickly."

She sighed. "I wouldn't get the chance. My father expects a long and very public courtship followed by a long and very public engagement culminating in a simple yet very public wedding."

She looked so crestfallen he couldn't help but smile. "I take it you object."

"I think falling in love is a private affair between the two people who are in love. It shouldn't need to be displayed to the whole community for their approval. Nor do I believe it has to be drawn out for more than a year. Do you agree with me?"

The sudden shift surprised him. "Most emphatically. I think two people can fall in love almost instantly, but getting married is never simple. There are questions to be answered, conflicts to be resolved that would become awkward if they had to be worked out in the public eye. Everybody would have their own opinion, but the only important opinions are those of the two people in love." He didn't want to think of what public opinion would say about his relationship with Laurie.

"I'm so happy you agree with me I could kiss you."

Her unexpected response caused Jared to chuckle. "That really would start the gossips going."

"I wouldn't care."

Jared had thought Martha was very pretty the first time he met her and hadn't hesitated to say so, but if she was *really* flirting, this was moving too fast even for him. Unexpectedly she stopped in front of her father's newspaper office.

"Thanks so much for helping me." She accompanied that with a brilliant smile. "One package is for my mother and the other for my father. They're both in the office today. The weekly newspaper is due out tomorrow."

"Is there anything newsworthy?"

She tilted her head to the right. "Do you think there should be?"

Jared was undergoing the unaccustomed experience of having a woman move so fast he couldn't keep up. It left him feeling unmanned. "As long as it's good news."

"Isn't love always good news?"

"Not always, especially in the eyes of others."

"Then I must be careful to keep it out of sight. Thanks again."

She went inside, leaving Jared feeling shell-shocked. He was used to women showing an open interest in him, but never had one appeared to pursue him so openly. He was even more surprised to find he wasn't comfortable with it.

∽

"I haven't made up my mind about the loan yet," Norman told Jared. "There are some things happening that make me uneasy about lending such a large amount of money at this time."

"What things?" Jared didn't think Norman was referring to a competing bank because Laurie had said that wasn't likely to happen.

"I'm not free to discuss them just now, but things could change at any moment."

Jared got the feeling Norman really was genuinely worried, but he didn't trust the man. "I can't wait much longer for you to make up your mind. The herd will be coming through the territory sometime in the next few weeks. If I don't have the money, I'll lose my chance to buy it."

"I still don't see why you insist on Herefords."

Jared struggled to rein in his anger and frustration. "I've already explained that."

"Tell me again."

Jared signed in exasperation. "The previous owner of the ranch said longhorns didn't carry the kind of weight he needed to make a profit with the limited grass in the valley. This ranch is a partnership that includes my nephew and the four men who work for me. We'll put every dollar we have left into the herd. Herefords are the only breed that can make a substantial profit here."

"How do you know? No one else has brought them into Arizona."

"They've been used with success in other dry areas."

"Why can't you buy a few and see how they do?"

"As you said, there aren't any Herefords in Arizona. The man bringing this herd intended to take them to California without realizing the difficulties. I believe he'll sell the whole herd here for a discounted price, but he won't sell part of it knowing he has to take the rest to California anyway. It's all or nothing, and I don't have enough money to buy them all."

Norman stared at his hands, his mind seemingly on something else.

"Is this about Laurie working for me?"

That brought Norman out of his abstraction. "I've made it plain from the first that I disapproved of Laurie working for you. It endangers her reputation."

"Are you saying you won't give me the loan as long as Laurie continues to work for me?"

"If you were married, there wouldn't be any need for Laurie to work for you."

Jared's thoughts skidded to a halt. "I haven't said anything about marrying. I haven't fallen in love with anyone."

"It's not necessary to fall in love to marry," Norman said. "To my way of thinking, it would be a distraction. Emotions are very fragile things that change without warning. It's better to think of marriage as a business proposition."

"Are you saying I ought to marry a woman for her money?"

Norman seemed to be losing patience. "I'm saying you shouldn't think of marrying Laurie for her money."

Jared took a moment while he struggled to swallow his instinctive response. "I'm not thinking of marrying anyone, with or without money. I certainly can't be planning to marry Laurie for her money. She's working for me because she doesn't have any. You have it all."

"That's not true," Norman announced with unnecessary emphasis. "It's simply a misunderstanding. Women can't understand matters of finance like a man can. I've explained that I will take care of everything for her, which is what my brother's will directed me to do."

"As Laurie sees it, she doesn't have any money. You shouldn't be surprised if she marries to change that."

"Laurie will remain a widow out of respect for my brother's memory," Norman declared. "That's why it's important that she stop working for you. It's embarrassing to have a Spencer working as a cook and housekeeper."

"Again, are you saying you won't give me the loan as long as Laurie works for me?"

Norman was still evasive. "I'm saying you ought to get married. Then you wouldn't need Laurie or any other woman to work for you. Be assured I am considering your request for a loan, but I can't give you a decision just yet."

Jared found himself outside on the boardwalk wondering just what it would take to convince Norman to give him the loan. It was clear he *wasn't* going to grant the loan as long as Laurie was working for Jared, but it wasn't clear that he *would* grant the loan if Jared asked her to leave. That put him in a difficult position.

If he used Laurie's money, which he was certain he would get, he wouldn't have the money to give Steve and the men the kind of stake for the future they deserved. He certainly wouldn't be in a position to marry. If he decided not to use Laurie's money, he had no assurance that Norman would grant the loan. He wouldn't put it past Norman to be using the loan as bait to get Jared to fire Laurie, then refuse to give Jared the money.

He could justify that if he was certain of the loan. It would be a difficult decision, but it would be a business decision. Laurie wouldn't like it. *He* wouldn't like it. Steve and the men would hate it, but everybody would understand.

He hoped.

Colby came out of the mercantile and was coming in his direction. Jared had a sudden thought. He walked to meet Colby.

"I can see from the look in your eyes that you're going to try again to convince me that we're brothers."

"I wish I could, but I know you're set against it."

"I'm not set against it. I just don't see any point in thinking about something that neither one of us can prove."

"What if we could?"

"If you had incontrovertible proof, I'd be happy to welcome you as one of my brothers. I've always wanted to know what happened to them, but that kind of proof doesn't exist."

"How do you know?" Jared tried again. "What did your parents tell you?"

"They wanted me to think of them as my only parents so it was best I forget about my real family."

"Do you still know where your adoptive parents live?"

"Yes."

"Would you write them and ask if they have anything, or know anything, that could be used to prove we're brothers?"

"This means a lot to you, doesn't it?"

"I thought it meant a lot to you."

"It did until I married Naomi and got a family of my own." Colby was silent for a moment. "It would be hard at this point in my life to learn to feel like a brother to you or anyone else. We have none of the years together, none of the shared experiences to build on. It would be like trying to become best friends when we might not have been friends at all."

"I've thought about this a lot. I understand the difficulties, but it's something I can't forget. Despite having Steve, I feel like I'm missing my family. I know this is an imposition, but would you write your family and ask?"

Colby hesitated so long Jared thought he was going to refuse.

"Okay, I'll do it, but I doubt they'll answer. I've had no communication with them since I ran away fifteen years ago. As far as I know, they never tried to find me."

"Thank you. If you don't get a reply, I promise I won't bother you with this again."

Colby's mouth twisted. "I don't believe a word of that. You'll discover we have the same ears or our big toes turn in the same direction, and you'll take that as incontrovertible proof."

Jared laughed. "No, but I might think your sense of humor is. My father always said I wasn't serious enough."

"That's not what I hear. Now I hate to be rude, but I've got eight oxen waiting impatiently to exhaust themselves hauling timber down from the rim."

As he watched Colby walk away, an idea came to

Jared. Colby was much too capable to spend the rest of his life hauling goods up and down the valley. The territory needed a marshal, and Jared still had some good contacts in the army. He would write and ask if they would give that job to Colby. With his knowledge of the territory and his relationship with the people in the area, he would be a perfect choice. Colby may not accept that they were brothers, but Jared was sure they were. What man wouldn't do something like this for his little brother?

Jared couldn't seem to get away from the questions that bedeviled him: Should he fire Laurie and hope Norman would give him the loan? Should he reject Laurie's offer for a partnership and try to make it with longhorns? Or should he keep Laurie's money and accept that he'd never have the kind of financial success he'd hoped? He had no one to blame but himself for getting into this situation. If he hadn't been so stunned by Laurie and the thought of having her around all the time, he would have stopped long enough to sit down and run the numbers.

The men had tried to tell him, but he'd been so excited about getting the herd—and spilling over with lust for Laurie—that he'd ignored their warnings. Now he'd put them and himself in a difficult position. Knowing what he knew, it wasn't going to be easy to face Laurie and the men over the supper table, but he was so late he wouldn't have time to come up with a strategy. He hoped he would be able to make them believe all was well.

Everyone was at the table when he entered the kitchen.

"Where have you been?" Steve asked. "I tried to get Miss Laurie to hold supper for you, but she said you knew what time she had to leave."

Without a word, Laurie got up and moved to fix a plate for Jared. He was relieved she didn't seem upset with him.

"She was right not to wait," he told Steve. "I got to talking with Colby and lost track of time."

"Did you convince him that he might be your brother?"

"No, but he did agree to write his parents to ask if they have anything that might help us decide one way or the other."

"I don't see why you care," Loomis said. "You don't know him. You might not even like him once you do."

"I've got four brothers," Nick offered. "You won't like them, but you can have any one of them you want."

Jared accepted the plate Laurie handed him and took his place at the table.

"What do you think Colby's parents might be able to tell him?" Laurie asked when she was seated again.

"I don't know, but anything would be more than we have now."

"I'm surprised Colby agreed to write that letter. He hasn't had contact with his parents since he ran away."

"What did you do to this ham?" Uninterested in whether or not Colby could be Jared's brother, Odell was savoring the ham like it was manna from heaven. "I've never tasted anything like it."

"Is something wrong with it?" Laurie asked.

"It's wonderful."

"Don't bother to ask how she cooked it," Nick said. "You won't be able to make it taste the same."

"I could try."

"Not while Laurie is within a hundred miles of this place," Loomis said. "She not only cooks a lot better than you, she looks a lot better, too."

"Hell, I look better than Odell," Nick said.

"Not so you would notice," Clay told him.

This led to a general discussion of which man was the best looking. Steve said they ought to disqualify Jared because nobody could beat him. Nick and Clay objected to that and appealed to Laurie to decide the issue. She declined because she said she would have to rule in favor of her boss, or he might fire her.

"We wouldn't let him do anything that crazy," Loomis insisted.

"He wouldn't anyway," Steve said. "He likes her."

"Not as much as I do," Nick declared. "In Sicily, she would be declared as beautiful as a Greek goddess."

"How would you know?" Jared demanded irritably. "I doubt you've ever been to Sicily."

"I was conceived in Sicily," Nick said. "It is in my blood."

Jared didn't share in the laughter that greeted Nick's assertion.

"I think you're all very handsome," Laurie stated.

"Not Odell," Steve insisted. "Even his horse doesn't like him."

More laughter only succeeded in exacerbating Jared's

temper. It was bad enough that they stared at Laurie like bug-eyed youths with their tongues hanging out. They didn't have to be so silly about it. And why was Laurie laughing and smiling at them? Didn't she know that only encouraged their foolishness? They were grown men who ought to know better. They didn't see him hanging on Laurie's every word and gesture like a lovesick puppy.

"I bet you're the most beautiful woman in the Arizona Territory," Steve said.

"That goes without saying," Loomis said. "You can include all the land west of the Mississippi."

"Why not include the whole country?" Jared wanted to know. "No need to stop there. Make it Europe, too, maybe even the whole world."

"Don't you think Miss Laurie's beautiful?" Steve asked his uncle.

"Of course I do. I'm not blind, but it's got to be embarrassing to her to have all of you gushing over her."

Loomis turned to Laurie. "Are we embarrassing you?"

She laughed lightly. "Not at all. I enjoy seeing all of you laugh and have fun. It's probably a sign of poor character in me, but I even like being told I'm attractive."

"None of us would ever be guilty of using such a poor word as 'attractive' when talking about you," Loomis said.

Jared wanted to smash his fist into Loomis's face and wipe away that besotted look. It was one thing to be appreciative of a woman's beauty. It was another to understand the proper ways to express it.

"I've always said she was beautiful," Steve informed everyone. "I'll keep saying it until I find a word that says even more than that."

"'Pretty' would be quite enough," Laurie said.

"Pretty is for girls," Loomis said.

"It's obvious Laurie is no longer a girl," Nick said.

Jared was sure he would have indigestion if he listened to another word. He thought Laurie was beautiful—he'd told her so many times he now felt embarrassed remembering it—but he hadn't done it in this overly saccharine manner. Nick tried to act like he was a Sicilian noble, and Steve was only a kid, but Loomis should know better.

"The way you boys talk, Laurie might think you wanted to marry her."

"I would marry her if she would live in the bunk-house," Nick said.

"None of us has enough money to buy more than a tent," Loomis explained.

"Miss Laurie has a house," Steve reminded them. "You could live there."

"A man likes to think he can provide a house for his wife," Jared said. "Not the other way around."

"What's wrong with a wife having more money than her husband?" Laurie asked. "Why would you condemn every woman of means to spinsterhood?"

Another problem Jared hadn't thought of until now. Not only would Laurie own more of the ranch than he would, but she had inherited her husband's estate. Norman was the richest man in Cactus Corner. It was doubtful his brother had been far behind. "I don't mean that a rich woman should never marry. I just mean that a man likes to think he can provide for his wife and children."

"But they would be her children as well. Shouldn't she be allowed to contribute to their support?"

Jared could feel himself sinking deeper and deeper into the hole he'd dug for himself. "A wife contributes by taking care of them and feeding them. According to my mother, that was more than enough for any woman."

"In Sicily, there is no such thing as a wealthy woman," Nick said. "Before she marries, the money belongs to her father. After she marries, it belongs to her husband. A man never has to feel dependent on his wife."

"I wasn't talking about a man depending on his wife," Laurie said. "I was talking about sharing."

"There is no sharing in Sicily."

"I'm glad I don't live in Sicily."

"But you would be a goddess there. Men would fight duels over you."

"I'd rather be a mortal and keep my money."

"I wouldn't care if my wife was rich," Steve said. "Would you care if your husband was poor?" he asked Laurie.

"I haven't given it any thought because I'm never going to marry again."

Thirteen

THE MEN STARED AT LAURIE IN SHOCK.

"Why not?"

"Never?"

"That would be a terrible shame," Loomis said.

"I'm not sure about that," Laurie told Loomis, "but I am sure I won't marry again. My father and husband controlled me in life, and now Noah's trying to control me from the grave. I'll never put myself in that position again."

The men engaged in a lively attempt to convince Laurie to change her mind, and Jared was surprised he didn't join in immediately. He intended to marry someday so why not consider Laurie? They weren't in love with each other, but he liked her, she liked him, and he certainly wouldn't find a more beautiful woman. She was an excellent cook and housekeeper, the men liked her, and she seemed happy working at the ranch.

He knew why not. With her money and looks, she could attract the attention of rich and powerful men. Why should she settle for a husband like Jared and a life of hard work?

But if she'd wanted to do that, why hadn't she moved to Tucson or even San Francisco? With all the gold discovered in northern California, the city would be flush with wealthy men looking for beautiful brides. She could end up living in a mansion with a dozen servants and a husband wealthy enough to buy thousands of Herefords rather than the few hundred he hoped to buy.

Would he want to marry Laurie if money wasn't an issue?

He didn't know. He hadn't seriously been thinking of marriage to anyone. He'd been too involved with his career in the army, trying to find his brothers, taking care of Steve after the death of his parents, and looking for a ranch that could support the two of them while providing his friends with the money to build lives of their own. The appearance of a woman like Laurie hadn't been in his plans any more than marriage had.

How could he marry a woman with more money than he could hope to have? People would believe he married her for her money. But that wasn't the worst of it. How would he feel knowing *she* was supporting *him* rather than the other way around? Would other men respect him? Could he respect himself? Since it was her money holding up the ranch, would she believe she ought to make all the business decisions? Could he endure that? Would the men continue to work for him? He hadn't been in the West very long, but he knew that Westerners believed a man had to be in control of his life or he wasn't a man. It hadn't been any different in Texas.

It looked like this was one thing he wouldn't have to worry about. None of the arguments the men advanced had succeeded in changing Laurie's mind.

"I think you'd make a charming husband," she said to Clay. "Odell would be steady, Nick would flirt outrageously without meaning a word of it, and Loomis would be as fine a husband as any woman could want, but I'm still not going to marry again."

"What about me and Jared?" Steve wanted to know.

Laurie tickled Steve under his chin, which caused the boy to blush vividly. "You're so sweet you'd do anything I asked."

"What about Jared?"

Laurie directed her gaze to Jared. She sat considering her answer for so long Steve grew impatient.

"Don't you like Jared?"

"You asked what kind of husband I thought he would be, not whether I liked him."

"Am I so terrible you have to ponder your answer for so long?" Jared asked.

"You're more complex," Laurie told him. "You have grand ambitions and are certain you know how to accomplish them, but you have to be the creator of your own destiny. At the end of the day, you want to be able to stand back and say *I* accomplished that, not *we*. You've seen what life has done to other people, and you're determined not to let it happen to you and Steve." Her gaze narrowed. "You don't intend to let anyone stand in your way."

Jared was shocked that Laurie understood him so well when he hardly knew anything about her.

Loomis looked from Laurie to Jared and back to Laurie. "A shrewd analysis. You're a dangerous woman."

Laurie shrugged. "I only see what everyone else sees."

"Yes, but you're able to see beyond that. Be careful. Some people won't forgive you for seeing what they can't see and wouldn't admit if they could."

"I'm a woman. Nobody ever asks what I think." Laurie stood. "It's time for me to go home," she said to Steve. "I'll put away the food while you bring the buggy."

Conversation lagged before turning to the work needing to be done tomorrow, but Jared couldn't forget what Laurie had said. Did he want to be the sole architect of his success? If so, did that mean he wanted a wife who would depend on him in every way, or did he want a wife who was a partner and companion, someone he would see as an equal?

Much to his shock, he didn't know. Without really thinking about it, he'd assumed his wife would be much like his mother, his sister-in-law, all the women he'd known growing up. He'd never had any reason to question that, probably because he'd never bothered to think about it. Laurie might not be interested in marrying, but the question of whether he would marry a woman like Laurie had made it clear he had to reevaluate his thinking. Or start *really* thinking for the first time.

And he'd better start doing it soon. If he had to be married, or at least in the process of getting married, to get the loan from Norman, he had to decide what kind of wife he wanted and start looking for candidates. He was reasonably good-looking and part owner of a ranch, but there were other men who were equally attractive as potential husbands. No woman was going to marry him just because he asked.

He hadn't worked everything out in his mind, but he knew he wanted more than a wife who would agree with everything he said, who had no opinions of her own, and who didn't *want* any. He wanted his wife to be young, innocent, and attractive. But even that wasn't enough. He'd never been in love so he didn't know how that would fit into the equation—his parents hadn't been in love with each other and his brother had married his best friend—but he wanted the kind of closeness he felt with Laurie, the give and take, the sharing.

There was something very natural about the relationship between them. It was easy, comfortable, and enjoyable. He also wanted a woman of firm character. He was haunted by the specter of his mother who had dwindled into little more than a kept woman after his father died, sleeping with any man who would take care of her. He also needed someone who wouldn't balk at hard work or the roughness of ranch life yet was intelligent enough to be a companion rather than a drudge. He wanted someone like himself.

How was he supposed to find such a woman in the short time left before he had to decide whether to accept Laurie's money, gamble on Norman granting the loan, or go it alone?

❧

Laurie felt guilty for not having finished the cleaning, but not enough to leave Jared's embrace. He would have to go back to work soon, so she wanted to take advantage of every possible minute. This was the second time they'd made love—she didn't count the time they were interrupted by Steve's return—but it was unlike the first because this time she'd been able to approach it, knowing what to expect and how to enjoy it to the fullest.

As much as she loved it when Jared made love to her, she enjoyed being cuddled even more. It gave her the feeling of closeness, belonging, being valued, that she'd missed most of her life. She burrowed into Jared's embrace, getting as close to him as physically possible. The thought of Norman's reaction if he could see her now surprised a chuckle out of her.

"What's so funny?" Jared asked.

"Nothing. Just a silly thought."

"Not about me, I hope."

She kissed him on the end of his nose. "Certainly not about you. I have only wonderful thoughts where you're concerned."

Jared pulled her closer. "I have impossible thoughts about you. How it's impossible to stop thinking about you even for a few moments. How it's impossible to stop wanting to make love to you. How it's impossible to imagine holding a more beautiful woman in my arms."

"You've got to stop telling me I'm beautiful."

"Why?"

"I'll start to believe it. It's nearly impossible to admire a woman who's impressed with her own looks. Only Cassie has managed it."

"Cassie is pretty. You're beautiful. It's not the same."

"Nevertheless, I'd rather you tell me about the

ranch. When are you going to show me around? Since I'll own half of it, I ought to know how to run it as well as you."

Laurie felt Jared stiffen, but she'd expected that. She didn't know anyone except Colby who was willing to accept a woman as an equal partner, and he'd fought against it in the beginning. She expected Jared would be even more reluctant, but she wasn't going to back down. Making love to him was pleasure. Being partners in the ranch was business, and she didn't intend to confuse the two.

"It would take several days just to give you an idea of what we do. Like I told Norman, you would have to spend the whole day in the saddle."

"I don't have to see everything at once. Besides, I can't cook supper if I'm gone all day. I can take a couple of hours one day and you can show me one of the things you do. Then I'll take a couple of hours another day and you can show me something else."

"You don't know how to ride. There are lots of places you can't take the buggy."

"Then I'll learn to ride. Colby bought Naomi a sidesaddle. I'm sure she'll let me borrow it."

Apparently Jared had lost all desire to cuddle. He pulled away and sat up. "We're not doing much right now beyond taking a count and making sure all the herd survived the blizzard and the flood. That's not a situation that's likely to occur again anytime soon."

Laurie wasn't ready to give up. "I don't want to see everything you do right away, but I have no idea what it's like to spend the day on a horse or where to look for cows and what to do when I find them. I've spent my life inside a house or inside a store. I think it would be wonderful to spend time in the fresh air, under a clear sky with the cool breeze on my face and the scent of flowers in the air."

"It's not nearly that romantic." Jared sounded grumpy.

"Neither is cleaning house and cooking meals, but you seem to think it's important."

"I don't have a horse that would be safe for you to ride."

"I can borrow Naomi's when I borrow the saddle."

Jared got out of the bed and reached for his clothes. "Won't she need it?"

"I doubt she'll be riding until after the baby's born."

Jared stepped into his pants and reached for his shirt. "It will be a little awkward to explain to the men."

"I'll have a half ownership in the ranch. Surely they expect me to want to know what's going on."

Jared sat to put on his socks and pull on his boots. "That's what makes it awkward. I don't have the money yet so technically you *aren't* a partner yet."

Laurie was beginning to feel irritated. "If they can put up with Norman riding all over the ranch, being rude and asking stupid questions, they can put up with me watching them while they work. I won't get in their way."

Finished dressing, Jared stood. "I think it would be best to start with a ride over the ranch to familiarize you with the herd and the limits of our range. Not all of the range is by the river. The cattle forage in the canyons and sometimes on the top of the rim."

"I would love to see the valley from the rim. Colby says it's a beautiful sight."

"He's right. The pine forest is wonderfully cool in the summer. It would be a great place for a summer picnic."

"I would like that."

Jared bent over to kiss her. "I'd better be going. I don't want the men wondering why I'm so late joining them. We'll talk about this later. But before we go anywhere, I have to make sure you will be safe on that horse and using a sidesaddle. Some of the trails are treacherous."

"Naomi stayed on a runaway horse using a side-saddle the first time she was on a horse. I feel sure I can stay in the saddle at a walk regardless of how treacherous the trail."

Jared's smile was strained. "I'm sure you can. Now I'd better go." He kissed her again, then left the room.

Laurie didn't move right away. There was a lot going on that she had to think about, and she didn't want to be distracted by work. The cleaning could wait until tomorrow, and she would have plenty of time to fix supper later.

She had expected Jared to resist showing her the ranch and teaching her how it was run. Every man she'd ever met assumed women were good only for having children, doing housework, or selling in the shops. The *real* work required a man. She was willing to admit she couldn't fell a hundred-foot tree, drag it out of the forest to a sawmill, or lift a twenty-foot beam. She had no desire to shoe a horse or break a wild mustang to saddle, but she didn't consider either impossible.

She absolutely could understand profit and loss

statements, plan a budget, and make orders. Noah had thought he'd done all the financial work for the mercantile, but she'd prepared the figures he used to reach the final decisions. She had done the same for payrolls, so she had no doubt she could understand the operation of the ranch as well as any man. However, she doubted she'd ever get a man to agree to that.

Yet that wasn't what disturbed her the most. She understood why Jared wanted to protect his sphere of importance. What worried her more was the effect Norman's offer to reconsider giving Jared a loan was having on him. She didn't have access to Jared's figures, but it was obvious that her fifty percent of the ranch would dramatically reduce his income, an income that had to be shared with Steve and the other men. That had to weigh heavily on him. It would for any man.

She was certain Norman was using the offer of the loan as a means to persuade Jared to send her away from the ranch. It wouldn't surprise her if Norman refused to give Jared the loan even if he did fire her. She hated the pressure it put on Jared to try to hide what was going through his mind. She couldn't blame him for the choices he was considering any more than she could the decision he would make. It was a business decision, but that didn't mean she had to like it.

Nor did she like the very real possibility that she could soon have no job and no way to invest her money without moving away from Cactus Corner. She couldn't depend on the possibility of a new bank causing Norman to change his mind. The man thought he was infallible. If Jared got his loan, she would be right back where she'd started—in Norman's heartless clutches and unable to do anything about it.

There was also a third problem. She was afraid she was becoming too fond of Jared. There was so much to like about the man it would have been unusual if she *hadn't* grown to like him. Setting aside the fact that he was breathtakingly handsome and a spectacular lover, he was kind, considerate, responsible, and ambitious, and he thought she was beautiful.

Okay, he didn't want to give up his monopoly on running the ranch, but she couldn't hold that against him. He'd unbent far enough to take her as a full partner though she was sure it went against the grain. He'd peeled potatoes, helped with some of the heavy cleaning, and comforted her when she was upset. But he didn't love her, and she was never going to marry again. The prudent thing to do was halt this attachment before it could turn into something troublesome. She had to face the possibility that he wouldn't need her if he got the loan. And if her instinct was right, firing her would be a condition of Norman giving him the loan.

Laurie sat up and reached for her clothes.

Saying she ought to put a stop to her infatuation and doing it were two very different things. She really did like Jared. They were comfortable together. He gave her support and confidence. He valued her contributions. And he was jealous of the attention the other men paid her.

That was a guilty pleasure. During her marriage, she'd gone out of her way to avoid attracting attention. She would have been petrified to have caused anyone to be publicly jealous of Noah. That would have made her life even more miserable.

She pulled her chemise over her head and reached for her dress. Fortunately she'd chosen a dress that fastened down the front. She was dressed in less than a minute. A couple of minutes to repair the damage to her hair, and she was ready to leave the bedroom. As she passed through the doorway, she turned and looked back. That small, plain room had been the arena for her physical and emotional awakening. Whatever happened, it would always have a place in her heart.

Laurie was excited. Jared was going to show her part of the ranch, and she would be riding rather than driving her buggy.

Naomi had been in favor of Laurie's desire to learn how to manage a ranch, but she had insisted that Laurie let Colby teach her to ride before Naomi would lend her horse or her sidesaddle. So for the last week, Laurie had spent her evenings with Colby teaching her how to stay in the saddle while Steve made fun of such an awkward way to ride horse. On Sunday they'd gone for a long ride after church. Naomi had borrowed Sibyl's horse, and Peter and Esther had ridden their ponies. They never went beyond a fast trot, but Colby had pronounced Laurie ready to handle the rougher terrain of the ranch.

Jared eyed the sidesaddle with disfavor. "Are you sure you can stay on a horse with this thing?"

"You know I can. You're just looking for an excuse to send me back to the kitchen."

Jared grinned at her. "I was thinking that you'd be safer riding double with me."

Laurie laughed. "I will not be seen riding in a man's lap. The thought of the gossip that would start makes me quake."

Jared sobered. "I don't think much of anything makes you quake."

Laurie wasn't sure how he meant that. "I'm learning to have a little courage. Now help me into the saddle. I want to see as much as I can before I have to come back and fix supper."

Once in the saddle, Laurie hooked her leg about the pommel and gathered the reins.

"You look like you've done this before."

"Naomi made Colby teach me before she would lend me her horse." She hadn't told Jared what she'd been doing because she wanted to surprise him.

Jared swung into the saddle. "We won't be riding on flat roads or alongside the river. Let me know if you start feeling uncomfortable."

Not unless she fell out of the saddle first. Riding gave her a sense of freedom, a feeling of control she'd never experienced. Maybe it was the speed. Maybe it was seeing the world from much higher up. Maybe it was no more than controlling an animal bigger and more powerful that herself. After feeling confined for so many years, she felt she could go anywhere she wanted, do anything she wished. She knew it wasn't true, but she loved the feeling.

"Where are we going?" she asked as they rode down the trail toward the river.

"Nowhere in particular. I thought we'd ride along the river and see if we could find anything interesting."

Laurie gazed up at the Mogollon Rim that rose

two thousand feet in the distance. "Are we going up there?"

"No. When it rained down here the other day, it snowed up there."

She could see snow on the pine trees. It formed a vivid contrast to the mild temperature on the valley floor.

"Okay, teach me how to run a cattle ranch."

The next hour was as boring as it was exciting. She didn't find talking about soil quality or the amount of rainfall interesting, but it gave her a new way of seeing the world around her. The Verde was no longer just a river. It was the foundation of life in this part of the territory. Grass was no longer a weed, and trees were important for more than lumber. A boulder-choked canyon became an oasis in the desert. Most important of all, a cow became interesting for more than its ability to provide meat.

An unexpected result was that the discussion gave her a new way to see Jared. The more he talked about the ranch and his plans for the future, the more excited he became. She could understand and value what Herefords could do for the quality of the herd, but Jared became so excited he bubbled with energy. His expression became so serious, so intense, she felt like a heathen and he the preacher trying to convert her.

"Do the other men feel the way you do about the ranch?"

His enthusiasm waned. "Steve and Odell like it okay, but the others are here only until they can earn enough money to get a start somewhere else."

"What will do you when they leave?"

"I don't know. It depends on whether Norman gives me a loan."

That was something they hadn't discussed. Now seemed like a good time, but noise in the distance gave her thoughts a different direction. Jared brought his horse to a stop. "What's going on?" she asked. "Can't we go see?"

He looked uncomfortable. "It's not something a lady should see."

"Why? What are they doing?"

"We're reducing the number of longhorn bulls. I don't want any left by the time the Hereford bulls arrive."

"How are you doing that? I don't hear any shots."

"We're castrating them."

She'd had a sheltered existence, but she knew about castration. "I want to see how it's done. I know it's what you do to make steers so they'll gain weight. It's something every rancher needs to know."

Jared hesitated.

"I'm not going to faint."

"It's not just that."

"What?"

"It's a dirty and dangerous job. The men don't watch what they say."

Laurie wanted to laugh, but she refrained. "It won't be the first time I've heard a curse. My father has never worried about his language around me or my mother."

"But the men will have to sit across the table from you afterward."

"Are you worried about me or them?"

"Both."

"I'll be fine. I expect the men will be, too. Now let's go."

When he didn't move, she started her horse in the direction of the noise. Jared caught up.

"Let me go ahead and warn them."

"I'd rather you didn't. I don't want to distract them, and I don't want them to think seeing me where they're working is anything unusual."

"It will be."

"Then it's time to change that."

She could see a cloud of dust before she could see the men. When they reached the clearing in the brush, she saw that the men had surrounded a large bull that was being held to the ground by ropes tied to the saddles of three horses. Clay held a fourth rope around its front legs. Odell was attempting to get a rope around the hind legs. Laurie brought her horse to a stop out of their line of vision. This was no time to cause a distraction.

Their language was colorful, but it was no worse than her father's when he was angry. The men were covered in dust, sweat had soaked Loomis's shirt, and Nick had lost his hat. Steve's face was flushed with excitement. Odell managed to get a rope on the bull's hind legs. He was jerked about like a rag doll until he was able to tie off the rope on a sturdy maple.

"Get the goddamned knife and make it quick," Loomis shouted at Odell. "This bastard is going to be mad as hell when we let him up."

A quick slash of the knife caused the bull to bellow in fury. Odell stepped away, tossed the bloody appendage in a bucket, and wiped his forehead with his sleeve.

"Let him up."

"Not until I'm in the saddle," Nick said. "We had bulls in Sicily. They could kill a man who was slow to mount up."

"We'd better get out of the way," Jared told Laurie. "That bull isn't going to care who he blames."

The animal sported horns that projected nearly three feet on either side of his head. Laurie didn't want to think of the damage they could do. "How will the men get away?" she asked Jared.

"They'll be on horseback before they release the last ropes. We just need to be a safe distance away. I'm not comfortable with you in that saddle."

"Would you be more comfortable if I rode astride?" He looked so shocked Laurie couldn't repress a laugh. "Don't worry. I wouldn't embarrass you like that. Now what else can we do? I have about an hour before I have to start supper."

Jared tried not to get his hopes up, but what other reason could Norman have for asking him to come to the bank than to tell him that he was giving him the loan and that they needed to discuss terms? If Norman meant to refuse, he needn't have bothered to meet at all. He certainly wouldn't have asked Jared to make the long ride to town. Jared was already trying to figure out how to tell Laurie he wouldn't need her money. That would be a lot easier than telling her she couldn't work at the ranch any longer. Norman had avoided making that a requirement for getting the loan, but Jared had no doubt that he would soon.

He would miss Laurie. Just thinking about not making love to her caused his body to ache in protest. He'd been with many women in his life, but not one of them came close to giving him the pleasure he enjoyed with Laurie. Her combination of youth, beauty, and physical lushness was almost more than his senses could bear. A man was lucky to find one of the three in most women.

To find all three provided in such generous amounts by the hand of Mother Nature was a miracle. Even now he could practically feel the softness of her skin and the warmth of her embrace. Her smile, whether from across the table or on the pillow next to him, had the power to render him unconscious of anything else. There was so much energy, so much life in her that it was impossible not to be drawn to her.

The men were completely under her spell, and all she had done was cook for them and smile while they ate. She never flirted or behaved improperly in any way, but each one of them felt she had a special fondness for him. She was a sorceress, as powerful as the ancient Circe, able to cast her spell on any man she chose. She had enraptured him more easily than the others and with even less effort. He was under her spell, ensnared in her net, her helpless slave, powerless to resist her.

Yet what if he must? Where would he find the courage and the strength of will to go against something he wanted as much as food to eat, air to breathe? He would give anything to be able to thumb his nose at Norman, but doing so would compromise the futures of the men and Steve, as well as himself.

Even if he had been willing to sacrifice his share, he couldn't do that to the others unless he had no choice. And he had choices. He just had to make the best one.

Part of his confusion stemmed from the puzzling coolness Laurie had shown him lately. It was hard to point to anything specific, but he could feel it. It hung in the air between them, invisible but undeniable. Her smile wasn't as warm and didn't always reach her eyes. She seemed to be giving more attention to the men and less to him. She didn't turn to him as quickly when he spoke to her, her answers were shorter, and she took longer to complete her work each day. Their talks in his study had dwindled to little more than an exchange of information about the day.

He couldn't figure out what he'd done to cause this change. When he asked her if she was upset, she assured him she wasn't and wanted to know why he thought she might be. He couldn't just come out and say she wasn't smiling at him as brightly or glancing at him as often. Theirs was a business relationship, not a romantic one. If he'd had any doubts or hopes that had changed, her repeated intention to remain unmarried, despite Steve's daily attempts to change her mind, would have banished them.

It wasn't that he was thinking of asking her to marry him—he hadn't seriously thought of marrying anyone until Norman mentioned it in connection with the loan—but she would have made a perfect wife for him. He hadn't said or done anything to make her think he had marriage in mind because she was adamant she would never marry again. However, things were different now. Would she change her mind if he asked? He wasn't sure. She had seemed to be so happy with him at first, but after making love several times, she seemed to lose interest in him.

But if he were to marry her, Norman wouldn't give him the loan and he'd never have the money he needed for Steve and the men.

His fruitless mental agonies came to a halt when he drew his horse to a stop in front of the bank just as Martha Simpson was emerging from it. She smiled when she noticed him.

"We don't see you in town very often," she said to him as he dismounted. "Are you afraid our weak, female hearts can't withstand the strain of having such a handsome man in our presence?"

"That's never been a problem. Actually, no one seems to have noticed my absence."

"Well, I have. As I said before, there can never be too many attractive single men in town."

Jared pretended to be scandalized. "I am *shocked* to hear such a statement from you, but you said you were a bit forward."

Martha threw him a provocative glance. "How unkind of you to remember my faults rather than my virtues. I do have some, you know."

Jared relaxed his frown and laughed. "I'm sure you have many. Maybe we could have dinner sometime and discuss them." He didn't know where that came from. He hadn't thought of Martha in a romantic way. But after Norman's demand, he had to start thinking of somebody that way. From her apparent interest in him, Martha appeared to be a good choice.

"Is that how you court a girl out West—invite her to dinner to discuss her virtues?"

"I don't know. I haven't been here much longer than you."

"No one else has shown much interest in my virtues." She appeared to be disappointed.

"I'm sure it's just an oversight." He looked up at the front of the bank and thought of his meeting with Norman. All desire to flirt evaporated. "I have to go in there, but I'd rather have dinner with you."

She leaned in to whisper, "I understand Mr. Spencer can be a difficult man."

"I've heard the same thing."

"At least he's not afraid to speak his mind." She scowled. "I'd better be going before my father begins to wonder what mischief I'm up to."

"Do you get into mischief often?"

"Not often enough. Bye."

Her salutation contained so much challenge it put a smile on Jared's lips. If he had to marry to get his loan, maybe he should think seriously about Martha. She was the first woman other than Laurie to make him smile. The smile disappeared soon enough when he entered the bank. Not even Cassie's cheerful welcome succeeded in restoring it. By the time he entered Norman's office, he'd forgotten it altogether.

"I noticed you talking to Miss Simpson before you came in," Norman said the moment Jared was seated.

"I arrived as she was coming out of the bank."

"She's a lovely young woman. Have you asked her to marry you yet?"

Fourteen

It was all Jared could do not to gape at Norman. The man must have lost his mind. "I've only met her a few times in the street."

"Have you met her parents? They're a solid, dependable pair, even if her father is a preacher."

"I've met very few people in town. I've been too busy at the ranch."

Norman leaned forward, a scowl on his face. "I heard you were dragging Laurie all over dangerous parts of your ranch on horseback. That was bad enough to expose an inexperienced rider to such danger, but what possessed you to let her stay where they were castrating a bull? That's nothing a woman like my sister-in-law should know anything about, much less be forced to witness."

How did Norman manage to know everything that happened at the ranch? Did he have spies? "Laurie wanted to see the ranch. She'd been asking me for days. I warned her about the castration, but she insisted on staying."

"You should have forced her to leave."

"Laurie has been *forced* too often in her life. She's a grown woman capable of making up her own mind."

"No woman is capable of making up her mind. That's why she has a husband."

Jared could see no future in trying to change Norman's mind about Laurie or anything else. "I'm not her husband so you can't expect me to tell her what to do."

"Of course you can. You're a man."

This was a dead-end conversation. "If you feel this strongly about it, I suggest you talk to Laurie."

"I have talked to her, as you well know, and she ignores me."

"If she can ignore you, her former brother-in-law and the executor of her late husband's estate, you can't expect her to listen to me. I have no hold over her."

"You can fire her. Then she'd have no reason to go near your ranch."

"We've already been over this. I need someone to cook and clean for us, and Laurie is the only woman who's been willing to take the job."

"Once you're married, you won't need anyone else to cook and clean."

"That may be, but I'm not married."

Norman leaned back in his chair, giving Jared an exasperated look. "Are you stupid, or don't you understand what I'm saying?"

"I'm not stupid, but I'm not sure."

"If you want this loan, you have to be married. Personally, I don't care whether you're married or not, but Laurie has to stop working for you. The only way I can be sure of that is if you're married."

Jared could hardly believe his ears. He'd thought getting Laurie to leave the ranch was the reason behind Norman's offer to reconsider his loan, but he hadn't expected Norman to turn it into a bald-faced command. "Do you seriously expect me to invite Miss Simpson to dinner and ask her to marry me before we've had dessert?"

"I don't care how you do it, but until I see your engagement announced in the newspaper, I won't give you the loan."

"I gather your meeting didn't go well," Cassie said when Jared emerged from Norman's office.

"Do meetings ever go well with him?"

"Not recently. Will you be meeting with him again?"

"I don't know." There didn't seem to be any reason until he could see if he could bring himself to ask Martha Simpson to become his wife.

❧

"Did you know Jared was seen having supper with Martha Simpson?"

Naomi was waiting for Laurie when she got home. She barely allowed her cousin time to take off her coat and hat, fix some coffee, and settle into a chair before coming to the reason for her visit.

"No, I didn't." Between being tired from the day's work and the afterglow of making love, Laurie wanted little more than to relax for an hour or two before going to bed. She also needed time to think. Jared had been reluctant to make love the last time. She'd practically had to seduce him. She hadn't wanted their relationship to become too serious, but she didn't want it to cease altogether. There was no reason Jared couldn't have dinner with anyone he wanted. She had no hold on him, but she was upset and a little jealous. Martha was young and beautiful. Marrying her might be the one thing to convince Norman to give Jared his loan. "Why are you telling me this?"

"Because you ought to know."

"Why?"

Naomi looked her straight in the eye. "Because you're in love with him."

Laurie set her coffee down before her trembling hand caused her to spill it. "What makes you think that?" she asked without meeting Naomi's gaze.

"By the way you talk about him. Your eyes light up. You smile like I've never seen you smile. You're animated, almost eager to talk about him."

Laurie knew her feelings for Jared had become too serious, but she had no idea anyone had guessed. "I like Jared," she confessed, "but it would be hard not to like him after being married to Noah."

"You just gave yourself away."

"How?"

"If you'd been talking about anyone else, you'd never have compared him to Noah. He's your boss, not the man you want to marry. Nor is he your lover."

Laurie prayed she didn't blush, but maybe it didn't matter. Naomi seemed able to see inside her head. Something must have given her away. Naomi's gaze suddenly intensified.

"He isn't your lover, is he?"

Determined to brazen it out, Laurie asked, "Why would you think that?"

"Because you look the way Peter does when he's in trouble. There's guilt written all over your face."

Still hoping to avoid confessing, Laurie said, "Okay, so I'm fond of Jared, but it doesn't mean anything. I'm not going to marry again."

"Does he know that?"

"Everybody at the ranch does. Steve has been trying to convince me to change my mind ever since I told them."

"Why would you tell everybody something like that?"

"We were talking during dinner. I don't remember how the subject came up, but Steve asked me, and I told him I would never marry again. Why would I? My father sold me into a marriage I didn't want, my husband became my jailer, and Norman is trying to turn me into a living monument to his brother's memory. The last thing I want to do is subject myself to another man's control."

"That won't happen if you find a man who loves you as much as Colby loves me."

"I figure there's only one Colby, and you got him."

"What if Jared is Colby's brother?"

"Being brothers wouldn't make them alike."

"What if Jared marries Martha or somebody else? Would you still have a job at the ranch? I don't know if Norman has anything to do with Jared having dinner with Martha, but I'm sure he won't give Jared his loan as long as you're working at the ranch. That would put you back where you were at the beginning, dependent upon Norman for every penny."

Laurie had already thought of that outcome. The only reason Jared had accepted her proposal for a partnership had been because he didn't have the money to buy the Herefords he wanted. Initially, he figured if the previous owner couldn't make a go of it with longhorns, he wouldn't, either. But since reaching his agreement with Laurie, he'd had time to study the former owner's records, and he had learned that the man had made some mistakes he could have corrected if his wife hadn't insisted on going back East.

Now Laurie wasn't sure he absolutely had to have Herefords to make a go of the ranch. She hadn't wasted her time over the years listening to Noah and Norman talk business. She understood finances enough to know he'd end up with more money by getting a loan from Norman than by giving her half the ranch's income.

Frustrated with Laurie's silence, Naomi asked, "Don't you care what's happening?"

"Of course I do."

"What are you going to do to stop it?"

"How can I stop it? More important, why should I try? I thought you hated my working for Jared."

"I did at first, but you've been happier than you've been in years. You smile all the time now. You and Steve laugh. You're Esther's favorite person after Colby and me. I like Jared and I believe love him. I think you ought to marry him."

Laurie gaped at Naomi, unable to believe what her cousin had said. She hadn't thought of marrying Jared. It was hard to believe Naomi had.

"Don't look at me like I've suddenly grown two heads," Naomi said. "You love Jared, and he's obviously very fond of you. If you married him, you'd have a husband to protect you, and you'd be beyond Norman's control."

Memories from the past flared into existence. "I don't want anybody to *protect* me. That was my father's excuse for marrying me to Noah and Norman's excuse for trying to control everything about me down to the food I eat. I'm not going to let anyone tell me what I must do or make me feel I have to apologize for the way I look."

"Does Jared do that?"

"No."

"Do you like him enough to marry him?"

"I haven't thought about it. But if I do marry again, it will only be because I feel I can't live without him."

"Do you think he's in love with you?"

"He can't be if he's paying court to Martha Simpson."

"Maybe he wouldn't be doing that if he thought you weren't set against marriage."

"If he were in love with me, he'd be doing everything he could to convince me to change my mind instead of wasting his time on Martha."

"He's done nothing to indicate he was in love with you?"

"Nothing."

"I thought he had. That quite changes my opinion of him."

"Why?"

"No gentleman would convince a woman to work at his ranch against the advice of all who hold her dear unless he was interested in her for a proper reason."

"He didn't convince me. I convinced him."

"That's not what you told me in the beginning."

Laurie was tired of carrying on half conversations. "There's something I have to tell you, but you must never tell anyone, not even Colby."

"You can't expect me to believe you've done anything that awful."

Laurie told her about the money. "I convinced Jared to take me on as a full partner. He only did so because Norman wouldn't give him a loan. Now that Norman has changed his mind, Jared would be worse off taking money from me."

At first Naomi was shocked, then worried. Finally she smiled. "I can't believe you had so much money all these years and no one knew about it. It's a wonderful joke on Noah. Where did you hide it?"

"In the drawer with my undergarments. I knew he would never go there."

Naomi laughed. "And Norman has no idea that you have this money or that you're planning to give it to Jared?"

"No. Investing with Jared was a perfect cover. No one would know it wasn't his money."

"They'd figure something was wrong when you started living like a queen off your ranch income and everybody knew Norman wasn't giving you enough to keep a squirrel alive. The only way to disguise it completely would be to marry Jared."

"Well, I don't love him, and we've established that he doesn't love me."

"We haven't established any such thing. I don't think you're honest about your feelings for Jared, and we don't know what he'd do if he thought you weren't opposed to marriage."

"You're forgetting that Norman won't give him the loan if I'm still working for him."

"If that's all that's bothering him, Jared could ask you to stay away long enough to get the loan, then marry you. Norman wouldn't know anything about the money if you could talk Jared into changing his accounts to Papa's bank. Your money would just disappear into Jared's account."

Laurie shook her head. This was getting too complicated. "I love you for being so worried about me, but you don't have to. Whatever Jared decides to do, I'll be just fine. I'm just never going to be under a man's control ever again. Not even love is worth that."

But as Laurie walked home, she began to wonder how far she'd wandered from the truth, which led her to wonder if she *knew* the truth. Did she really understand Jared's position, or was she merely saying that to keep from having to deal with her feelings about it? What were her feelings? Did she feel betrayed, abandoned, forgotten, used when needed and cast aside when no longer useful? Did she have the right to feel any of that when Jared had every right to put his interests and those of his men ahead of her? He hadn't promised her anything beyond a business arrangement, which was exactly what she'd insisted on. She had promised him the money, but she hadn't given it to him. Could he have started to wonder if she actually had it?

He believed in her, or he would have said something before now. The business had gotten sidelined by their physical relationship. Each was so attracted to the other that they hadn't talked about anything else. They'd been trying so hard to pretend, for the sake of her reputation, that nothing was going on that they'd failed to talk about their feelings. Or had they failed because they didn't *want* to have to deal with their feelings? What were their feelings for each other? Did she know? Did he? Did it matter since he seemed to be interested in Martha Simpson?

She reached her house and went inside. "Steve, are you here?" She wasn't surprised when she received no answer. Steve liked spending time with Ben Kessling, which was good for both boys, but she could have used some distraction from her thoughts. Making coffee and thinking about what to fix for supper wasn't enough.

What did Jared feel for her? She'd never been courted in the traditional fashion, but when they were alone he treated her the way she thought a man would treat a woman he liked very much. But would he have tried to keep his feelings secret from others if he loved her? There were lots of reasons why a boss would do that, but none why a lover would. She guessed that answered her question. As she suspected, he wasn't in love with her, which was okay. She hadn't wanted love, only proof that she was desirable. The hours in his arms had proved that. She wouldn't marry, but she no longer had to feel ashamed of herself. She would never be able to thank him enough for that.

But how did she *feel* about Jared? Not the love-making, not his saying she was beautiful and desirable. What did she feel about *him*? He loved his nephew, respected his friends, was a good boss, and worked hard to ensure their futures. That caused her to admire and respect him, but was that the limit of her feelings toward him? Could Naomi have seen what she couldn't?

The answer surprised her. That was only the beginning. Her feelings went far beyond that. She liked being with him. She only had to think of being in his arms and she went soft and hot inside. Bringing his face to mind invariably caused her to smile. She always felt protected when she was with him. Much to her surprise, she'd started to feel more at home at the ranch than in her own house. She preferred being there, might have moved there if it wouldn't have caused such an uproar. Why should she feel that way when she had her own home and prized her independence?

Because she loved him.

❦

Jared didn't know what to make of Dr. Kessling coming to the ranch. He went down the steps to greet the doctor as he tied his horse to the hitching post. "I'm glad to see you, sir, but I don't think anyone here is in need of a doctor."

Kessling extended his hand in greeting. "It seems our community believes being a doctor isn't enough to take up my time. They think I ought to become a banker."

"I was surprised when I heard that."

"Glad it has affected you the same way it did me. Let's go inside. Winters out here are crazy. It's cold one day then hot a few days later, only to go back to being cold again. It's a miracle half the town isn't sick. But they're all healthy, so I have time to learn what it means to handle other people's money."

"I'm surprised Norman hasn't tried to have you murdered."

The doctor laughed. "I'm sure he would if he thought there was any chance I would succeed."

"Why are you doing this?"

"Let's sit down with a cup of hot coffee, then I'll tell you. It's a long story. Where's Laurie?" he asked when Jared returned with the coffee.

"She's so determined to learn how to run a ranch she talked Steve into showing her around this afternoon. She thinks I'm too protective."

"I don't know how she can think that when the first thing you showed her was a bull being castrated."

Jared couldn't help being irritated. "Is there anything that happens here that everybody in Cactus Corner doesn't know?"

"Not much. We've known each other all our lives, so we're famished for anyone new to talk about."

"Sounds like where I grew up in Texas."

"I guess all small towns are the same. Or at least they were before the war." The doctor sighed. "That changed a lot for us. You, too, since you didn't go back to Texas."

"I might have if my family hadn't died. That made the quest to find my brothers all the more important."

"Naomi said Colby was resistant to the idea."

"But he agreed to write his parents. Maybe he'll find something to help."

"Don't get your hopes up. Colby says they did

everything they could to make him forget he had any other family." The doctor took a swallow of his coffee. "Now to why I'm here."

Jared set his coffee down and turned to face the doctor.

"You know Norman has refused to give Laurie access to her inheritance because of the will Noah left. He could have given Laurie a generous allowance and still honored the spirit of Noah's will, but Norman can't do anything without trying to prove he's in control. It doesn't matter that he continues to infuriate people. But you don't want to know all of that. People in town are really angry about this, angry enough to do something. And that something has been to start a new bank. And they'd decided I'm the one to do it."

"I agree with them," Jared said. "You are universally liked and trusted."

"That might not continue to be true if I manage to pull this bank business off. In any case, what I have to do first is find enough depositors to actually open a bank. I'm here to ask if you will transfer your accounts to us and if you'll use your influence to get Fort Verde to do the same."

It hadn't taken Jared long to guess the object of the doctor's visit, but he hadn't expected to be asked to talk to the people at the fort. It left him in a ticklish position.

"I'll be frank with you. I hope you succeed. Norman needs the competition and everybody else needs a banker who's at least polite to his customers, but I can't help you. I'm hoping Norman will give me a loan. Helping you would guarantee he would turn me down again."

"Suppose the new bank could give you the money you need?"

"You can't."

"You need that much?"

"Yes."

"Everybody knows you want to buy Herefords, but are you sure spending that kind of money is wise when you already have longhorns?"

Jared supposed he'd have to get used to everyone knowing his business, but he wasn't going to like it. "It's an investment in the future."

"Whose future?"

Jared could guess that people in town might suspect his relationship with Laurie had developed into something more. It was time to set the record straight. "This ranch represents everything my nephew and I could salvage from Texas as well as the little money the men working for me were able to scrounge up. It represents all our futures. Longhorns would enable us to make a bare living. That might be fine for me, but not for Steve and the others. They're not ranchers. Herefords would give them a chance for a life of their own choosing."

"I wish you success, but I hate to see you depending on Norman."

"So do I, but it's our best chance."

The doctor set his coffee down and rose. "I won't bother you any longer. But if you change your mind—or Norman changes his—come see me."

Jared laughed, but he didn't feel lighthearted. "If Norman turns me down, you can be sure I'll do everything I can to get the fort to give its business to you."

"And Laurie?"

"What about her?"

"You've got to know Norman won't give you that loan as long as she's working for you. She took a gamble with her reputation by coming here. It hasn't helped her relationship with Norman, either."

Jared decided it would save time and confusion if he convened a town meeting every time he wanted to discuss his private business. "Laurie is a wonderful woman who deserves everyone's respect and admiration. I hope Norman will treat her more generously if she stops working here."

"I understand you're courting Martha Simpson. How does Laurie feel about that?"

Jared struggled to keep command of his temper. "I'm not *courting* Martha. We only had dinner once."

"In Cactus Corner, that's courting."

Jared decided it was useless to argue that. "Norman has made it plain that I won't get the loan as long as Laurie is working for me. Laurie has made it equally plain to all of us she has no intention of marrying again."

"Have you asked her?"

Jared was finding it nearly impossible to keep a civil tongue in his head. What made this man think being a doctor gave him the right to pry into people's personal business? "I haven't asked *anybody* to marry me."

"Then it's about time you consider it. Endangering one woman's reputation won't enhance yours. Endangering *two* will get you ostracized."

Jared wanted to say he'd never done anything to

endanger either woman's reputation, but he knew that wasn't true. He could only stare mutely at the doctor.

"Martha is new to our community," the doctor told him, "but Laurie has been one of us since her birth. The mere fact that we would attempt to start a bank in competition with Norman should show you how strongly we feel about her."

"Why are you asking me these questions? Have either Laurie or Martha said anything to indicate they're upset with me?"

"You don't know Laurie very well if you think she would complain about you to anyone."

"I *do* know her, which is why I'm confused."

"Laurie had an unfortunate marriage which makes it hard for her to see clearly sometimes. We're just looking out for her."

"And you think I'm not?"

"Have you talked with her about this loan and how it will affect her?"

"I've been trying to think of a way of saying it."

"What's wrong with telling her Norman won't give you the loan unless she stops working here? She might not like it, but she can certainly understand the position you're in."

There were so many things wrong with doing that Jared didn't know where to begin, but nearly every explanation would make him look selfish and uncaring. He would admit to being selfish for the benefit of Steve and his men, but he wasn't uncaring of Laurie's feelings. That's why he hadn't talked to her yet.

Honesty compelled him to admit that wasn't the only reason. He liked Laurie and enjoyed being around her. And it wasn't simply because she was a great cook or the most satisfying sexual partner he'd ever had. She could be funny and serious, ambitious and accommodating, shy yet forceful, uncertain yet know exactly how she felt or what she wanted. For the first time in his life he had found companionship and physical satisfaction in the same woman.

"It might look like an easy thing just to say it like that, but it's not. Steve adores Laurie. I don't think he would speak to me if he thought I'd caused her to leave. You couldn't find four more different men than those who work for me, but they would lay down their lives for her. For them, breakfast and supper are the best times of the day. And not just because Laurie is a great cook. She listens to them, asks questions, and remembers what they say. They know she cares about them. This place wouldn't be the same without her."

The doctor showed no sympathy. "They're going to be without her, so you might as well bite the bullet. Putting it off isn't going to make things any easier."

"And what if I tell her she has to leave and Norman decides not to give me the loan? Do you think she'd come back?"

"Norman will do what he wants despite its effect on others, so I can't help you there. I don't know what Laurie would do, but you've got to talk to her."

"I know. I'm being selfish. You can't know what a difference she's made in our lives."

"Then tell Norman to go to hell, and ask her to marry you."

"I'm not in love with her, nor is she in love with me. Not that it matters since she says she won't marry again."

"That's what she told Naomi, too, but Naomi doesn't believe it. In any case, talk to her."

With that, the doctor took his leave.

Jared watched him mount up and ride away, but his mind wasn't on the doctor. It was where it seemed to be most of the time lately—on Laurie. Jared wondered how it was possible to be so powerfully affected by a woman he didn't love. He admired her, respected her, wanted her, and found it nearly impossible to face being without her. Just thinking about her caused his body to swell with desire. It was difficult trying to imagine being married because no other woman could measure up to Laurie. Did that mean he was condemned to be single for the rest of his life?

❦

"I wondered how long it would take Norman to come to you about the bank," Naomi said to Laurie. "I hope you told him to go to hell."

Laurie laughed at her cousin's indignation. The meeting with Norman had actually been fun. "I told him it was his own fault, that no one would have thought of opening a new bank if he had given me my money or a decent allowance."

"What did he say?"

"The same thing he always says, that he's following the provisions of Noah's will."

"What did you say to that?"

"I told him I had nothing to say to him until he decided to give me complete control of my money. He finally said he would think about it if I would agree to keep the money in his bank. I told him it wouldn't be complete control until I was free to withdraw it any time I wanted." Laurie sighed. "I'd agree to keep it anywhere he wanted as long as he would give me a signed agreement that he could no longer deny me access to it."

"You know he'll renege."

"He must be desperate. He even said he might drop his opposition to my working at the ranch, but I know that wasn't the truth. Norman is just like Noah. He'll promise anything, but once he makes up his mind about something, he'll never change it."

They were interrupted by Colby coming into the house accompanied by Peter and Esther. The children raced to Naomi.

"Papa got lots of packages," Peter announced.

Esther was equally excited. "They're in the wagon outside. You gotta come see."

Naomi hadn't missed Colby's stunned and puzzled expression. "What's this about? Who's sending you packages?"

"My mother."

Fifteen

"YOUR MOTHER!" NAOMI EXCLAIMED. "I CAN'T BELIEVE it. Show me her letter. What did she say?"

"She didn't say anything. She's dead."

Naomi pointed to the envelope in Colby's hand. "But you said—"

"There's no letter in the envelope. Both my parents are dead. The packages were sent from the sheriff's office."

"If she didn't leave you a letter, what's in the envelope?"

Colby pulled out a sheet of paper and handed it to his wife. "A statement from a banker in Albuquerque saying he's holding an account in my name with nearly thirty thousand dollars in it."

Both women gasped. Naomi stared at the paper in disbelief. "I'm surprised you didn't faint. I'm not sure I won't yet. I can hardly take a deep breath."

"Apparently my father died about a year ago. When my mother got sick, she sold everything and put the money in a bank account with my name on it."

"I thought she hated you," Naomi said.

"So did I. She certainly acted like it."

"Maybe she had a change of heart after you ran away."

"Maybe, but I wouldn't have thought it likely. I never heard either of them talk about family. Maybe they had no one else to leave it to. I guess I'll never know. Oh, I almost forgot. The sheriff is also sending a trunk she left for me."

"Maybe there'll be something in it to prove you and Jared are brothers," Laurie said.

"I don't want you to say anything that might get Jared's hopes up," Colby said to Laurie. "My parents insisted I forget I had another father and mother. They wouldn't even tell me my name."

"It's none of my business, but what are you going to do with all that money?" Laurie asked. "You could buy half the town."

"I don't know, but I'll start by depositing it in the new bank."

"But that won't help Laurie," Naomi protested. "Maybe you could promise to deposit it with Norman if he'll give Laurie her money."

"Do what you want with your money," Laurie told Colby. "You don't have to worry about me."

"But if Norman gives Jared his loan—"

"I'll be fine," Laurie insisted.

"I think Naomi's idea is a good one," Colby said. "I'm sure it would convince Norman to hand over control of your money."

"Then Papa wouldn't need to start a second bank," Naomi said.

"Please don't," Laurie begged. "Norman has tyrannized this town long enough. It's time something was done to change that. I believe a second bank is the only thing that can penetrate his smug certainty that he's better than everyone else."

"But what about you?" Colby asked.

"Naomi will tell you why I'm not in immediate danger. Now I think I'd better go home. I'm not feeling very well."

"I'll have my father check on you," Naomi offered.

"Don't bother him. If I don't feel better tomorrow, I'll go see him myself."

❧

Laurie went into Jared's office intending to tell him she wasn't feeling well and thought she should go home early. He was reading a letter and looking so pleased with himself she put aside what she'd come to say. "That must be really good news," she said. "I've never seen you look so happy."

Jared turned to her, his face wreathed in smiles. "It's the best news I've had in a long time."

Laurie pulled up a chair next to him. "Tell me about it."

"It's about Colby. I was thinking he's much too capable to spend his life hauling stuff from one end of the valley to the other. From everything I've seen and what people had said about him, he'd be a perfect marshal for the Arizona Territory."

"Wouldn't that mean he'd have to move to Prescott or maybe Tucson?"

"I don't know. Since he'd be marshal of the whole territory, maybe he could live anywhere he wanted."

"Wouldn't he have to be gone a lot?"

"Yeah. I guess Naomi wouldn't like that."

"Colby wouldn't, either. He's crazy about Naomi and adores his children. Have you talked to him about it?"

"No. I still have some influential friends in the army, but I didn't want to raise his hopes until I was sure." He handed her the piece of paper. "This letter says I have an inside track on nominating a man for the position."

Rather than attempt to read the letter, which had been written by someone with very poor penmanship, she glanced down the page. She was about to hand it back when she saw a name that sent chills down her spine. She looked for an explanation, but it wasn't on the page Jared had given her. "Why is Josiah Sinclair's name in the letter?" she asked.

Jared showed surprise. "Do you know him?"

"No. I've just heard about him. Why is he mentioned in the letter?"

"He's apparently wealthy and powerful enough to bring pressure on the army to find out what happened to his son, Raymond. The army said he and another soldier deserted during the war after stealing an army payroll, but Sinclair says his son would never do that. He says his son was romantically involved with Sibyl Spencer. He's convinced that someone from Spencer's Clearing knows what happened to his son. The appointment is mine to offer Colby. All I have to do is find something that will satisfy Sinclair." Jared paused, staring at Laurie. "What's wrong? You look like you've seen a ghost."

"I know Colby wouldn't want a job that would take him away from Naomi and his children."

"Maybe not, but I have to offer it to him."

"But according to what you just said, you can't do that until you find a way to satisfy Josiah Sinclair."

"I suppose that's true."

"You can't let that man come here. He hates everybody in Cactus Corner because Sibyl refused to marry Raymond."

"I'm sure he won't come here himself. He'll send someone to investigate for him."

"You can't let that happen."

"Why not?"

"He hates us. He only wants to humiliate us."

"It has to be more than that. You look like you're about to throw up."

Laurie had known that someday she'd have to tell where she'd found the money. She'd finally relented and told Naomi. It never entered her mind that the money could have had any connection to Raymond Sinclair's disappearance. If Josiah Sinclair sent an agent to Cactus Corner, it would be worse than the time the army colonel came to Spencer's Clearing.

"I can't tell you," Laurie said. "You just have to tell them you've changed your mind."

Jared took her hands in his. When she looked away, he gently turned her gaze back to him. "Tell me what happened. I'm sure you didn't do anything wrong."

"You can't know that."

"I know you."

"Well, I *did* do something wrong. Only I didn't know how wrong it was at the time."

"You'll have to explain that."

"I will if you promise not to turn me over to the army."

Jared chuckled. "You'd have to have killed someone for me to do that."

"I didn't, but someone I love as much as I love anyone did."

Jared sobered. "Then I know it can't be as bad as you think."

Taking a deep breath, she said, "Naomi shot a soldier who killed our grandfather and robbed him, and I kept the money I found in his saddlebags." There, she'd said it. She couldn't take it back. Whatever happened was now out of her hands.

Jared took a moment to absorb the unexpected revelation. "If the soldier really did kill and rob your grandfather, Naomi had every right to shoot him. I'm sure the army agreed."

"We never told them."

"Why not?"

"I don't know. The men decided that. I wouldn't have known anything about it if I hadn't been told to put the house back in order. Colby said we should have told the army. He said Naomi wouldn't have been arrested because she was trying to defend her grandfather."

"Colby knows?"

"Naomi doesn't keep anything from him."

"Good for her. But what I don't understand is why you think this soldier is connected to Raymond Sinclair."

"I don't know anything about what Raymond did or what happened to him, but that soldier came to Spencer's Clearing the same night the army said Raymond disappeared. If they were working together, the money I found must have been part of the army payroll. They could put me in jail for stealing."

"You didn't steal that money. You found it. They can't put you in jail for that."

"How do you know?"

"I was in the army for seven years. I had command of troops. I know the rules."

"Did you have to decide what to do about a woman who killed a soldier or a woman who kept stolen money?"

"No, but—"

"Then you can't be sure. If Raymond's father is powerful enough to force the army to keep investigating Raymond's disappearance when they don't want to, he's powerful enough to get us arrested."

"He's a civilian. He can't force the army to do anything."

"He already has. And what if Raymond's disappearance is somehow connected with the soldier Naomi shot? Something else happened that night."

"Why do you think that?"

"Sibyl was in love with Raymond. She swore she would wait for him until the end of the war if she had to. Yet she married Norman Spencer without a single protest the day after they buried our grandfather. She didn't like Norman any more than anybody else did, but when I asked why she married him, all she would say was that she'd changed her mind."

"You don't believe her?"

"No. She doesn't love him, and he doesn't like her much better."

"What are you suggesting?"

"I'm not suggesting anything because I don't *know* anything. I'm just worried something terrible will happen if you don't write back and tell them you can't help Josiah Sinclair."

"You don't think Colby would take the job if I offered it to him?"

"Not if it meant he would have to be away from Naomi and the children. I doubt he would agree to move, either. We've given him the family he never had. He's not going to give that up easily."

Jared pondered a bit before replying. "If Colby wouldn't take the job, I don't see any reason to risk upsetting everybody. I'll write back and say there's nothing I can do for Mr. Sinclair."

Laurie was so relieved she jumped up and kissed Jared. Taking advantage of the situation, Jared drew Laurie into his lap and kissed her thoroughly. When he came up for air, he asked, "Is there anything else worrying you? I really like the reward for getting rid of it."

Laurie laughed and gave him a quick kiss. "I'll be sure to think of something, but right now I'd better start on supper so I can head home early. I started feeling bad yesterday. I want to see the doctor."

Jared attitude turned serious. "Why didn't you tell me?"

"I was hoping it would go away. I'm never sick."

"I'll drive you."

"There's no need for that. I'm not *sick*. I just don't feel well, and I don't like it. It's probably just a cold or something like that."

"I don't care. I'm going with you."

But a short while before Laurie was ready to leave, Steve came rushing back to the house. "We found another cougar kill. You said I was to come get you and the rifles so we could go after it before it was done feeding."

"Go on," Laurie said when Jared hesitated. "Steve can go with me."

"Go where?" Steve asked, clearly worried he might miss going after the cougar.

"Laurie's going home early because she's not feeling well. I was going to take her."

"That's my job," Steve declared, the lost chance to be part of the hunt for the big cat regretted but put firmly behind him. "Are you sick?" he asked Laurie.

"No, but this queasy feeling is hanging on, and I want to talk to the doctor about it."

"I'll hitch up the buggy. You and the boys have to remember every minute of the chase," Steve told Jared. "I want to hear all about it at breakfast."

"Bloodthirsty brat," Jared said affectionately. "You be sure to get Laurie safely to the doctor. Now I'd better collect the rifles and go. I don't want a single cougar left on our range when the Herefords get here."

❧

"I started feeling bad last night," Laurie told the doctor. "It caught me by surprise. I never get sick."

"Everybody feels bad from time to time," the doctor said, "even healthy young women."

"But this came on so sudden."

"Describe your symptoms as precisely as you can."

Her symptoms weren't hard to describe—they even didn't sound very bad, but the doctor's expression showed shock, grave concern, then a kind of resignation.

"What is it?" Laurie asked. "Am I going to die?"

"No. You're going to have a baby."

Laurie was overwhelmed by so many contradictory feelings she couldn't have said how she felt. *Shock.* How could this have happened? Why hadn't she been more careful? *Fear.* What was everybody going to say? What would Jared say? *Embarrassment.* How could she hold up her head in public when everyone would know what she'd been doing? What would she say when Norman and her father pointed a finger and said they'd been right about her all along?

Happiness. She could hardly wait for the baby to be born. She hoped it would be a boy who would grow up to look just like his father. *Worry.* Where could she go and how soon should she leave? *Resolve.* She refused to live her life as a scarlet woman, nor would she allow her child to be stigmatized because of its birth.

"Are you going to say anything?" the doctor asked.

Laurie gathered her thoughts and pulled her courage around her like a protective shield. She was on her own. What she decided now would determine her future. "What would you like me to say?"

"That you and Jared are secretly married."

Laurie sighed. Did she wish that were true? If so, did she wish it for herself, Jared, or just for the baby? "You know we're not married."

"Then I'd like you to say you'll be married by the end of the day."

She could just imagine the scene if she told Jared he had to marry her before nightfall. He would be shocked, cornered with no way out. "That's not possible. Jared isn't in love with me, and I'm not—"

"Save your breath. If Naomi is convinced you love Jared, that's good enough for me."

"It doesn't matter what I feel. Jared doesn't love me, or he wouldn't have been seeing Martha Simpson. If he marries me, Norman won't give him his loan."

"Would he put a loan ahead of you and his baby?"

"I don't know what he would do, but I'm not going to ask him. And you aren't, either. I don't want anyone to know about this baby, not even Naomi."

"What are you going to do?" The doctor had moved beyond shock and disapproval. He was looking at her with the love and concern of a father for his daughter.

"I don't know, but I'm not going to drag a man to the altar against his will. That happened to me, and I would never do that to anyone."

"This isn't the same."

"It's close enough. Now I have to go. Steve is worried I'm going to die, and I'm sure the men are hungry because they won't eat anything Odell cooks."

"But you can't—"

"The last time someone told me what I couldn't do, I ended up married. That's never going to happen again."

"You've got to think about your baby."

"I am, but I'm also thinking about its mother. I'll be okay, Dr. Kessling. I know you don't think so, but I will."

Laurie desperately wanted some time alone to absorb the knowledge that her whole life had changed, but she had no idea what to do about it. Steve was waiting for her as she left the doctor's office, his face a study in youthful concern.

"I'm okay," she said when he jumped up and started toward her. "It's just some nausea which will go away after a while. You need to return the horse and buggy to the livery stable. I'll meet you at the house."

He wanted to ask questions, but she shooed him away and headed home. She found herself inside her house without remembering how she got there. Her head was too full of questions she couldn't begin to answer.

Except one. She *was* in love with Jared.

                            ❧

"What are you doing out so late?" Jared asked when he opened the door to find Dr. Kessling coming up the porch steps. The doctor's expression was so full of anger Jared forgot what he meant to say next. "What happened? Is something wrong?"

"I need to speak to you privately."

"Sure, but if it's about helping with your new bank, my answer hasn't changed."

After growling, "Save your breath. I don't want your help or your money," the doctor stormed past Jared and into the house.

Stunned and confused, Jared followed him into the study. "Would you like some coffee?" he asked the doctor.

"I don't want anything of yours. I just want to say

what I have to say and leave before having to look at you makes me so angry I attack you."

Completely at a loss Jared asked, "What's wrong? Did Steve do something? Laurie didn't say anything about it."

"As far as I can tell, Steve is the sweet, innocent boy he appears to be, which is more than enough reason to have him removed from your house."

Out of patience and overcome with curiosity, Jared demanded, "Tell me what's happened to make you so angry at me."

The doctor rounded on him. "You have no idea?"

"No."

"If I told you Laurie was expecting a baby, would you still have no idea?"

A fist to the jaw wouldn't have sent Jared reeling like the impact of that news. Not only would Laurie's reputation be shattered beyond redemption, but it had consequences that would reverberate through the life of the child they'd so carelessly created. He wanted to collapse in a chair, reach for a bottle of whiskey, or saddle his horse and ride until he was too exhausted to think. Instead he asked, "When did she know?"

"She came to me a couple days ago complaining of a weak stomach and wondering if it was caused by something she ate. She was too innocent to realize that is a classic sign of pregnancy."

Jared almost asked how the doctor could be sure it wasn't Noah's child, but then he remembered Laurie had said Noah had never touched her. That's why Laurie had longed to feel desired, and Jared had let his lust take advantage of that need. "Did Laurie say—"

"Laurie didn't say anything, but I've known Laurie all her life. Hell, man, I'm the one who delivered her. She's not the kind of woman to give herself to a man she didn't care for greatly. If you had to take advantage of her, couldn't you at least have been careful?"

"I'm not going to deny what I did or try to defend myself, but I didn't take advantage of Laurie. I would never do that. I'm too fond of her. She wanted it as much as I did."

The doctor seemed to sag, the fight going out of him. "You've got to marry her. There'll still be a lot of gossip, but it's the only solution."

Jared was caught between two realities. Laurie had said she would never marry, and Norman wouldn't give him the loan as long as Laurie had anything to do with him. But he wouldn't let himself think about Norman, the loan, or the future of the ranch. Laurie was more important than all of that. "She told us she'd never marry again. She was insistent, no matter how much anyone argued against it."

"Did *you* argue against it?"

"Steve and Loomis didn't give me a chance. They kept after her for days, but she never changed her mind."

"Do you love her?"

Jared didn't know what to say because he'd never asked himself that question. It seemed that part of keeping their relationship secret had been not thinking or talking about it. If they didn't talk about it, they didn't have to acknowledge it existed. And if it didn't exist, there couldn't be any complications. Only it did exist, and there was a major complication.

"I don't know." He had to be honest. "We've never talked about our feelings for each other."

"You slept together often enough to create a baby, but you never talked about your feelings?"

Jared shook his head. Why had he and Laurie believed they shared no feelings beyond their lust for each other? He had thought it was enough for him, and it seemed to be enough for her, but would they have talked about their feelings if their affair hadn't been secret? That was a stupid question. Women like Laurie didn't have affairs. Men like him didn't marry the women they slept with to satisfy their physical needs.

So what the hell had happened between them? He didn't know what Laurie felt about him, but she was far more than a means to satisfy a physical need. Had he been so preoccupied with buying Herefords, trying to convince Colby they were brothers, and worrying about the loan that he'd paid no attention to his feelings? He hadn't always been that stupid.

"Laurie told me not to tell you," the doctor told Jared, "but I felt I had to. Norman will make her life so miserable she won't be able to live in Cactus Creek once this gets out."

"She won't have to. I'll ask her to marry me."

The doctor didn't look relieved. "How is that going to work? She says she doesn't love you, and you don't know what you feel for her."

"I don't know, but we'll work something out."

The doctor turned to leave. "She'll know I told you, so don't try to keep it a secret." He sighed. "I appreciate your desire to make things right. I just wish you were a man of greater integrity. After Noah, Laurie deserves better."

The doctor's comment angered Jared, but he was in no position to defend himself. Laurie was a young widow coming out of a bad marriage. Everyone would believe he'd taken advantage of her at a weak moment—but wasn't that exactly what he'd done? It didn't matter that she was as strongly attracted to him as he was to her. It should have been his responsibility to preserve her reputation, to protect her from men like himself. He deserved the doctor's scorn.

"I've told her to stay home if she doesn't feel better," the doctor said as he was leaving.

"I ought to see her tonight. I'll follow you into town."

The doctor grunted—whether in approval or disgust Jared was unable to tell—and took his leave.

Jared's instinct was to grab a drink and take a few moments to absorb the news and try to assess the changes it would inevitably cause in his life, but he knew that was cowardice. He would have more than enough time during the ride into town to do that. It was more important that he see Laurie right now. He turned away from the door only to come face to face with Loomis. The man was so consumed by rage he was shaking.

"You bastard!" he shouted. "You yellow-bellied, coyote-livered son of a bitch!"

Stunned by this uncharacteristic outburst from his friend, Jared asked, "What's wrong with you? What are you talking about?"

Instead of offering an explanation, Loomis threw himself at Jared, both fists flailing at the bigger man.

Jared avoided Loomis's initial attack, but the man

didn't give up. "Stop it!" Jared shouted. "Why are you attacking me? I haven't done anything to you."

Jared's protests just drove Loomis to greater fury. Jared tried to keep from fighting back with his fists, but it quickly became clear that was the only way he would be able to stop Loomis. The brief struggle left both men bloody, but the outcome was inevitable.

"What caused you to go loco?" Jared asked when he had Loomis down on the floor. "I've never seen you like this."

"She was a sweet, innocent girl, and you took advantage of her."

Loomis was so choked up Jared could hardly understand him. The only *girl* Jared could bring to mind was Martha. "I've only had dinner with her twice. I haven't even kissed her." He'd tried, but he couldn't make himself do it. It made him think of Laurie, and that made him feel like a traitor.

"I'm not talking about that gal you're seeing on the sly. I'm talking about *Laurie.*"

Jared's blood ran cold. How did he know about Laurie? Did the other men know, too? "What are you talking about?"

"I heard what the doctor told you. You got her pregnant while you were messing around with another woman. I won't work for a man like that. I'm quitting right now. You can give me my money when you have it, but I'm riding out tonight."

Jared could think of nothing to say to defend himself, but he didn't want to lose a friend of so many years. "I'm going to marry her. That will make it right."

Loomis struggled to break Jared's hold. "Nothing can make what you did right. You're disgusting."

Jared wasn't proud of himself, but he thought "disgusting" was a bit strong. "I'm going to let you up, but I don't want to fight you anymore."

"Don't worry," Loomis sneered. "You're not worth it."

The words stung, but any response Jared might have made was cut off by the entrance of Nick and Clay.

"What the hell is going on?" Nick asked.

"Nothing." Loomis got to his feet and straightened his clothes. "I fell down and Jared was helping me up."

"That's bullshit," Clay said. "You're both bloody. You've been fighting."

"I said I fell down," Loomis snarled. "I guess I hit Jared on the way down."

Clay turned to Jared. "Are you going to tell us what happened?"

"I think Loomis made it plain enough. I have to go into town. I expect I'll be late coming back."

"What's up?" Nick asked.

"I'll let you know when I get back." Jared gestured to Loomis. "Makes sure he gets cleaned up. It was a nasty fall."

He didn't need to see their skepticism to know they didn't believe a word of what Loomis had said, but he had more important things to do. He could deal with them later. He just had to make sure he didn't ruin any more lives.

❧

Laurie knew the doctor had broken his promise the

moment she opened the door and saw Jared on her porch. Without a word, she opened the door for him.

"Let me send Steve over to see Ben. Then we can talk."

With the sensitivity young people often displayed when the safety of their world was threatened, Steve sensed something important was up. Laurie had to promise to fill him in later before he would agree to leave.

"You can't tell him," Jared protested.

"Everyone will know before long. Without Steve, I wouldn't be working at the ranch. He deserves to be among the first to know. I'll fix coffee. I'll be back in a few minutes."

Laurie didn't want any coffee, but she needed time to gather her thoughts. She knew what she wanted to do—what she *had* to do—but seeing Jared so unexpectedly had shaken her resolve. He had to be here to ask her to marry him. To everyone else, that would seem the perfect solution, but it wasn't enough for her.

She hadn't endured one loveless marriage to step into another. And it didn't matter that she was in love with Jared. She knew he liked her, but that wasn't enough, especially when he'd been paying court to Martha Simpson. This wasn't the time to start going over her options, none of which she liked. She'd have plenty of time to do that in the coming days.

The coffee seemed to have gotten ready in half the usual time. She had to face Jared long before she was ready. She decided to let him speak first.

"The doctor came to see me tonight. Why didn't you tell me about the baby?"

"Why should I? We're not married."

"I'm its father."

"How can you know that?" That was hard to say. It made her seem like something she wasn't.

"Because I know you. You would never have slept with me if you hadn't been vulnerable and I hadn't been thoughtless enough to take advantage."

Laurie sat up, her spine ramrod straight. "I may have been vulnerable, but you didn't take advantage of me. It was my choice. Whatever may have been your desire, you would never have forced yourself on me. As a matter of fact, I believe *I* persuaded *you* the last two times."

"That doesn't change anything."

"It doesn't change the fact that I'm going to have a baby, but it changes everything else. This baby is my responsibility, not yours."

"It is *our* responsibility. I want to marry you."

"Are you saying you're in love with me?" Laurie threw the question at him without warning, knowing it would catch him off guard. Despite knowing he wouldn't, she had hoped he would say yes. His hesitation was all the answer she needed. "Don't bother to say anything. I knew the answer before I asked the question. I asked it because I wanted you to stumble, mumble, pause, or look like you were choking on the words. You're a good man, Jared Smith, an honest man. I would never want to make you lie."

"I like you very much," Jared hurried to assure her. "I think we would get along very well together."

"There are several reasons why I'm not going to accept your offer," Laurie said. "First, you don't love me. I was married to a man I didn't love, and I know how miserable it made me. I would never do that to another person. You would come to resent me, probably dislike me, and that wouldn't be good for the baby. Then there's the loan. I know you can make more money for yourself and the men if you borrow from Norman rather than giving me half of the ranch. I was thinking only of myself when I proposed the loan. I realize now you only accepted because you thought you had no choice. Norman has said he won't give you the loan if I continue to work for you. You can't imagine he would change his mind if I married you."

"I don't care about Norman or the loan."

"You say that now because you're upset, but you don't mean it. I felt a coolness these last weeks. I also know you've been seeing Martha Simpson. She's a beautiful young woman who would make you a marvelous wife."

"No decent woman is going to want to marry me when she finds out I turned my back on my own child." Jared shook his head in frustration. "That's not what I meant to say. I couldn't respect myself enough to ask a decent woman to marry me."

"You don't have to worry about that. I'm going to leave Cactus Corner before anybody else knows about the baby."

"You can't do that."

"I can and I will. I will sell my house and invest all my money in the new bank. Norman will be forced to give me a decent income or risk losing his customers. I will have more than enough money to support the baby and me. Besides, I think I would like to work. I quite enjoyed feeling useful."

Jared advanced several arguments as to why she should marry him and why she would regret leaving Cactus Creek. The more he tried to persuade her, the harder it was to stick to her resolve, but he never did the one thing that would have caused her to change her mind. He never said he loved her with the passion and genuineness of a man so deeply in love that he couldn't imagine not marrying her. The more he tried to persuade her, the more she was certain her heart would break. Finally, she could stand it no longer.

"There's no point in saying anything more. I'm not going to change my mind. I won't be coming to the ranch anymore, so you might as well take Steve home with you tonight. He won't want to go, but I trust you'll find a way to persuade him. I don't want him to know what I'm going to do until it's done."

Jared tried to continue his argument, but she told him she wanted him to leave. "I'm tired and want to rest. I have a lot to do in the coming days."

She thought he was going to refuse to leave, but he said, "I'll be back. I'm not giving up. I know I've done this all wrong, but that child will be my son or daughter. I want to be part of its life."

Laurie thought of the agony Colby had gone through knowing he had a child he'd never seen. For a moment she almost weakened, but she steeled her nerves. She was doing this for Jared as well as the baby. Someday he would have a wife and more children. She didn't want her mistake to be a dark cloud hanging over his future. When she didn't respond, he left the house.

Laurie slumped back in her chair. Her coffee was cold, but she didn't care. She'd get up and throw it out in a while, but right now she didn't feel like she had the strength to move. Keeping to her resolve had drained her energy. She would just sit and let the reality of her future sink in. It wasn't a terrible future. It just wasn't the one she wanted.

Laurie didn't know how long she'd sat quietly, but no more than five minutes could have gone by before she heard someone knocking at the front door. She didn't want to see anyone, but she was afraid it might be Steve. She didn't know what she could say to him, but she couldn't refuse to let him in. She wasn't prepared to find Loomis on her porch.

"May I come in?"

Sixteen

ORDINARILY SHE WOULD HAVE BEEN RELUCTANT TO let anyone in this late in the evening, but she could tell Loomis was suffering under a great emotional burden. She hadn't the heart to turn him away. "Come on in, but you can't stay long. It's getting late."

Loomis followed her into the sitting room.

"I would offer you some coffee, but it would be wasteful to brew a whole pot." She was sorry Loomis was upset, but she didn't want to encourage him to stay.

"I don't want any coffee," Loomis said. "Jared came to see you." When she didn't answer, he went on. "I saw him leave."

Laurie stiffened. She liked Loomis, but wasn't comfortable knowing he was watching who came and went in her house. Nor could she figure out why he would care. "I don't understand why that should be any concern of yours." Loomis looked so upset she was worried he'd either start sobbing or fall into some sort of fit. "Are you feeling okay?"

"No!" The word exploded from him. "I'm so angry I can hardly think."

She'd never seen Loomis like this. He had always been calm and rational. "What's wrong? Can I help?" She had no idea how his anger could concern her or what she could do to help him.

"I know why Jared came," Loomis said. "I over-heard the doctor talking to him."

Laurie could feel the heat flame in her face. She was so shocked she didn't know whether to stand her ground or run from the room. Her father was right. Make a serious mistake, and everyone would find out about it.

"I think what he did was truly horrible," Loomis said. "I tried to knock him down, but Jared is bigger and stronger. I just made a fool of myself."

"I'm sure you didn't. It was very brave of you." Laurie had to pull herself together. She was mortified Loomis knew about her situation, but she was more upset to learn she was the cause of Jared and Loomis getting into a fight.

"Did Jared ask you to marry him?" Loomis asked.

The question made her even more uncomfort-able, but since he already knew about the baby, there was no point in refusing to answer. "Yes, he did, but I refused."

His emotions were so out of control she couldn't tell if he was upset or relieved.

"Will you marry me? I don't have a ranch and I don't have much money, but I'll do my best to make you a good husband and the baby a good father."

Laurie was glad she was sitting down. The whole situation was turning into a fiasco. "It's very sweet of you to offer, Loomis, but I can't marry you."

"Why? I'm not as big or handsome as Jared, but—"

"It has nothing to do with that," Laurie assured him. "If I loved you and you loved me, it would be different. But we don't. That's the same reason I won't marry Jared."

"You don't love him?"

"He doesn't love me."

For the first time this evening, Loomis seemed to regain some control over his emotions. "Did he tell you that?"

"No, but when I asked him if he loved me, he hesitated. He had the look of a man who was about to be cornered."

Loomis thought for a moment. "I think maybe he loves you. In fact, I'm sure he does, but that doesn't mean I think you ought to marry him."

Laurie was disgusted at the fountain of hope that gushed forth within her. Was she so desperate to be loved that she'd latch on to a *maybe*? What happened to her resolve to be an independent woman, to never marry again? Why should hope resurrect itself based on Loomis's opinion? He couldn't know what Jared felt for her any more than she could. She doubted Jared knew what he felt. "He's been seeing Martha Simpson. What clearer evidence could you want that he doesn't love me?"

"That doesn't mean anything. Norman said he wouldn't give Jared a loan unless he was married or his engagement had been announced in the paper. He made it clear that person couldn't be you. But you had told us you'd never marry again so Jared started looking around for someone else. He likes Miss Simpson, but he doesn't love her. He wouldn't have had supper with her if it hadn't been for the rest of us."

"What do you mean? What does Martha Simpson have to do with you?"

"Jared is a natural leader, but he's not as strong on financial planning. It wasn't until after he'd accepted your offer of a partnership that he realized there wouldn't be much money left over. He doesn't care about himself, but he promised us if we would help him get his ranch established, he would give us enough money to go out on our own. Odell is the only one who likes cows. The rest of us can't stand them. Jared's even more worried about Steve. Everything the boy has is invested in that ranch."

Laurie tried to gather her thoughts. "Are you trying to tell me Jared wouldn't be trying to get a loan from Norman if he weren't worried that giving me half of the ranch's income wouldn't leave enough for Steve and the men?" She had suspected something like this, but this was the first time she knew for certain.

"Yes. He has to have Herefords to make a significant profit, but he can't buy them without your money or Norman's. If he uses your money, there's not enough left for the rest of us."

Stupid man! Why hadn't he explained all of this before? If he loved her enough to marry her, she'd give him the money. She'd only wanted it as a means to gain her independence and freedom from Norman's stinginess. If she married Jared, she wouldn't have to worry about Norman ever again.

She needed Loomis to leave. She had a lot of thinking to do. She didn't know if it would change *everything*, but it certainly did *some* things. "Thank you for telling me all this," she said to Loomis. "I appreciate your offer, but I can't accept it. Now you'd better head back to the ranch before it gets too late."

"I'm not going back. I quit."

She hadn't expected that. Jared and Loomis had been friends for years. "Why?"

"I couldn't stay after the way Jared treated you."

More embarrassment. Would the consequences of her need to feel desirable never end? "You can't blame Jared for what happened. He didn't force me to do anything I didn't want to do. I'm sorry if that destroys your image of me, but I'm far from a perfect woman."

"You did it because you *loved* him. He did it because…"

Loomis appeared reluctant to ascribe Jared's motives to pure lust. She couldn't—or wouldn't—either. She said, "The only person who knows the answer to that question is Jared."

Had she loved Jared so much even then that Loomis and the others could tell? She'd been strongly attracted to him from the beginning, but could she have fallen in love so quickly without realizing it? Couldn't you feel desire without love, or did both have to come together? Maybe attraction and desire were early stages of love that could be mistaken for something less because they came so quickly.

Yet why hadn't she been able to tell when they turned to love? They were her feelings. She should have known before anyone else. Was it because she was too busy concentrating on trying to get beyond Norman's control, too busy insisting she would never marry again because she was determined to be independent of any man's control? She would probably never know the answer. All that really mattered was that she loved Jared now. But did he love her?

"I hate to think I've caused a rupture between you and Jared. I wish you'd return to the ranch. He depends on you."

"Well he can stop depending on me. I never meant to stay."

She hoped Loomis would change his mind when he calmed down. "What will you do?"

"I don't know yet, but I'll figure out something. Now I'd better go. I don't want my hanging around to give you a bad name."

He couldn't do any worse than she'd already done. "Don't worry about me. I can take care of myself."

Loomis favored her with a long look. "You know, I think you can."

～

Laurie was about ready to climb into bed when she heard another knock at the front door. She was tempted not to answer it—she'd already had more than enough interruptions to her evening, and more than enough things to think about—but she was afraid not to. In such a close-knit community, it could mean someone needed her help. When she found Norman on her porch, she was tempted to close the door in his face.

"What do you want? Do you realize how late it is?"

"I have to talk to you."

For a moment, she had a terrible fear he knew

about the baby, but she realized he couldn't have found out already. No one who knew would have told him under anything less than torture. "Come back in the morning." She started to close the door, but Norman put his foot in it.

"It can't wait."

Realizing that the only way to get rid of Norman was to let him say what he'd come to say, she opened the door and stepped back. "You've got ten minutes. After that, I'm going to bed."

"It's about this new bank."

"I knew it would be," Laurie said as she settled into a chair. "What do you expect me to do about it?"

"You've got to make them stop."

"If that's what you want, you've got to talk to Dr. Kessling. I have nothing to do with it."

"They're doing it because of you."

"No, they're doing it because of *you*. You've used your money to tyrannize this community as long as I can remember."

Norman looked insulted, the way he always looked whenever people disagreed with anything he'd done. "I lent money on easy terms to anybody who asked for it when we settled here. Everyone would still be living in tents if it weren't for me."

"Everyone is thankful for what you did. As important as that was, it's the only instance of thoughtfulness to stand against your attitude of superiority and rudeness. Has it ever occurred to you that other people have feelings, too?"

Norman acted like he hadn't heard a word she said. "I built the memorial to Toby." He had commissioned a large vine-covered arbor in the center of town with a water fountain and trees that would one day offer precious shade during the heat of summer.

"It took you nearly a year."

"I couldn't find the materials I wanted. I knew everybody wanted it to be special."

"Is that why Colby had to tell you if it wasn't finished within a month, he'd build it for you and use it as a headstone for your grave?" Norman was naive if he thought there were any secrets in Cactus Corner.

"I'll change." He said the words like each one tasted foul.

"No, you won't. You're still refusing to give me a reasonable allowance and using Noah's will as an excuse. You're refusing to give Jared the loan he needs because you don't want me working for him."

Now he was back on firmer ground. "It's not suitable for my sister-in-law to work as a cook and housekeeper."

"I'm no longer your sister-in-law, and I have to work because you won't give me my own money."

"I'll double your allowance. No, I'll triple it." She could only guess how much it cost him to say that. Norman never backed down from a position once he had taken it.

"And cut it back once you get what you want? No, Norman. It's time someone put a stop to your cruelty. Rather than try to stop the new bank, I'll do what I can to encourage people to use it. And in case you didn't know, Colby's parents left him more than enough money to open the bank."

"That's impossible. They haven't spoken in years."

"Talk to Colby if you don't believe me, but starting tomorrow you'd better try being a lot nicer. If not, people are going to borrow money from the new bank to pay off your loans. That will leave you a very rich man but without customers or friends." Laurie got to her feet. "Now I'm going to bed. You have to go."

Norman stood, his features twisted by anger and frustration. Maybe even fear. "You hate me, don't you?"

Laurie paused a moment. "I don't think so. Most of the time, I try not to think of you at all."

❧

"I shouldn't be meeting you again so soon." Martha admonished him. "People are going to start thinking we're courting."

Jared had asked Martha to meet him for coffee in an attempt to clear his conscience. Learning Laurie was going to have a baby had forced him to confront several truths, all of them uncomfortable and embarrassing. One of those was that he couldn't bring himself to marry Martha, even for the sake of Steve and his men, and he felt guilty for trying to give her the impression he did. He was even more ashamed of himself for planning to use her to get Norman to give him the loan. What kind of man would do that? Certainly not the kind of man he thought himself to be.

"I suppose it is a bit unusual, but not improper," he said.

Martha's laughter was easy and uncomplicated. "How could it be improper when we are in public and half the people in town stop to speak to one of us?"

"Speak to you," Jared corrected. "I'm not so

pretty." He wanted to bite his tongue. He was here to clean up the mess he'd made, not make it worse with suggestive comments.

"Well, I'm glad you did. I like being seen with a handsome man. Besides, you're old enough you don't stare at me with your mouth open. I'm well aware that single women are at a premium in town, but that's no reason for young men to lose their power of conversation."

Jared was used to Martha's way of flirting, but this was a little unusual even for her. Instead of treating him like a potential husband, she was making him feel like a father figure or favorite uncle, which was a blow to his vanity. "I'm not that old."

Martha laughed. "You know what I mean. I'm thankful you helped me understand boys my age."

When had he done that? "Why was that so important?" Jared was feeling older by the minute. When they'd met before, they'd talked in general terms about the difficulties of a young woman stuck in a small town in the West. "Stuck" was Martha's word. She'd complained about the inability of young men to express a coherent thought and the taboos against women doing just that.

He'd explained the reverence in which young men held a young woman who was both beautiful and genteel. He'd also encouraged her to be more assertive, not to hesitate to say and do what she wanted. At the time, he'd considered it a subtle way to court a young woman without *really* courting her. From the beginning, he'd be ashamed of what he was doing. He'd only managed it by focusing on Steve's future.

"A young woman needs to know what a man feels for her," Martha said. "That's difficult when he's incapable of speech."

"I've never been incapable of speech."

Martha laughed. "I don't mean *you*. I'm talking about young men."

Jared felt he'd suddenly gone gray and aged three decades. In frustration he asked, "Are you talking about any young man in particular?"

"Ted Drummond." Martha blushed. "I thought you knew."

Jared recalled Martha mentioning Ted—Jared sometimes had trouble keeping his mind on their conversations—but the boy was so handsome every woman mentioned him sooner or later. He'd met Ted a couple of times but didn't find him remarkable in any way except his looks. "What about him?"

"You told me to speak my mind, let people know what I thought. Well, I told Ted what I felt for him." She laughed. "I thought he was going to faint or run away, but he pulled himself together and we had a good talk."

"Good. What did you talk about?"

"Us. His future. *My* future. Everything." Martha flashed a brilliant smile. "We're engaged, and I owe it all to you."

Jared was suddenly afflicted with the aforementioned shortcoming of the younger generation. He was speechless. Everyone knew Martha was a flirt, but how could he have so misjudged their conversation? Was he so busy thinking about Laurie that he hadn't paid enough attention to what Martha had been saying to know she wasn't thinking about him? Apparently she had talked so freely because she saw him as an older cousin or friend of the family. As much as this punctured his vanity, he was relieved that his selfishness hadn't hurt Martha. "Have you told your parents?"

Martha frowned. "They're not happy that I want to marry a stable hand. They would rather I marry someone much older, like you."

Jared wasn't sure how much more pounding his ego could take, but he decided to stick it out. "Ted's not really a stable hand. He's more like Morley Sumner's partner."

"That's what I told Papa. Will you talk to him? He'll listen to you."

Now he was going to have to play go-between for this modern-day Romeo and Juliet. Jared doubted Reverend Simpson would care what he thought, but after what he'd tried to do, he owed it to Martha to talk with her father. "Let me know when will be a good time. Just don't blame me if he doesn't listen."

"I'm sure he will. Everybody respects you so much. Now I have to run away. Mama has given me several errands."

A smiling Martha Simpson jumped up from the table, gave him a kiss on the cheek, and scurried away. Feeling like he'd stepped into the midst of a funnel cloud, Jared shook his head in bewilderment. He'd gotten off easier than he deserved. Even more remarkable, he'd actually helped Martha and Ted.

As for the kiss on the cheek, it wouldn't cause any trouble. Not after Martha announced her engagement.

Besides, would anyone seriously believe Martha could be romantically interested in such an old man?

~❦~

Steve met Jared at the door when he returned to the ranch. It was clear the boy was very upset.

"Loomis says Miss Laurie isn't coming to the ranch today. He says she's *never* coming to the ranch again, and it's not because she's sick. I knew something was wrong when she made me leave the other night. What did you do to her? Loomis won't tell me. All he said was you were the most stupid man he'd ever met. Then he packed his saddlebags and rode off."

Jared didn't know what to tell the boy. He hadn't seen Loomis since the fight. He didn't know how he could have known anything about what passed between him and Laurie. Still, what Loomis did or didn't know wasn't important. Laurie being pregnant with their child was all that mattered. As long as Laurie refused to marry him, he didn't know how to resolve the situation. Jared headed for the kitchen with Steve trailing behind.

"Laurie isn't sick, but she isn't feeling well," he told the boy. "I'll go back to see her tomorrow. Maybe she'll feel better by then."

He was lying again. Well, not lying exactly, but certainly giving a false impression. He'd been a straightforwardly honest man his whole life. The way he'd tried to take advantage of Martha Simpson wasn't typical of him and he was ashamed, but what he'd done to Laurie was much, much worse. How could he have ended up in such a morass when his intentions had been so good?

Because he'd let his desire for Laurie outrun his sense of decency. It didn't matter that she had been willing. It didn't matter that she appeared to have enjoyed it as much as he did. It only mattered that his behavior had put her in a position that would ruin her reputation and cast a shadow over the life of their baby.

He struggled to absorb the fact that he was going to be a father. What kind of role model would he be? He'd sold up in Texas to come west looking for brothers he knew nothing about and had very little chance of finding. He'd bought a ranch that couldn't succeed without Herefords he didn't have the money to buy. He'd signed a business agreement that severely limited his potential income then decided to get out of it by courting a woman he didn't love. No wonder Laurie didn't want to marry him. He didn't deserve a woman like her.

"I want to go with you," Steve said.

"Where?" Jared had been so deep in thought he'd lost the thread of their conversation. He'd also forgotten he'd come into the kitchen to make coffee. He reached for a pot to fill with water.

"To see Miss Laurie," Steve reminded him. "Maybe she'll come back if I talk to her. I know she likes it here. I'll starve if I have to keep eating Odell's cooking. If she comes back, maybe Loomis will, too."

That was something else. He'd lost the respect of his best friend. Loomis would never work with him again. "I know we all liked Laurie," he said to Steve, "but—"

"I loved her," Steve declared emphatically. "I thought you loved her, too."

Jared put the pot on the stove and lit the fire. "The way you would love her and the way I would love her aren't the same."

"I know that," the boy stated. "I'm not stupid, but all of us saw the way you looked at her. Nick was hoping you'd ask him to be best man, but I told him you'd choose Loomis."

Jared was shocked to know the men had been discussing a wedding between him and Laurie. Had he been so bowled over by Laurie that he'd completely lost touch with everyone else? "How many times did Laurie tell you she would never marry again?" He went into the storage room to get the coffee beans.

"Lots, but she didn't mean it. She'd marry you if you asked her. Did you ever tell her you loved her?"

"No," he shouted back at Steve.

"Then you don't know what she would have said."

"There are things you don't know."

"If you're going to tell me I'm too young, you can stow it," the boy replied, angrily. "I saw the way she looked at you."

Jared put the coffee in the grinder. "She looked at everybody else just as much, sometimes more," he said over the noise.

Steve moved to the doorway. "Of course she did. You didn't think a woman of her character was going to throw herself at you, did you? She was waiting for you to speak first."

"Why would I say anything? I was courting Martha Simpson."

Steven snorted in disgust. "You weren't courting Martha. You were running away from Miss Laurie."

Done grinding the coffee, Jared came out of the storage room and closed the door. "There are some things I should have told you earlier."

"What?" Steve looked like he was prepared to question anything Jared said.

"I made a miscalculation when I agreed to give Laurie a full partnership."

"What kind of miscalculation?"

"Giving Laurie half the ranch cut everybody's share in half."

"We knew that, but it didn't matter."

"But the men wouldn't have enough money to start over on their own. You wouldn't have enough money to go back East, maybe go to college."

Steve shook his head. "Loomis said you were so head-over-heels in love with Miss Laurie you couldn't think straight. If having Herefords can double our profits, we'll end up with the same amount of money. That water is boiling. Are you going to make coffee, or just let the water boil away?"

Jared took the pot off the heat and dropped the coffee into the pot. "We don't know having Herefords will double our profits. Besides, we don't have them yet."

"We were willing to take the chance because we thought Miss Laurie was worth it. We thought you did, too."

He opened his mouth to say he thought Laurie was worth more than that, but he closed it again. Why should Steve believe him? He'd taken advantage of Laurie, then turned his back on her when things didn't turn out like he expected.

That wasn't exactly right. He hadn't turned his back on her. She was adamant she would never remarry so he had to look for another way. No, that wasn't right, either. He hadn't said he loved her, hadn't asked her to marry him. As Steve said, he didn't know how she would have answered. Would she have married him?

"If I had asked Laurie to marry me, she'd have thought I was doing it just for the money," he told Steve.

"Would you?"

"Would I what?"

"Have been marrying her just for the money?"

Jared had been about to pour his coffee, but he paused. "Of course not."

"Why would you have been marrying her?"

"I wouldn't ask any woman to marry me unless I loved her."

"So if you asked her to marry you, you'd have been in love with her. Right?"

"Yes."

"Did you ask her?"

"Yes."

"What did she say?" the boy asked eagerly.

"She refused me."

He looked crestfallen. "Why?"

"She doesn't believe I love her."

"You do. I know you do. You told her you did, didn't you?"

The words he was about to utter caught in his throat. When Laurie asked if he loved her, he'd hesitated because he'd never stopped to ask himself what his *true* feelings for her were. Was it merely lust, desire, or was it more? Of course it was more, but how much more? What *kind* of more?

"You didn't answer my question," Steve reminded him. "Did you tell her you loved her?"

The answer was simple. "No."

Steve stared at him in disbelief. "Why not? You've been in love with her almost from the beginning. Even Odell knew it, and he can't see anything that isn't shoved under his nose."

He didn't have an answer except to say he'd been a complete fool. The most wonderful woman in the world had stepped into his life, and he hadn't the sense to realize it. He *was* in love with Laurie. He probably had been after her first day at the ranch, but all he had been able to think about was her face and her body. Why would she want to marry a man like that? More important, why hadn't he known he was in love with her?

He'd been given every indication. He couldn't stop thinking about her. He missed her when she wasn't around. When he was working, he would think of things he wanted to tell her as soon as he got home. When she left each evening, he practically held his breath until she returned the next morning. When he was with her, he couldn't think of anyone else.

"I've been blind," he told Steve. "And stupid. I should have talked to you and the boys. And Laurie. Especially Laurie. I can't understand how I could have missed what everyone else knew, but I'm going to make sure it never happens again."

"Does that mean Miss Laurie will come back?" Steve's eyes shone with eagerness.

"I'm going to do everything I can to see that she does, but I need your help."

"I'll do anything you want."

"I need the other guys, too."

"They're as eager to get her back as I am."

"Good. Now here's what I want you do to."

Seventeen

NORMAN ROSE FROM HIS SEAT BEHIND HIS HUGE DESK. "I was going to come out to the ranch this afternoon," he said when Jared was ushered into his office. "After seeing the kiss Miss Simpson gave you at lunch yesterday, I've decided to give you the loan."

"I'm glad I could save you a trip and clear up a misunderstanding," Jared replied without sitting down. "Miss Simpson is going to marry Ted Drummond. What you saw was a kiss of gratitude because I'd given her some helpful advice."

Norman sat back down. "Then you're not going to marry her?"

"No."

Norman looked like a petulant child who'd lost a favorite toy. "Then I withdraw my offer of a loan."

"That's okay. The reason I came in was to tell you I'm no longer interested in a loan from you."

The transformation that swept over Norman was stunning. He looked vulnerable, possibly even scared. "You've got to get your loan from me. You can't go to that new bank."

Jared had to restrain an impulse to gloat. "I

don't have to get my loan from you. In light of the conditions you imposed, I'm ashamed of myself for considering it. I was a coward, but it won't happen again. I hadn't thought of approaching the owners of the new bank, but thanks for the suggestion."

Norman looked defeated. "Why are you doing this? Do you hate me, too?"

Jared was surprised by the question. "I don't know you well enough to have any personal feelings for you one way or the other, but I do think you're an unprincipled businessman who would do anything to make money. On top of that, you're a malicious person who enjoys manipulating people. After the way you've treated Laurie, I'm surprised people in town still talk to you. If you didn't have Cassie working for you, I expect you'd have lost half your customers by now." Jared paused. "I can sympathize with you, though. I've been blind, couldn't see what was obvious to everyone else. I thought I was right so I pushed ahead, but I was wrong. Now I've come close to losing the most important person in my life."

"Laurie."

"See, even you knew it before I did. I'm not worthy to be her husband, but I'm going to do everything I can to convince her to marry me anyway, even if it means I'll never be able to buy those Herefords. If she does marry me, you can be sure I'll never put money, anything, or anybody ahead of her again."

❧

"Don't blame Papa," Naomi was saying to Laurie. "He was so worried, I knew something was wrong. I wouldn't give him any peace until he told me."

Laurie didn't know whether she was more angry or relieved. It was a comfort to have someone to talk to, but she was upset Naomi knew of her predicament. She had intended to leave Cactus Corner before anyone other than the doctor knew.

"Have you told anyone else?"

"No, not even Colby."

Naomi hadn't told Colby yet, but she would. They were so closely attuned he would know something was wrong and worm it out of her. Not that it would take very long. It was impossible for them to keep secrets from each other.

"Have you seen Jared?"

"Yes. He asked me to marry him, but I refused."

Naomi's reaction was so extreme it was comical. "Are you crazy? You're in love with him."

"But he's not in love with me. I swore I would never marry again after Noah died. I certainly wouldn't make the mistake of marrying a man who didn't love me."

"I think he does love you," Naomi insisted.

"Then why is he seeing Martha Simpson?"

"Because she's a lovely young woman who flirts with every single man in town."

"Jared is not a child. Not even a lovely young flirt can make him do something he doesn't want to do."

"Don't be ridiculous. Most men are helpless when up against a pretty young woman who's generous with her smiles."

"Thanks for trying to make me feel better, but I'm not going to marry Jared."

"What are you going to do?"

"I'm going to leave town. I'm trying to decide whether to move to Tucson or even farther away."

Naomi gripped both her cousin's hands. "You can't do that."

"You can't think I'd try to rear this child in Cactus Corner with everybody knowing his father was married to another woman. Maybe you could brazen it out, but I can't."

"No, I couldn't do that," Naomi confessed, "but you can't move away."

"I can't see any other alternative."

"There has to be something. We've got to think."

"Thinking is not going to change the fact that I refuse to raise my child with the stigma of being illegitimate."

"You should have thought of that before you slept with Jared."

Naomi tried to apologize, but Laurie wouldn't let her. "Of course I should have. I've said worse things to myself than you ever will. At the time, I felt what I was doing was important. I even convinced myself it was necessary if I was ever to have a normal life, but now I know it was foolish. I can try to blame it on my marriage to Noah, Norman's stinginess, or my father selling me to the highest bidder, but it was my decision. I was too blinded by having freedom to see what anyone else would have seen as an inevitable result." Laurie laughed softly. "Loomis followed Jared into town. When he found out I had refused Jared, he offered to marry me."

"Do you love Loomis?"

"Of course not, and he doesn't love me. He was just being kind."

"There must be someone you would like to marry besides Jared."

"I love Jared, but I'm still not sure I want to marry. If I weren't expecting a baby, I wouldn't be considering it now."

"Not even though you love Jared?"

Laurie laughed guiltily and blushed. "I considered being his mistress rather than his wife."

"Laurie Hale Spencer!" Naomi exclaimed. "I can't believe I heard you say that."

"Neither can I. And if you tell anyone, *anyone,* and that includes Sibyl, I'll deny it."

The two women stared at each other. Laurie tried to keep a straight face, but Naomi looked so serious she couldn't. First she twisted her mouth to keep a smile from forming. Then she pinched herself to suppress a snicker. Moments later a gurgle of laughter burst from her. Naomi looked horrified before laughter overcame her.

"You're horrible," Naomi said, "and I'm just as bad. Who would ever have thought you'd turn into a lewd woman?"

Laurie wiped her eyes. "I always wondered what it would be like to be able to choose the men I slept with. I guess my father was right to be worried about me."

"Don't get me started on your father. That man—"

A knock on the front door interrupted their conversation.

"I wonder who that can be," Laurie said.

"It could be anyone coming to check on you. Everybody knows you haven't gone to the ranch for two days. They're bound to think you must be sick."

"Well, I'm not. I want you to assure everyone I'm in perfect health."

The knocks came again, more insistent this time.

"You'd better see who it is," Naomi said. "Then we can get back to discussing what to do."

Laurie reluctantly got to her feet. "There's no discussion. I'm moving."

"There's got to be another way."

"There isn't, so stop worrying."

Laurie had been prepared to greet one of the women in town. She wasn't prepared to find Jared on her porch. She must be a stupid woman who couldn't learn her lesson even when it was obvious. Despite her dilemma, just seeing him sent her heart racing and her spirits soaring. It wasn't just his handsome face or his imposing physique. He looked so worried, so tense, she wanted to put her arms around him and assure him everything would be all right.

"I'm coming in," he announced and proceeded to do exactly that.

"What do you want?" Laurie asked. "We said everything last night." But she didn't mean it. However much it hurt to know it wasn't likely to happen, she couldn't relinquish the hope that he had come to love her.

"You may have said everything you wanted to say, but I didn't." He stopped in his tracks when he saw Naomi.

"Don't think I'm going anywhere," Naomi said, grim determination writ large on her face. "I'm going to pay close attention to every word you say. They'd better be good. If not, you're in big trouble."

"I'm glad you're here," Jared said. "Maybe you can talk some sense into Laurie."

"Why *are* you here?" Laurie asked Jared.

Jared crossed to Laurie and took both her hands in his. "I want you to marry me."

How could the words she longed to hear hurt so much? "I've already told—"

"This has nothing to do with the baby. I was in love with you before you knew about that. I was just too stupid to realize it."

Naomi didn't give Laurie a chance to answer. "She's in love with you, too. Don't let her deny it."

"I can speak for myself," Laurie said to her cousin.

"You haven't been doing very well, so I thought I'd give you a little help. We've gotten to the part where Jared loves you and you love Jared. Don't stop now."

"Do you *really* love me?" Jared asked Laurie.

"You know I said I was never going to marry again."

"That's not what I asked. Do you love me? Because I love you very much."

Laurie wouldn't let herself believe it just yet. "What about Martha Simpson?"

"I'm embarrassed to say I let Norman's threats and her smile cause me to behave very foolishly."

"What did I tell you?" Naomi asked Laurie.

Laurie had never wished her cousin at the other end of the earth until right now. "Do you mind if we have this conversation without interruption?"

"Okay, as long as you don't get sidetracked on things that are irrelevant."

"Martha Simpson isn't irrelevant."

"She is if you love Jared and he loves you."

"She's right, you know," Jared said to Laurie. "I've never been in love with Martha nor she with me. She only wanted advice on how to deal with a young man who was hesitant to say what was in his heart. Apparently I convinced her it was all right for her to say it for him. So now she's engaged to Ted Drummond."

Laurie was surprised—and relieved. "Why was she reluctant to marry Ted? He's the most handsome man I've ever seen."

"More so than me?"

"I love you, but I'm not blind. At least not where Ted's looks are concerned." Oops! She'd committed herself before she was absolutely sure that *he* loved *her*.

"We're getting off track again," Naomi warned.

"I'm liking your cousin more and more," Jared said. "She never forgets what's most important."

"And what is that?" Laurie asked.

"You agreeing to marry me. You still haven't given me an answer."

Laurie met his gaze, her heart in her throat. "Can you tell me that this has nothing to do with the baby, the money, or the loan, that you would want to marry me if none of that had ever happened?"

"I can do better than that," Jared said. "I not only love you unconditionally, I'm *going* to marry you. I think we ought to do it today."

Laurie's heart started beating so fast it was hard to breathe. "I can't get married five minutes after I say yes."

"Of course you can. All you have to do is say *yes*. The boys are waiting for us at the church along with Reverend Simpson. I've already got the license."

Naomi jumped to her feet. "I've got to get Colby and Sibyl. Papa, too. We're not going to miss this." She was out of the house before Laurie could collect her wits.

She heard the words, saw the love in Jared's eyes, but could hardly believe this was really happening. Five minutes ago, she was planning to leave Cactus Corner as soon as possible to avoid disgrace. Now, in the next five minutes, Jared wanted her to become his wife. "Are you sure you want to do this?" she asked.

"Didn't you hear me when I said everybody was waiting? All you have to do is say yes."

Laurie hesitated.

"I know it's an awkward situation. I wish I could change that, but I can't. I can only try to assure you that I would love you regardless of the circumstances. You're the most beautiful, the most remarkable, and most wonderful woman I've ever met. All the men adore you. Everybody in Cactus Corner adores you. Why wouldn't I?"

"Not one of them wants to marry me."

"Loomis told me he asked you to marry him."

"He was feeling sorry for me. He doesn't love me."

"I'm not so sure."

"I don't love him, so it doesn't matter." She shook her head to clear it. "Why are we talking about Loomis?"

"Because you're looking for every excuse to keep from saying you'll marry me. I can wait all day, but I doubt the preacher will."

"Do you really have the boys and the preacher waiting?"

"You'll soon be able to see for yourself."

"How could you be sure I'd marry you?"

"I couldn't, but I was determined to take advantage of any momentary weakness or indecision."

"You'd marry me on those terms?"

"I'll marry you on *any* terms."

She scanned his face and looked deep into his eyes. What she saw there erased all her doubts. "I believe you would."

"I'm ready to prove it if you'll just give me the chance."

"I have one condition before I'll give you my answer."

"Anything."

"The money I was going to give you for the partnership—"

"I don't care about the money. I've told Norman I don't want his loan. I'll try to make it with longhorns. If necessary, I'll go back into the army."

"You didn't let me finish."

"Okay, but you can give that money away for all I care."

"That's what I intend to do."

Laurie grinned when Jared looked shocked. She was glad he wasn't entirely altruistic. She liked him better with a few faults. "I'm going to give the money to you. That way you can buy your Herefords and the men can have their original share of the income."

"But it's your money."

"If I marry you, it'll be *our* money just as it will be *our* ranch."

"Will you stop saying *if*. I'm about to go crazy waiting for an answer."

"If I marry you, will you teach me how to run the ranch?"

Jared was becoming frustrated. "Yes, I'll teach you how to run the ranch and anything else you want."

"I want to learn to ride astride, castrate a bull, and everything."

Jared gulped. "I'm not letting you anywhere near a bull that's being castrated. Not only is it dangerous to you and the men. Everybody in this town would think I was a callous fool."

"You say the sweetest things."

"Would you be serious!"

"I am."

"No, you're not. You're just looking for ways to put off giving me an answer."

"Actually I'm trying to decide what dress to wear. You don't think I'm going to get married looking like this, do you?"

Apparently having gotten the answer he wanted, Jared decided talk was no longer necessary, so he grabbed Laurie and covered her with kisses. Laurie agreed with his decision.

❧

When Laurie and Jared entered the church, she found it packed with virtually every person in town. Cassie met them at the door.

"I'm the flower girl," she announced. "Naomi is waiting inside to be your matron of honor. Sibyl wanted to be one, too, but they were afraid two might scare Jared off."

"The only thing I'm scared of is Laurie changing her mind before I can say *I do*."

Dr. Kessling stepped up to join them. "Steve is going to be your best man," he told Jared, "and I'm going to give the bride away."

Jared turned to Laurie. "I had hoped we'd have a small wedding."

"Laurie is related to half the people in this town," Naomi said. "There's no way she gets married without us being here. No more procrastination. Martha is about to play a wedding march. When you get inside, make sure your answers are loud and clear. Everybody wants to hear them."

Jared looked at Laurie, his eyes spilling over with love. "Even if I shout them, they won't convey how important this day is to me."

"I'd prefer you don't shout," Laurie said. "Everybody would think I was pinching you to get you to say yes."

"The way you're looking at each other right now, nobody could possibly doubt that you're in love," the doctor said. "Now get going. I hear music."

❦

Later, Colby came up to Jared. "I hate to interrupt you at your wedding reception, but I've got something to show you."

Jared didn't know how she'd done it, but Sibyl had managed, with the help of every woman in town, to pull together a party to celebrate his wedding. There was cake, punch, and more sweet things to eat than he'd ever seen at one place. He had married into one incredible family.

"You look so serious," Jared said to Colby. "Is something wrong?"

"No, but I thought you ought to know. I'd have told you before, but I didn't get it until today."

"Get what?"

"Come outside. I'll show you."

Jared didn't want to leave Laurie, but he was certain Colby wouldn't have asked him to step outside if it hadn't been important. "Colby wants to see me outside for a few minutes," he said to Laurie.

"What's it about?"

"I don't know, but he said it wasn't bad news."

Laurie gave him a quick kiss. "Don't be gone long, or folks will think you've deserted me on my wedding day."

"Not a chance of that." Jared gave her a kiss in return. "Just don't let Loomis poach on my preserves. I don't trust that look in his eye."

"It's whiskey, not lust. Now go."

Colby was waiting by a wagon when Jared went outside. "I wrote my family like you asked," he told Jared. "I didn't expect an answer, but I got a letter a short while ago telling me my parents were dead and that I had a lot of money in the bank."

Jared wasn't sure that this had to do with him, but he was listening.

"I couldn't believe they'd leave me anything, certainly not money, but the letter said they were sending a trunk my mother left to be sent to me if I ever tried to contact them." Colby pointed to the trunk in the wagon. "This is it."

"What's in it?" Jared asked. It was a little trunk. It couldn't hold much.

"Not what I expected. There's nothing about

their family or where they came from, just some things I had as a baby. Clothes and a couple of toys." Colby reached into his pocket and pulled out a piece of paper. "And this. My parents were Randall and Betty Holstock. My name was Kevin Holstock. I'm your brother."

Jared had wondered how he would feel when he finally found one of his brothers. Now that it had happened, he found it impossible to put into words. But when he saw tears streaming down Colby's face, he knew it meant even more to him. Without hesitation, he stepped forward to embrace the brother he'd lost so long ago. Soon tears were running down his face, too.

He tried to think of something to say, but no words were as powerful as his brother's embrace. He finally had a family, someone who was a part of him, someone *he* was a part of. He wasn't sure he'd ever thought it would happen. Now that it had, it would take some getting used to.

"What are you men doing out here? Come inside. Everybody's asking for Jared."

When the two men separated, it was obvious they'd been crying. Immediately worried, Naomi hurried down the step to her husband.

"What's wrong? Did somebody die?"

When Colby couldn't speak, Jared answered for him. "He just got some information from his mother that proves we're brothers."

Naomi let out a shriek and threw her arms around Colby. Both of them were crying, which started Jared tearing just in time for Laurie to come outside.

"What's taking so long?" When she saw Colby and

Naomi embracing and crying, she hurried down the steps. "Why is everybody crying? What's happened?"

Jared wiped away his tears. "Nothing's wrong. Something wonderful has happened. Colby got a letter from his mother proving we're brothers."

Laurie looked from her husband to Colby and back to Jared. Then she smiled and kissed her husband. "I'm so happy for you because I know how much you wanted to find your family, but I hope you won't be upset if I'm even more happy for Colby. At least you had a family that loved you. Colby had nothing."

"His name is Kevin," Jared said. "Kevin Holstock."

Laurie looked to where Colby and Naomi were still locked in each other's arms. "You can't begin to know how important that man is to us. He's probably the only reason any of us are alive today. To us he'll always be Colby Blaine." She paused. "Am I going to be Laurie Smith, or Laurie Holstock?"

Jared hadn't thought about that. As long as he could remember, he'd been a Smith. The name connected him with the only family he had. "Colby and I will have to talk about that someday. Until then, you're Laurie Smith and your husband is Jared Smith. We don't need a name to make us a family."

As soon as Naomi and Colby released each other, Laurie turned to Colby. "Welcome, brother-in-law. You can't know how happy it makes me to know you're my husband's brother. Now let's go inside before our guests think we have abandoned them. We have something really special to celebrate." She reached for Colby's hand. "I know the whole town will want to celebrate with us."

So they walked back into the church, the two brothers with one arm over the other's shoulders and their other arms around their wives' waists.

Epilogue

LAURIE SAT QUIETLY ASTRIDE HER HORSE, WATCHING more than four hundred white-faced Herefords begin to spread out over the Green River Ranch. "They don't look like they're in good condition," she said to Jared.

"That's the only reason I was able to buy them so cheaply. The owner didn't think they'd make it to California."

Laurie reached over to grasp her husband's hand. "I was glad Colby offered to give you the money if you needed more to buy the whole herd."

Jared squeezed his wife's hand in response. "He said we'd missed twenty-nine years of doing things together as brothers. Offering to be partners in the herd was his way of trying to make up for lost time."

Laurie knew that the two men would never make up for the years they'd lost, but asking Jared to be the godfather of the child Naomi was carrying was a first step. She was certain Jared would ask Colby to be the godfather of their child. Laurie's hand moved to her stomach. Her body hadn't begun to swell, but she could feel the baby's presence within her. Jared hadn't wanted her to ride, but she'd insisted. She relished the time she spent in his arms at night, but she wanted to spend as much of her day with him as possible.

The sound of hammering drew her attention to a rise about a quarter of a mile from the river. A new house was going up, one big enough to hold all the children they hoped to have. Jared had said it didn't need to be so large, but now that Norman had relinquished control of Noah's estate, Laurie intended to spend her money on her family. It was hard for Jared to accept her affluence, but Steve had told him not to be an idiot, that if Jared didn't want Laurie's money, he'd be glad to take it. But Laurie intended to be very careful how she used her money. Jared's pride and self-respect were as important to her as they were to him.

Jared turned to his wife. "Colby told me he had stopped trying to find his brothers because Naomi and the children gave him all the family he needed. I didn't understand him then, but I do now." He reached for Laurie's hand. "I'm glad I found Colby, and I'm glad I have Steve, but it wasn't until I found you that I knew what being part of a family really meant."

Laurie squeezed her husband's hand. "My parents sold me into marriage, and my husband disliked what I was. Despite being related to half the people in Cactus Corner, I never felt worthy of love until now."

Jared leaned out of the saddle to kiss his wife. "I don't know of anyone more worthy. And I'm going to do my best to make you believe it."

Laurie could think of no better way to spend the next fifty or so years.

Read on for an excerpt from

To Have and to Hold

The Santa Fe Trail, 1865

COLBY RODE WITH A LOOSE REIN.

It didn't matter where he was going or when he got there. No one was expecting him and there'd be no welcome when he arrived. But that didn't bother him. That was the way things were, and Colby had learned to accept life as he found it.

His eyes narrowed to slits to keep out the glare of the blazing June sun. The dry air absorbed the perspiration as soon as it dampened his shirt between his shoulder blades. It was more than a hundred degrees on the plain, too hot to hurry.

There was no breeze. Nothing moved except the shimmering heat waves. Even the grass protested the heat. A wet spring had produced luxuriant growth, but the searing summer sun had turned green and gray to gold and brown. Stiff stalks brushed against his boots with the dry rattle of seedpods while the grass's rough edges tugged at the underbelly of his long-limbed Appaloosa stallion.

But Colby's thoughts weren't on his surroundings. He was entering a land of ghosts, the land of his past.

His destination was a rocky bend in a shallow tributary of the Cimarron River. Two graves lay hidden deep in the shade of a cottonwood grove, his parents' graves, parents he had never known, parents whose love and kindness hadn't been there to lessen the pain of growing up. A childless couple had taken him in, but they hadn't liked the boy he became. He left home at fifteen.

Eight years of drifting had earned him little beyond a horse, gear, and a distrust of women. Things hadn't been any better in the army. He had been too open in his contempt of incompetent men unfit for the ranks they held. He left the day the war ended.

Now he was drifting again.

The only place he'd ever felt at home was a cottonwood thicket, his only family the mounds of stones. He had had two brothers, but he'd never been able to find any trace of them. He would stay a few days, sleeping under the trees by day, walking the river by night. The graves had no past and no present, no hope, no expectation. They could mean anything he wanted them to mean, what he needed them to mean.

One corner of Colby's mind—the part always busy receiving and digesting information gathered by his alert ears, constantly moving eyes, and acute sense of smell—never forgot to be vigilant. He was in Comanche territory.

It had been a Comanche raiding party that killed his parents.

Colby glanced down at wagon ruts cut through the

buffalo grass. He'd been following them for two days. It was a small train of just over a dozen wagons, but they had taken the Cimarron Cutoff. Did they know Comanche raids had closed the cutoff during the war? Nobody traveled this route without army protection. Colby scanned the horizon from north to south. He could see no sign of movement, but he didn't expect to see the Comanches until they were upon him. He grasped the reins more tightly, and the powerfully muscled horse between his legs snorted in protest.

"Easy, Shadow."

Colby slowed his mount to a fast walk. The stallion sniffed the air and snorted. Apparently the scent of the train animals was still strong. They couldn't be more than a few miles ahead. As he studied the thin line etched into the dry sod of the plain, Colby felt his skin contract and the muscles in his stomach flutter. An odd foreboding settled over him. Senses honed through years of fighting told him something was amiss.

The crack of a rifle shot caused him to pull up. In the vast quiet, the sound was unmistakable. The wagon train was under attack!

Colby didn't stop to ask himself what one man could expect to do against a band of Indians. He thought only that some other child might be deprived of his family, might be forced to live a life of bitter loneliness.

Gripping the reins firmly and digging his heels into Shadow's flanks, Colby let out a yell that sent the powerful stallion into a flat-out gallop.

Naomi Kessling stumbled over a gopher hole as she walked beside the lead yoke of oxen. Muttering angrily as she regained her balance, she raked the back of her hand across her forehead to wipe away the drops of perspiration that seeped through her eyebrows and lashes to sting her eyes. She jerked her yellow gingham sunbonnet farther down, but it didn't help relieve the glare from the relentless sun. Stifling another curse she wouldn't have wanted her father to hear, she pushed her way through the dry grass that snatched at the hem of her dress, crushing it beneath her boots to clear a path for those who followed.

Her father dozed inside their wagon. He'd been up all night with Wilma Hill, who was expecting her first child in a matter of days. Ben, Naomi's younger brother, walked before her, beating the grass to scare away rattlesnakes. Mr. Greene, their guide, had ridden ahead to find a suitable stopping place for the night. His son drove the lead wagon while his son's wife and small son slept inside.

The Kessling wagon was second. Fourteen other wagons followed close behind, men and boys guiding the oxen and mules or herding the livestock, women and children huddled inside to escape the merciless sun. The journey had turned into a nightmare punctuated by the preparation of tasteless meals, fruitless attempts to rest, and one crisis after another. Tempers flared, anger burst from between compressed lips, and fear-haunted eyes searched the horizon for their familiar forested and well-watered hills. But every morning the ruthlessly unforgiving prairie stretched before them—flat, dry, and empty.

Until today.

There was no warning of the attack. The Indians seemed to rise out of the ground like morning mist from the surface of a pond. The first arrow knocked Abe Greene backward off the seat. The second buried itself in the ground at Ben's feet. The third missed its target because Naomi had already turned back to reach for her father's rifle.

So swift and unexpected was the attack that the Indians might have slaughtered them at once if Ethan, Naomi's seventeen-year-old brother following in the train's wake hoping to bag a sage hen for supper, hadn't knocked the leader off his pony with his first shot.

"I'll get the Greenes' wagon!" Naomi shouted to her father. She yanked Ben from where he stood paralyzed with shock, staring at the arrow buried in the ground, and shoved him behind the Greenes' wagon. Using the oxen as a shield, Naomi turned the wagon to start forming a circle.

Inside Cassie Greene screamed over and over again.

Somehow, despite the hail of arrows, the cries of the wounded, the gaps in the ranks, they completed the circle. Men crouched under wagons. Some lay flat on the ground; others shot from behind flapping canvas. Ethan, wide-eyed and breathless, came running up to join Naomi. Kneeling back-to-back in the grass under their wagon, they fired as rapidly as they could reload.

Naomi knew nothing about fighting Indians. She had listened to the stories Mr. Greene told of surprise attacks, but she hadn't taken them seriously. Thousands of wagons had traveled the Santa Fe Trail for nearly forty years.

Yet here they were, in the middle of a searing hot plain, some of their friends dead or wounded, she and her brother fighting for their lives from underneath a wagon.

The agonized moans from various parts of the train threatened to draw Naomi's attention from the attackers, but she couldn't worry about them now. Their wounds wouldn't matter if they didn't come out of this alive.

But would they? There could be as many as fifty Indians out there. She couldn't see through the thick grass to count them. She didn't know if any of them had been killed besides the leader. Even before the acrid smoke cleared, she aimed her rifle and pulled the trigger.

Medicine bag in hand, her father jumped down from their wagon and climbed into the Greenes'. A moment later Cassie began to cry with high keening wails. Naomi's father left the Greenes' wagon and turned his attention to other wounded.

Naomi knew Abe Greene was dead.

Suddenly the Indians pulled back. Accurate shooting and the constant boom of Morley Sumner's repeating rifle had enabled them to break the first attack. Now the train might have a chance.

Ben came running around the corner of the wagon to join them in the grass. "Abe's dead as a mackerel," he said, the pallor of his skin betraying the fear he tried to hide. "He's got an arrow sticking out of his eye. There's blood and goo all over his face. Cassie's gone crazy."

Naomi pushed Ben down in the grass. "I don't

want to hear about it," she said, fighting off nausea. "Can you load a rifle?"

"Sure," Ben said, proud of his skill.

"Then load for Ethan and me. And keep down. Those Indians could come again any second."

Norman Spencer stuck his head under the wagon. "Where's your father?" he asked.

"I don't know," Naomi answered.

"We've got people hurt."

Mr. Spencer had been the most important man in their hometown of Spencer's Clearing. Back in Kentucky he'd seemed like the natural choice to lead their community, but Naomi doubted he knew any more about crossing the prairie or fighting Indians than she did.

"Abe's dead," Ben announced. "Got an arrow sticking out of his eye."

"Toby Oliver, too," Mr. Spencer said.

Toby! He was only nineteen, fresh home from the war and hanging around Polly Drummond with more than stealing kisses in mind.

"Will they attack again?" Ethan asked.

"I don't know," Mr. Spencer said.

"I think they will," Naomi said. "If they hadn't been meaning to, they'd have left by now."

"Your sister's probably right," Norman agreed. "You'd better keep your guns loaded."

"You think they're just waiting?" Ethan asked after Norman had left.

"Yes," Naomi answered. "I expect they'll attack again any minute."

But they didn't. The minutes crawled by and the

attack still didn't come. She had heard that sometimes if the defense was strong enough, Indians would go away rather than lose braves. But she was certain they weren't going to let them escape. The Indians meant to kill them.

The heat under the wagon was stifling. The tall grass prevented the breeze from reaching them. Bits of dried stalk, ground to a powdery dust under the feet of the restive oxen, coated her skin. Drops of perspiration washed furrows as they raced down her face or burned into her grazed knuckles. Naomi wiped the sweat from her eyes, her unwavering gaze on the circling Indians.

"How much ammunition do we have left?" she asked Ethan.

"We've used a lot already."

"Don't shoot unless you have to."

One of the Indians suddenly spurred his pony in the direction of the wagon, zigzagging as he came. Black hair flying behind him like the mane of a wild stallion and his face distorted by rage, he looked like a monster out of a nightmare. Naomi struggled to hold her fear at bay at the sound of his maniacal screams.

She fired and missed.

The Indian loosed an arrow that buried itself in the flesh of one of their oxen. As the animal bellowed in pain, the Indian turned and galloped off.

Furious at the attack on the team he cared for with such pride, Ethan crawled from under the wagon. Standing, he took careful aim and fired at the retreating Indian's broad, muscled back. When the smoke cleared, the pony was riderless.

The wounded ox bellowed and lunged against the traces. Worried the brake would come loose and they'd be crushed under the wagon's iron-rimmed wheels, Naomi thrust an ax handle through the spokes to lock the wheels.

The arrow had sunk halfway up the shaft just behind the ox's left shoulder. Naomi was certain it had entered his heart. One leg folded beneath the animal's weight. The ox fell to the ground and rolled on his side. He lifted his head to deliver a final bellow of protest, but the sound that came out was a death rattle from deep in his throat.

"The bastards!" Ethan's voice was thick with emotion. "The heartless, stinking bastards!"

When he started forward, Naomi yelled, "Stay back!" and pulled on the straps of his overalls. "You can't do anything now."

She wondered if the Indians intended to kill their oxen so the settlers would be stranded and die of thirst. It had been two days since they crossed the Arkansas River—it would take them nearly a month to cover the remaining four hundred miles to Santa Fe—and the water in their barrels was low. They had to do something, but what?

"We've got to get away after dark," she told Ethan. Her throat was so choked with dust her voice was little more than a whisper.

"Where can we go?"

"I don't know. But they'll kill us if we stay here." Suddenly, the air was rent by earsplitting yells and the Indians charged from all four directions.

"Get behind me," Naomi shouted to Ben.

Their shots turned away three attackers, but the fourth came on, jumping down from his pony to get a better line of fire at the people under the wagons. Chalky colorings of black, white, and blue turned his face into a mask of terror. He had colored his body with a red stain, streaked his chest with a dark brown that made Naomi think of dried blood. More than a dozen strings of beads hung around his neck. Two scalps dangled from the string that held up his loincloth.

The Indian ran a few strides toward them, dropped to his knee, and loosed an arrow at Ethan. It found its mark with a sickening impact. With a cry of rage, Naomi snatched up the rifle Ethan dropped and thrust it up toward the Indian now only a few feet from her.

She fired, and the savage fell to the ground clawing at the gaping hole in his throat.

Fighting against the waves of nausea rolling through her, Naomi turned to her brother. Ethan lay huddled in the grass, his face ashen, his body motionless, the arrow protruding from his leg.

"Is he going to die?" Ben asked, rigid with fear. His eyes seemed to be entirely white.

"No." Ethan struggled manfully not to give in to the pain. "I just got hit in the leg."

Naomi wondered if the Indians had more arrows than everyone in the wagon train had bullets. She counted the boxes of shells. Six left. The sun was still high in the sky. Night was several hours away.

The Indians stopped to regroup. Once more Naomi was forced to watch and wait.

How long? A minute? Half an hour? Time seemed

to stop. It was so hot under the wagon at times she could hardly breathe. The images before her eyes grew faint and indistinct, but she fought off the dizziness that threatened her.

The smell of blood from Ethan's wound filled her nostrils and made her sick to her stomach. She shooed the flies away.

A cry from Cassie Greene riveted Naomi's attention. She looked out on the plain. The Indians had lined up for another charge. How many were still out there, twenty? Thirty?

It didn't matter. There was no more suspense. No more fear. They would all die. She could face the certainty of death, but her pride wouldn't let her face it cowering under a wagon. She would meet them on her feet, a rifle in her hands.

"Load for me," she ordered Ben. Her voice was hoarse now, barely an intelligible whisper.

"They'll kill you," Ethan protested, pulling her back as she started to crawl from under the wagon.

Naomi turned on him. "They're going to kill us anyway." She heard her voice as though from a distance. She sounded slightly hysterical, but she felt utterly calm. Her gaze bored into him, and her voice dropped to a rasping whisper. "Don't let them take me alive. I can stand anything but that."

Ethan turned his eyes away. "You know I can't do that."

She grabbed him, made him look at her. "Promise me." It was no longer a request.

He averted his face. "Christ!"

She seized his chin and forced him to look at her.

"I know what they do. I'd go mad."

It was an awful thing to ask of a man. It was especially cruel to ask of a seventeen-year-old, yet Naomi didn't hesitate. Her gaze, intense and resolute, locked with Ethan's. "You've got to promise me."

"All right," Ethan replied, but he didn't look at her.

"Swear it! I'll haunt you if you don't."

"I said I would." This time Ethan looked straight into her eyes, and Naomi knew he meant it. She rose to her feet.

At almost the same moment, the Indians charged along a broad front. Naomi lifted her rifle, but before she could bring it level, a series of thundering shots rang out and Indians fell from saddles like toys knocked over with the back of an angry child's hand. Naomi stared dumbfounded as the attackers divided into two groups, wheeled in panic, and galloped off in opposite directions.

"What's happening?" Ethan asked Naomi.

"Over there!" Ben cried, pointing.

In the distance Naomi could see a man's head above the grass. Then he burst into full view. A rider on a great Appaloosa was galloping toward them.

No one followed him. He was alone. He had attacked the Indians all by himself. He had to be crazy.

Naomi looked to where she had seen the Indians disappearing, but they weren't running away any longer. Attacking from opposite directions, they formed a semicircle around the rider. His only chance was to reach the wagons before one of their arrows buried itself in his back. His horse was magnificent. Such an animal could easily outrun the Indian ponies, but could he outrun the Indians' arrows?

The whooping and screaming warriors loosed their arrows to no avail. Naomi was hopeful he would reach the wagons when she saw the closest Indian draw his bow. She fired at him but missed.

"Shoot him!" she shouted to Ethan, who had dragged himself from under the wagon to kneel next to her. "Hurry before it's too late!"

Ethan didn't hit the Indian, but he caused the brave to drop his bow. Before she could sigh with relief, an Indian rose out of the grass not thirty yards away.

The Indian leader she thought Ethan had killed! He drew his bow and aimed for the stranger's back. Before she could shout a warning, she heard the twang of the bowstring, the zing of the arrow through the air, and the sickening thud as it buried itself in the man's back.

Rifle fire burst from all around her, and the Indian fell to the ground, truly dead this time.

With a tremendous leap, the Appaloosa jumped over the Kessling oxen and landed inside the ring of wagons. The stranger toppled to the ground virtually under the hooves of the frightened, milling animals.

About the Author

Leigh Greenwood is the author of the popular Seven Brides, Cowboy, and Night Riders series. The proud father of three grown children, Leigh resides in Charlotte, NC. He never intended to be a writer, but found it hard to ignore the people in his head, and the only way to get them out was to write. For more information visit www.leigh-greenwood.com.

To Have and to Hold

Cactus Creek Cowboys
by Leigh Greenwood

USA Today bestselling author

A stranger to the rescue

Colby Blaine has been a loner his whole life. And he isn't about to change now. But that doesn't mean he can ignore people in trouble. When he rides up on an inexperienced wagon train under attack, he doesn't hesitate to jump into the fray. It's only after the raid that he really lands himself in hot water...

Naomi Kessling is certainly grateful to Colby for saving her family and agreeing to lead their train to safer territory. But the man has an infuriating way of knowing just how to get under her skin—he asks too many questions about a past she doesn't want to remember, and his touch makes her long for far more. Yet the more time they spend together, the more Naomi sees that perhaps it's Colby who needs rescuing the most...

Praise for Leigh Greenwood:

"Leigh Greenwood is one of the best." —*RT Book Reviews*

For more Leigh Greenwood, visit:

www.sourcebooks.com

Heart of a Texan
by Leigh Greenwood

❦

In the wrong place...

Roberta didn't mean to hurt anyone. But the night that masked bandits raided her ranch, it was hard to tell friend from foe. She didn't know Nate Dolan was only trying to help when she shot him in the chest. And when he offers to help her catch the culprits, she only feels guiltier. The absolute least she can do is nurse the rugged cowboy back to health...

with all the right moves

Nate has been on the vengeance trail so long, he nearly forgot what a real home looked like. And Roberta is mighty fine incentive to stay put for a while—even if she has a stubborn streak as wide as the great state of Texas. She might be convinced she's healing the wound in his chest, but neither of them know she's also soothing the hurt in his heart.

❦

"Readers will enjoy the battle of wits between these two stubborn protagonists." —*RT Book Reviews*, 4 Stars

"Strap yourself in for a wild ride with this cowboy and the stubborn love of his life." —*Fresh Fiction*

For more Leigh Greenwood, visit:

www.sourcebooks.com

Texas Pride
by Leigh Greenwood

---❧---

A prince among men

Carla Reece had never met anyone more infuriating in her life. The blond giant who swaggered up to her door had no right to take over half her ranch—no matter how stupid her brother had been gambling it away in a high-stakes poker game. Her new foreman claimed to be some foreign royalty who promised to leave in a year. Still, a year was way too long to spend with a man who made her madder than a wet hen and weak in the knees all at the same time.

A hellion among women

Ivan may have charmed everyone in town into thinking he was the perfect gentleman, but Carla knew better. There had to be a chink in his armor—a red-hot passion under that calm, cool gaze. But once she finds it, she may be in for more than she ever bargained for…

---❧---

Praise for Leigh Greenwood:

"For a fast-paced story of the Wild West, Leigh Greenwood is one of the best" —*RT Book Reviews*

For more Leigh Greenwood, visit:

www.sourcebooks.com

Texas Mail Order Bride

Bachelors of Battle Creek

by Linda Broday

New York Times bestselling author

——————— ✇ ———————

Rancher Cooper Thorne thinks his life is finally on an even keel—until Delta Dandridge steps off the stagecoach and claims she's his mail-order bride. Brash and quick-witted, the meddling Southern belle is everything Cooper thought he never wanted…and everything his heart is telling him he needs.

But Cooper swore long ago that he'd never marry, and he aims to keep his word…especially now that the demons from his past have returned to threaten everything—and everyone—he holds dear.

——————— ✇ ———————

Praise for Linda Broday:

"Takes me back to a West that feels true. A delightful read." —Jodi Thomas, *New York Times* bestselling author

For more Linda Broday, visit:

www.sourcebooks.com

Desperate Hearts
by Rosanne Bittner

USA Today bestselling author

— ✍ —

She's a woman with a secret

Elizabeth Wainright is on the run. Accused of a murder she didn't commit, she has no choice but to cut ties with her old life and flee west. The last thing she wants is attention, but when her stagecoach is attacked, she suddenly finds herself under the fierce protection of one of Montana's famed vigilantes…whether she likes it or not.

He's a man with a code

Lawman Mitch Brady is sworn to uphold justice in the wild lands of 1860s Montana. He's never met a man he's feared, and he's never met a woman more desperately in need of his help. Something's shaken the secretive Elizabeth, but as he gets to know the beautiful city belle, he finds the only thing he wants more than her safety…is her trust.

— ✍ —

Praise for Rosanne Bittner:

One of the most powerful voices in Western romance." —*RT Book Reviews*

For more Rosanne Bittner, visit:

www.sourcebooks.com

Paradise Valley
by Rosanne Bittner

—— ❧ ——

Maggie Tucker has just gone through hell. Outlaws murdered her husband, looted their camp, and terrorized Maggie before leaving her lost and alone in the wilds of Wyoming. She isn't about to let another strange man get close enough to harm her.

Sage Lightfoot, owner of Paradise Valley ranch, is hunting for the men who killed his best ranch hand. But what he finds is a beautiful, bedraggled woman digging a grave. And pointing a pistol at his heart.

From that moment on, Sage will do anything to protect the strong-yet-vulnerable Maggie. Together, they'll embark on a life-changing journey along the dangerous Outlaw Trail, risking their lives…and their love.

—— ❧ ——

Praise for Rosanne Bittner:

"A wonderful, absorbing read, with characters to capture the heart and the imagination…it's a romance not to be missed." —Heather Graham on *Outlaw Hearts*

"Power, passion, tragedy, and triumph are Rosanne Bittner's hallmarks." —*RT Book Reviews* on *Wildest Dreams*

For more Rosanne Bittner, visit:

www.sourcebooks.com